The Fourth Angel

G. P. PUTNAM'S SONS *New York*

THE

Fourth

Angel

SUZANNE

Chazin

G. P. Putnam's Sons
Publishers Since 1838
a member of
Penguin Putnam Inc.
375 Hudson Street
New York, NY 10014

Library of Congress Cataloging-in-Publication Data

Chazin, Suzanne.
    The fourth angel / Suzanne Chazin.
        p.   cm.
    ISBN 0-399-14705-5
        1. Women fire fighters—Fiction.   2. Fire marshals—Fiction.
    3. Arson   investigation—Fiction.   4. New York (N.Y.)—Fiction.
    I. Title.
    PS3553.H3468 F68   2001   00-055941
    813'.6—dc21

Printed in the United States of America

10   9   8   7   6   5   4   3   2   1

This book is printed on acid-free paper. ∞

Book design by Victoria Kuskowski

ACKNOWLEDGMENTS

I am deeply indebted to the following people, without whom this book never could have been written:

First, to my quartet of "heroes": *Reader's Digest* Assistant Managing Editor Gary Sledge, who encouraged me through the long years before publication. Few are as privileged to have such a talented and nurturing mentor.

To my agent, Matt Bialer, a man of infinite patience, kindness, and support who has, more than once, saved me from my own "improvements."

To my editor at Putnam, David Highfill, whose instincts are so good, his delivery so tactful, I wish I could bottle it. I'd make a fortune and never have to rework a first draft.

And most of all, to my husband, FDNY Deputy Chief Thomas Dunne, without whom none of this would have been possible, personally or professionally. Through him, I've come to understand what being a firefighter, a leader, and a partner is all about.

My deepest gratitude goes to the men and women of the New York City Fire Department who have been unfailingly gracious in helping me with this book. I have tremendous respect for all of you. In particular, I'd like to thank Supervising Fire Marshal Randy Wilson for his tireless good humor in shepherding me all over the city; retired Assistant Chief of Fire Marshals Denis Guardiano and retired Fire Marshal Gene West for their enthusiastic sense of story and character; and retired Fire Marshal Tom "Jacko" Jakubowski for always knowing the right person to speak to. A special thank you to Fire Lieutenant Marianne Monahan, Firefighter Cathy Riordan, and retired Fire Marshal JoAnn Jacobs for their early valuable insights and inspiration.

Thanks to the Seattle Fire Department for providing me with the tape of the Puyallup test fire, and to retired Seattle Fire Department Investigator Richard Gehlhausen for his forthright and thorough explanations of HTA fires and investigation techniques.

I am indebted to ATF Special Agent and Certified Fire Investigator Jessica Gotthold for her eye for critical detail; to Ellen Borakove at the New York City Medical Examiner's office; to Dr. Ned Keltner of Ktech Corporation in Albuquerque, New Mexico, who clued me in to the science behind HTA fires; to Harvey Eisner of *Firehouse Magazine;* and to Ed Perratore, who saved my computer more than once.

And finally, thanks to Janis Pomerantz, Warren Boroson, Elena Serocki, Sharon Djaha, and the "book club" for being there when no one else was.

TO MY PARENTS,

SOL CHAZIN AND LILLIAN MORAGHAN CHAZIN,

FOR GIVING ME THE COURAGE TO DARE

AND THE FOURTH ANGEL POURED OUT HIS VIAL UPON THE SUN;

AND POWER WAS GIVEN UNTO HIM TO SCORCH MEN WITH FIRE.

—Revelation 16:8

Shortly after midnight on January 17, 1984, firefighters in Seattle, Washington, responded to an all-hands call for a fire in an unoccupied warehouse. The twenty-five-thousand-square-foot Carpet Exchange had concrete walls and flooring and a steel truss roof. Yet it collapsed in nineteen minutes in a conflagration so extreme that it melted the building's steel supports and severely damaged the concrete floors. Worse, attempts to extinguish the flames only served to *increase* their intensity.

A postfire examination revealed that an arsonist had used some sort of flammable mixture (an accelerant) to start the blaze, yet no identifying residue could be found. Tests later confirmed that given the fire's superheated temperatures—in excess of 3,000 degrees Fahrenheit—even state-of-the-art safety gear would have offered emergency workers less than three minutes of protection, dooming anyone trapped inside. Neither the accelerant nor the arsonist was ever identified.

Since 1984, as many as twenty such fires have been reported in the United States and Canada. They can't be readily extinguished. All rescue attempts are futile. All traces of arson evidence are destroyed. The deadly infernos have claimed the lives of two firefighters and completely destroyed every building. Fire investigators call them HTA (high-temperature accelerant) fires. All remain unsolved, and the accelerant a mystery.

Every fire starts with a spark—a small, innocuous burst of heat and light. It craves seclusion, lying low at first, quietly sucking up oxygen, exhaling carbon monoxide. Its lethal breath slips unnoticed through the cracks of doors and vents, slowly choking off air and light.

Minutes or hours later, the first plume of bright orange flame erupts. It climbs on quivering tentacles, following predictable paths—up walls, across ceilings, through open doors, and out windows. Upward, ever upward, it climbs, consuming everything it touches. Then, when it has grown so large that no one person can destroy it, the fire turns bold, roaring like a brawny drunk, smashing windows and setting whole rooms alight in an instant of fury. Anyone unfortunate enough to look upon it at that moment would believe he was staring into the gates of hell.

The Fourth Angel

CHAPTER *One*

It was the eerie insistence of the sound that first caught the young woman's attention. A shrill bleat, remote yet unremitting, began when she turned on the ladies' room faucet. It reverberated through the drain and up the white-tiled walls, a haunting counterpoint to the party chatter and samba rhythms wafting in from the magazine's sixth-floor lobby. Air in the water pipes, the woman told herself. Old New York buildings have a lot of strange noises.

She bent over the sink and splashed cold water along the caramel contours of her face, trying to stave off another bout of morning sickness—a misnomer, she decided, given that it was already eleven on a Monday night. An amulet jingled from a silver-plated chain around her neck, three rose-colored quartz crystals in a filigree cage. A gift from her father when she was a little girl, and the only part of him that stuck around. Men leave, her mother had always told her. The young woman stared down at her champagne-colored chemise, stretched tightly across the small, telltale bulge of her belly, and shook her head. She was learning that herself now.

She turned off the spoke-wheel faucet, but the sound continued, breaking into two distinct noises: one whistling like steam, the other buzzing like an alarm clock. She stiffened, finally allowing herself to hear the naked urgency in the tones. The flat, ceaseless warning.

Fire.

A smoke detector outside the bathroom joined in the jarring squeal. In the magazine's lobby, the music stopped. Footsteps scrambled in all directions, punctuated by gasps and garbled words. But what scared the woman most as she headed for the bathroom door was the peculiarity of the voices. They were high-pitched and mono-syllabic—even the men's.

The lights flickered once, then went out, turning the windowless bathroom into a tomb. She pounded the walls until she felt a slide bolt. Less than five minutes ago, it had slid across with ease. Now the bolt refused to budge.

"Come on, girl," she cried, panic lacing her soft southern drawl. Strange odors, like copper pots left too long on a stove and burned bacon, assaulted her. A pepperiness crawled into her windpipe. She knew the old caveat about escaping a smoke-filled room—get down low and crawl. But the bolt could only be reached from a standing position, so she alternately stood and yanked, then sat and coughed until her lar-ynx ached. Finally, on her fifth try, the bolt gave way and she flung her-self out of the bathroom.

A wave of heat and dense smoke rolled over her, sucking the air from her lungs, making her arms and back feel as if they'd been stung by a swarm of bees. Quick shallow breaths were all she could manage, but each one felt as if she were inhaling through a cocktail straw. Her hand brushed against the sandpapery stubble of a beard and she recoiled, falling back against the hem of a dress, the sharp edge of a pair of glasses, a cascade of braided hair. The dead and dying were every-where.

Far-off, anguished voices cried out. But they were increasingly drowned out by a rumble like an elevated train. A slimy casing now covered the woman's toffee-colored legs. Suddenly, the realization hit her: that casing was all that was left of her skin. She was burning alive.

The pain bit deep into her. She scrambled over shards of glass with-out feeling them. Through the veil of black smoke, she made out the dim shape of one of the loft's fourteen-foot windows. She was sixty feet in the air—a jump meant almost certain death—but she didn't care anymore. She'd die quickly. That's all she wanted now.

With seared fingers, she crawled nearer the ledge. The roar was getting closer. Small, bright orange flames rolled across the high, pressed-tin ceilings like waves upon the ocean, each one bigger than the one before. The monster on her back was ripping huge chunks of flesh off her now. From somewhere far away, she thought she heard a siren. She turned.

A flash of light exploded out of the elevator vestibule. As loud as a blast of napalm, it ignited for only a second. But when it was over, for the young woman, there would be no more pain and suffering.

There wouldn't even be a recognizable corpse.

CHAPTER *Two*

No one tells you the basics about being a woman in the New York City Fire Department. Sure, it's the usual stuff. Proving you've got guts. Not getting bent out of shape over some *Penthouse* pinup in the locker room or the water-filled condom tucked into the pocket of your turnout coat. But it takes a woman to truly understand the most fundamental problem with being female in the FDNY.

There's no place to pee.

Not in the firehouses with their communal bathrooms. Not at a fire scene where you can stand for hours, kidneys burning, while the guys sneak around the corner and do it against a wall. And God knows, not when you are a fire marshal speeding to an eight-alarm blaze right after downing two large mugs of coffee.

It wasn't like Georgia Skeehan had a choice in the matter. The big guns would be at a fire this size—Frank Greco, the chief of department; William Lynch, the commissioner. Her partner, Randy Carter, wasn't about to hang around the Dunkin' Donuts while she lined up for the bathroom. (Is there ever *not* a line in a ladies' room?)

Carter drove, leaning on the horn of their dark blue, department-issued Chevy Caprice as it barreled south down Ninth Avenue, sirens wailing. Through the windshield, Georgia made out the cloud of dense gray smoke rising above Manhattan's SoHo neighborhood. A static of dialogue crackled across the department radio. Dispatch confirmed a 10-45, code one. Then another.

And another. There were bodies in this fire, and it sounded as if no one knew how many.

"Did you see the progression on this thing?" Georgia asked Carter, studying a rough chronology she'd scribbled from dispatch reports. "The fire went from a second alarm to an eighth in under ten minutes."

Carter nodded, tugging at the sleeve of his gray pinstriped suit. He was the only marshal Georgia knew who wore anything better than a Sears sports jacket to work.

"Body count's up to eighteen already." He frowned, deep lines etched into dark skin.

Georgia could deal with the carnage. It was the smells she never got used to. Rancid human smells. The sickly-sweet stench of charred flesh. The bitter, coppery odor of burned hair and coagulated blood. She popped a peppermint Tic Tac in her mouth and offered one to Carter. He waved it away.

"Artificial flavors and sweeteners," he explained in a voice still tinged with the rural North Carolina of his boyhood.

"You're going to be getting a mouthful of carbon monoxide and God knows what else in a moment, anyway. What's the difference?"

"You choose the way you want to die. I'll choose mine." Carter floored the accelerator through a red light, narrowly missing a yellow cab. Georgia braced herself against the broken glove compartment.

"I don't have a choice about the way I die," she reminded him. "You're driving."

He allowed the faintest grin to cross his lean, craggy features, which pleased her. They had been partners for nearly a year now. Georgia never asked, but it didn't take a rocket scientist to figure out that somewhere in this ex–Marine drill sergeant's seemingly spotless thirty-year career with the FDNY, he must have ticked off some well-connected chief. Anybody that senior who got stuck with a female rookie partner had to be on someone's shit list. Of course, it also didn't help that he was black.

"At least I don't ride some Hells Angels motorcycle," he ribbed her. "Next thing I know, you'll be getting a tattoo—"

"If I do, it'll be in a place you'll never see."

One-thirty-one Spring Street was cordoned off for two blocks in every direction. Trucks, engines, and rescue rigs jammed the pavements, their ruby flashers throbbing with almost physical force against the low, darkened buildings. An early-April drizzle pearled across the Caprice's windshield, refracting the red lights like splatters of blood. Georgia shivered. Easter was less than two weeks away, but it didn't feel warm enough yet to be spring.

"Better put your gear on," Carter cautioned. "This one's gonna be a doozy."

"Doozy, right." Georgia watched Ladder Nine's tower ladder rain high-pressure water on the smoldering ruins. Her bladder felt like Niagara Falls behind a dam of Popsicle sticks.

"Randy," she ventured hesitantly. "I gotta go."

"Go where?" His gaze narrowed as it sank in. "Man, Skeehan. I'm gonna start calling you The Faucet. Seems every time we get a run, so do you."

"What do you want me to do?"

"Start wearing Depends."

"Not helpful."

Georgia stared at the men in fire helmets and bulky black turnout coats swarming the pavement. Each thickly padded coat boasted three stripes of gray reflective tape across the torso, sandwiched between fluorescent yellow bands, plus two more on each sleeve. The tape gleamed in the spotlights of hovering camera crews. So much for privacy. Georgia relieved herself behind a foul-smelling Dumpster as a television chopper whirred overhead. Her son would probably pick her out on tomorrow's news.

Carter was fumbling around in the Caprice's trunk for the PET— physical examination tools—kit when Georgia returned. The kit contained tape measures, hammers, claw tools, and screwdrivers, everything needed to pull apart the wreckage to determine how and where the fire started. Determining a fire's cause and origin, or C&O, is the first step in any investigation.

"While you were, uh, you know—" Carter stammered. "Relieving yourself . . ."

"What?"

He shrugged on his turnout coat without meeting her gaze. His deep-set eyes had the sorry look of a basset hound's. "Word's gone around. One of our guys didn't make it."

She would always be twelve when she heard that phrase. "Who?" she asked softly.

Carter slipped his gold marshal's shield on a chain around his neck. "A brother named Terry Quinn. From Fifty-seven Truck. Twelve years on the job. You didn't know him, did you?"

"No, but that's Jimmy's company. You know, Jimmy Gallagher? My mother's . . ." Georgia hesitated. She always felt funny saying "boyfriend." "My mother's companion."

Carter nodded. "Humdinger, this is. Some kind of fancy party was going on on the top floor. A lot of important people were inside, including this Chinese dude—Wong or Wing or something—"

"Wang? Rubi Wang? Holy . . . The founder of *Nuance*?" Only a man over fifty, like Carter, wouldn't instantly recognize the fashion designer's name or his magazine.

"Yeah." They finished suiting up. At the police barricade, they flashed their badges and picked their way across the spongy ash, past firefighters packing up hose lines. Shattered glass crunched underfoot like soda crackers. On a charred side wall were small mounds of what appeared to be human body parts—some of them black with burns, some greasy and grayish-white.

In order to uncover the fire's point of origin, Georgia and Carter knew they would have to trace the blaze's V-pattern—its widest path of destruction back down to its narrowest and lowest—in this case, the basement.

The basement, or what was left of it, was as filthy as a coal mine. Charred and melted debris. Ankle-deep puddles of black water. Air gauzy with smoke and oily with the residue of burning plastics. Carter squatted before a cast-iron radiator, grimacing at a newly acquired stain on his pants.

"We're doing the grunt work so those Arson and Explosion guys over at the NYPD can waltz in here tomorrow and grab all the headlines," he complained. Only marshals are allowed to examine physical evidence at a fire. If an arson includes a homicide, however, jurisdiction can often turn into a political slugfest between cops and firefighters. "If A and E takes this, they're buying me a new pair of pants."

"Hey, they have extras," Georgia noted dryly. "You can't go on TV as much as they do in the same suit."

Carter grinned as he pulled on a pair of latex gloves and brushed a hand across the radiator. His smile abruptly vanished. One of the coils was encrusted with white ash, as fine and brittle as chalk. Two others were partially fused together.

"What kind of fire melts cast iron?" Georgia had meant the question to be rhetorical. She forgot Carter was the only marshal who could recite the flashpoint of almost any substance.

"A fire with a core temp of at least twenty-eight hundred and fifty degrees Fahrenheit," he said without meeting her gaze. Georgia started. Fires that level whole buildings average no more than about 1,500 degrees. This blaze was nearly double that. *Mother of God, what are we dealing with here?*

Carter swept water off a patch of concrete and shone his flashlight across it. Georgia noticed an irregular black stain, darker at the edges and clear in the center, like a dye that had bled outward.

"That looks like a pour pattern," she told him excitedly. Pour patterns are stains left when an arsonist uses a flammable liquid to start a fire. The liquid—typically gasoline or kerosene—tends to protect the surface beneath when it burns, charring mostly at the edges.

"Something burned here," Carter agreed. "But it's not a pour pattern." To prove his point, he directed his flashlight to a grouping of identical stains on another part of the floor, then to a similar drip down a brick wall burned clean from the intense heat. "Pretty clever torch to get a fire started halfway up a wall, I'd say."

"If it's not a pour pattern, what is it?"

"Probably tar stains from when the roof melted. We'll get it tested, but I'll buy you lunch if it's anything else."

Georgia looked up through what had once been the rafters to the halogen-lit night. *Roofing tar.* She wondered if she'd ever get good at this job.

A thick Brooklyn accent crackled over Carter's handie-talkie. "Carter, Skeehan, come in."

Carter rolled his eyes and mouthed the words, "Man of Action." Frank Greco's nickname. Georgia grinned. In five years as the chief of department, Greco's most notable accomplishment was changing the shade of blue in the officers' dress uniforms.

Carter depressed his speaker button. "Here, Chief."

"The commissioner needs a COA for the cameras. So does Mr. Michaels. What can you pull together in fifteen minutes?"

"What's a COA?" whispered Georgia. She thought she knew all the department jargon.

"Condensed overview analysis," said Carter, shaking his head. "Greco-speak. Gives the chief something to do at headquarters all day besides play with himself. Rest of us peons call it a briefing."

"Oh. Who's Mr. Michaels?"

"Beats me." He shrugged, then depressed the speaker button. "Chief? This *Mr.* Michaels? Does he own the building?"

"*And* the Knickerbocker Plaza Hotel. *And* half of New York besides. That's *Sloane* Michaels. You copy, Carter?"

"Ten-four. We'll get right on it." Carter clicked off the speaker button, then added, "You bald-headed, butt-kissing, can't-decide-your-way-out-of-a-paper-bag bureaucrat."

Georgia laughed. "So that's how you ended up with me, huh? Forgot to turn off the speaker first?"

"Something like that."

They split up to look around. Georgia shone her flashlight across a pile of rubbish where one of the building's timber support beams should have been. Hundred-and-twenty-year-old lofts typically boast beams thirty to forty feet long and a foot thick. Even in the worst fires, the wood does little more than become blackened and segmented on the surface— a condition known as alligatoring. Yet here all she could find was a huge mound of charred splinters, none more than six inches in length.

"Randy, this is incredible," Georgia called out, sloshing over. "I think the fire disintegrated the timber supports."

Carter had his back to her. He was staring at something in his hand. She was nearly on top of him before he looked up, startled. He slipped whatever he was looking at into his coat pocket.

"Is something wrong?" she asked.

"I'm trying to do my goddamned job here. How 'bout doing yours for a change?"

Georgia froze. Not once in all their time working together had Randy Carter ever lost his temper—not the tour when he took a shot to the jaw from a drug dealer. Not the night some bozo firefighter started peeing on crime-scene evidence. Not even when the other marshals ribbed him about having a rookie girl for a partner.

"Are you all right?" she asked softly.

He tipped back his black fire helmet and ran a hand from the top of his receding hairline to the bottom of his graying mustache. "Yeah." He exhaled. "I'm sorry. I'm just having a bad tour. Look, maybe y'all better handle the briefing."

"Me? Brief the commissioner?" In the eighteen months since she'd been promoted from firefighter to marshal, Georgia had investigated nothing bigger than a few tenement torchings. Though on paper they were equal partners, in practice she almost always let Carter take the lead. "What do I say?"

"As little as possible."

"We don't even know if it's arson."

"Yeah, we do. *I* do." The statement stopped Georgia cold. Carter never made definitive judgments this early in a case. He must have read the shock on her face, because he beckoned her over to a swirling bluish-green depression on the basement floor, about fifty feet from the stains they'd noted earlier. It was shiny and sleek, almost like glass. And it was etched deep into the concrete, as permanently as a tattoo.

"You see this pretty burn?" He ran his fingers across the mark. "Something very bad and very deliberate caused it."

"Nothing burns concrete," Georgia insisted. "That's why they call concrete buildings fireproof."

"Fireproof," Carter mumbled. "Well, maybe y'all gonna have to change the term." He straightened with the groan of a man who suddenly felt too old to be crawling around burned buildings on his hands and knees. "Go to the command post and talk to the brass for me, will you? I'm going to get some air, see if I can round up any witnesses."

As Carter hoisted himself out of the basement, something fell from his turnout coat pocket. Georgia picked up a tiny piece of blackened metal melted around a pinkish stone and called to him, but he was already out of earshot.

Georgia frowned at the stone flickering lazily in her palm. Randy Carter could tell the difference between accelerant and roofing tar from ten feet away, yet he hadn't bothered to bag evidence even a rookie would know how to handle. She couldn't read him tonight.

THE COMMAND POST was like a war zone. Cigarette butts and Styrofoam coffee cups littered the ground. High-ranking chiefs and aides conferred on handie-talkies. Big men in helmets and turnout coats pushed past Georgia, their faces granite masks of concentration.

What am I doing here? she wondered. No one in the upper echelons of the FDNY knew her, least of all the commissioner. And all she knew about William Lynch was what she'd heard from other firefighters—namely that Lynch, a lawyer by trade, had never come within fifty feet of a speck of ash. That's why his white helmet stayed so shiny.

He was talking to Frank Greco, the chief of department, when she came upon him. Georgia introduced herself to both men and saluted. Lynch gave her a puzzled look. The chief of department, a head taller, frowned.

"Where's Carter?" Greco asked, squinting into the crowd on the assumption that a gray-haired black man would be easy to spot in a sea of Irish and Italian faces.

"Talking to witnesses, Chief. He asked me to brief you, but I can radio him, if you'd prefer."

Greco's enormous black handlebar mustache twitched nervously. The Man of Action hated decisions.

"Oh, for Chrissake," Lynch said finally. "Look, young lady, just tell me what you know. I'm doing the goddamned press conference in five minutes."

Georgia launched into a brief description of the melted cast iron and burned concrete found at the scene, and the 3,000-degree temperatures the evidence suggested.

"A gas leak?" the commissioner interrupted.

"There's too much destruction—"

"So you're thinking arson?"

"At this point, yes," said Georgia. Greco shot her a murderous look. She hadn't realized she wasn't supposed to offer opinions. The chief quickly stepped in.

"What the marshal is trying to say is that the department will need a specialized task force to assess the impact of the damage and prioritize the various scenarios—"

"Put a lid on it, Frank," the commissioner growled. Georgia stifled a grin. She was beginning to like Bill Lynch, lawyer or not. He turned to her now.

"Arson, you say. . . . Then what's the motive, Marshal?"

"Motive, sir . . . ?" Georgia stammered.

"Wouldn't the building have been just as much of an insurance loss at fifteen hundred degrees as at three thousand?"

"I suppose," said Georgia.

"And wouldn't everyone inside have been killed from carbon monoxide in a fire with a core temp of only eight or nine hundred?"

"That's true . . ." She'd forgotten that Lynch, a former DA, had probably prosecuted a fair number of arson cases in his day. Motive would've been one of his first considerations.

"So how do you explain a three-thousand-degree inferno? It's like using ten bullets to kill a man you could've killed with two."

A cloud of stinging smoke drifted overhead. Georgia stared at the pavement where body bags were being stacked like carpet remnants. The death toll was now up to forty-three.

"Maybe," she ventured softly, "someone really liked pulling the trigger."

CHAPTER Three

"Yo, Chief! You goin' to work?"

"I sure am, squirt." The blond man hoisted two large spackling buckets and a couple of paint cans into the back of his beige, graffiti-covered Ford Econoline van and smiled at the six-year-old boy. Scabby knuckles, two front baby teeth missing, but at least no black eyes or bruises. Ramon's mother had finally found a boyfriend who didn't use her and her kids as punching bags.

"How come you're not in school?" It was a Tuesday morning in early April. No holiday he was aware of.

"Teacher conferences, Chief." Everyone called the blond man "Chief" up here in Washington Heights—even the drug dealers. Thirty-nine years of age, with a boyishly round, smooth face, sawdust-colored hair, and pale blue eyes, he was one of only a handful of white people left in this upper-Manhattan neighborhood. Almost everyone else was Dominican.

The chief wiped his hands down the sides of his white, paint-splattered carpenter's pants and checked his watch. "I've got an hour before I have to be at a job in TriBeCa. You get Luis and Bobby and I'll take you hotshots for ice cream."

"All right!" said Ramon. He disappeared into the dim recesses of the building and came bobbing back down the stairs with his obese seven-year-old cousin, Bobby, and Luis, Ramon's tall, gangly eight-year-old half brother. Luis was trying to maneuver his black-and-chrome dirt bike down the stoop.

"Hey, little man, let me get that for you," the chief said, grabbing the bike with one hand and balancing it for the child on the cracked sidewalk. He knew the bike well. A BMX all-terrain he'd bought the boy last year when his shabby hand-me-down got stolen. He'd bought a sturdy combination lock as well so this bike would never stray.

"Me and Bobby'll walk with you," said Ramon. "Luis is gonna bike."

"That's cool," said the chief.

There were no trees along this block in Washington Heights, not even any weeds to signal the onset of spring. The dilapidated tenements and low brick apartment buildings were bathed in shadow on even the sunniest of days. Luis, normally a talkative child, biked silently alongside the trio. He had been acting strangely lately. The chief was worried about him.

"How's that bike holding up, Luis?"

"Okay," the boy mumbled.

"He won't give me no rides," complained Ramon.

"Hey, Luis." The chief frowned. "You gotta look out for your little brother. Loyalty. Fraternity. All that stuff we talked about. You wanna be a fireman one day, don't you?"

Luis shrugged. That stopped the chief cold. The boy had wanted to be a fireman since they'd first met, three years ago. That was all he ever talked about.

"What's going on, son? Is Orlando doing something to you he shouldn't?"

He'd threatened the boy's mother, Celia Maldonado, once before with calling child welfare, after her last boyfriend beat the kids. The chief didn't do it, of course. Celia's taste in men had always been poor, but she was basically a good mother. And besides, if the city really did take her boys, Celia would probably go off the deep end. The children would most likely be split up, and God only knew what hellhole of a foster home they'd end up in.

"Luis," the chief said softly. "You know what touching is, don't you?"

The boy frowned. "Orlando ain't doin' nothin' . . ."

"You'd tell me the truth, wouldn't you?"

"No one's hassling me, okay?" The child got on his bicycle and pedaled ahead. The chief gave the other two boys quizzical looks. Bobby shrugged. Ramon looked at his sneakers. "Orlando told Ma you weren't really a fireman," the child blurted. "And Ma told Luis."

The chief's easy, handsome smile flickered for only for a moment. Then he took off down the street. He was a good runner, despite having been asthmatic as a child. Twice, he had completed the New York City Marathon in just over three and a half hours.

He planted himself in front of Luis's bike, then put two strong arms between the handlebars, forcing the child to stop.

"You lied," Luis muttered. "Orlando says you didn't leave the fire department because you got hurt rescuing somebody. He says you weren't even a firefighter."

The chief squatted in front of the bike and gently pulled at the boy's chin until their eyes met. Luis was crying.

"Son, I'd never lie to you." He pulled out a bandanna from his back pocket and wiped the boy's tears. "Didn't I buy you this bike?"

Luis nodded.

"And when your ma gets short of cash, don't I always take you guys to Mickey D's?"

Again the child nodded.

"So why would I lie to you? Why would I hurt you?"

The boy thought a moment. Then he sniffed back tears and braved a smile.

In the cramped bodega, the chief bought three ice-cream sandwiches for the children and a copy of the *Daily News* for himself. HELLFIRE! screamed the front-page headline. Beneath, a full-page photo showed a giant hole in SoHo where a building had stood until eleven P.M. last night. Fifty-four people were dead.

"I gotta go to work," said the chief, squeezing Luis's shoulder. "Don't worry about anything, son, you hear me?" The boy smiled warmly at the man.

The chief tucked the newspaper under his arm and left the store. Outside, he bent down beside Luis's bike to retie the laces of his paint-spattered work boots. He fingered the bike's combination lock idly. *35-62-27.* He'd bought that lock. He'd protected Luis. He'd always protected Luis. In this neighborhood, the bike would be gone in a heartbeat without it. *35-62-27.* He turned the dial and felt the familiar click as the lock gave way.

The chief can giveth, yes. But the chief can also taketh away.

CHAPTER Four

The bagpipes wailed on a gathering breeze. "Amazing Grace" floated in a high, reedy tenor above the sea of midnight-blue uniforms and white caps that lined the hilly Yonkers boulevards Terry Quinn once called home.

Georgia Skeehan and Randy Carter gathered their somber dress blues around them as a sharp gust lifted off the Hudson River, past the tumbledown row frames, gray factories, and bars with neon-green shamrocks blinking in the windows. They were both dog-tired from having been up all night, but a firefighter's death wasn't something you shrugged off.

"Was it like this for your dad?" Carter asked softly, taking in the carpet of dark blue extending a half mile in every direction.

"Yeah, I guess. It's sort of a blur to me," Georgia admitted. "I saw the whole thing through a twelve-year-old's eyes."

She looked up to the steps of the dull redbrick Roman Catholic church where Quinn's widow and two little girls were standing. The older girl had to be about six. She was crying. Her sister, three, looked blissfully unaware as a gleaming red fire truck, bearing the flag-draped casket of her father, rolled toward the packed congregation.

"I still miss him a lot," Georgia confessed. "It's crazy, you know, but for years, his death felt like a kind of abandonment to me. Like he'd just up and left me to grow into a woman without him. I really needed him, growing up. I guess every girl does."

Out of the corner of her eye, Georgia thought she saw Carter fighting back tears. She turned and touched his sleeve. "Are you okay?"

"Yeah, sure." His voice was hoarse and labored. She studied him now. His basset-hound eyes seemed sunken and glassy, and there was a slight stoop to his normally ramrod-straight posture. His chin bore two small scabs from a hasty shave. And Carter, the neat freak, had dirt under his nails.

"What's wrong, Randy? Something's eating you, I know it. C'mon, tell me. You've heard every goddamned inch of my life."

"I'm fine. Really." He waved her off. "I'm tired from last night, that's all. I just need to walk around, get some air."

Before Georgia could argue with him, she felt a meaty hand on her shoulder. She turned. A burly man with hair the color of spent charcoal gave her a bear hug. "Hello, love," said Jimmy Gallagher. For a man of fifty-six, he was still surprisingly strong.

Georgia gave him a peck on the cheek, then turned back to Carter. "You want me to come with you, Randy . . . ?"

"No. I'll catch up to y'all later. Jimmy . . ." He tipped the brim of his white dress cap at Gallagher, who returned the gesture, then frowned as Carter disappeared into the crowd.

"Did I interrupt something, love?" he asked, fumbling for a cigarette in the pocket of his uniform jacket.

"Does Randy look different to you? He's been very subdued since the fire."

"*Everybody's* subdued today. You think the guys at Ladder Fifty-seven look any better? Quinn was from our house."

"Did you know him well?"

Gallagher sneaked a few puffs of his cigarette and nodded. "Yeah. We were friends. Worked with him last night. One minute he was there, the next he was gone. Good, God-fearing family man. Born in the old sod, like me." Gallagher's parents had left Ireland when he was seven. He didn't have a brogue, but his voice still carried all the Irish inflections. He wore them like a badge of honor, which, in the FDNY, they sort of were.

"Quinn's name's familiar to me from somewhere," Georgia mused.

"You're probably thinking of that court fight here in Yonkers about a year ago. The county wanted to build a halfway house for sex offenders in his neighborhood. Quinn headed a citizen's committee to stop them. They got a lot of television coverage."

"I recall the headlines, but not the outcome."

"Place burned down before it could open."

Georgia raised an eyebrow.

"I know what you're thinking, love. And no, the fire was ruled accidental."

"So he saves his neighborhood and dies of carbon monoxide poisoning a year later—with half a tank of air still strapped to his back."

"Fire didn't get him, at least. His widow was able to have an open casket at the wake this morning." Gallagher nodded at this small blessing. "He looked good."

"How could he look good?" moaned Georgia. "He's dead."

"I've seen it the other way. Trust me, it makes a difference to the loved ones, it does." Gallagher stubbed out his cigarette with the heel of a polished black uniform shoe and gave her a kiss on the cheek. "I gotta go inside now."

"You're too late to get a seat."

"Don't want one. I'm standing in back. The sight of all that brass gives me a headache."

Georgia smiled. Jimmy Gallagher was a great firefighter, smart enough to have made chief by now, had he studied his way up the ranks. He never wanted to. Being a firefighter—doing the tough, dirty, brutal work himself—was in his blood. He was never one to put much stock in titles. She touched his arm.

"Why don't you come over for dinner tonight? Ma's only ever really happy when you're around. And Richie wants to finish that slot car you guys are building."

"Ah, no, love," he stammered. "Another night." Georgia pursed her lips.

"You're going drinking with some of the firefighters after the funeral, aren't you?"

"You make it sound like a party."

"That's what it is."

"No, love, it's not. It's a chance to honor the dead and celebrate the living—"

"Did you drink after my father died?"

Silence.

"I'm sorry," Georgia apologized. "That came out wrong."

Gallagher took a minute with it, then looked at her squarely. "If I *did* drink, and that was eighteen years ago, then it was to commit to my heart one of the bravest men I ever knew. I pray to the heavenly Father that one day, *half* as many firefighters lift a glass in my memory as did for George Skeehan."

"Pray it's not for many years."

He winked at her and grinned. "That's for God to decide." He checked his watch. "I have to go. Tell your mother I'll call her tomorrow. And tell Richie we'll get that slot car done before the memorial mass, I promise."

"But that's only six days away," Georgia called after him.

"I promise." He snaked through the crowd, glad-handing half a dozen firefighters along the way. Then Georgia saw him bend down extra low and gesture in her direction. She gave him a confused look until she caught the glint of Walter Frankel's wheelchair. Frankel was the department's forensic chemist. He was also a close friend. She maneuvered through the crowd to greet him.

"I can't believe you're here," she said, giving him a kiss on the cheek.

"I go to department functions," he said indignantly, pushing his horn-rimmed glasses up the bridge of his nose.

"Functions, yes. Funerals, no."

"I'm not into the Irish style of grieving. Can't tell the difference between their funerals and their keg parties."

A few organ notes resonated from the church. Voices hushed. Men removed their caps and bowed their heads. The funeral mass was beginning.

"You want the scuttlebutt I'm hearing?" Frankel whispered.

Georgia bent over and put a finger to her lips. "Not now."

He plunged ahead anyway. "You've seen the autopsy report on Quinn, right?"

"Walter," she chided. "We're at the man's funeral."

"And what better time to talk about how he died? He had a cheater in his pocket and no facepiece." Cheaters were illegal tubes fashioned by firefighters to get air from their tanks without having to wear the bulky facepiece.

"I know about the cheater. I was there last night, remember?" said Georgia. "And I know—surprise, surprise—that he didn't turn on his PASS alarm, either." A personal alert safety system—or PASS alarm— is a yellow beeper that fastens onto the straps of an air tank and goes off if a firefighter remains motionless for thirty seconds. Georgia had yet to meet a firefighter who routinely turned his on.

"Okay, okay," said Frankel with a trace of annoyance. "But I'll bet you didn't know this: Quinn didn't smoke—"

"So?"

"He apparently always wore a seatbelt. He was a goddamned Irishman—accent and everything—and he didn't drink."

"You know, Walter, that's an ethnic slur. Not every Irish person drinks."

"You're right. Some are in AA. Look, you can edit me for PC later. What I'm saying is, don't you find it strange that a man this cautious about his health would use a cheater instead of a facepiece?"

"This isn't the place," she said disapprovingly. "Or the time." Snippets of the mass swirled overhead in the blustery cold. "The commissioner's delivering his funeral address."

"This is the part where he says that an ordinary fireman is an extra-ordinary man."

Georgia made a face and straightened, just in time to hear Lynch speak the same words. Frankel shrugged.

"I've heard his speeches before. They're all canned, you know."

"You're a cynic."

"I'm a realist. Lynch is killing time in this job until he can get appointed to something better. He wants a few headlines for his scrapbook. When he gets them, he'll move on."

They remained at attention until the doors of the church were finally opened wide, and the gleaming mahogany casket of Terry Quinn was borne through them. A lone trumpeter played taps. Then the bagpipes started up again, their plaintive chorus echoing down the long blue corridor of men.

The fire engine bearing Quinn's casket, with its crown of white lilies, proceeded slowly up the boulevard. A phalanx of uniforms snapped their white gloves in salute. Georgia lifted her hand as well. Frankel, she noticed, did not seem as moved by the display. He was a civilian. As much as she cared for him, that would always be the difference between them. He could distance himself from the tragedy. She couldn't.

The crowd soon began dispersing. Georgia and Frankel tried to find Carter but couldn't, so Georgia wheeled Frankel to his van.

"These funerals . . . they must be especially hard for you," he said softly.

Georgia smiled sadly and nodded. It was one of the things she liked best about her relationship with Walter. They knew each other so well, all the big stuff could be pared down to a sentence or less.

"Terry Quinn was only thirty-five—four years younger than my dad when he died," Georgia noted.

Frankel shook his head. "Such a senseless loss."

"It's a loss," said Georgia sharply. "But never senseless. He was a firefighter. He died doing his job. Maybe he didn't save anybody, and maybe he was too cavalier with his safety, but he had a purpose in being there."

"That's not what I meant." Frankel sensed he'd touched a nerve, so he said nothing as he aligned his wheelchair with the van. A ramp from underneath the carriage slowly lifted him into position. "Are you still on this investigation?"

"There's no official word, but I doubt it," said Georgia.

"I've got some material you might want to take a look at. When you see it, you'll know why I said Quinn's death was senseless, why it didn't have to happen. Not for him—not for any of those people."

"Better send it to headquarters," said Georgia. "The NYPD's already jockeying for the case. And even if our people get to keep it, Chief Brennan's going to put someone higher up the food chain on this."

"Mac Marenko?"

Georgia made a face. "Hard to think of him as higher up in anything."

Frankel laughed. "Georgia, do me a favor? Bring that new motorcycle of yours over to the lab tonight and take a look at my stuff. I send it to Marenko, he'll bury it—the way the department's buried all the others."

The wind had picked up. Georgia was certain she'd misunderstood him. "Others?"

Frankel fixed a dark, sad gaze on her. "You didn't see the first blaze of this kind in New York. And God help us, you may not have seen the last."

CHAPTER Five

Georgia had planned to grab a short nap after the funeral, then help her son, Richie, hang Easter eggs on the lilac bush out front. But by the time she awoke, the sun was melting into a filmy butterscotch light, and a scattering of garishly colored eggs already weighed down the lilac's bare branches. She'd have just enough time to eat and meet Frankel at the lab.

She found Richie downstairs, sprawled out on the living room couch, tossing a basketball in the air with a steady, rhythmic motion. He didn't stop, even after his hazel eyes registered her presence.

"The eggs are hung," he said flatly.

Seeing his profile—the smooth, creamy cheeks, the perfect bow of his lips—still brought to mind the chubby toddler who used to melt into her arms at the first crack of thunder, the bark of a dog, or the gaze of a stranger. Now, at nine, he seemed more concerned with the pedestrian aspects of their relationship—her physical, mute presence at "mom" functions, her willingness to be a chauffeur on demand.

"You did a great job, honey," said Georgia. "Sorry I overslept."

He propped himself up and gazed out the window. "Those eggs always look so dorky. I'm not hanging them next year."

Georgia wasn't sure if he wanted her to agree with him or protest his indifference. Only last year, he was kid enough to cry when he got the flu and had to miss the school's egg hunt. It wasn't that many years ago he had believed a six-foot rabbit actually hopped through his window. Georgia looked down, searching for something neutral to say, and noticed his feet, still clad in sneakers, perched on the armrests of the couch.

"Richie, this isn't a locker room. Please take your shoes off the furniture."

"Grandma doesn't mind."

"But I do."

The boy rolled his eyes and made an elaborate show of shifting his feet to the floor. "You slept all afternoon, and you're still cranky."

"I was up all night. I slept for two hours. Two hours isn't all afternoon."

He propped the basketball on his finger and attempted to spin it. It wobbled around once before careening across the floor, barely missing the laminated-oak coffee table and a glass hutch full of her mother's Hummel figures. Georgia grabbed the ball.

"Does this look like a gym?"

The kitchen door swung open.

"For heaven's sake, Georgia. He's just a boy."

Georgia pursed her lips at the short, shapely woman with auburn hair, standing in the doorway, wiping a paring knife on a towel. The knife was part of a twenty-piece cutlery set her mother had won in a magazine sweepstakes last year. Margaret Skeehan was always winning things. Everything from the complete recordings of Engelbert Humperdinck to a vibrating back massager. Useless stuff, mostly. It was the winning her mother liked, that sense that fate was on your side for one shining moment.

"Ma, basketballs don't belong in the living room. I don't recall you letting me bring so much as a softball glove in here when I was a kid."

"You would've broken something."

"How would you know? You never let me do it." Georgia flinched at how easily she and her mother fell into old patterns. Living in the house she'd grown up in created an uneasy alliance. Margaret Skeehan was a woman with fierce green eyes and the kind of Gaelic determination that shows its love through loyalty and stubborn faith more often than words or touch. Georgia had always been more drawn to her father's warm, easygoing nature. He would've understood why, four months ago, she'd bought that fire-engine-red Harley Davidson motorcycle with its raked front end and polished chrome handlebars. He would've understood that sometimes being a mom isn't enough. Sometimes you just have to escape.

Richie sat up straight now and put the basketball between his legs. "Do you want me to play outside?" The question was addressed to Margaret. He didn't even look at his mother.

"Would you, on the driveway? There's a good boy," she cooed. "Practice for that big game Thursday night."

Richie gave his mother a dirty look, stuffed the basketball under his arm, and disappeared out the front door. Minutes later, Georgia heard the thump-thump on the blacktop. Might as well have been a hammer to her heart.

"He never listens anymore," she said softly, watching him from the kitchen window.

"Do you listen to him?"

"Of course I do. He's got a three-subject range: basketball, Pokémon, and the Mets."

Margaret sighed. "If you really believe that, then you're not listening. It's just like shooting pool. It's all in the approach."

Margaret Skeehan was a champion pool player, a fact that seemed entirely at odds with her petite frame and reserved nature. Her father, Jack Reilly, had owned a pool hall when she was a kid, and she still competed occasionally in local tournaments. Georgia and Gallagher always got a kick out of watching some swaggering, tattooed hulk being roundly defeated by a five-foot-two-inch fifty-five-year-old grandmother.

"I've got enough problems figuring out how to talk to *guys*," moaned Georgia. "Now I have to figure out how to talk to my son?"

Margaret took a cucumber out of the refrigerator and began to slice it. "Sometimes I think you're too hard on Richie. Too hard on men in general. You don't trust them."

"I trust men—"

"And that's why you show *all* your first dates your gun?"

Georgia shrugged. "Some men have trouble dating a woman who packs firepower. Might as well get it out on the table, so to speak." Georgia took the cucumber from her mother. "Here, let me do that."

Margaret gave her the knife and Georgia noticed, as always, how beautiful her mother's hands were—manicured nails, soft skin smelling of Pond's cold cream and Yardley's lavender soap. Georgia's nails were ragged and colorless, her skin a tapestry of scrapes and bruises.

"Georgia, it's not about *you* anymore. It's about Richie. He needs a father. It's not like Rick's ever . . ." Margaret let her voice trail off.

"Ever what? Coming back? You don't think I know that? Ma, he walked away seven years ago. He's married with another kid now."

"But you don't try very hard to find a replacement."

"I don't see Prince Charming knocking. If he did, it'd probably be to do his laundry."

"See? there you go again." Margaret cleared a stack of contest entry forms from the kitchen table. She was always entered in at least twenty. "Maybe you need to be Princess Charming first."

"Okay," said Georgia. "Let me practice." She pitched her voice an octave higher: "'Can I get you another six-pack for your fourth football game of the day, dear?' Or maybe this: 'Tell me more about your sixty-four-kilobite Intel Pentium processor. It's soooo fascinating.' And let's not forget the all-time winner: 'What a thoughtful gift. I always wanted a muffler for my birthday. And a surprise, too, since my birthday was last month.'"

Margaret laughed and shook her head. "I wish you'd joke less and date more."

"Hey, I do both. I date the jokes—it kills two birds with one stone."

"Seriously, dear," her mother insisted. "There *are* nice guys out there. Maybe if you did more traditional things, like coming with Jimmy and me to the memorial mass . . ."

Georgia rolled her eyes. "We're not going to start that again, are we?"

"My goodness, Georgia, I don't understand why, every year, you refuse to go. They're honoring dead firefighters—men like your father."

"I honor Dad in my own way. And I don't need the Catholic Church, the Emerald Society, or the Ancient Order of Hibernians to do it." The Emerald Society was the fire department's Irish fraternity; the Ancient Order of Hibernians was a national Irish-heritage organization. The annual memorial mass was less about mourning and rememberance than about posturing and politics. "Every one of those groups is a bunch of self-important men. And besides, I'm not looking to meet a firefighter. I deal with enough of them already." Georgia nodded to her mother's stack of contest entry forms. "Hey, maybe you can win me somebody decent. No purchase required, void where prohibited and all that . . ."

"You forgot the most important condition: you must be present to win. With a man. With your son."

Through the window, Georgia watched Richie shooting hoops. His sneaker laces were undone. She fought the urge to run out and tie them.

"If you're referring to my not hanging the eggs, I already apologized. And not for nothing, Easter's still almost two weeks away—"

"I'm talking about Thursday night," Margaret interrupted.

"Richie's basketball team's season finale," Georgia droned, as if by rote. "I haven't forgotten. Eight-thirty P.M. Saint Aloysius Auditorium."

"Good. Because if you don't make that game, you'll break your little boy's heart."

CHAPTER Six

"I could've been a mugger," scolded Georgia. "Don't you at least lock your doors?"

Walter Frankel looked up from his ancient microscope, lost in thought. A half-eaten chicken salad sandwich beside him was either the remains of his lunch or the extent of his dinner. He no longer bothered much with food since his wife, Doris, died last year.

"You said you were coming at seven P.M. It's seven. What's to steal?" He gestured to beakers and jars of various colored solutions lining shelves along the walls.

The Bureau of Fire Investigation's Criminal Forensics Lab was a misnomer. The name implied a sophisticated laboratory with state-of-the-art equipment. In truth, the lab was nothing more than a couple of rooms with some high school chemistry cast-offs in a warehouse on West Thirteenth Street, a block from the Hudson River. In summer, the stench from the nearby meat-packing warehouses was unbearable, and rodents as big as cats wandered freely. In winter, transvestite prostitutes who prowled the area warmed themselves in doorways over open trash-can fires. Every year, the FDNY talked about folding this one-man operation into the much more sophisticated NYPD lab in Jamaica, Queens. And ever year, Frankel managed to hold on.

"Did you bring the bike?" he asked with excitement.

"I thought it might rain, so I drove the clunker instead." A Ford Escort. Eight years old. Once red. Now rust.

"Oh," he said. She didn't think he'd be so disappointed.

"I'm still getting the hang of being on two wheels," she apologized.

"Me too."

Georgia smiled at his stab at black humor. Ten years ago, when Frankel was forty-two, doctors diagnosed him with an aggressive form of multiple sclerosis. Two years later, his legs gave out for good. Since then, he'd undergone every torture imaginable, from bee-sting venom and huge doses of steroids to experimental diets. Last fall, after Doris died, he had entered a special intensive program at New York Hospital, funded, like so many other things in the city, by real estate tycoon Sloane Michaels. Frankel raved about the program, but Georgia had yet to see any improvements.

"So, what besides company am I here for?" she asked, flopping into an orange vinyl chair repaired with duct tape.

Frankel rummaged through an enormous stack of papers. Behind him, a movie poster of Arnold Schwarzenegger as the Terminator loomed, two rounds of machine-gun ammunition crisscrossing his sculpted torso. The Austrian muscle man was Frankel's idol. Schwarzenegger's body never failed him.

"That blaze in SoHo was no ordinary fire, and you know it," Frankel said. "The moment that thing was lit, it was *Hasta la vista, baby.*"

"So I gather. Randy told me it was definitely arson, and he never makes statements like that."

"How's he doing?"

"I wish I knew." Georgia sighed. "I called his house this afternoon. Marilyn said he disappeared after the funeral and wouldn't even tell her where he was going . . ."

"Girlfriend?"

"Randy? He's straight as they come. No, Walter. Something scared him at the fire."

Frankel shrugged. "Look, don't worry. Carter's a survivor. Believe me, I know. He's been through worse." He unearthed a black videocassette box from underneath a pile of papers. "This was what I wanted to show you."

"I'm not gonna have to sit through another Schwarzenegger flick, am I?"

"I've got something here that would turn Arnold into a Bavarian cream puff. C'mon."

Georgia followed Frankel into the small office adjoining his lab. He slipped the tape in the VCR. A uniformed figure flashed on the screen. *Chief, Fire Department, City of Seattle* was printed in amateurish type-face beneath the head shot. The man rattled on in a stiff and overly rehearsed way about something he called high-temperature accelerant fires, or HTA for short. Georgia yawned. She'd had enough training films at Randalls Island to last a lifetime.

The camera zoomed in awkwardly on a vacant strip-shopping center. Underneath, the location was identified as Puyallup, Washington, but it could have been anywhere. Georgia had passed hundreds just like it on highways from Long Island to New Jersey. It had a concrete foundation, plyboard-and-gypsum walls, plate-glass display windows, and a tongue-and-groove wood roof supported by steel beams. Except this one had nothing in it. From end to end, it was broom-clean, save for a random scattering of large boxes spread across the linoleum floors. She counted perhaps ten of these boxes. In the center, someone had draped open a firefighter's turnout coat. At the right-hand corner of the screen were small red numbers. Whatever was about to unfold was going to be timed.

"The Seattle Fire Department's going to torch the place?"

"Watch," Frankel commanded.

The camera zoomed in again through the plate-glass windows. Someone in uniform laid a small gauge that Georgia took to be a thermometer underneath the turnout coat. Georgia grew restless. The video had all the panache of a home movie. Then, from off camera, a voice shouted, "Fire in the hole!"

Suddenly, a blinding white-hot column of flame like the tail of a rocket shot up from inside the structure as the red numbers began a second-by-second count. In the blink of an eye, murky gray smoke filled the main section of the building.

"Where's the fire load?" asked Georgia. "The building's empty. There's nothing in there to burn."

"It's burning itself. It's burning the concrete, the gypsum board, the wall studs."

At the twenty-second mark, smoke was already banking down from the ceiling. At one minute, the heavy metal front door exploded into the parking lot. Georgia had heard about really bad fires from veterans—PCB meltdowns, five-alarmers in supermarkets with bow-truss roofs that collapsed without warning. Nothing could compare to this. Those took hours to work themselves into a frenzy. They burned because they had plenty of kindling in the form of gas or tires or furniture. This fire raged on nothing at all.

Suddenly, a hoarse, jittery voice behind the camera spoke. "It just fried the coat. It friggin' fried the coat."

Frankel leaned into her. "The department used a thermocouple to measure the temperature under the turnout coat left inside," he explained. "They just got a reading of five hundred degrees. At *floor* level."

Georgia looked at the red numbers on the screen. One minute and forty-two seconds had elapsed since the fire started. Any firefighter caught inside that building wouldn't have stood a chance. At 500 degrees, blood boils, lungs scorch. Even if the skin doesn't fry, the organs poach from the inside.

Frankel read her face. "Like I said, *Hasta la vista, baby.*"

Only two minutes into the blaze, the entire length of stores burst into one solid wall of orange-yellow flame. Windows shattered. Flames up to forty feet high danced across what was once the roof. Georgia shifted in her seat.

"Why don't they put it out now?" she asked as the roof collapsed in on itself.

"Because they can't. If you put water on a fire that hot, it'll split instantly into hydrogen and oxygen atoms, and the oxygen will feed the flames. Water will just make the fire hotter."

"How do you extinguish it, then?"

"Basically, you wait until all the accelerant has burned off. Then the temperature of the fire drops from about three thousand degrees Fahrenheit to a standard fifteen hundred degrees, which you can douse with water."

The movie's final moments recorded what was left of the wreckage after the flames had been extinguished. All that remained was a depression of concrete with glassy blue-green stains and a few mostly vaporized steel beams. Timber supports had disintegrated into five-inch splinters. Frankel flicked on the lights.

"What the hell is that stuff?" asked Georgia. "Rocket fuel?"

He shook his head. "Rocket fuel is a carefully controlled substance, like dynamite. But if you mean does it act like rocket fuel? Absolutely. It has its own oxidizer, or built-in source of oxygen, just like rocket fuel. That's why it doesn't need a fuel load to burn. It'll burn concrete if you let it."

She thought about the burned concrete and melted cast iron at the Rubi Wang fire on Spring Street. "If it's not rocket fuel, what is it?"

"In the test? A cocktail of ammonium nitrate, potassium perchlorate, metal alloys, diesel fuel, and aluminum powder, with a little magnesium thrown in to make those pretty white sparks."

"And these are carefully controlled substances too, right?"

"Ammonium nitrate is a commercial plant fertilizer. Potassium perchlorate is used in flash powder. Ground aluminum is sold by paint dealers." Frankel took off his thick glasses and wiped them on his shirt. "I could probably find a recipe for HTA on some computer bulletin board and almost every ingredient needed to start a fire like this at Kmart. Anybody who's had high school chemistry is competent enough to mix the ingredients, and you don't need a lot of the stuff, either, like with an explosive. Even a couple of shoe boxes' worth work nicely. These fires give a hell of a bang for the buck."

"Fires—plural? You mean a bunch of these have occurred?"

"Under two dozen over the last two decades. Mostly in Washington State and California, with a couple in Canada and the Midwest."

"What about in New York?"

"None that we know of," he said, returning his glasses to his face, "until now."

"The Rubi Wang blaze. So Randy was right about it being arson."

Frankel breathed in, a raspy hollow breath suggesting to Georgia that perhaps his lungs, too, were beginning to suffer the wrath of his disease. His lips parted as if ripe with thought. Then they closed again. He was tired. No—"weary" was the word. A long sleep couldn't lift the burden of his thoughts.

"C'mon, Walter. You didn't bring me all the way down here to tell me that that fire *wasn't* HTA."

Frankel wheeled himself to a file cabinet in his outer office, where he unearthed an accordion folder crammed with reports and newspaper clippings. He fished out a plastic evidence bag. A single piece of lined notebook paper was inside. "Here," he said, handing her the bag. "Read this."

Georgia studied the small, excessively neat, linear print.

And the fourth angel poured out his vial upon the sun; and power was given unto him to scorch men with fire.

"This was mailed to fire department headquarters in early December, four months ago," Frankel explained.

Georgia furrowed her brow. "I don't get it."

"Hey, you're the parochial school graduate. It's from the New Testament. The Book of Revelation, to be exact. It arrived the day after a very hot fire turned a vacant Manhattan furniture warehouse into a parking lot."

"You think the letter and fire were connected?"

"I didn't—until the second letter arrived."

"The second?"

He handed her another letter in a sealed evidence bag. Same handwriting. Same lined notebook paper.

And the voice which I heard from heaven spake unto me again, and said, go and take the little book which is open in the hand of the angel which standeth upon the sea and upon the earth.

—THE FOURTH ANGEL

"This one arrived at headquarters in late January—on the heels of another superhot fire," Frankel explained.

"In Manhattan?"

"Uh-uh. This one was in Red Hook, Brooklyn, at a vacant five-story apartment house."

"Any casualties?"

Frankel scanned his notes. "One squatter. The building was probably used as a crack house. A few days after that letter, this one came." He handed her a third letter.

The second woe is past; and behold, the third woe cometh quickly.

—THE FOURTH ANGEL

"The day *after* this letter arrived, there was a big fire up in East Tremont in the Bronx. Also a vacant apartment building. Also one squatter death."

Georgia studied the three letters. "You think these fires were HTA?"

"You tell me. Three vacant buildings leveled in under half an hour each. No fire load. No accelerant residue. No discernible points of origin. I saw the angle iron on that building up in East Tremont—it was melted like a Hershey bar left in the sun."

"Did you put this stuff in your reports?"

"I attached copies of the letters. I never heard about them again."

"The building owners must have cared . . ."

"The two apartment houses were on city-owned land."

"Any code violations?"

"You tell me."

Georgia frowned at him. "Didn't you look at the building inspection reports?"

"There were none. I went back and forth with the Buildings Department three times. There are no reports in the files. Nada. Zip. It's as if the buildings never existed."

Georgia sank into the chair and stared up at the ceiling. Loose paint and water stains covered the perimeter. "What the hell's going on here, Walter? How come three buildings have gone up in high-temperature blazes and nobody in the fire department wants to talk about it?"

"That's what you've got to find out."

"Me?" Georgia straightened.

"I've got two years to go before I can retire with full benefits. The department's got ample reason to yank my rear out on disability before then. I'm trying to hang on, Georgia. But you? You're young and smart, and you need a challenge, or you're gonna spend the rest of your career fighting off those ghosts roaming around in your head."

She flinched. Her ghosts were her own business. "You've never gotten anyone killed, Walter. You've never faced death firsthand."

"I haven't?" His gaze fixed on her, and Georgia felt instantly foolish. She looked down at him, past the black polyester pants that hid his sticklike legs where the muscles had long since atrophied. Lately, his doctors had been suggesting he invest in a motorized chair that would hold up his neck when he couldn't any longer.

"I'm sorry," she said softly. "I just meant that things haven't gotten any easier for me. I thought leaving the firehouse and becoming a marshal would help."

"You made a deal with God, yes? You figured if you just kept filling in those little job tickets, that your guilts about Ferraro would disappear, that one day you'd wake up whole again." Frankel slapped his painfully thin thighs. "God's the worst bookie in the business, let me tell you. He never keeps his end of a bargain."

He held out the brown dog-eared folder. "You have to hand over the preliminary report on the Rubi Wang blaze to Chief Brennan, anyway. Read my stuff. If you don't feel there's a pattern, fine. You don't have to mention it. Just take a look."

The folder weighed down Frankel's bony arm. Georgia took it, more to relieve him of the burden than anything else.

"I'll read it," she promised.

"Tonight," ordered Frankel.

Georgia made a face, then shrugged. "Okay, okay. Tonight."

CHAPTER Seven

ARTHUR P. BRENNAN, CHIEF FIRE MARSHAL, BUREAU OF FIRE INVESTI-GATION, FDNY, read the black stenciled lettering on the door. Brennan was on the phone when Georgia entered, his beefy frame stuffed in a swivel chair aimed at the grime-encrusted window. Beyond headquarters loomed the squat, gray skyline of downtown Brooklyn. The Bureau of Fire Investigation was the law-enforcement arm of the New York City Fire Department. Every marshal had once been a firefighter, and some went back to it after a year or two. For those who stayed, a series of civil service exams took them up the ranks—from fire marshal to supervising fire marshal to assistant chief. The chief was usually appointed.

Brennan wore a department uniform—dark blue jacket with brass buttons and medals on the pocket—which made him look something like a navy general. It had the desired effect, for though he made no move to acknowledge her, Georgia remained at attention, ready to salute.

"You stand like that long enough, you're liable to attract pigeons."

The voice came from behind the door. Georgia turned, her concentration broken. Supervising Fire Marshal Mac Marenko was slouched in a chair, a toothpick wedged in his mouth. Though his rank entitled him to more clout and pay, it didn't automatically make him anyone's boss—least of all hers.

"Am I interrupting something?" Georgia asked.

"Nope." He grinned. "I'm just a fly on the wall."

"Then how about you find a nice pile of manure and make yourself at home?"

"Clever, Skeehan. I like a girl who's clever." Marenko rose. He was a big man, easily six-two, in good physical shape, with a mop of wavy blue-black hair that needed trimming and a nose made all the more striking for its appearance of having been broken. "The chief asked me to stay. Besides, I know why you're here. The prelim report on the Rubi Wang fire, right?" He moved toward her. "Can I see it?"

Georgia shot a quick, nervous glance over at Brennan, who was still on the phone.

"For Chrissake, Skeehan, I'm heading the investigation. I'm gonna see the report anyway."

"Oh. I thought the NYPD had the case."

"So did they."

She wanted to offer congratulations, but the words wouldn't squeak past her lips. Marenko, she knew, considered women a liability in the fire department. It was hard to root for a guy like him. She extracted the report and handed it over.

"Thanks." He pulled the toothpick out of his mouth and flicked it into a waste basket. "And thanks, too, for your warm show of support."

"You want support, Marshal, buy a jock strap."

"Ouch." He feigned injury. "That was hitting below the belt." He opened the report, and Georgia realized that two pages of Frankel's notes had somehow gotten lodged under the front cover. If Brennan or Marenko got so much as a whiff that Frankel was feeding her information, he'd be out on disability before he could say *hasta la vista, baby.* She lunged for the papers. Marenko caught her wrist.

"Ah-ah-ah. Didn't your mother ever tell you not to grab?"

"That stuff doesn't concern you."

"I'll be the judge. First tell me what it is."

"Some background on other fires that resemble Monday night's blaze."

"What *other* fires?" The voice boomed, startling even Marenko, who let go of Georgia's wrist. Chief Arthur Brennan was off the phone. He fixed his beady blue gaze on Georgia. Frank Greco, as chief of department, was higher ranking, but he was more politician than commander. To really feel your knees quake, there was nothing like a good session with the chief fire marshal.

"A furniture warehouse in upper Manhattan last December, sir." Georgia licked her lips. Her throat felt parched. "And two vacants—one in Brooklyn; one in the Bronx. All appear to have been started by something with the same intense heat and destructive power as Monday's fire."

"Says who?" The rosacea on Brennan's face, normally just a bumpy red sheen on his cheeks and nose, looked particularly florid right now. Georgia sensed she was the reason.

"It's in the reports from each of the fires." She patted the side of her folder. No reason she couldn't have looked up the reports herself—without Frankel's help. Brennan couldn't prove otherwise. "All of the fires occurred in New York City within the last five months. So far, none has yielded even a trace of accelerant residue."

"And you think one person is behind them?"

"There's a pattern," she said, relaxing a bit as she gathered steam. "We're talking about combustion temperatures high enough to melt iron and turn concrete into glass. I'm assuming these are arson jobs, but the accelerant is a whole lot fancier than kerosene or diesel fuel—"

"This is, of course, your *expert* opinion." Georgia saw the smile, swift and faint, travel from Brennan to Marenko. She had no friends in this room.

"Sir, I know I'm a rookie here—"

"Damn straight, Marshal. You *are* a rookie, and don't you forget it." Brennan spread two large palms on the edge of his desk and rose, his girth straining at his white uniform shirt, his face growing redder and puffier right up to his thinning silver hair. "Who gave you authorization to go looking through other marshals' investigations?"

"I was just being thorough . . ." Georgia stammered.

"Thorough? By trying to show people up? Undermining their credibility?"

"Not at all . . ."

"Well, that's what it sounds like. Sounds to me like you're saying everybody else was sitting on their brains while half of New York burned to the ground. And lo and behold, with only—what? A year and a half in this bureau? Seven, tops, in the FDNY?—you've got everything solved."

Georgia swallowed. *Why did Walter ever get me into this?* "What if something was overlooked? Are you saying you don't want to know?"

"What I'm saying, Skeehan, is that your input here is over. Do I make myself clear?"

She felt weak and nauseated, anxiously aware of the bitter coffee she'd gulped this morning. In Brennan's mind, she was now a backstabber. As long as he sat in that chair, she could count on writing fireworks summonses for the rest of her career.

"Something wrong here, Arthur? I could hear you bellowing all the way down the hall."

Fire Commissioner William Lynch was standing in the doorway. Georgia had forgotten his office was on the same floor. Though Lynch was easily a half foot shorter than the chief, Brennan's expression of panic reminded her of a humbled schoolyard bully's. Lynch had the power to hire and, if not fire, at least retire anyone who sufficiently ticked him off.

"It's just a small department matter, Bill," said Brennan, nervously patting the air.

Lynch ignored him, shifting his gaze around the room. "Good to see you again, young lady." He nodded to Georgia. He passed a fleeting glance over Marenko, who seemed to be trying to melt into the dingy beige of the walls. By the time Lynch settled his eyes back on Brennan's, they were hard. And in that instant, Georgia knew. The commissioner and the chief fire marshal hated each other.

Lynch turned his attention to Georgia.

"Refresh my memory, Marshal. The name is . . . ?"

"Skeehan. Georgia Skeehan."

"Have you been with the bureau long?"

Probably about thirty more minutes, if Chief Brennan gets his way. "Almost nineteen months, sir," she replied.

"So you'll be part of the Rubi Wang investigation?"

Brennan cleared his throat. "I've appointed Supervising Marshal Marenko here to head the investigation. He's been with the bureau for ten years. He's a sixteen-year veteran of the FDNY with two Class B citations—"

"What brings you to headquarters, Marshal Skeehan?" Lynch asked, pointedly ignoring Brennan.

"It's like the chief says, Commissioner. Just a department matter."

"Oh, really?" Lynch pulled up a chair from the conference table and sat down with a casual slouch that suggested he wasn't going anywhere. "I'd like to hear about this *department* matter."

Georgia shot a sideways glance at Brennan's acne-scarred face. He was giving her a hard look. She could deliver an Oscar-winning performance and still wind up dead. Maybe it was time to try a different tack.

"Commissioner, have you ever heard of high-temperature accelerants, or HTAs?"

Lynch shook his head, so Georgia gave him a brief sketch of the pattern of fires. Brennan interrupted.

"Bill, I can assure you my men will consider every lead. But for a rookie to assume these fires are related without any shred of evidence—"

"Except the letters," Georgia mumbled. The room went silent. Brennan shot a quizzical look at Marenko, who spread his palms and shrugged.

"The letters. The three letters," Georgia stammered. "From someone calling himself the Fourth Angel." She turned to the commissioner.

"Twenty-four hours after the first two fires and twenty-four hours *before* the third, a letter arrived here at department headquarters." She fished copies of the three letters out of a folder and handed them to the commissioner. Lynch studied them carefully, then handed them to Brennan.

"You haven't seen these before?" he asked the chief.

"No." Brennan wiped a hand across his ruddy face and held the packets up to Marenko, who also shook his head.

Now it was Georgia's turn to be surprised. Frankel had insisted he'd made the letters known. Marenko might not have been aware of them, but Brennan? That seemed impossible. The chief handed the letters back to Georgia.

"Where did you get these?"

"They were supposedly part of the original reports."

"Not that I saw," Brennan countered.

"Commissioner, may I say something?" Marenko had been remarkably quiet until now, Georgia noticed. Lynch nodded for him to continue.

"I don't know where these letters came from or who wrote them. But I'll tell you this: there are dozens of wackos in New York—harmless wackos—who do nothing but write threatening letters. And tracking them down won't solve the Spring Street arson. Somebody offed Rubi Wang because they were sore at him. Or his magazine. Or somebody at his party. The odds are very good that this fire was a jealous-lover, Happy Land sort of thing." In March 1990, eighty-seven New Yorkers died after a jilted boyfriend set fire to gasoline he poured into the Happy Land social club in the Bronx. It was one of the deadliest arsons in city history.

"I've already gotten hold of a surveillance tape from a warehouse across the street from the fire," Marenko continued. "It shows a guy in a cowboy hat leaving the building at eleven P.M.—just minutes before the first alarm was called in. We're circulating a sketch through the media. Our boy shouldn't be hard to find."

Lynch steepled his fat fingers under his double chin. No one spoke. Georgia could hear herself breathing.

"Tell me, Marshal Skeehan," the commissioner said finally. "What would *you* do if you were part of this investigation?"

"But sir, I—"

"Indulge me."

She sucked in a deep breath. "I would certainly follow up on the surveillance tape, as Marshal Marenko is suggesting. But I still think it's a hell of a coincidence that four very hot blazes with all the earmarks of HTA have taken place in New York City within a five-month period. I think the connections bear investigating. I think the letters do, too."

Lynch's smooth, blank features betrayed no emotion. Then, all at once, he clapped his hands.

"I agree," he said. "And since you're the only one here with the guts to pursue this, I want you on board."

"Sir?"

"You heard me. I want you to be part of the Rubi Wang investigation."

Brennan was on his feet immediately. His complexion had gone from red to ashen. "She'll be a drain on manpower and resources . . ." the chief stammered.

"My best guys are gonna end up baby-sitting her," Marenko protested.

Georgia tried to quell the trembling in her voice. "Sir, this is a great honor, believe me. But I'm really not qualified—"

The commissioner slammed his fist on the conference table.

"This lousy department wouldn't even *have* the investigation if it weren't for me. You think the NYPD just rolled over and played dead? I went into debt with the mayor big-time, so don't even *think* of telling me who I can and can't appoint."

A dull throb began to form at Georgia's temples. A capricious appointment by a hated outsider could doom her entire career in the FDNY. But that was something the commissioner probably hadn't considered. Lawyers, she reminded herself, play by a different set of rules.

Lynch glanced at his watch, a clear sign the meeting was over. "There's a cocktail party I've been asked to speak at tonight, at Sloane Michaels's hotel, the Knickerbocker Plaza. Michaels is a good friend of mine. It was his building that burned on Spring Street. I would appreciate it, Marshal Skeehan, if you'd accompany me and help calm everyone's jitters over the situation."

"Uh, yessir," Georgia choked out.

"Good. The event's at eight P.M. Black-tie. Please give my secretary your address and my car will pick you up at seven-thirty." He gave Brennan a parting look. "And Arthur, you try to sabotage Marshal Skeehan or any part of this investigation, I won't only go after *you,* I'll go after your nice fat pension. . . . Civil servants, my ass," Lynch muttered as he left. "Three years running this godforsaken bureaucracy, and I haven't met a civil one yet."

Lynch's footsteps disappeared down the hallway. Georgia fought the tightening in her throat. "Chief, it was never my intention to undermine—"

"Shut up," said Brennan icily. "Shut up and listen good." He pointed a fat finger at her. "You're window dressing on this investigation, you hear me? Keep quiet and do as you're told, and maybe I'll just forget this ever happened. But if you do anything to make me look bad, I swear, EEO or no EEO, after this is over, you won't have the authority to piss out a match in this city. Got that, Skeehan?"

"Yes, sir. I got it."

CHAPTER *Eight*

Georgia was so shaky from the morning's encounter that she missed her turn on the Brooklyn–Queens Expressway. While she was crawling through traffic, she dialed Walter Frankel from her cell phone and told him the news.

"*Mazel tov*. Lynch has more brains than I gave him credit for."

For a smart man, Frankel could be deliberately obtuse at times. "Walter, I'm in a no-win situation. If I do my job well, they'll say I'm looking to upstage them. If I do nothing, they'll say, 'See? She was just a political appointee.' "

"You want some advice? Follow the letters from the Fourth Angel."

"Hey, news flash. Brennan and Marenko say they've never seen them before."

"They're lying."

"Funny, they'd probably say the same about you."

He laughed. "Keep me in the loop."

"Yeah, the hanging kind."

She hung up and made her way into Manhattan and across town to Engine Two in the West Village. Engine Two, the site of the new task force, was a squat, heavy redbrick firehouse, two stories high, with cornices pockmarked from years of grime and exhaust. The red enamel apparatus door was open, and the engine in quarters. A burly young firefighter sat at a desk near the entrance.

"Yeah?"

"I'm Fire Marshal Georgia Skeehan. I'm part of the new task force."

He knew the back story already. She could tell by the sour, distant look in his eyes. *Telephone, telegraph, tell-a-firefighter.* News travels fast in the FDNY.

He pointed to a metal staircase across the apparatus floor with the word BROADWAY taped to the wall behind it. Underneath, someone had pasted a picture of a naked woman. Boys will be boys.

On the second story, gray light oozed in through an old airshaft, dribbling across wainscoting painted with too many coats of mud brown and plaster walls as cracked and gouged as a child's scabby knees. Long ago, a battalion chief had been stationed here, in a small room across from the brass sliding pole. The frosted-glass door to that room now had a piece of lined notebook paper taped across it. FIRE AND ARSON-RELATED TACTICS SQUAD, it read. Georgia didn't know the task force had an official name. Then she made the connection. In this acronym-happy bureaucracy, the men had dubbed this the FART Squad.

Mac Marenko was already inside, hunched over a compact figure with broad shoulders and coppery skin who was puffing a Newport Light at a computer terminal. Neither of them bothered to acknowledge her, though Georgia recognized the seated marshal immediately. His name was Eddie Suarez; he was a crackerjack investigator, fluent in Spanish, with a good ten years in the bureau. She wasn't surprised to find him on the investigation. She closed the door and breathed a sigh of relief when she saw another marshal poke his face out of the evidence locker: Randy Carter. He still looked dazed and drawn, but at least they would be working together.

Carter's eyes met hers. He offered a quick, faint smile, which Georgia returned, though she was surprised at his tentativeness. His tie appeared hastily knotted, and there was a slump to his shoulders she had never noticed before. It occurred to her suddenly that Carter might be ill.

She walked over. "I called your house twice yesterday. You never called back."

"Sorry," he mumbled. "I got home late." He attached a log book to the front of the evidence locker without meeting her gaze, then meticulously recorded the date on the top sheet. He seemed aware of Georgia's shadow, hovering expectantly, but made no move to speak.

"Okay, *fine.*" She hissed. "*Don't* tell me what's going on. Shit, Randy. You can recite the names, occupations, and personal tics of every one of my dates from hell. . . . When Ma found that lump on her breast last fall? Before we knew it was benign? You baby-sat me on the job—and off. For Chrissake, *you* can tell when I'm on the rag. What is it you can't share with *me*?"

Carter sighed and shook his head. "I would, Skeehan. If I could tell anybody, I . . ." He fumbled around for something more to say. But his hurt—deep and profound and unspeakable as it apparently was—had seemingly robbed him of the ability. He squeezed her shoulder. "I'm sorry, girl. I gotta work this one out for myself."

"I'm just worried . . ."

"I know you are. I appreciate that."

Marenko, his tie loosened and his shirtsleeves rolled up, breezed by and pointedly slammed a box of supplies at Carter's feet. "There's ten more where that came from."

Georgia faced Marenko. "What would you like me to do?" she asked.

"You don't want me to answer that one, sweetheart," he said, then turned on his heel and went back to unloading supplies.

Georgia threw her jacket on a chair and walked up to him. He was standing in front of a file cabinet, attempting to open the top drawer, which was stuck.

"Look Mac," she said. "I realize we didn't start off too well today, but if you'll just give me an assignment—"

Marenko banged on the side of the drawer and cursed, pointedly ignoring her.

"I'm eager to learn and I won't get in anyone's way."

He didn't give any hint that he'd heard. So Georgia stepped between him and the file cabinet. From a black leather bag she wore around her waist, she extracted a small screwdriver she always carried, poked it in the drawer, grabbed the handle and lifted. The drawer slid smoothly forward.

Marenko, nearly a foot taller, made a face and patted his empty shirt pocket searching, it seemed, for a cigarette. "Everybody's got a talent," he said sourly. "Yours seems to be showing people up."

"I was trying to help."

"I'll just bet you were." He grabbed a toothpick from a drawer and jabbed it in his mouth.

"You gotta excuse Mac," said Suarez, flicking ashes in an empty Coke can. "He just quit smoking. What is this, Mac? Your fifth try?"

"Why don't you just discuss my sex life while you're at it."

"I would if you had one."

Georgia followed Marenko around the room while he checked paper supplies and set up mail bins and key locations.

"C'mon, Mac," she reasoned. "Give me a chance. I'll do a thorough job. Randy will tell you—I'm no slouch. We make a good team."

Marenko, squatting to count cartons of fax paper, stopped in mid-count, grinned, and shook his head.

"What's so funny?"

He stood up. "Carter may be your partner when this investigation's over. But on *my* task force, sweetheart, *I* decide who partners with who. Carter's with Eddie Suarez."

"So who's my partner?"

The frosted glass door burst open, and a heavy wheezing and shuffling resonated from the hallway.

"Did youse guys know they don't make raspberry jelly doughnuts after nine A.M.? The creams and powdereds, they make all day. . . . Like, what's with the jelly? Nobody in New York eats jelly after nine A.M.?"

Georgia's heart sank. She knew the heavy Brooklyn accent even before she turned.

"Marshal Skeehan," said Marenko, with a gallant wave of his muscular arm, "meet your new partner."

Gene Cambareri dropped a box of doughnuts on an empty desk, then licked powdered sugar off his stubby fingers. He was sixty-two, balding, and suffered from bunions that made him walk so slowly that he'd earned the nickname "Lightning," typical firehouse black humor. Most days he spent gossiping and playing gin rummy with the old warhorses on the job. At least sixty pounds overweight, he hadn't made a collar in years and, with just three months to go before retirement, wasn't about to make any waves now.

Cambareri shuffled over and extended a sticky hand. "Pleased to be working with youse, Georgia." A cheap tie rode halfway up his belly, and his white shirt sported a grease stain across the pocket. Georgia shook hands, then shot Marenko a murderous stare as Cambareri lumbered across the room to greet Carter and Suarez.

"Nice move, Mac," she muttered. "You think this one up all by yourself, or did Chief Brennan help your gray matter along?"

"Hey, a rookie can learn a lot from an experienced hand." He shrugged, stifling a grin. "That means anywhere you go, Gene goes too."

"Oh goody," Georgia said dryly. "And where, exactly, are we going?"

"Site protection."

Georgia gritted her teeth. Site protection was a fancy name for standing around the scene of the fire all day, making sure no civilians decide to grab a couple of souvenirs from the debris. It was the job of a rookie beat cop, not an assigned member of the task force.

"You're a prince, Marenko. Anyone ever tell you that?"

He popped a stick of gum in his mouth and blew a large bubble. "Anytime you wanna quit the task force, just say the words."

"I'd sooner die."

"A few days of this, sweetheart, you'll wish you had."

CHAPTER Nine

Three P.M. Wednesday afternoon. Gene Cambareri was slumped in the driver's seat of their department-issued Chevy Caprice, snoring. It felt to Georgia like she had been parked across from the fire scene on Spring Street for four hours. In reality, it had been only forty-five minutes.

The crime-scene tape was up, the place well barricaded from prying eyes. Every time Georgia saw a pedestrian peering through the plyboard slats at the charred site, she left the car, flashed her badge, and asked her standard questions: *Were you here the night of the fire? Did you see anything? Do you know anyone with any information?* She paid special attention to people who brought flowers and religious medals or lit candles. Arsonists love to revisit the scenes of their crimes.

No one had seen or heard anything. Georgia punched the Caprice's dashboard.

"I'll bet Marenko's at the task force now, laying out the entire investigation with Randy and Eddie," she fumed. "And we won't know zip because we're here."

Cambareri opened one eye. "Georgia, what are youse killing yourself for? Anything Marenko wants us to know, he'll tell us."

"He doesn't want us to *know* anything. That's the point."

"You can't get in trouble with what you don't know. Take it from someone who's been on the job thirty-five years." He yawned and scratched his belly. "Youse want something to eat? I know a great little diner around the corner. Best coconut cream pie in the city. Show 'em your badge and they'll give you a ten percent discount. We can get a table near the window, have coffee, watch the building from there . . ."

Georgia shook her head. "You go, Gene. I don't mind."

"Youse worry too much for a young girl. Hey, you know Larry Mancuso? Fire marshal up in the Bronx? He worries about everything, just like you."

"I don't know him," said Georgia irritably. She wasn't interested in Cambareri's gossip.

"Yeah, well, Larry, see? He got behind on his paperwork. And he had these buildings that were supposed to be condemned or something. I mean, who's got time for that stuff? And he put the paperwork aside, and bam! One day, one of the buildings turns into a parking lot. Real bad fire. A street mutt dies and Larry's all worried. He's thinkin' he's gonna lose his job 'cause that building shouldn't have been there."

"So?" Georgia asked impatiently. "What's your point?"

"My point?" Cambareri said, spreading his fleshy palms. "Larry made himself sick about this fire. And he didn't lose his job. Didn't even get a reprimand in his folder. The department just buried the thing— end of story. So you see? Things work out. Have some coffee and pie with me. We can play a hand of gin rummy."

"Some other time, Gene," said Georgia. "I promise."

"Youse sure?"

"I'm sure."

Cambareri got out of the car and waddled down the street. Georgia watched him, feeling bad she wasn't being nicer. It was Marenko she was frustrated with.

In the rearview mirror, she caught sight of a white woman in her early twenties, carrying a scraggly bouquet of daisies. Her hair was dyed the color of eggplant. She wore a ring through her nose. And she was dressed entirely in black, though it looked expensive, not thrift-shoppy. Some rich Westchester girl—a Sally—trying to look downtown cool. The young woman crossed the street and tenderly laid the bouquet on top of several others at the fire site. Georgia got out of the Caprice and flashed her gold shield.

"Hey, can I talk to you?"

The young woman looked up, her mascara-caked eyes widening as she took in the badge. Then she did something Georgia was totally unprepared for. She ran.

"Hey!" Georgia sprinted after her, cursing the weight of her holstered nine-millimeter as it repeatedly banged into her right hip. No point in radioing Cambareri for help. With his bunions, Lightning wasn't likely to give chase, anyway. She caught up to Miss Eggplant and yanked her over to a warehouse wall by her dyed hair.

"Are you a cop?" the woman gasped as Georgia frisked her.

"Fire marshal." Georgia went through the woman's pockets. No weapons—just a plastic bag full of pills. "And I suppose these are vitamins, huh?" She waved the bag in the woman's face.

"Please don't bust me. My parents will kill me."

Georgia wasn't about to tell her that the NYPD, not fire marshals, usually made drug arrests. The woman's driver's license said her name was Alison Simon. She had a Saks Fifth Avenue credit card and a Parsons School of Design student ID in the same name. Definitely a rich Sally from the 'burbs, Georgia decided.

"You put flowers down back there. Why?"

"I knew Fred, the building super? He died in the fire?" Georgia stifled the urge to roll her eyes. Alison was one of those people who turned every statement into a question.

"Do you know anything about how the fire started?"

Miss Eggplant didn't answer. Georgia spun her around. "Maybe you want to think about it while you spend a night in slam for the, uh, vitamins," she bluffed.

Alison twirled a strand of purplish hair around a black-painted nail. "It's not me you wanna talk to. It's my boyfriend, Jose."

"Why's that?"

"Fred and Jose were sort of . . . business partners . . ."

"Business partners?"

Alison shifted feet nervously. "Yeah. Fred hired Jose to fix things? You know—locks, door hinges, that kind of stuff in the building. But Jose was also, like—"

"The local supplier." A pretty common side occupation in lower Manhattan. Georgia knew full well that a lot of handymen dealt drugs, and building superintendents sometimes took a cut. She made a note to get the super's full name and address off the building records and interview his next of kin, if Marenko hadn't done that already.

"So, why should I talk to Jose?"

"Jose told me that Fred was pissed. He was gonna lose his job? On account of the drugs? He, uh, told Jose he wished he could burn the whole friggin' building down."

"The superintendent at One-thirty-one Spring Street threatened to torch the building?" Georgia tried not to betray her rising excitement.

"Yeah. That's what Jose told me."

If it was true, it was a tremendous break—one Georgia couldn't afford to let slip away. Unlike police officers, fire marshals have the authority to take sworn statements—affidavits, admissible in court—on the spot. Georgia wrote up Alison Simon's statement in her notebook and had her sign it. She pictured Mac Marenko's shocked expression when she placed this little piece of evidence on his desk. The day wasn't turning out so badly after all.

"Where can I find your boyfriend? His name's Jose . . . what?"

Alison shrugged.

"He's your boyfriend and you don't know his last name?"

"He moves around a lot," she said, twisting her hair more vigorously around her finger. Georgia's heart sank. Without a direct witness to the super's remarks, Alison Simon's statements were little more than hearsay. And, for all she knew, "Jose" wasn't even the guy's real name. No doubt *he* didn't have a Saks Fifth Avenue credit card.

"Does Jose have a phone number where I can reach him?"

"He's got a cell, but . . . like . . . you call him on that, he might take a walk, you know?"

"Why? Are the cops looking for him?"

Alison shrugged. "He's, uh, got a couple of outstanding bench warrants."

"For selling drugs?"

"Yeah." This college friend was probably one Miss Eggplant's parents had never met.

"I've gotta talk to him, Alison. As soon as possible. It's vital."

The young woman sighed. "I can probably get him to contact you tomorrow if you promise not to bust him."

"Tell him I'm a fire marshal—not NYPD. If he plays it straight with me, and the bench warrants are what you say they are, I won't ask him about anything except the arson."

CHAPTER Ten

The chief heard the commotion at six P.M. Wednesday evening, right after he got home from work. Celia Maldonado's boyfriend, Orlando, was screaming in Spanish. Ramon was crying. He couldn't hear Luis or Bobby. They had vanished—just as Luis's bike had the day before.

The chief opened his apartment door and stood in the stairwell. He still had spackling compound on his hands and paint flecks in his blond hair from the TriBeCa job. Police sirens were screeching in the street. Curious neighbors were crowding the doorways.

Ramon was clinging to his mother's hips, his large, dark eyes nearly swollen shut from crying. He looked up and saw the familiar paint-spattered white work pants.

"Chief! Chief!" the little boy wailed. "Don't let them take me."

The chief squatted before the boy. "What's going on, squirt?"

"Somebody said Orlando was bad. But it ain't true."

"Of course it's not true."

"Now we got to go away," sobbed Ramon.

The chief straightened and stared down at the short, beefy black woman who had been trying to separate Ramon from his mother. "What do you think you're doing?" he demanded.

The woman frowned at him, suspiciously taking in his white skin in a neighborhood where Anglos were outsiders. "Who are *you*?"

"A neighbor . . . Look, I live above the family. I'll vouch for 'em. Orlando's great with the kids. And Celia's a good mother . . ."

"I'm afraid we've had a complaint, sir . . ."

"From whom?"

"Complaints to the Bureau of Child Welfare are made anonymously. I couldn't tell you even if I knew."

"The kids can stay with me," he pleaded.

"I'm afraid that's impossible. There's nothing anyone can do until this is straightened out. Now, please let me do my job." The woman carried the screaming child down the stairs. Orlando, meanwhile, was spitting and throwing things at police while other tenants looked on.

"I never laid a hand on those kids," he shouted. Celia clung to him, sobbing, but he seemed not to notice. His dark eyes were full of confusion and rage. Two cops finally managed to back him against a wall and cuff him. Celia spoke soothingly to him in Spanish, but he didn't answer. The chief could already see it in the man's eyes: no matter what the outcome, Orlando would never be coming back.

Out front, Ramon was being ushered into the back of a dark blue sedan, where Luis and Bobby were already strapped in. The chief got to the street just in time to see Ramon's toothless face pressed against the rear passenger window, tears and mucus streaking the glass. Orlando, his hands cuffed behind his back, saw it too. He flicked his sad eyes at the chief, a brief, questioning appeal in his stare. The chief looked away. Then a cop shoved Orlando into the backseat of a cruiser and they were gone, with only the bleating wail of the siren to mark their absence.

The upstairs hallway was empty, the neighbors back behind locked doors. Celia was rooted to a spot by a window, staring out at the thickening darkness. When she did finally sit down on the stairway landing, it was with a finality that suggested she might never get up again.

"They took my babies. They took my man," she cried, head in her hands. "For what? He didn't touch nobody. First decent man I ever had . . ."

The chief sat on the grimy step beside her and put a muscular arm around her shoulder. Her bones felt so brittle, he was sure he could snap them in two if he tried.

"Hey, Orlando'll be back," he lied. "The cops will realize it's all a big mistake and release him. A few house visits, and those rug rats will be tearing up the halls again."

She palmed her dark eyes and looked at him hopefully. "You really think?"

"Of course." He shrugged. "I'll make a few calls. Pull a few strings. I've got tons of connections where it counts in this city. Cops, fire-fighters—you name it. If I don't know 'em, then my old man, God rest his soul, did. Orlando will be out in twenty-four hours, tops. We'll get the kids back by next week."

"Oh, thank you. Thank you," Celia sobbed, hugging his paint-spattered sweatshirt. "You always been so good to my boys. They worship you. You a hero to them. I don't know what we'd do without you."

The chief smiled and patted her back. "That's what I'm here for. To help."

CHAPTER Eleven

For a blue-collar girl from Queens, it was a once-in-a-lifetime event. Georgia knew that even before she entered the enormous Renaissance-style suite in Sloane Michaels's new luxury hotel, the Knickerbocker Plaza. Yet it still awed her to be forty-eight stories above the twinkling lights of Manhattan, at a party hosted by a multimillionaire and peopled with network anchors, Broadway actresses, athletes, and models whose faces screamed at her from billboards across New York.

"Quite a crowd, isn't it?" asked Lynch, looking even more portly than usual in his tuxedo.

Georgia breathed in deeply. "Yes, sir." She made mental notes of the celebrities she saw, knowing her mother and Gallagher would salivate over every juicy detail. But those faces she didn't recognize—for the most part, the heavier-set, older men—radiated an even more profound sense of stature. Georgia guessed that these were the investment bankers, CEOs, and art patrons whose money and power quietly and steadfastly ran the city when all the razzle-dazzle of the stars had faded.

Snippets of their conversations drifted over from a marble bar decked out in pink tulips and white freesia: *Their house in the Hamptons just made the cover of* Architectural Digest. . . . *They're on the priority list for tables at Balthazar. . . . He's leaving Dalton for Phillips Andover next year. . . .*

What am I doing here anyway? Georgia wondered. Her black silk chemise had soaked up so much static from the commissioner's limo that it puckered like shrink wrap around her thighs. Her fake patent-leather pumps from Payless Shoes squeaked across the parquet floors. She still had that stupid screwdriver in her handbag. And heaven help her if she opened her mouth. That would be a dead giveaway. Or, as people from her neck of the woods said, *Fugedabowdit.*

To make matters worse, Lynch kept introducing her to party guests as "the department's star investigator." Each time he said it, Georgia reddened, picturing the marshals in the FART Squad guffawing.

People were gracious. They asked questions, seemingly fascinated by the work she did. Yet Georgia found herself holding back, fearing—perhaps irrationally—that the drama and pathos of her job couldn't be communicated over bites of smoked-salmon sushi. No one here, after all, had ever had to look at a charred cadaver up close, peel a flailing junkie off a burning bed, or hold a sooty child and watch her die. They saw death from afar, in sanitized, two-column obits prominently displayed in *The New York Times,* in formal lavish funerals, in dedications to museums and scholarships in the departed's honor. To offer up her very real and gut-wrenching experiences in the guise of entertainment would only serve to cheapen them. She'd hate herself in the morning.

She had no idea, however, that her regrets were about to start even earlier than she could've imagined. An hour into cocktails, Sloane Michaels introduced the commissioner to the crowd. Georgia had expected Lynch to deliver a short boilerplate speech. She'd forgotten Frankel's warning that the commissioner was in this job to grab a few headlines. With network anchors and prominent media people standing wall to wall, he couldn't have picked a better place.

"The fire on Spring Street may have been started by an unusual substance that burns at extremely high temperatures," Lynch told the audience in a lawyerly tone which suggested he had personally come to this expert conclusion. "Since last December, there have been several similar, unexplained fires across New York—"

Already, a well-known television reporter was shouting out a question. "Are you suggesting that one person set all these fires?"

Georgia flinched. *Please don't answer,* she thought, looking at Lynch. *It's too early to speculate.* But the commissioner was on a roll.

"Do the math. I'm saying that there's a possibility—and I stress, *possibility*—that all these extremely rare fires are related. So the answer is yes."

Noises of shock and concern arose from the audience. Veteran journalists excused themselves to phone their news organizations. *And what if this angle doesn't pan out?* thought Georgia. Alison Simon's statement earlier today suggested the fire might be nothing more than the work of an angry building super. The guys at the task force would think Georgia was behind this little stunt. She retreated to the bathroom, feeling sick.

When she emerged, Sloane Michaels was standing before her, holding out a martini. He was shorter than the images Georgia had seen of him on magazine covers and television. She looked over her shoulder, assuming the drink was for someone else, then blushed when she realized it was for her.

"I haven't had a chance to meet you yet this evening, Marshal. My apologies. You looked like you could use a drink." He slipped the glass into her hand.

"Thank you," Georgia mumbled shyly. She didn't drink martinis. But hey, this was Sloane Michaels. You didn't say no. And besides, right now, she needed something stiff.

"Is what the commissioner said true? That the department thinks a serial arsonist burned down my building and killed all those people?"

Georgia took a gulp of the martini. The olive sank to the bottom of the glass. It was the only part she wanted, but she decided against fishing it out with her fingers. "I'm sorry, Mr. Michaels, I'm . . . not at liberty to say."

"But the commissioner—"

"Has to answer to the mayor only. I have a string of higher-ups who would roast me alive for speaking out of turn."

"I understand." He nodded thoughtfully. "And I respect that." The silver flecks in his hair and close-cropped beard sparkled under the chandelier lights. Crow's feet at the corners of his root-beer-colored eyes, so artfully underplayed on camera, were obvious when he smiled. Still, he posed a striking presence for a man of fifty. "Is there something I can do to help, at least?"

She thought a moment. "Actually, yes. The building super at Spring Street—what was his name?"

The smile left his lips. "Fred Fischer, why?"

"Did you have any problems with him? Did he ever threaten you?"

Michaels closed his eyes and placed his right thumb and forefinger on the bridge of his nose. A diamond-studded college ring glistened in the light. "It's a long, complicated story." He sighed. "You want to walk and talk?"

"I don't want to drag you away from your party."

"Trust me, you aren't." He lifted his gaze to two assistants standing discreetly out of earshot and pointed to his watch. Then he ushered her out a side door to a bank of elevators. "So, you used to be a firefighter, huh?"

"That's right. For five and a half years."

From a pocket in his tux, Michaels produced an electronic key card and inserted it into a special panel in the elevator which opened to reveal a series of color-coded buttons.

"Ever rescue anybody?" He caught her look of discomfort. "I guess that's like asking a combat veteran about his war experiences."

"I'm sorry," she apologized as they stepped into the elevator. "It's my fault. I'm just not comfortable being the FDNY poster girl. I don't know how to speak the language."

"And what language is that?"

Georgia felt the lift in her feet as the elevator plummeted forty-six stories. "Your language. The language of the people at the party. It's like . . ." She searched for an analogy. "You ride in a limo, I ride on a Harley . . ."

"Fathead or Evo?"

"Huh?"

"Personally, I prefer the Fathead engine. More torque. More throttle."

"You ride?" Georgia asked with amazement.

"Every chance I get."

The elevator delivered them directly into a handsome suite of offices on the mezzanine level. The walls were paneled in cherry, the ceilings were high and rimmed with dentil moldings, the furniture was over-stuffed leather and brocade. It had the look of old New York, despite having been built less than a year before.

Michaels put a finger to his lips and assumed a pensive pose. "Let's see, I'm going to guess you ride a Harley Softail Custom—"

She reared back. "How would you—?"

"Classic twenty-one-inch laced front wheel, solid-mounted Evo engine, thirteen-forty cc's, modified cam. . . . And I'll bet it's fire-engine red, right?"

"I can't afford to modify the cam, but you got the rest right. How?"

"I figured, being a firefighter, you're athletic. Not afraid of big machinery. If you're going to ride, you're not going to do it halfway. No eight-eighty-three-cc Sportster for you."

"Okay . . ."

"Women who ride tell me they like the Softail. It's moderately priced, so it's within your budget. It's a model that's not overloaded with a lot of testosterone toys. And, for a firefighter, I figure it's gotta be red."

"You're good."

He winked at her. "You're only saying that because you don't know me yet."

A call came in on his cell phone, and Michaels excused himself to take it. Georgia played name-that-face with the photos of famous people on the wall of his office. There were the politicians, the movie stars, the foreign dignitaries. Michaels wore a practiced cheerfulness in all of them. Like he wanted to be somewhere else.

On his desk—a gleaming antique mahogany—she expected to find a perfectly posed portrait of his wife. But when she looked at the desk photo now, she was struck by something far more powerful.

The framed photo was indeed of a woman whom she guessed to be his wife. But it was an unposed shot—an enlarged snapshot, really—of Michaels and her at some kind of formal social gathering. Michaels wore a tux and looked a little more boyish and a little less gray. His wife was reed-thin with short dark hair. She was an unremarkable-looking woman in a forgettable black evening dress. Definitely not a trophy wife.

Georgia guessed the shot was probably five or six years old. The quality was poor, and neither Michaels nor his wife looked particularly stunning in it. Yet the more Georgia looked at the picture, the more struck she was by something so deep, so personal, that she felt as if she were reading someone's diary. For in this shot, Michaels wasn't looking at the cameras. He was looking at his wife, with his arm wrapped so protectively around her brittle, narrow shoulders that it seemed he was holding her against a force that threatened to take her away. The vulnerability of it touched Georgia. She wondered what it felt like to be loved like that. She didn't think she'd ever know.

"Amelia was a runner," said Michaels, nodding to the photograph as he put down the phone. "She won medals. Now she can't walk. My wife has MS."

"I'm so sorry." Georgia averted her gaze from the photo. She didn't want him to know the longings it spoke to in her own life. "I have a good friend with MS. He's in that program you fund at New York Hospital."

Michaels sighed. "I wish money could make them better. This"—he gestured to the cherry-paneled walls around them—"is glorious. But it can't give my wife back her legs . . . or all those people at Spring Street their lives."

Georgia asked him to tell her about Fred Fischer. "You had problems with him?"

Michaels smiled sadly and shook his head. "He didn't set the fire, Ms. Skeehan."

"What makes you so sure?"

"Two reasons." Michaels walked over to his bookshelf, pulled down a gold-framed black-and-white photo of two boys, and handed it to her.

Georgia stared at the older figure, a lean, dark-haired youth of about twelve. "Is this you?"

"Uh-huh. And the little guy"—he pointed to a tow-headed child of about four, giggling beside him—"was my half brother, Fred."

"Fred Fischer was your *brother*?"

Michaels retreated behind his desk and toyed with a paper clip without meeting her gaze. His voice was hoarse when he spoke. "Fred was going through some problems. I figured the super's job might keep him straight. I didn't even know he was in the building until I got the call yesterday to come down to the medical examiner's office and ID his body."

"Oh, Mr. Michaels, I'm so sorry." It struck Georgia suddenly how many losses the man was dealing with—his wife's illness, his brother's gruesome death, the guilt of all those people dying in *his* building. Maybe she'd been too quick to judge him earlier. Maybe deep down, they didn't speak such a different language after all. "Were you and Fred close?"

Michaels tossed the paper clip across his desk in disgust and tried to regain his composure. "I'd be dishonest if I didn't tell you it was up and down." He sighed. "Sober, Fred was a really decent man. But lately, he wasn't sober all that often. First, it was booze. Then it turned to cocaine . . ."

"Did you try to get him help?"

Michaels nodded. "He didn't want my help."

"I have a witness who says Fred threatened to burn the building down."

"Fred threatened lots of stuff when he was stoned." Michaels's face clouded over. "I know what you're thinking, Marshal. That I'm just protecting my brother's memory. . . . Look, I told you there were *two* reasons I knew why Fred didn't set that fire. One is 'cause he's my brother and I *know* him."

He yanked open a desk drawer and pulled out a sheet of paper. "Here's the second. I got this in the mail a few weeks ago. Fred couldn't have written anything like this."

Georgia looked at the sheet. It was a mimeographed copy of a piece of lined notebook paper with an eerily familiar scrawl across the top.

And the fourth angel poured out his vial upon the sun; and power was given unto him to scorch men with fire.

"I don't know if it's related to the fire or not," said Michaels. "But it scared me."

Georgia didn't blink. Her training would never allow her to divulge that Frankel had already shown her the original of this same letter. "Do you have the envelope it came in?"

"No. I didn't know what I was reading until I was reading it."

"Any other unusual occurrences? Things missing? Employees or business associates recently threaten you? You fire someone? Evict or sue somebody?"

"You left out 'beat a stray dog and steal money from a blind widow.' "

"This isn't a character assessment, Mr. Michaels. In my experience, stuff like this happens when someone's looking for revenge. So my question is, who'd want revenge?"

Michaels sank into his chair and put his head between his hands. "No one. Except for my brother, no one was particularly pissed off at me. Hell, I don't even know what the letter means."

"It means," said Georgia, "that you'd better watch your back."

CHAPTER *Twelve*

Thursday morning, Georgia and Cambareri had already been on their first wild goose chase of the day. Marenko had sent them out to Great Neck, Long Island, to interview a former disgruntled business partner of the late Rubi Wang. Not only had the guy already *been* interviewed by the NYPD's Arson and Explosion squad right after the fire, but he had an airtight alibi: he was getting gallbladder surgery that night. A check of his credit cards, phone calls, and electronic toll bridge receipts confirmed his story.

Cambareri thought the morning hadn't been a total waste. They had passed his favorite Brooklyn pizzeria on their way back to Manhattan. Thursdays, the sub sandwiches were half price, and he was eagerly tearing into a meatball parmigiana now as they sat in the car.

"This really stinks," said Georgia, tossing the remains of a slice of pizza into a paper bag on the backseat.

"Oh," he said. "You shoulda had the meatballs. Lotsa garlic. Wanna bite?"

"No, I don't mean the food. I mean what Mac's doing here. Do you realize we've got no idea what's happening on this investigation? We don't know if they've come up with any physical evidence to tie the fires together. We don't know if they've found that guy in the cowboy hat who was on that warehouse surveillance tape. I put that report on Mac's desk about Alison Simon and her boyfriend, Jose, and I don't even know if he's read it."

"Why youse wanna know everything?" asked Cambareri. "It'll just get youse in trouble. Look what happened to your old partner there . . ."

"Randy?" Georgia's ears pricked up. "You know what's eating him?"

Cambareri licked tomato sauce off his fingers and shrugged. "Naw. I'm talking 'bout maybe six, seven years ago. Before you were on the job. . . . He never told youse about Broph?"

Georgia shook her head.

"I shouldn't tell youse neither, then."

"Why?"

"Ancient history. And you know Carter—he keeps himself to himself."

"Was Randy in some kind of trouble? C'mon, Gene, if it's ancient history, what's the harm in talking about it?"

Cambareri sighed. "Carter had this partner, Paul Brophy. And . . . uh . . . Broph liked to gamble. Got himself into a jam. Found out he could clear his debts by looking the other way on an arson job at a dress warehouse in lower Manhattan. Broph was the lead investigator—"

"He took a bribe to label an arson accidental?" Unlike cops, fire marshals have the authority to decide if a crime has even been committed. Which means a crooked marshal, though rare, can wield a lot of unchecked power.

"Yeah. Only Carter decided it didn't all add up. So he went back over the evidence and started questioning his partner. When he didn't like the answers he was getting, he took the case to the IG." Inspector general's office—the equivalent of police internal affairs. "Broph broke down, admitted the bribe, and got fired."

"Randy did the right thing."

Cambareri pointed to his chest. "*I* agree with youse. But right's got nothing to do with it. A lotta guys think Carter shoulda tried to talk Broph outta what he was doin' or, if he couldn't, put in a request for a different partner. Carter broke the code of silence. Bad stuff happens when you do that."

Cambareri finished the last of his sub and wiped the grease from his lips. "I used to have this partner, see? Louie Frantangelo. He retired a couple of years ago. We used to go fishing on Long Island Sound together. They had sea bass three feet long out there in them days . . ."

Georgia rolled her eyes. Another Cambareri story. This should take up the afternoon.

"Louie and me, see? We get this call one day 'bout a small fire at this hotel up in Harlem. You know, not a hotel like you'd go on vacation or nothing. Like, they charge by the hour, know what I'm saying?"

"A whorehouse," said Georgia without interest.

"Yeah." Cambareri blushed. He didn't like talking coarsely around women. He reminded her of Jimmy Gallagher in that regard. "So's we get there and all these badges start coming outta the place."

"Badges?"

"One of 'em's a battalion chief, and he tells me, 'You didn't see me here.' Me? I wanted to walk around the block, grab some coffee, and come back. But Louie, he says, 'No, man. I got a job to do, brass or no brass.' "

"What happened?"

"We went in and arrested a two-bit pimp for setting a closet fire. He was out in six months—and Louie got lifted to Brooklyn. Ended up spending his days collaring street mutts who burn their old ladies' clothes for cheating on 'em."

"What are you saying, Gene? That Randy and Louie Frantangelo were wrong? That we shouldn't do our jobs?"

"Youse *are* doing your job, Georgia. This"—he pointed to their stuffy Caprice, reeking of tomato sauce and garlic—"*is* your job. See, maybe the department's got good reasons for you not to know something. That superhot fire last December at that Washington Heights furniture warehouse? The locals used to run a numbers joint in the basement there. Cops and firefighters got a ten percent discount. On paydays, the cruisers and rigs would be parked two deep at the curb. And that East Tremont building? That was my friend Larry Mancuso's job. How you think it's gonna look for him to have to admit that a building that wasn't supposed to be standing burned down on his watch?"

Georgia turned and looked at Cambareri for the first time—the tomato sauce splattered across his double chin, the rumpled creases in his white polyester dress shirt, the outline of a sleeveless white T-shirt beneath. For thirty-five years, he'd been trading doughnuts, card games, and gossip with guys in every firehouse in the city. If anyone knew the department's secrets, it was him.

"Gene, are you saying that the building Mancuso was supposed to have ordered condemned and demolished was the site of one of the HTA fires? And another occurred at an illegal gambling haunt of cops and firefighters?"

Cambareri waved his bearish paws in front of him. "Why youse wanna go making problems? Especially for a decent guy like Mancuso? He ain't no Paul Brophy."

"I don't want to make problems for anybody. But if the department's covering up something—is that why the building records are missing? Because the department doesn't want anyone to know that the East Tremont building shouldn't have been standing? That the paperwork was bungled? Or that an illegal gambling den was frequented by cops and firefighters?"

"I don't know about any of that stuff." Cambareri frowned, shaking his head vigorously like a little kid. "And I don't *want* to know."

"What about that superhot fire in Red Hook?"

"I'm taking youse back to Manhattan now," he said, ignoring her question. "We're supposed to pick up the autopsy reports from the medical examiner's office and deliver 'em to the task force. And that's *all* we're doing, Georgia. I'm not saying no more."

CHAPTER Thirteen

In New York, the living meet sudden death in the strangest of ways. Some slump over white linen tablecloths in four-star restaurants; others sprawl on park benches, or lie prostrate in bed beside a poor choice of lover. They meet death in fits of rage, in pleas of forgiveness, in cries of denial, and with nary a blink. In life, they could be princes or paupers, heirs or felons, geniuses or lunatics. In death, they share equal berths beside one another in the bowels of an unassuming eight-story turquoise-and-steel building at Thirtieth Street and First Avenue—the office of the Chief Medical Examiner of the City of New York.

"Follow the bodies," Carter always told Georgia. "Buildings will only tell you how they burned. They won't tell you why." People, however, were another matter. They were doozies. Georgia wished Carter were here now, using some phrase no one this side of eighty would understand.

The door to the chief medical examiner's office opened now, and a fireplug of a man with bushy black eyebrows thrust out a hand.

"Greetings. I am Dr. Kaplov." He rolled his *r*'s like some mad scientist in a Cold War–era movie. "You are marshals on the Spring Street investigation, yes?"

Georgia had been to the ME's office dozens of times and never met Kaplov. Assistants handled the smaller cases. She and Cambareri flashed their badges and handed Kaplov their business cards.

"We don't want to take up all youse time," Cambareri said quickly, shooting Georgia a warning glance. "We'll just take the reports. Our supervisor, Mac Marenko, will call youse later."

"That's fine," said Kaplov. "I'll ask my secretary to get them."

Kaplov buzzed her on the intercom while Georgia let her eyes wander the length of one of the walls of Kaplov's office. Mounted on it was a large framed medieval print depicting a group of young people on horseback coming across a pile of dead bodies in various horrific stages of decomposition. The dead had little bubbles of dialogue coming from their mouths. The words appeared to be in Italian.

"You are intrigued by the artwork, I see," said Kaplov.

The secretary knocked on the half-open office door and thrust a thick, bound report in Kaplov's hands, which he handed off to Georgia. "The print's a reproduction of a Francesco Traini fresco, painted in the fourteenth century, at the height of the bubonic plague. It's called *Triumph of Death.*"

"Pretty graphic," noted Georgia.

"I like the sentiment. Do you speak Italian?"

"I'm afraid not."

"The corpses say here, 'What you are, we once were. What we are, you will become.' "

"Comforting."

Kaplov grinned like a little boy who'd just scared his sister. Then he clasped his hands together. "You want to take a moment in my office to look through the report? Discuss anything with me?"

"No," Cambareri interjected. "Thank youse anyway." He made a move to the door. Georgia took a seat and defiantly began to flip through some pages. Cambareri folded his short, fat arms tightly, then leaned against a bookshelf, wheezing. Kaplov looked from Georgia to Cambareri and shrugged, like a man caught in the middle of a marital spat.

"On this page?" said Georgia, holding up a mimeographed section labeled *Cause of Death.* "For the firefighter Terry Quinn, you wrote 'Cause undetermined, pending police investigation.' "

"That's correct," said Kaplov.

"I thought Quinn wasn't wearing his facepiece, took too much smoke, and died of carbon monoxide poisoning."

"With contributing factors," explained Kaplov. "He *did* have lethal amounts of carbon monoxide in his blood. But he also presented a subdural hemorrhage on the right side of his skull."

"I don't follow."

"A subdural hemorrhage is bleeding into the brain. Quite possibly, he lost consciousness and fell on something, or something fell on him. But the angle is also consistent with blunt force trauma."

"Blunt force trauma?"

"Being hit—deliberately or not—with some blunt external object. There was pressure from your department to release him quickly so as not to prolong the family's suffering. Our offices, of course, obliged. But I will not allow my people to list a cause of death they're not satisfied with."

Kaplov's phone rang. He picked it up. Georgia massaged her temples and avoided Cambareri's frown. She tried to picture Quinn's last moments of life. Black smoke. Heat that even low to the floor was probably approaching 350 degrees. He was crawling around, taking puffs off his air tank with the cheater in his mouth. No mask, his PASS alarm off. He banged into something. A pipe. A two-by-four. Maybe his helmet came loose, and something fell on him and knocked him out. The jolt forced the cheater from his lips. Without his PASS alarm on, no one could find him in the smoke. It would take only four to six minutes to die that way. No grand mystery—just bad luck. She rose from her chair, to Cambareri's great relief.

"Just one more question, Doctor," said Georgia as Kaplov got off the phone. "Have all the bodies been identified?"

"All except for one," he replied. "A female—thirty to forty years of age. African-American. She's still downstairs. We can't track her through the guest list, and no one's come forward. Oh, and one more thing—she was pregnant."

"Really?" Georgia sat back down. Cambareri blew his nose loudly. On purpose, she surmised.

"The world is changing, yes?" said Kaplov. "Perhaps there was no husband. Maybe not even a boyfriend. But in my experience, when a pregnant woman dies violently, I always like to know where the baby's father is. And since no one's come forward, I have to wonder whether this man may know something about this fire, don't you think?"

"May we take a look at her body?"

"I'll have my secretary buzz the attendants in the basement to get her ready," he said.

"Georgia, we gotta get back," Cambareri pleaded.

"It'll just take a minute." Georgia looked over at Kaplov, who was speaking into the intercom. She could tell something was wrong by the way the doctor's black eyebrows knitted together like two fuzzy caterpillars.

"Apparently," said Kaplov, rearing back from the intercom, a note of surprise in his voice, "a man is in the process of identifying the woman's body now. I believe if you hurry, you might still be able to catch him."

"I'm on my way," said Georgia. She turned to Cambareri. "Meet you downstairs." She wasn't about to wait for Lightning and his bunions.

Until 1989, the process of identifying a body in New York City was a nightmare. Relatives who came in to make an ID were led down a narrow metal staircase to a side door off the basement morgue. There, they would stand on the antiseptic blue tile, shivering in the 38-degree temperature while some attendant wheeled a gurney over, often within earshot of orderlies joking about the "floaters" and "jumpers"—suicides—they had seen that day.

After half a dozen mothers suffered heart attacks, seeing their kids on a slab of steel, someone finally got the bright idea to create a viewing room, a soothing, plushly furnished room where relatives could see the body behind glass. To make the process even more humane, attendants also took instant photos, so families didn't even have to ID the body—they could do it via photos.

Georgia knew this. She ran straight past the lobby with its maroon velvet couches and pen-and-ink sketches of New York, and into the viewing room. But the room was empty. She found a receptionist and flashed her badge.

"Where's the guy making the ID on the Jane Doe from the Rubi Wang fire?" she asked breathlessly. The receptionist looked puzzled. "The guy," Georgia repeated. "Where is he? Did he leave?"

"He's downstairs. With the technician."

"He's *downstairs*?" Only cops and marshals went downstairs anymore. Not that there was anything gory about the body vaults, per se. In fact, they had the look and feel of storage lockers at an airline terminal. But there was no denying their grisly contents.

Georgia took the elevator down and stepped into the basement. An unsettling odor of formaldehyde permeated the air. Along one side of the blue painted walls were several autopsy rooms, their only windows facing inward to the six rows of shiny steel vaults spread out across the antiseptic interior. Georgia scanned the well-lit aisles, looking for an attendant. In the third aisle, she found a short Indian man in a white coat, nonchalantly zipping up a body bag. He could've been wrapping a chicken, so blasé was he about the contents. Georgia walked over and flashed her badge.

"Is that the Jane Doe from the Rubi Wang blaze?" The attendant nodded. "Where's the guy who ID'd her?"

"In the men's room, getting sick." He shrugged.

Georgia could see why. The body was hairless, as powdery in parts as spent charcoal. Gray-white bone protruded from sections of the face, and the lips and eyelids had melted away, leaving eyeballs that looked to Georgia like overcooked egg yolks. The face had a gaping stare, as if poised to scream, the result of vaporized muscle tissue. There were no ears. On what looked like the remnants of a hand, there were no fingers, only some gnarled nubs curled into a retracted claw. The smell was the worst—an ammonialike stench, as acrid as pepper in the nostrils, but with a fatty, putrid undertone that seemed to settle on the tongue like candle wax. She felt bad for anybody who had to see a loved one like that. *Why the hell did he insist on coming down here?*

Georgia found the men's room at the end of the aisle and planted herself squarely at the exit, her gold shield gripped and ready. The door opened slowly. She saw the familiar basset-hound eyes first. Only today, the rims were red and swollen. His mustache and hair seemed to have gone a shade grayer overnight, and his cheeks were gaunt and cut with new lines. Georgia took a step backward, tried to speak, but couldn't mouth the words.

"Randy . . . ?"

As soon as he met her gaze, his knees gave out. He leaned against a wall for strength, then slowly sank to the floor, dropping his head into his hands. Georgia couldn't hear his sobs, but she saw his bony shoulder blades beneath his suit jacket jerk and twitch as waves of grief wracked his body. She knelt beside him and lifted a hand to comfort him, but her fingers simply dangled in midair. He was like a raw wound that she could only make more painful by touching. She sat next to him for a long time without speaking.

"Who . . . ?" she asked finally. She didn't have the energy for more words.

". . . Cassandra," he choked out, "my daughter."

Georgia started. Carter had been with Marilyn for twenty years. He'd raised her two children like they were his own. They called him Dad. Those were the only kids he'd ever mentioned. Carter wiped the sleeve of his suit across his eyes.

"I was in the Marines," he explained in a raw voice. "Cassie's momma and I never married. I left the service, moved to New York, and . . ." His voice trailed off. He reached for his wallet and pulled out a creased, dog-eared photo of a young black man in military fatigues with a little toffee-skinned girl on his knee, her hair in cornrows. "When she came up this way later on, I tried to be part of her life. . . . I guess it was too late." A new wave of tears welled up, and he hung his head, embarrassed. "Now it'll always be too late."

Georgia reached out to stroke his arm. He didn't pull away. "Are you sure it's her?"

He nodded. "At the fire, I found part of the rose quartz necklace I had made up for her when she was little. I didn't want to believe she was dead, so I checked out her apartment. When she wasn't there, I knew. Dental records came up today from North Carolina. It's a match. Now I'm gonna have to tell her momma."

"Oh Randy. God, I'm sorry." The words seemed so inadequate. "Did you know she was—" Georgia panicked. *Was it possible the attendants hadn't told him?*

"Pregnant?" His voice cracked, and he shook his head. "Not until I got here today. I know so little about Cassie's life." He looked as if he might cry again. "I have no idea who the father was." He took a deep breath. "Please Georgia, don't tell anybody about this."

"But why?"

"Marenko will take me off the investigation. It's standard procedure. You *know* that."

"Maybe you should be . . ."

"No," he said angrily. "She's my kid. All her life, I wasn't there for her. At least let me be there for her now. Please, Georgia. Please give me that. You know what it's like not having your father looking out for you. You told me so yourself."

"Okay." Georgia sighed, feeling a familiar stab of pain at the mention of her dad. She helped Carter to his feet. "You're my partner and my friend, Randy. I'll always back you up."

CHAPTER Fourteen

"So, youse find out who ID'd the Jane Doe?" Cambareri asked Georgia as they walked back to the car from the ME's office. The sun was strong, the rumble of traffic along First Avenue deafening.

"He was a relative of the victim's mother in North Carolina, I think. He'd already left the viewing room when I got there."

At a kiosk, Cambareri bought a Snickers bar and a lottery ticket. Georgia inhaled the smell of hot pretzels at a vending cart nearby. It felt good to be out among the living. She wondered if Carter would ever feel that way again.

"Then how come," Cambareri took a bite of candy, "youse went down to the morgue basement? You was there a while."

"I wanted to take a look at the body—all right, Gene?" A First Avenue bus rumbled by, and they both got a mouthful of diesel fumes. "Not for nothing, but aren't you the guy who always tells me not to ask so many questions?"

Cambareri crumpled the candy wrapper and grinned. "You're learning, young lady. You're learning."

Back at the firehouse, Cambareri wandered into the kitchen to sample the lasagna. Georgia trudged upstairs. Marenko was on the phone. His blue denim shirtsleeves were rolled up; his navy blue wool tie dangled over the desk. She could see the silky black hair on his sinewy forearms. She handed him the medical examiner's reports, which he scanned without a thank-you while he was on the phone, then put to one side. When he hung up, she planted herself in front of him.

"I'd really appreciate the opportunity to track down Alison Simon's boyfriend, Jose."

Marenko pushed back from his desk and clasped his hands behind his head. "Why?"

"Because it's a good lead. You know it is, Mac."

He rummaged in his desk drawer for a toothpick and jabbed it in his mouth. "Suarez is already handling it."

"You gave Eddie *my* lead? Why did you do that?"

"Do you speak Spanish?"

Georgia threw up her hands. "What's that got to do with it? I'll bet neither does Alison Simon. For all I know, neither does Jose."

"The point is," said Marenko, reaching across his desk, "you don't believe Fred Fischer had a hand in this fire anyway."

"What do you know what I believe?"

He tossed her a fresh copy of the *Daily News.* FIRE OFFICIALS SUSPECT SERIAL ARSON, exclaimed the headline.

"That wasn't me," she countered. "That was the commissioner who made that statement at the party last night. What was I supposed to do?"

"Tell him he's wrong. You're good at giving superiors your opinions."

"At least I'm trying here. Not like you. As soon as Gene and I walked out of this office yesterday, you put together your game plan. You eliminated all the fire's accidental causes, broke down the evidence, and divvied up the important interviews. For all I know, you've got the suspect in cuffs already."

"Close." He smiled, rolling the toothpick in his mouth. "And he ain't no serial arsonist, sweetheart. I'll tell you that." Marenko rummaged through a pile of papers on his desk and threw a report at her. It was from the Bureau of Alcohol, Tobacco, and Firearms's national laboratory in Washington, D.C.

"What's this?"

"A couple of marshals in Brooklyn still had some containers of untested evidence from that fire in Red Hook last January—one of the ones *you* claim is HTA," Marenko reminded her. "So I sent it to the ATF's labs and asked them to do a search for hydrocarbon accelerants. You see their conclusions?"

Georgia flipped through the report. Marenko had yellow-highlighted the senior forensic chemist's words: "Sample tested positive for diesel fuel."

"They found diesel fuel at that HTA site in Red Hook?" asked Georgia, amazed.

"They sure did. And you know what that means? It means that that building in Red Hook wasn't burned by HTA. Diesel fuel, even if it *had* been one of the firebomb's ingredients, couldn't have survived an HTA. It's what I've been telling you, Skeehan—the fires *aren't* related."

Georgia slumped against the edge of his desk, put the report down, and shook her head. *Brennan and Marenko were right,* she thought. *I am a rookie in over my head.* "Okay, Mac." She sighed. "You win."

Marenko leaned forward. "Listen, Skeehan. You probably think I'm being a prick here. But I'm just trying to save you—and this department—from looking really stupid in the press." He patted her hand. His palms were callused and firm.

"You want me to quit the case?" she asked.

He pursed his lips together and opened his palms expansively. "Think about it, okay? You don't have to make any decisions today."

Georgia stared at him and said nothing. Marenko misread her silence as consent. "Hey, it's not your fault." He shrugged. "Lynch and Brennan were playing a game of whose dick is bigger. You just happened to get emotionally caught up. Maybe you were having one of those women's days—"

"A 'woman's day'? You mean my period?" She frowned, feeling a churning in her gut.

"Or PMS, or whatever," he stammered.

He'd almost had her. Almost. But like most men, he never knew when to quit. "I don't get PMS," she said quietly. "I don't take Prozac. I don't suffer from father envy, penis envy, or the need to get in touch with my inner child."

The words were rolling now, and she was powerless to stop them. "You want me to quit? Fine. But before I do, I'm going to have to explain to the commissioner why it is that one of the buildings that burned in a fire you say *isn't* HTA and *isn't* related shouldn't have been standing in the first place."

Marenko reared back in his chair, openmouthed, the toothpick wedged into the corner. "Say what?"

"That vacant apartment house in East Tremont. It was supposed to have been demolished. The paperwork never went through. The building records are missing—on purpose, I suspect. And that furniture warehouse in Washington Heights? No one investigated that fire too closely, either. Could it have been because the badges liked gambling there so much?"

Marenko looked up at the ceiling and cursed. "Lightning told you." It wasn't even a question.

"You were right, Mac." Georgia reached over and yanked the toothpick from his astonished lips, then threw it in the wastebasket. "A rookie like me *can* learn a lot from an experienced hand."

He stared at her now, gaping like a schoolyard bully who didn't quite know how to fight a girl. Slowly, he ran a hand through his wavy mop of hair and let his eyes wander the length of her body, beginning at the band of skin separating her navy blue pumps from the hem of her pants and resting a half beat on each curve, all the way up to the silky white collar of her blouse. Then he laughed. It was a deep, rich sound. Totally unexpected. She'd never heard him really laugh before, and it caught her off guard. He threw an eraser at her playfully, and she threw it back.

"You win, Skeehan." He grinned, shaking his head. "You're all right for a girl." He rose and grabbed a blue twill sports jacket off a coat tree in the corner. A set of keys jangled in the pocket. He tossed them up in the air and caught them with the reflexive grace of an athlete. "C'mon," he said with a wink. His eyes were as blue as the denim of his shirt.

She hesitated. "Where are we going?"

"You wanna work this case for real, or not?"

CHAPTER *Fifteen*

The chief hadn't been out to Howard Beach, Queens, for months—not since his old man died. He sipped a Styrofoam cup of bitter black coffee to steady his nerves and rolled down the windows of his graffiti-covered van.

A strong breeze lifted off the marshy flats of Jamaica Bay. Overhead, a plane roared as it began its descent into Kennedy Airport. If the chief closed his eyes on this warm, balmy April Thursday, he could still drink in the sensation of sitting in his dad's motorboat, the sun on his fair skin, the smell of diesel fuel, listening to big, leathery men with smoky voices talk fire over cigarettes and beer.

Even then, it was all he craved. And by rights, it should've been his—would've been his—if things had gone the way they were supposed to. Late at night, in Washington Heights, when sirens wailed like cats in heat and bullets punctuated the darkness, the what-ifs seemed to have the power to physically crush him.

He turned onto a quiet street of tidy bungalows with grottoes of the Virgin Mary on postage-stamp lawns. Near the end of the block stood his dad's old firehouse—a rectangular sandstone-colored structure, two stories high. To its left, inside a gate, firefighters' cars were crammed at odd angles. To its right, separated by a narrow airshaft, was a three-story row-frame apartment building with a flat front and flat roof.

The building, covered in dark green asphalt shingles, looked like an upended shoe box. Six families lived there, and despite its drab appearance, it had always been well maintained. Fake geraniums sprouted in window boxes, and Easter bunnies were taped to the glass panes. Out front, two little girls with blond braids were drawing chalk figures on the pavement, just as he once had.

In front of the firehouse, a firefighter was hosing down the engine. The chief recognized him now: Sean Duffy, a probie, or first-year firefighter. Six-foot-three, twenty-four years old, he had a broad, square face, a neck like a tree stump, and a crew cut the color of bark. Duffy's older brother, Tim, a homicide detective, had gone to school with the chief. His father, Ted, and uncle Dennis were firefighters. Sean Duffy did a double take at the sight of the van and waved. The chief pulled over to the curb and reached across the passenger seat to shake Duffy's hand.

"Hey, stranger," said the probie, wiping his wet hands on his blue uniform pants. "Long time, no see."

"No see, all right." The chief grinned. "You're putting on weight."

Duffy rubbed a small ripple of excess flesh bulging beneath his navy blue uniform shirt. On his left shoulder, the red flame of the FDNY insignia glistened in the sun.

"Firehouse cooking, man. And not enough work." Duffy waved to the little girls giggling next door. From the right front pocket of his uniform trousers, he produced a candy bar. "Hey, Molly," he called out to one of the girls, a freckle-faced child of about five with long blond lashes and bright green eyes. "Wanna share this with your friend?"

The child skipped over and snatched the bar from Duffy's outstretched hand. He towered over her, but she seemed perfectly at ease. *Like Ramon,* thought the chief. He wondered idly what hellhole the kid was in. Orlando was out of jail, but not back with Celia. He almost felt sorry for her.

"Thank you, Sean," said the little girl now, in an accent that sounded faintly Irish. Duffy patted her golden hair and returned to his conversation. "Good kids, but I swear, I coulda gotten more action if they'd put me in a graveyard."

"Hey, your old man probably pulled strings to get you someplace safe. You've got years to see action."

The probie's face clouded over. "Listen, I heard about what happened. I'm real sorry, man . . ."

"Yeah, well, my dad was getting on . . ."

"That, too, of course," said Duffy, his eyes taking in the chief's paint-smeared clothes. "But I meant the other stuff." The probie shook his head. "If it was me, I'd want to kill that chick. You helped her. You taught her the ropes and then she does that . . ."

"It's not the first time that's happened to me."

"Yeah, but you just *know* if things had been the other way around, she'd have been hollering harrassment or some such crap."

The chief forced a tight smile. "I'm trying to put it behind me, Duff. Get on with my life. I pull in good money as a painter these days. So I'm okay about it."

"You're a better man than I am," said the probie. "Hey, you coming to the . . . um, celebration tonight?"

"I thought the firehouse got in hot water over last year's little party."

"The brass was pissed off for a while, especially since Chief Greco's son is one of our engine officers. But downtown did their damage control. And you know those guys—if it didn't happen on television, it didn't happen. This year, they're having it around the corner, at the VFW hall."

"What about the guys on duty?"

"They're all going and bringing their radios. Me? I'm still a first-year probie. I don't think it'd look right to be over there and all . . ."

"You should go," the chief urged. "What's anyone going to do to you when Greco's own son is there? You just said nothing happens around here."

Duffy considered the point and nodded. "You're probably right. The guys in the firehouse are telling me the same thing. It's gonna be a wild night, I think."

The chief smiled. "I'm sure it will be, Duff. I'm sure it will be."

CHAPTER Sixteen

"Do you mind telling me where we're going?" Georgia asked as Marenko eased one of the department's dark blue Chevy Caprices northbound onto the West Side Highway. Traffic was at a crawl. The afternoon sun shimmered like crushed glass across the Hudson River.

"It's all here," he said, tossing her a folder labeled *Ronald Glassman.* "But first you gotta understand something . . . about that other stuff."

"You mean those embarrassing little sidebars to the HTA fires?"

Marenko winced, then tried to collect his thoughts. "Screwups happen," he said slowly. "Anybody in this department long enough knows where the bodies are buried. But you go to the commish with that, you'll make it sound like a cover-up."

"That's what it is."

"No," he said, running a hand through his hair. "Incompetence, yeah. Guys being guys, yeah. But Skeehan, Lynch'll just use this for his own political ends. Brennan'll screw you big-time and it won't solve the Spring Street arson. Look, trust me on this one. I'm trying to save your ass here."

"You want to save *my* ass?" She laughed. "Now there's something I can take to the bank. . . . So who's Ronald Glassman?"

"The cowboy on that surveillance tape. I got a positive ID from the guy's secretary this morning. Judging from the tape, it looks like he left One-thirty-one Spring Street as the fire started Monday night. We're heading up to his house in Westchester to find out why."

"I don't get it," said Georgia, studying the folder. Marenko's notes said Glassman, an advertising-agency sales director, was married with two daughters and lived in Chappaqua, an affluent town about forty miles north of Manhattan. "If this guy was at the party, why didn't he come forward?"

Marenko made a face. "Think about it, Skeehan. It doesn't take a rocket scientist—"

"Okay, okay." She rolled her eyes. "So he was there with another woman. And you're figuring maybe he's a witness."

"Witness, my ass. He's got motive—enough to hang him. That black chick down at the ME's office? A relative from North Carolina ID'd her as Cassandra Mott. She used to work at the same ad agency as Glassman. Glassman's secretary said it was rumored they were getting it on. She died four months pregnant. I'll bet you this jerk knocked her up and maybe didn't like that he was gonna have to pay for it. We can do the DNA, simple enough, if it comes to that. I left word for Carter to contact the family in North Carolina and find out what he can about her and this guy."

Georgia closed her eyes and bit her lower lip. *What was this news going to do to Randy?* Bad enough his little girl died in a horrible fire, but to think that some rich, white, married guy did this to her on purpose?

Georgia thought about Cassie Mott now. They were so much alike in so many respects. They'd both reached adulthood without their fathers, then turned around and fallen for men who packed up themselves when fatherhood came a-calling. Rick, at least, didn't try to kill her. She smiled darkly, thankful for small favors.

Marenko reached inside his blue twill sports coat for a pack of gum. He offered her a stick. She declined.

"Still not smoking?" she asked.

"Trying not to. Every time I quit, it's just as hard. I'm always hungry, which reminds me, when we get to Chappaqua, we'll get a bite to eat. My treat."

"That's not necessary."

He read the concern in her eyes. "It's a meal, Skeehan. An apology for giving you a hard time. I'll say one thing about you—you've got guts. I don't think I could've stood up to Brennan like you did yesterday in his office."

"I hadn't planned to, believe me." She stared out the window as the road opened up, flanked on either side by deep thickets of woods and grassy meadows. "Mac, was what you said in Brennan's office yesterday true? That you'd never seen those letters from the Fourth Angel before?"

"Yep."

"How about Brennan? Was he telling the truth?"

"Far as I know."

"So where did they come from?"

"Beats me." He turned the knobs on the radio until he got WFAN, an all-sports station. The NHL playoffs were under way, and some guy named Jocy from Brooklyn was spouting off about the Rangers' defense. Guys and sports.

"See, you've got to realize," Marenko said, "crazy people write letters. It doesn't always mean they set fires."

"Why won't you at least *consider* the possibility that there's a serial arsonist out there?"

"Because the MOs on all these fires are entirely different. Different kinds of buildings, different parts of the city. And there are other problems," Marenko continued, ticking them off on his fingers. "You've got the traces of diesel fuel in Red Hook that aren't consistent with HTA. In East Tremont, our Bronx guys found the bottoms of three plastic buckets in the ruins. The whole friggin' place burns to the ground and we've got these three plastic buckets. How does anyone explain that? Especially since there was nothing like that in Spring Street."

"You never told me about the bucket bottoms," Georgia said stiffly.

"Hey? I'm telling you now. So you understand why the fires aren't related. Walter Frankel gave you those letters. And don't tell me he didn't."

Silence.

"Okay, so you're protecting him, fine. But he's setting you up—"

"He was trying to help me—"

"Yeah. Help you right out of a job, I'd say."

"You think I'm naive," she offered.

Marenko shifted his eyes off the winding road and gave her a long, searching look. The skin beneath those azure lakes was mottled and beginning to take on the wrinkly texture of unironed rayon.

"In some ways, yeah. I'd say you're as naive as a Girl Scout. Nice quality in a woman. Bad one in a cop. My motto is: nobody tells anybody everything."

"Even you, huh?"

"Especially me, Scout." Marenko winked at her. From anyone else, she would have bristled at the nickname. From Mac, it seemed oddly sweet and well intended—certainly better than things he'd called her in the past.

In Chappaqua, they found a Chinese restaurant with red paper lanterns in the windows and sat down to watch the ebb and flow of small-town life. Georgia ordered sweet-and-sour pork and a Diet Pepsi. Marenko ordered Szechuan chicken and a Budweiser. Georgia frowned.

"You gonna tell me that one beer's gonna keep me from doin' my job here? Man, in a firehouse, I'd just be gettin' started."

"Were you like that as a firefighter?"

"Me?" Marenko touched his chest. "Uh-uh. I was always stone-cold sober on the job. Went home and drank. So I ended up with a couple of commendations in my folder and a big, fat legal bill from my divorce." He took a gulp of beer and wiped his mouth with the back of his hand. "How about you?"

"How about me, what?"

"You're divorced, right?"

"No . . ."

"Separated?"

She took a sip of soda and shook her head. "Never married."

"But you've got a kid." Marenko caught her sharp gaze. "Sorry. I wasn't trying to judge. I guess I'm just old-fashioned."

"Me too." Georgia laughed. A woman with a small boy wandered past the restaurant, making her think with a pang of Richie. "I wanted to marry Richie's dad. He just didn't want to marry me."

"Then he was an asshole. Better off without him."

The food came and Marenko made a brave stab at using the chopsticks, but finally opted for a fork. He ate with gusto, entertaining her with an assortment of X-rated Chinese dish names.

"You get the cultural sensitivity award of the night," she told him between giggles.

"Hey, I ain't prejudiced. My insults are equal opportunity," he explained. "You must've known a guy like that when you were a firefighter in Queens."

Petie Ferraro. Her smile faded. The pork suddenly tasted like carpet underpadding. She could barely choke it down.

Marenko stopped chewing. "I say something wrong?"

"You reminded me of a firefighter I knew. He was killed in the line of duty."

"Was he the guy you tried to save?"

She put her chopsticks down. It never occurred to her that he would've heard. "You know about Petie Ferraro?"

"I recall something about you getting a medal for helping to rescue a firefighter before you got promoted to marshal."

Georgia rolled her chopsticks under a sweaty palm without meeting his gaze. Like a water main that had sprung a leak, images of Petie spurted up from the recesses of her memory. The thickset body that shook like a bowl of Jell-O when he laughed. The black Fu Manchu mustache that he stroked when he told a funny story. He loved to build slot cars and race them with his three kids. He loved camping and fishing with his wife, Melinda, in the Adirondack Mountains every summer. He smoked the foulest cigars, told the dirtiest jokes, and made the best chicken parmigiana in the world.

The waiter came by with a dish of fortune cookies and the check.

"You know," said Marenko, misreading her silence, "lots of guys feel bad when someone they save dies. It's just that much harder when it's one of our own. But hey, you can't do more than put your life on the line for a brother. That's what the job's all about."

Georgia pushed her meal away and glared at him. "You think, huh? You think all that training, all that bullshit talk about brotherhood and bravery and pride in the uniform is gonna carry it. And then that moment comes and you meet yourself face to face and you can't even recognize who you are."

He reared back.

"I'm sorry," she apologized. "I'm not mad at you. I'm mad at myself. This thing's still eating me alive." She sighed. "I'm just tired of making excuses."

It had been almost two years since that fire, but Georgia remembered every detail. "Ferraro and I were doing a second-floor search at a house fire in Queens. I got turned around in the smoke, started running out of air, and I couldn't find the exit."

The house had been part of a row of sagging, dilapidated frame structures, sided with gray asphalt tiles. Out front, a rusted red tricycle lay overturned on a patch of bare dirt. The dirt was covered with shards of glass from the windows firefighters had to break.

"Petie threw me out of a room as it blew. Saved my life. Then suddenly, I heard this loud crack. I looked back, and he started dropping through the floor behind me. I don't know if I was in shock or what, but I thought he could scramble out by himself. I was choking, so I ran to a back window, smashed it open, and gulped for air. Then it hit me. He *needed* me to pull him out. I'd deserted him, crapped out, run away."

"But you got a medal," Marenko said softly. "They don't give medals for crapping out."

"Yeah, I got a medal. I radioed for help, crawled back to that hole, and lowered myself down a rope. It was probably no more than three minutes since I'd run, but it was enough. He was in bad shape, and I was burning up pretty good down there, too. Guys came and helped me pull him up. Petie never regained consciousness and died the next day.

"There were reporters on the scene," Georgia remembered. "And the chief in charge, without even talking to me, told them I'd rescued Ferraro. I was in the hospital getting treated while this was going on. When I came out, it was all over the news."

A siren sounded in the street. Georgia caught the outline of an ambulance whipping by. In the suburbs, that shrill wail was rarely attached to a fire truck. But to Georgia, the sound would forever speak of a past that couldn't be rectified, a wrong that couldn't be righted.

"I felt bad to begin with," she said softly. "Then to get that medal— that was the worst day of my life. Petie's widow, Melinda, came up to me at the ceremony and thanked me. I didn't know what to say. Obviously, no one had told her the truth. To this day, I've never been able to bring myself to visit her and her kids."

"Did you ever go back to the firehouse?"

"Uh-uh. Once I ran at the fire, I just kept on running. I stayed out on medical leave for a while, then did some light duty work at headquarters. I'd taken the fire marshal's exam a year earlier. Three months after the incident, I got the call that the job was mine. I thought it would make the nightmares go away."

"But it didn't."

"No." She sighed. "Not even a little."

They sat in silence while Marenko drained his beer and Georgia watched the light fade from the sky. He checked his watch.

"We should probably head up to Glassman's house." He reached for the check. Georgia offered to pay, but he waved her away. "A deal's a deal. I said I'd buy you dinner."

In the car, Georgia finally broke the uneasy silence. "You think I'm a pretty pathetic excuse for a firefighter, don't you?"

Marenko shrugged. "I wasn't at that fire, with my air running out and the place burning up. I can't say I'd have done any different."

"But deep in your heart, you don't think you'd have ditched a brother. Admit it, Mac."

"No, I don't think I would've. But you're, what? Five-foot-four? And you weigh what?"

"One-twenty," Georgia answered, shaving a few pounds off the truth. No woman admits what she really weighs.

"Well, I'm six-two and I weigh two hundred. So I know if I'd have been there, I could've pulled him back up. You didn't know that."

"Perhaps . . ."

"Which is why women don't belong in the FDNY. I think maybe you cost Ferraro his life, but I think it's because you're a woman, not a coward."

Georgia slammed her fist against the dashboard. "Oh, great. I never should've told you any of this. I've just confirmed every petty, Neanderthalic belief in your pea-size, testosterone-driven brain. First of all, I *did* get him out of there—all five-foot-four, hundred and twenty aerobically conditioned pounds of me. I just did it too late. I can bench-press a hundred and thirty pounds. I can run a five-minute mile. And I could drag your sorry ass out of a building. I just don't know if I'd want to."

"Yeah? Well, I guess we'll never know." He reached across the dashboard, opened the glove compartment, and thrust a crumpled piece of paper into Georgia's hands. "When you're through nagging, maybe you could read me the directions to Glassman's house."

"I'm not nagging."

"That's what my ex-wife always said."

"Maybe that's why she's your ex-wife."

CHAPTER Seventeen

It took Georgia and Mac twenty minutes to find Ronald Glassman's house. The roads just outside of Chappaqua were long, winding, and poorly marked. The house was at the end of a long driveway up a steep hill. Marenko wanted to pull into the driveway. Georgia insisted it was more polite to park on the street.

"Polite, my ass. What if I get bit by a rabid raccoon?"

"Don't tell me a six-foot-two, two-hundred-pound *man* is intimidated by a teensy-weensy raccoon?"

"Fuck, yeah."

"Well, I think we should walk. And another thing: curb that mouth of yours. These aren't a bunch of firefighters."

At the end of the steep driveway was a three-car garage adjoining a cedar-sided contemporary. The palladium window over the entrance was two stories high. The roof was pitched at odd angles, resembling something constructed from children's blocks. Marenko couldn't resist a peek in the garage. He let out a long whistle.

"He's got a Land Rover, a Mercedes convertible, *and* a Lexus. This guy's loaded."

"Did we come here to buy a car or conduct an interview?" snapped Georgia. She rang the bell. A dog barked noisily from somewhere deep inside the house as a slim, bottle-blond woman answered the door. Marenko and Georgia flashed their badges, apologized for the intrusion, and asked to see Glassman.

If the woman was surprised to see them, she gave no hint of it. Instead, she took their coats and led the marshals into a two-story, cathedral-ceilinged living room with plush white carpets, a white damask sofa, and a fieldstone fireplace that looked as if it had never been used.

"Can I get you anything to drink?" the woman asked. The dog continued to bark and growl from some unseen room. Georgia asked for some tea. Marenko shook his head. "Where's your dog?" he asked nervously.

"Mitzi? She's just a little Pomeranian. She's in the kitchen. We keep her there because she's so difficult to catch once she gets outside. She won't bother you."

The woman went to fix tea and Georgia grinned.

"What's so funny?"

"So, one of New York's Bravest is afraid of raccoons and yappy little Pomeranians. Remind me never to ask for your assistance if I'm cornered by a rabid animal."

"I wouldn't dream of getting between you and your boyfriends."

Marenko paced the carpet and peered through French doors that led to an inground swimming pool off the patio. "This joint's enormous. How much you think it costs?"

Georgia frowned at him just as Ronald Glassman appeared in the archway of the living room. He was a handsome man, in a steely sort of way—early forties, slate-gray eyes, and just the faintest beginnings of a receding hairline. He wore a neatly pressed oxford shirt and pleated khaki trousers that contrasted nicely with a fading tan.

"I was under the impression that I'd given you detectives all the information you needed the other day." Glassman extended his hand and Georgia and Marenko shook it in turn, but his tone was brusque and businesslike and his handshake felt more like a weapon than a welcome.

"We're not detectives. We're fire marshals," Georgia innocently corrected. Marenko gave her a dark look. She was reminded of Chief Brennan's words—she was just window dressing here.

"How long is this going to take?" Glassman made a point of looking at his wristwatch.

"Not one minute longer than it has to," Marenko shot back. Clearly, the two men had already had some prickly dealings.

Glassman sat stiffly on the couch, twirling a rubber band between his fingers. Georgia studied him with fascination. *So you're the man who had an affair with Randy's little girl,* she was thinking. *Did you tell her you loved her? Did she always know you were married? And what did you do when she told you she was pregnant?*

Actually, she could guess at the last one. She recalled it in Rick's eyes like it was yesterday instead of a decade ago. The staccato pause. The frozen stance, as if the words he'd heard couldn't have been the right ones. The forced, lame smile. But most of all, the dumb questions: *How pregnant?* Like any woman's a little bit pregnant for long.

Glassman's wife appeared with tea, then sat beside her husband on the sofa with her hand on his knee. Marenko and Georgia traded looks. Spouses and parents were absolutely the worst people to have around, because a suspect would never admit to anything under-handed in their presence. Until they got Ron Glassman alone, they'd never be able to work him. Georgia was through being window dressing.

"Mrs. Glassman?" She turned to the wife.

"Wendy."

"Wendy. This is a very informal conversation. We just need your husband to verify some facts. Marshal Marenko and I don't want to tie up both of your evenings."

"Nothing is more important than being here with Ron," she insisted. Georgia looked helplessly at Marenko.

"You got a bathroom in this place?" Marenko asked.

"Off the kitchen, to the right. I'll show you," said Wendy.

Georgia hoped Wendy might tail him, but she was back within seconds, so Georgia began rattling off a mundane list of questions for Glassman: Where was he the night of the fire? What was he working on? Were there witnesses?

Glassman rolled his eyes. "I've told these people all this before," he said to his wife. "This is why the city's going down the tubes. The right hand doesn't know what the left is doing."

A crash of what sounded like steel mixing bowls in the kitchen interrupted their conversation. The dog began yapping, then the yaps turned to growls, growing more distant by the second. Marenko returned to the living room.

"I don't know how it happened, but I think your dog got out, ma'am," he said sheepishly.

Wendy jumped up in a panic. "Oh, dear. She's impossible to get back inside."

"I saw her running past the neighbor's house," Marenko said, his face as earnest as an altar boy's. "I hope you can get her back all right."

Georgia licked her lips and lowered her gaze, hoping to wipe the grin from her face. Marenko got further on sheer audacity than anyone she knew. While Wendy looked for Mitzi, they'd have the suspect all to themselves.

Glassman, however, had other ideas. "I think you people have done enough damage for one evening," he said, rising. "Barging into my home and harassing my family. I'm on close terms with the Westchester County DA. One call from her and I could get both your badges."

Marenko stepped forward. He was taller than Glassman, more powerfully built, and quicker tempered. Georgia felt certain things would spin hopelessly out of control at one word from him. She stepped in and spoke quickly.

"Mr. Glassman, no one wants to harass you. Please try to understand our point of view. Fifty-four people are dead. We're desperate for information."

"I can't help you," he said, throwing the rubber band on the coffee table.

"Hey, no problem," said Marenko, opening his palms in an exaggerated gesture of magnanimity. "You don't have to talk to us. You know your rights. We'll leave."

"Good," said Glassman.

Georgia stayed rooted. She knew more was coming. Marenko bit the inside of his cheek and shrugged. "We'll just run the DNA on the dead chick's baby at the morgue. Then maybe we'll tell *Wendy* what we found." Marenko neglected to tell Glassman that, without a court order, no one could compel his DNA to complete the test. Georgia knew Marenko was banking on panic over reason. Cops do it all the time.

Glassman froze. A sheen came over his eyes. He sank back on the sofa and put his head in his hands. Marenko hunched next to him. Georgia followed suit on the other side.

"You were pissed at her, weren't you?" Marenko said softly. "I mean, who wouldn't be? This chick had you over a barrel."

Georgia knew what Mac was doing—depersonalizing the victim in order to gain the suspect's confidence and wangle a confession. Still, it stung to think of Randy's daughter as a "chick." Georgia tried to push the image of Carter, collapsed and sobbing at the ME's office, from her mind. Cops and marshals always handle cases from a dispassionate distance, she reminded herself. She couldn't be dispassionate on this one.

"That chick . . . what was her name?" Marenko asked. He knew damn well what her name was. He just wanted Glassman to say it. To ID her, and so establish a motive and connection.

Glassman shifted his gaze to the family room. His kids were in there. "The porch," he said stiffly, gesturing to a screened patio off the living room.

The night had grown cold. Their breath drifted in the moonlit darkness. Shadows of leafless trees raked the outside wall. It would be so easy to rush things and get back to where it was warm. But if there was one rule about investigating, it was never fill the silences.

Glassman paced the terra cotta tiles. "Her name was Cassandra Mott . . . Cassie Mott," he mumbled. "She was a receptionist at my ad agency for a while. She was also a nightclub singer."

"Yeah . . . Cassie Mott," said Marenko, like he'd just remembered it himself. "Well, that singer was gonna put a swan song to your beautiful life here."

Glassman stopped pacing and grimaced at Marenko. "You think I set the fire."

"To scare her, right?" Marenko prompted. "To get her to terminate the pregnancy. You didn't think it would go this far. Hey, you're a good family man. Anyone can see—"

"Fuck you," Glassman muttered through clenched teeth. "You come in here with your accusations. You don't know shit, mister. I'm just some guy in a suit you're looking to hang so you can go back to bowling or whatever it is you do with your fire buddies."

Georgia noticed Marenko's fists curling at his sides. It was taking all his powers of control not to belt the guy. Georgia stepped in.

"Mr. Glassman, don't you care that she's dead? That you may have information that can help us here?"

"I care. A whole lot more than you people. To you, she's just a name on a file. What do you know about her, anyway?"

"She was born and raised in Mount Airy, North Carolina." The words came unbidden, as if Georgia were reciting them from her own life. A cool gust of wind whipped past her, forming large goose bumps on her arms. She shivered. "Her dad was in the military. He never married her mother and left when she was five. She wore a rose quartz amulet on a silver-plated chain that he'd given her as a child. He still keeps an old picture of her in his wallet. He has no other biological children, and is devastated by her loss."

Glassman reared back. Marenko's jaw dropped. Both men stared at her. "So you see, Mr. Glassman," said Georgia softly. "We *do* care."

"You were at Rubi Wang's party on Monday night," Marenko prodded.

"N-no," Glassman stammered. "I told you yesterday. I was working late."

Georgia and Marenko exchanged surprised looks. Obviously, Glassman had no idea about the surveillance tape. If he could lie about being at the party, what else could he lie about?

Glassman must have read his misstep in their faces. His voice took on a sudden, desperate edge. "Do you honestly think I'd kill fifty-four people?" He laughed nervously. "I'm not some street punk with a fourth-grade education, you know. Maybe you can run mental gymnastics around those guys, but not here."

"So tell us the truth, then," Georgia offered.

Glassman sighed and shook his head. "I want to help you, but I . . ." He looked back at the living room now. Wendy was clearing teacups from the coffee table. He took a deep breath, like a man waking up from a trance. "I can't lose all this, do you understand?"

Georgia nodded sympathetically. Marenko, however, had had enough. He folded his arms across his chest. "Hey, we're not your therapists, okay? The sooner you come clean about what went down, the better it's gonna be for you, pal."

Georgia gritted her teeth. They'd come so close. Even in the darkness, she could see Glassman's resolve hardening.

"If you marshals had anything to arrest me on, you'd have done it already. As far as I'm concerned, from this moment on, you're not talking to me or my family without a lawyer present. Now get out, before I have the local police come and show you a little Chappaqua hospitality."

CHAPTER Eighteen

Firefighter Sean Duffy adjusted the volume on his department radio. It was hard to hear the dispatcher's voice above the noise inside the VFW hall. And it was hot, too. The place reminded him of a high school gym. Sweat glistened along the dark shafts of his crew cut and trickled down the collar of his long-sleeved navy blue uniform shirt.

Lieutenant Danny Greco put a hand on his broad back. Greco, Duffy's commanding officer, was a stocky, balding man with a thick mustache and a beer belly. He was also the chief of department's son.

"Go ahead, Duff. Have a beer." The officer gestured to a long oak bar. The beer was flowing like water. Dozens of firefighters—on and off duty—were gathered in clusters, drinking, smoking, and raucously discussing everything from the Yankees' pitching to who was going to the memorial mass. "One beer's not gonna hurt a big guy like you," said Greco. "It'll just cool you down."

"Thanks, Lieu." Duffy nodded. "But I really don't feel like it. I'd like to go back to the firehouse, if that's all right with you. Maybe man the housewatch desk."

Greco shrugged. "Dispatch knows where to find us. We've got our radios. But if it makes you feel better . . ." The lieutenant took a gulp of his own beer. "You'll miss the floor show, you know," he said with a wink. "It'll be starting any minute."

"That's okay." Duffy wasn't sure he wanted to see it anyway, but he kept those thoughts to himself. The annual floor show was a tradition at the firehouse, the theme always something with a crude or insulting edge to it. Last year, shortly before Duffy got assigned here, the theme was Hasidic hairstyles. The men got drunk, donned coffee filters like yarmulkes, and taped long paper sideburns to their heads as they danced with hired strippers. Some bright spark got the idea to film it. Fortunately for the FDNY, Chief Greco happened to get wind of the tape before it reached the media, so the event never went further than downtown, though everyone in the trenches knew about it.

Duffy cringed when he thought of this year's theme: "Louis Farrakhan Appreciation Day." He was afraid to even *think* about what the guys would be cooking up.

He grabbed his turnout gear off the truck in the parking lot and told Lieutenant Greco he'd be around the corner, at the firehouse front desk. Then he walked into the damp night, shedding the commotion of the VFW hall like a down parka on a balmy day.

He wasn't exactly sure why he felt relieved to have left the party. Part of it was embarrassment. He didn't think he'd be comfortable with the strippers who were surely going to be part of the event. He never cared much for crude jokes, ethnic slurs, or slobbering drunkenness. But part of it was, quite simply, a sense of duty. He'd always wanted to be a firefighter, just like his dad and uncle. He pictured himself racing up tenement stairs in Harlem to rescue a trapped child, or dangling at the end of a rope in a crumbling Bed-Stuy housing project to lower some elderly person to safety. And even if all he did was sit at the firehouse front desk and flip channels, at least he wasn't at some party with guys who'd rather chug a cold one than take a walk in the smoke.

Up ahead he could see the firehouse. Every light was on—the too-bright wattage that reminded him of hospital emergency rooms. The street itself was empty. In this family neighborhood, most people were inside before eight P.M. Soft lights glowed from bedroom windows and televisions flickered.

Duffy punched the code that opened the firehouse door, then gazed over at the three-story apartment house next to it. A strange light in the row frame's basement caught his eye. It shimmered in an oddly asymmetrical way—bright in some parts yet shadowy in others, as if some sinewy thread of darkness were stitching it up piece by piece. Duffy stepped closer to examine it. Gauzy black tentacles floated in midair, like the appendages of some giant squid, soaking up the incredible whiteness of the light.

Smoke.

Fire.

The young firefighter fumbled with his department radio. "Ten-seventy-five," he sputtered to the dispatcher, giving the code for a working fire, along with the address. He slipped into his turnout gear, but decided against fetching an airtank and mask next door at the firehouse. The fire was only in the basement. Better to get the people out. He had time.

He raced up the row frame's front stoop and into the building. It had to be under a minute since he'd first spotted the blaze. Yet heat and black smoke were beginning to filter through the first-floor landing like dust motes on a shaft of sunlight. Duffy had never seen a fire move so fast. Even the smoke detectors had no time to react. Only now, one by one, did they start to buzz.

He banged on apartment doors. People crowded the halls. They all knew Sean Duffy. They wanted information. They wanted assurances. They wanted Sean to stop the smoke detectors from waking their children or to help them carry their most precious belongings to the curb. But already, the young firefighter could see that the smoke and heat were outrunning him, seeping up from air shafts and floorboards, teasing him into thinking he had more time than he did. He took a carton out of one mother's hand, threw it back in the apartment, and shoved her and her children to the exit.

People don't understand how fast fire travels, he thought. *They never think it can happen to them.* Duffy recalled a story his dad, Ted, had told him about an old man who made it safely out of a fire, then went back to retrieve his daughter's graduation photo. The old guy was found an hour later, dead on his living room floor, photo in hand.

He bounded up the second-floor stairs now, past families coughing and gagging, black snot running from their noses. The panic, in just thirty seconds, had grown palpable, along with the thickening smoke. Duffy's eyes stung. His lungs pleaded for air. A woman tugged on the sleeve of his turnout coat. It was Mrs. Corcoran, Molly's mother, holding the girl's little brother. But Molly wasn't there.

"I can't find my daughter," she sobbed in a strong Irish accent as a wave of unexpectedly intense heat pushed toward them. A second later, the lights went out.

"Go. Stay close to the floor," Duffy choked out, giving her a spare flashlight from his pocket. "I'll get her."

The Corcoran apartment was to the left of the stairs. Duffy crawled inside, feeling under beds and couches. Even on his belly, even with the window open and smoke billowing out, the temperature was probably hovering near 300 degrees. Lightbulbs burst. Bottles on countertops shattered. Plastic cups melted into a sticky ooze. The realization brought a stab of panic. Duffy looked up. Black smoke was banking down from the ceiling, collapsing visibility inch by inch. Soon there'd be no oxygen left in the room. He wished now he'd gone back for his airtank.

Then his boot brushed against an object that felt like a doll. He waved his flashlight beam across the floor and caught the glimmer of a soot-streaked braid. *Molly.* He grabbed the little girl's limp body and held her to his chest. He didn't even want to consider that she might be dead. He opened the window wider and kicked out the screen. They were twenty feet in the air. *He* could jump to the firehouse roof. But with Molly? He might crush her. Or drop her.

In the distance, he could hear the wail of sirens, but he couldn't hang on. In the hallway, spiky flames shot eight feet in the air, barking and spitting like a pit bull on a chain. Black smoke poured over his shoulder. More objects exploded in staccato bursts from the heat, sending molten projectiles through the apartment. He could feel himself becoming disoriented, his body and mind giving in to the waves of orange rolling across the ceiling, like an ocean from hell. He had to do something right away.

Then he saw a heavyset man wobbling up to the building with a twelve-foot aluminum ladder. A neighbor, he presumed. There were several in the street now.

"Over here," Duffy yelled, dangling the unconscious child out the window by her tender, twiglike arms.

The man hurriedly threw the ladder against the green asphalt shingles, climbed up and grabbed the child as well as he could, then carried her down. Duffy, disoriented, leaned over the window ledge and retched. He lifted a leg to climb out and make a stab at jumping to the firehouse roof.

The explosion came out of nowhere—so swift and fierce that the young firefighter had no time to react. It barreled out of the blackness, a locomotive of superheated gases, hurtling sinks and light fixtures that had been bolted to the walls. When Sean Duffy landed on the roof of the firehouse, he thought at first that he'd beaten it.

He shuddered, feeling cold and numb, like a sailor hit by a North Atlantic wave in February. The fierce explosion took his breath away, and try as he might, he couldn't get it back. But as the sensation passed, a more terrible one kicked in. His lungs and legs throbbed with blistering agony. And across his back he felt . . . nothing. Like it wasn't even there. He got to his knees, feeling as if he were sloshing about in a body encased in Saran Wrap.

When he looked down, he saw all that was left of his turnout pants: a film of puckered black fabric. His canvas gloves had melted to his hands. He studied his wrists. The skin beneath didn't even look like his skin—all blotchy and black, streaked with an inhuman shade of pink. It looked like a slab of barbecued meat.

He tried to stand, but a searing jolt of pain tore at his legs. He crawled farther from the fire on the tar roof, which was now bubbling and sticky from the intense heat. His mind foggily tried to comprehend where he'd left Molly. His clothes felt three sizes too small, like he was some kind of cartoon character doubling in size every minute.

He didn't recall the fire trucks arriving. He didn't remember being carried to the pavement. He couldn't even be sure whether the moan he heard was coming from his lips or someone else's. All around him, people groaned, their clothes seared and in tatters, their blackened skin sliding off their bodies in long, pasty sheets. Blood and body fluids oozed across sidewalks filled with kids' chalk drawings, as the injured babbled and rocked or lay silently, wide-eyed in shock. Many had no clothes or hair, or hair that was as prickly as razor wire. They looked like grotesque store mannequins.

Duffy saw Lieutenant Greco hovering over him now, working on him with two other guys he knew. More sirens screeched in the distance. He was aware of a crowd forming at the perimeter, of several of them stepping forward in the lamplit darkness, rolling up their sleeves.

"Get Ted Duffy," someone murmured.

"Get a priest," said another.

A convulsive shaking began somewhere deep inside Sean Duffy's body until it felt as if all four limbs were one large tuning fork. He vomited, curling into a fetal ball and closing his eyes at the sickly-sweet stench of what he guessed to be his own burned flesh.

"Molly," he croaked. He wanted to cry, but the tears wouldn't flow—probably burned up along with everything else.

"She's gonna make it," said Greco, easing him down on a stretcher.

"I forgot my airtank, Lieu. I messed up," Duffy muttered through melted lips.

Tears came to Greco's eyes. "You didn't mess up, kid. Don't worry about nothing. You did good. Real, real good."

CHAPTER *Nineteen*

"*So you think* you're pretty clever, don't you?" Marenko asked Georgia as he gunned the motor south along the Saw Mill River Parkway. They were headed back from Ron Glassman's house in Chappaqua.

"What are you talking about?"

"That stuff you made up about that chick."

"I didn't make it up."

Marenko studied her face as if he'd never really seen it before—the full lips, the large hazel eyes, the curly reddish-brown hair that fell almost to her shoulders, the faint band of freckles that made her look perpetually twelve. Then he turned his eyes back to the road and shook his head. "It didn't work anyway."

Georgia couldn't contain herself any longer. "Well, it just might have, if you hadn't pounced all over him. Maybe you're a hell of a firefighter when the flames are licking your rear end. Maybe you can bully some street mutt into a confession. But you don't know zip about talking to people. Everything's not black and white in this world. Not everybody's a hero or a coward, a good guy or a bad guy."

He shot her a long, searching look. "This isn't about Glassman, is it?" he asked softly. "It's about what I said earlier, about you and that firefighter, Ferraro."

"It's about everything."

He turned on a sports radio station, filling the air with Brooklyn accents passionately debating baseball lineups like they were White House cabinet posts. Just before they reached the bridge to Manhattan, he pulled off the highway and into a diner parking lot.

"Where are you going?"

"I want to get a cup of coffee, use the can, make a few phone calls," he explained. "You coming?"

"Why? It's not like you're going to tell me anything," she shot back.

"Hey, it's a two-way street, Scout. What you knew about that chick—"

"She's not a chick, all right?" yelled Georgia.

Marenko threw up his hands. "Suit yourself." He slammed the car door with more force than was necessary.

Georgia sat in the car, fuming. Marenko had taken her to Chappaqua to appease her—*appease the chick,* she could hear him saying—nothing more. It was only by chance that he'd happened to mention the bucket bottoms at that fire in East Tremont. Anything she wanted to learn about this case she was going to have to find out on her own.

But couldn't I always? she realized with a jolt. Walter Frankel was handling all the forensics on the investigation. And he was just a phone call away. She had her cell phone with her. It was only seven P.M. Frankel might still be in his lab. He always worked late.

He picked up on the first ring. He seemed delighted to hear her voice.

"They're freezing me out of this investigation," she complained.

"That's Brennan's doing. Does Lynch know about this?"

"Oh, there's a good idea—complain to the commissioner about my boss, the chief fire marshal. I've always wanted to spend my career checking smoke detectors."

"But Georgia, you *have* to let the commissioner know what's going on."

"What *is* going on, Walter? You're the only one who swears those letters from the Fourth Angel are legit. You told me all four fires were HTA. But Mac showed me a report from the ATF on that Red Hook fire. Did you get a copy of the results? There was diesel fuel on that sample of concrete—"

"Yep," he said. "There sure was."

"And at that Bronx fire? The marshals there found three plastic bucket bottoms in the wreckage—"

"Absolutely."

"So how can those two fires be HTA?"

"Georgia, the diesel fuel was a postfire contamination. They used a power saw to cut the sample, and microscopic particles of diesel contaminated it."

"How can you be so sure?"

"Because I know Dale Kessler, the ATF forensic chemist who did the sample. And what Mac *didn't* tell you was that before Dale found the diesel fuel, he did a test called petrographic microscopy."

"What's that?"

"That measures the minimum temperature a piece of concrete would have to be exposed to for the documented changes to occur. You know what the minimum was that Kessler found? Twenty-eight hundred degrees Fahrenheit. That's the *minimum*. So the diesel fuel stains happened *after* the fire."

"What about the bucket bottoms? Don't tell me they're postfire as well."

"No," said Frankel. "The bottoms appear to be from plastic hardware-store containers. I think they may actually indicate the fire's point of origin."

"Hardware buckets? C'mon, Walter. Those things are made of recyclable plastic."

"High-density polyethylene, to be exact."

"They should melt at temperatures of—what—two hundred and fifty degrees Fahrenheit?"

"Two-fifty to two-seventy-five," he agreed. "Then again, it seems entirely possible in a very hot, fast-moving fire that the coolest place— the most protected place—might be a covered surface directly below the point of origin. It's the same principle that explains why the floor directly beneath a burning liquid often shows little or no damage."

"Were the bucket bottoms found only in East Tremont?"

"I'm going through the records again now. But I believe one or two may also have been found at the warehouse in Washington Heights and at Red Hook, though no one put it together at the time."

"What about Spring Street?"

"No. Nothing. You saw the site first. Did you find any?"

"No," said Georgia. She looked up from her cell phone and saw Marenko heading to the car. "I gotta go, Walter. I'll talk to you later." She disconnected.

Marenko had a big smile on his face when he got into the car.

"What are you so happy about?"

"We hit paydirt, Scout." Marenko slipped the car into drive and nosed back onto the Saw Mill River Parkway. "Suarez did a criminal background check on our buddy Glassman. Turned up an interesting little item. At eighteen, he was arrested for criminal mischief. Would you like to know what that criminal mischief was?"

"What?" asked Georgia unenthusiastically. They were crossing into Manhattan now.

"Setting a fire . . . in a trash can outside a girls' dormitory at Cornell. The university kept it quiet. Glassman's family got a good lawyer who pleaded the charge down to a misdemeanor and got him off with a year's probation. But for my money, any guy who could do that at eighteen could definitely do Spring Street at forty-two."

Georgia stared out the window and said nothing. To her right, the George Washington Bridge sparkled like a string of diamonds on a gaudy dowager. Through the car's front windshield, Manhattan highrises shimmered in the night sky.

"Hey," said Marenko. "I thought you'd be pleased with this development. I'm *sharing* the case with you, Scout. Isn't that what you wanted?"

"You lied to me," she said softly. "About that lab report from the ATF. The results *don't* rule out a connection between these fires. You knew that when you showed it to me. Maybe Ron Glassman *is* the Spring Street torch. But how can I trust anything you say when you never tell me the whole truth?"

Marenko didn't answer. They cruised down the West Side Highway, an uncomfortable silence between them. "You still don't get it, do you?" he asked finally.

"Get what?"

They were a few blocks west of the firehouse now, but instead of turning, he parked the car by a deserted, tumbledown pier overlooking the Hudson River.

"Why are we stopping?"

He killed the engine. "Let's go for a walk. I want to talk to you."

The pier was old and rotting. Soft, spongy boards sagged beneath their feet and turned-up nails jabbed into the soles of Georgia's shoes. Marenko stuck his hands in his pockets, jingling change and keys as he stared out at the black swirling currents.

"Whoever set that fire on Spring Street—Glassman or Fred Fischer or somebody else—we'll fry him, I promise. But you gotta leave those other fires alone. You could get hurt on this one."

"Why?"

A car drove by, its high beams temporarily blinding them. In its wake, Georgia could see swift-moving shadows scurrying along the pier's lower timbers. *Rats.*

"Mac, you've got to tell me what's going on."

He patted his shirt pockets, then remembered. "Jesus, I could use a cigarette."

"Did you know about the missing building records? Those letters from the Fourth Angel?"

"I don't have to know all that stuff to figure out what's going on. Scout, listen to me." He turned to her now, his blue eyes flashing in the moonlight. "The bureau's got two hundred and twenty marshals in a city of eight and a half million people. We've got twenty-two thousand fire investigations a year, four thousand of them bona fide arson cases. Who's got time to go rummaging around dangerous abandoned buildings, filing elaborate reports and contacting landowners? Especially if the owner is the city. Even if a marshal put the time in, the Buildings Department is so swamped, they'd never get around to demolishing the place. What happened in East Tremont and Red Hook could've happened to any of us."

A tugboat drifted by in the distance. Georgia stared at it, trying to comprehend what he was saying. "So, two and a half to three months ago, two vacant, city-owned apartment houses went up in flames. Even though, on paper, they were already supposed to have been demolished. That's why the building records and letters from the Fourth Angel are missing, isn't it? The department wants to pretend those fires weren't part of a string of HTAs, just so nobody *looks bad* for neglecting to put in the paperwork."

Marenko said nothing.

"What about the fire in Washington Heights?" she asked.

"Nobody knew that was HTA . . ."

"At the time, perhaps. But *everybody* knew there was an illegal gambling den in the basement that cops and firefighters liked to frequent. That made revisiting the blaze a trifle inconvenient, wouldn't you say? Didn't it bother *anyone* that some kid could've died at one of these fires?"

He made a face. "No kids died. The world is full of ifs—"

"I can't accept that. I have to find those records and figure out who's behind this." She began to walk back to the car.

"Scout." He raced after her and grabbed the sleeve of her black leather motorcycle jacket. "Don't be stupid. When I say you could get hurt, I don't just mean jobwise."

"What are you saying? That I have to fear my own department?"

He didn't answer, but his look was cold and eerie. She checked her watch. It was seven-forty-five. Richie's basketball season final was in Queens at eight-thirty. She'd promised to be there.

"Take me back to the firehouse, please." If she jumped on her Harley as soon as they arrived, she might make the opening tip-off.

HER CHANCES WERE looking good as she settled herself across the soft, low-riding black leather seat and turned onto the FDR Drive. She could feel the deep, resonant purr of the engine as she roared up the east side of Manhattan. This was one place she could call her own, one place she was in control.

She got as far as Ninety-sixth Street when an unmarked car with flashing lights and sirens came up on her tail, motioning her to pull over. She checked her rearview mirror. The car was familiar—too familiar. Marenko was behind the wheel.

"What the hell do you think you're doing?"

Marenko showed her his beeper. A five-alarm fire had been called in in Queens fifteen minutes ago.

"It's a bad one, Scout," he said breathlessly. "A firefighter's dead, along with a bunch of kids and families. The marshals in Queens think it might be another HTA. They want us to have a look. C'mon, we'll ditch your bike at the nearest firehouse, grab some gear, and head over."

"But my son's basketball game . . ."

Marenko looked at her sharply.

"All right." She sighed.

"It better be."

CHAPTER Twenty

It looked worse than Spring Street, if that was possible.

Maybe it was the choice of target—a modest building full of families and kids—now blackened and caved in on one side like a loaf of bread somebody had stuck a fist through. Maybe it was the hordes of firefighters—on duty and off—clogging the smoke-charged streets. Or maybe it was just that no one thought it could happen again so soon.

"Six dead, including a brother. Fourteen wounded," Marenko yelled to her, cupping a palm over his handie-talkie to drown out the television choppers overhead. "A battalion chief's got witnesses telling him the building went from no smoke to fully charged in under five minutes. And Scout," he added, looking at her gravely, "the first marshals on the scene are saying there were white-hot flames and sparks when they arrived."

"HTA?"

Two fire department EMTs carried a screaming woman past them to an ambulance. Her face was beginning to blister and swell, her eyes disappearing into terrified slits. When she lifted her hands, Georgia saw that they were blackened to the wrists.

"I don't know, Scout." Marenko kicked at a child's chalk drawing on the sidewalk, now covered with soot. An Easter bunny delivering eggs. "But if it is—as far as the serial-arson angle goes—you've made a believer out of me."

Georgia frowned at the firehouse just five feet away from the burned row frame. It was surface-blackened on one side, but otherwise undamaged. The incongruity taunted her. *Help was so close. So close.*

"I hear the firefighter who died was just a probie," said Marenko, shaking his head. "He saved a little girl. The kid's not hurt too bad, but the probie was a mess when they got to him. The fire burned right through his coat."

"I don't get it, Mac," said Georgia. "Why was he up there alone?"

The roar of helicopter blades beat directly overhead. When Georgia looked up, she could see the letters FDNY emblazoned on the side.

"The brass is here." Marenko sighed. "The commish, Greco, Brennan. Everyone's in deep shit on this one." He touched her sleeve and nodded to a couple of firefighters by the side of a rig, hastily rinsing out their mouths and popping breath mints. "The truck and engine weren't in quarters . . ."

"Where were they?"

"There was some kind of party going on at a VFW hall around the corner."

"A lot of them have been drinking, it seems," Georgia noted. "Off-duty guys *and* on."

"Tell me about it." Marenko rolled his eyes. "One of 'em's the chief of department's son."

Georgia fastened the clasps of her turnout coat and slipped on fire-retardant gloves. "Would you like me to poke around the wreckage a little?"

"Yeah. I'm gonna talk to our Queens guys and witnesses, find out what I can."

They split up, and Georgia walked the perimeter of the row frame, which was now more skeleton than building. The roof was gone. The windows sported sooty black eyebrows and jagged edges of broken glass. In the rear, a charred cellar hatch had been ripped off its hinges, revealing a basement ankle-deep in soggy debris. Georgia shone her flashlight down there. Water dripped along splintered black beams. She stuffed her pants into her fire boots and descended into the slippery muck.

So many things in a basement could spontaneously start a fire. Old rags soaked in linseed oil. A spark from the boiler. A carelessly stored can of gasoline. Outdated electrical wiring. The list was endless. It could take days to sort out all the possibilities. She didn't have days.

Something metallic caught her eye. A chain. She fished it out. The links appeared to be made of heavy-gauge stainless steel, yet three had melted like candle wax. Stainless steel couldn't melt in temperatures of less than 2,600 degrees Fahrenheit. Georgia shuddered. She had to be looking at another HTA blaze.

Then she noticed something else strange poking out from the debris. It was a thin, pliable disk, maybe a foot and a half in diameter. White at the center, it had burned along the edges until they were charred and curly.

Georgia turned the disk over and brushed off the soot, revealing a stamped triangle of arrows with a 2 in the middle—a recycling designation—along with the initials HDPE. High-density polyethylene.

She stared at the disk, dumbfounded. Here she was in the wreckage of a fire hot enough to vaporize stainless steel, yet somehow not hot enough to melt a disk of recyclable plastic. Even allowing for the variations that can exist at different levels in a burning room—where temperatures along the floor can be a relatively cool 300 degrees, yet climb to 1,200 degrees or more at ceiling height—the evidence was extraordinary. And puzzling.

Marenko called her on the radio now. "Brennan and the commish want a meeting with us, ASAP."

"Us?"

"The commish wants you there." He paused. "So do I."

The command post was across the street, surrounded by fire trucks parked two deep. Ash drifted overhead like snowflakes. Though the sky was dark, the glare of generator-powered spotlights gave it a washed-out color—like a navy blue shirt, laundered too many times. Even the red flashing lights from emergency vehicles, normally so brilliant, lost their dazzle beneath the strange, artificial glare.

Greco, Brennan, and Marenko were already at the command post when Georgia arrived. Lynch was in the middle, a head shorter than the others. Only his spotless white helmet could be seen, bobbing up and down as he paced between them.

"What the hell is going on here?" the commissioner yelled at the chief of department. Greco cleared his throat and stroked the ends of his black handlebar mustache, which sported ridiculous little curlicues. He looked like the baritone in a barbershop quartet.

"We had a Level One emergency, Commissioner. All units were deployed in a timely and strategic manner—"

Lynch spun around and poked a finger at Greco's chest. "Don't hand that bureaucratic bullshit to me, Frank. Do you think I'm stupid? A firehouse is five feet from a major blaze—*five feet*—and it takes *four and a half minutes* for anyone other than a probie to respond? I checked with dispatch. They weren't out at another alarm."

"I'm told the men were getting the meal. They responded as soon as dispatch notified them . . ."

"Did this meal happen to include a few cases of beer?"

Silence. Georgia looked at Marenko. Marenko looked at the pavement.

"There was a uniformed-members event at the VFW hall," Greco stammered. "The men may have put in an appearance—"

Lynch cut him off. "A uniformed-members event? It was a fucking *keg* party, Frank. And you are going to order every man on duty here tonight to take a Breathalyzer. ASAP. Any man who doesn't pass is fired. On the spot. No ifs, ands, or buts—not from the union and not from you. And Frank"—Lynch paused—"that includes your son."

Greco opened his mouth to speak, but Lynch had already turned his back. The commissioner missed the curb, accidentally sinking an expensive-looking Italian loafer into an icy-cold puddle of hose runoff. When he pulled the shoe out, his sock was soaking wet, and a ring of white plaster dust had penetrated the fragile leather—*fire marshal ring*, as the guys jokingly refer to it. It was the badge of a catching investigator. Georgia must have ruined half a dozen pairs of shoes and pants the same way.

Lynch's jowls thickened in disgust. He sloshed up to Brennan and barked, "Arthur, are we dealing with another HTA here?"

"Commissioner, it's too soon—"

"Too soon? Do you realize what this department looks like to the mayor right now? To the media? The NYPD's *already* prepping to take over. They do that, and the mayor's gonna wonder why he needs a Bureau of Fire Investigation at all. So if you want to keep your job, you'll answer me. Are all these fires related—yes or no?"

Brennan's jawline hardened. The halogen lights illuminated every crevice of his rosacea-scarred skin. "No," he grunted finally, his eyes boring into Georgia's. "Marshal Skeehan was mistaken the other day when she told you these fires were related. We've received independent confirmation from the ATF to the contrary. As for this fire, I'm going to venture it's not related, pending further investigation—"

"Chief," Georgia interrupted. "I just found melted steel in the basement across the street. And those ATF findings? They were based on contaminated samples." If Marenko could've misled *her* by highlighting the wrong information in the report, he could've misled Brennan as well.

"As I said before, Skeehan," the chief uttered through clenched teeth, his beady blue eyes smoldering with rage. "You were mistaken."

Georgia furrowed her brow at Brennan as it sank in. *So you know— you know the fires are related. You know the ATF report supports that. Do you know where the building records are, too?*

"What the hell's going on?" Lynch demanded, shifting his glance from the chief fire marshal to Georgia, then back to the chief.

"I'll tell you what's going on, Commissioner," Brennan answered tightly, never taking his eyes off of Georgia. "Marshal Skeehan is a rookie with a hero complex, making unfounded allegations to distort her own importance in this investigation."

"I wouldn't do that," she protested.

"You wouldn't make yourself into a hero?" Brennan smiled icily. "Why don't you tell the commissioner how you crapped out on a fellow firefighter in Queens a couple of years ago, then had the gall to accept a medal for your cowardice."

"I . . ." Georgia opened her mouth to speak, but the words wouldn't come. Nothing could erase the hollow sense of having failed the only real test she'd been given in her life. She hung her head. *So Brennan knows about that, too—has probably known all along.* How could she justify her actions to the chief—to the commissioner—when she couldn't justify them even to herself?

Marenko threw down his helmet and stepped between them, giving Brennan a sharp look. "Everybody's pissing on one another and it's not helping," he said. "We—that is, *I*—didn't take the serial-arson angle seriously enough until now. Marshal Skeehan may have had the right idea all along. If this fire turns out to be HTA, I'll take responsibility for the mistake and change the direction of the investigation."

"You'll do better than that, Marshal," said Lynch. "From this point forward, I want Georgia Skeehan to head the investigation."

There was a pause, as if Georgia, Marenko, and the chief all refused to believe their ears.

"You're not serious," said Brennan. "She's a rookie—"

"You'll destroy the men's morale—" Marenko sputtered.

"Not to mention embarrass the department," the chief added.

"Sir," Georgia pleaded. "The chief's right. I'm really not qualified . . ."

Lynch held up a hand to silence them. "I don't give a shit who likes this arrangement and who doesn't. This is the way it's going to be." He turned to Georgia. "Look, young lady, you seem pretty sure of yourself, and I'm not really interested in what you did or didn't do as a firefighter or how many Cub Scout badges you have. If you think you can put these arsons together, then do it."

The commissioner gave a parting scowl to Brennan. "Arthur, I want you to hand over everything—and I do mean everything—having to do with this investigation. I'm tired of screwing around."

CHAPTER *Twenty-one*

The chief counted up the stories of the brown brick apartment building until he got to nine. The windows were still dark on this Friday morning. She was probably sleeping.

He cooled down from his morning run through Central Park, found a pay phone, and dialed her number from memory. Her voice was gravelly when she answered. He pictured her now: a tall, cool, dark-haired beauty with wide-set eyes and a smoky voice. She said hello a second time.

"I send you flowers and you don't say thanks?" Easter lilies. For spring. And funerals.

There was a pause. There was always a pause. As if she couldn't quite believe it was him. That pause made him tingle. "You don't like flowers anymore?" he asked.

"Why are you doing this?"

"I just wanted to tell you I'm not sore about what happened."

"I . . . I'm glad . . ."

"Hey, it was fun while it lasted."

She didn't answer.

"So," he said jovially, "how about a cup of coffee for old time's sake?"

"No . . . I don't think so. That's not a good idea." There was a catch in her voice. The chief heard it right away. She wouldn't accuse him. It would seem too rude. "Look, I . . . I've had some very strange things happen to me lately. I think it's better we don't . . ."

"What things? You can tell *me.*"

"Just *things,* okay? I've got to go. Please don't call me anymore or send me anything." She hung up.

The chief smiled to himself as he replaced the receiver. He could picture her now, racing around her Upper West Side apartment, making sure the doors and windows were locked, turning on all the lights, calling friends. She'd debate again what to do. Tell her supervisors? Call the police? And tell them what? That a guy she used to work with sends her flowers and asks her out for coffee?

He crossed the street to the park behind the Museum of Natural History to stretch out his hamstrings. A fire engine sped past. A Seagrave pumper. His heart clenched at the rumble of the diesel engine, the gleam of chrome and red enamel. The memory was a decade old, yet it taunted him, a wound that wouldn't heal. The chief could still picture that sweaty high school gym in Brooklyn, those drill instructors with their beady eyes and sharpened number-two pencils, that nervous twitch of energy in all the wanna-be recruits. Their entire futures boiled down to a series of measurements: *How fast can you run? How high can you jump? How much can you lift?* Seconds counted. Inches counted.

The chief checked his pedometer. He'd run ten miles this morning—not bad. He was in peak condition for a man of thirty-nine. Fast. Strong. Able to pass the toughest physical fitness test the department could dish out. But it no longer mattered. He was too old. No one took him seriously anymore. Not even the woman in 9E.

He left the park and walked into a dry cleaner a block from her apartment. He'd watched her come in here often enough to know she had an account.

"Can I help you?" asked the small Asian woman behind the counter.

"Yeah." The chief turned on his most handsome, winning smile. People always gave him what he wanted when they saw that face. "My girlfriend's sick and she asked me to pick up her dry cleaning."

"You have ticket?"

"Aw, man!" He smacked his forehead. "I knew there was something I forgot. She's leaving for a business trip first thing tomorrow. She really needs the stuff."

The woman studied him a moment. The rugged build, the blond hair damp from a morning run, the paint-flecked sweatshirt. He grinned ruefully, blue eyes twinkling.

"What's her last name?"

"Nolan . . . geez, thanks, ma'am. You're the best."

The bill came to $40 for two pairs of pants, a blazer, a blouse, and a silky peach nightshirt. The chief paid in cash. A block away, two sanitation workers were loading garbage into a compactor. When they turned, he threw everything but the nightshirt into the truck.

He folded the shirt into a ball under his arm and found a stationery store where he purchased a small padded envelope, then smiled his winning smile at the cashier and asked if she'd be kind enough to address the envelope because he was having a problem with double vision. The woman obliged, neatly printing out the address he rattled off. At the post office two blocks away, he had the package weighed and stamped, but didn't seal it.

It was nearly nine A.M. by the time he crossed back into Central Park and found his way into one of the park's deserted tunnels. There, he shivered in the damp air as he fumbled in his pockets for a butane lighter.

Seconds later, a warm orange flame glowed invitingly in the darkness, its light shimmering across the nightshirt. The chief could almost picture her in it now, that long, dark hair oozing like molasses over her shoulders. That pale porcelain skin disappearing into the folds of silky peach fabric around her cleavage. She had such a fair, unblemished complexion. He would bet she burned easily. *So easily.*

He touched the lighter to the back of the shirt. A flame flared up the middle. It grew quickly, jagged teeth tearing into fragile silk. Then he threw the shirt on the damp, filthy cement and stamped on it until the flames were extinguished. A charred slash ran down the back. A hideous scar. He opened up the mailing envelope and stuffed the shirt inside.

Her delicate white shoulders would tremble when she saw it. She'd know right away who it was from—and what it meant.

First the shirt, it would whisper. *Then you.*

CHAPTER *Twenty-two*

Georgia awoke with a start. A strong breeze snapped
loudly at the vinyl shades across her windows. She massaged her
throbbing temples and took stock of the time. Nine A.M. She'd had
three hours of shut-eye in the last twenty-four. She realized now
that she'd been dreaming of the dead firefighter, Sean Duffy. But
in her dream, the face was her father's.

Grief sat like an anvil on her chest. Every dead firefighter
seemed to bring that painful day back. Sean Duffy had saved that
little girl, she'd heard. The child was going to be in the hospital for
a few days, but she'd recover. Georgia wondered if Duffy's family
ever would.

She went downstairs to the kitchen and forced a stale jelly
doughnut on herself, hoping to stem the queasiness in the pit of
her stomach. The house was quiet. Richie was at school; her
mother, at her secretarial job. The plastic Easter eggs on the bare
lilac out front swayed in the breeze. Forsythia bloomed along a
chain-link fence.

On the kitchen table was a pile of papers. Bills, mostly,
addressed to her. Some contest entry forms addressed to her
mother. A folded orange sheet caught Georgia's eye. It was Richie's
basketball program from last night. When she opened it, a gold-
plated medallion tumbled out, with the words MOST IMPROVED
PLAYER etched across it. Richie had gotten an award—and she'd
missed it.

Damn, thought Georgia, shaking her head. *It's not like I was out
with some guy or drunk in a bar.* Lives were at stake—many, many

lives. And besides that, she had to put food on the table. She was here, goddamnit. Not like Rick. She was here.

She poured herself a cup of black coffee and roughly shoved the papers to one side of the table. An envelope thudded to the floor. Georgia picked it up. It was blank on the outside and unsealed, but inside there was a sheet of lined yellow paper filled with Richie's painstaking scrawl. Richie hated writing. She had to bribe him to pen thank-yous.

She unfolded the paper. A school photo dropped from the creases. Her throat went dry. Her eyes blurred with tears as she read it:

To My Dad,

Hi. My name is Richie. I'm 9. I never wrote a letter like this before. But I guess you never read one like it, so we are even.

I always wanted to know something about you. My grandma used to tell my mom I look like you. Here's my school picture. What do you think? If I walked down the street, would you know me? I wouldn't know you. That makes me sad.

It's okay if you don't want to be my dad. You don't have to, like, play ball with me or anything. But maybe we could just be friends or something. Maybe call each other on our birthdays and Christmas. When is your birthday? Mine is May 13th. I like to play basketball and collect Pokemon cards. I like reading Goosebumps books. Do you like these things?

Please write me. You don't have to send me presents or nothing. I got plenty of stuff. But a letter from you would really rock.

Your Friend,
Richie Skeehan

Georgia gripped the table for equilibrium. She wiped the tears away clumsily with the sleeve of her nightshirt.

You don't have to send me presents or nothing. I got plenty of stuff. But a letter from you would really rock.

Her fingers curled into a fist, and she pounded the table. She could taste the bitter bile of anger and guilt as it traveled down her gut. The only thing Richie wanted was the one thing she couldn't give him. She stuffed the letter back in its envelope and glared at it, silently cursing it as if the man himself were standing there.

But he never would be. Not for her. Not for Richie. It had been seven years since she'd seen Rick, but the memory of him never quite faded in intensity. He would always be twenty-five, with a mane of dark hair and a body as lean and taut as new rope. Hell, she couldn't even afford the luxury of hating him today—not with one of the biggest arson investigations in department history hanging over her head, and two dead firefighters haunting the recesses of her brain.

The phone rang now and she picked it up.

"You see? What'd I tell you? Another HTA." Walter Frankel never bothered identifying himself. "The department can't stick its head in the sand about these fires anymore."

"Oh, goody for me," said Georgia dryly. "Two firefighters are dead in less than a week, the civilian body count's up to—what? Fifty-eight? And now I get the keys to this broken-down jalopy." She was still numb from Richie's letter. She wasn't in the mood for Frankel's enthusiasm. "What's up?"

"Obviously not you."

"Hey, when I want guilt, I'll talk to my kid."

"Listen, I've got some good news. That bucket bottom you uncovered last night in Howard Beach? I managed to lift a thumb latent off it."

"A fingerprint survived that heat?"

"Actually, under the right conditions, heat can permanently affix a fingerprint to a surface. I'm running the print through AFIS now." The Automated Fingerprint Identification System, or AFIS, was a national clearinghouse of fingerprints. Anyone who'd ever been arrested, or served in law enforcement or the military, had their fingerprints stored in AFIS.

"Any matchups?" Georgia caught her reflection in the chrome of the stove and made a face. Her hair looked like a feather duster.

"So far, no. Which means our guy's not a criminal, ex-military, or one of New York's Finest or Bravest." He giggled. "Or drunkest."

Georgia groaned. "I can't believe those assholes last night. I think they *should* get fired."

"They won't."

"How do you know?"

"Because the Breathalyzers were administered by fire department EMTs," said Frankel. "Those guys won't screw a brother, even if he was seeing pink elephants. Greco'll probably lift the entire house and scatter the guys throughout the city, but I'll bet you anything, they'll *all* pass their Breathalyzers."

Georgia tried to run a comb through her hair, then gave up. Who was around to care, anyway? "Have you noticed, Walter? A lot of these fires seem to have caught the department with its pants down . . ."

"Not hard to do," he reminded her. "Screwups happen all the time. They're just more noticeable on a high-profile case."

"I don't know," she said. "I get the feeling it's not random. It's like somebody *wants* to make the department look bad. And who'd want to do that except an ex-firefighter?"

"Then how do you explain Spring Street? Nothing embarrassing there. Look, if it makes you feel any better, I'll ask AFIS to manually scan the fingerprints of New York City Fire Department personnel again. Maybe a print was smudged and we missed a match."

"Yeah. Have them do that," said Georgia. "Of course, even if you do find a matchup, it doesn't prove the guy who handled that bucket set the fire."

"Actually, combined with the right evidence, it just might. Come see me later, I'll show you why."

Georgia sighed. "I gotta go face the firing squad first." Frankel knew what she meant: the task force. "I'm scared, Walter. I can't run a major investigation. And if I fail, I'm going to let so many people down. The families of those firefighters, the civilians . . ." *And Randy,* she thought. *What if I mess up and can't find his little girl's killer?*

"Darling, you won't fail if you stand your ground," Frankel assured her. "My father taught vocational high school in the Bronx for thirty years. He dealt with gang members, drug addicts, kids from mental hospitals—you name it. His motto was 'Don't demand to be liked. Demand to be respected.' You remember that, they won't push you around."

"Yeah, but your dad worked with emotionally disturbed *children.*"

"So?" Frankel laughed. "Don't you?"

CHAPTER *Twenty-three*

Georgia could feel the chill as soon as she walked through the doors of Engine Two. Firefighters stopped talking when she passed. No one said hello.

Upstairs, voices grew hushed at the sound of her footsteps. Inside the task-force office, Eddie Suarez was planted in front of a tabletop television by the window, smoking a cigarette while he watched news coverage of the Howard Beach fire. Gene Cambareri was wolfing down a jelly doughnut and picking out guys he knew over Suarez's shoulder. Marenko was running something through the fax machine. Only Carter acknowledged her, and he did it by pretending to throw something in a wastebasket behind the door where she was standing.

"Watch out for yourself, girl," he muttered as he leaned over. "Mac's out for blood."

"Thanks for the warning," Georgia whispered. "You holding up?"

"Yeah." He sighed. "I'm still walking and talking, so I guess I must be."

Georgia hung up her jacket and threw a folder of papers on her desk. Marenko trudged over, carrying an enormous cardboard carton. He plonked it on her desk.

"The commissioner said to give you everything," he said coolly. "Here's everything."

"Mac," she pleaded. "Please don't do this."

He turned away and walked over to the television where Cambareri and Suarez were flipping daytime news channels, trying to pick up other coverage of the fire. Carter was sitting at his desk staring dully at the screen, his mind seemingly a million miles away. Georgia took a deep breath and strode toward the group.

"Okay," she said tentatively. "We're going to need to speak to the Howard Beach landlord, tenants, and neighbors, review the crime-scene photos, and supervise the Queens marshals' dig for evidence at the site. . . ."

No one heard her. They were all focused on the television. Cambareri was passing out doughnuts. Suarez was poking fun at Greco's handlebar mustache. Georgia tried again, making her voice more forceful this time.

"Guys, listen up. We'll need to streamline what we have on each of these five fires, so we can compare them at a glance. And we'll need to get a list together of firefighters and ex-firefighters who've faced disciplinary action or dismissal during the past year in case our guy's FDNY. . . ."

Carter bit his lip and looked at the floor. The rest of them didn't even seem to hear her. A rage churned inside her now. Georgia planted herself behind the set, determined to get their attention, but the men chatted away, oblivious. Her pant leg brushed against the television's electrical cord. A raw impulse seized her. She reached down, ripped one end of the cord out of the wall, the other out of the set, then opened the alleyway window and threw the cord to the pavement.

The talking stopped. The men flicked gazes at one another, then stared at Georgia in stunned silence. Cambareri's doughnut dripped jelly down his tie. He didn't even bother to wipe it off.

"If that's what I have to do to get your attention, so be it." Georgia paced in front of them now, her heart beating wildly. "All I've wanted since I got here was to be a productive member of this team. And you guys did everything in your power to shut me out. So if you're looking to blame somebody for what's happened, blame yourselves."

She took a deep breath, feeling her mind and body picking up a rhythm. "Now, we've got two firefighters and fifty-eight civilians dead, and I *care* about that deeply. I know you do, too," she said, shooting a quick, piercing glance at Carter. "I want interviews. I want someone to go out to Queens and oversee the collection of evidence. And I want to know about firefighters with a beef against this department. So you guys can start helping me *work* this case, or you can get the hell out and I'll find four other warm bodies who will."

The men shifted uncomfortably in their seats and looked at Marenko. What he said, clearly, they'd all go along with.

"You don't know *how* to run a case, Skeehan," Marenko said finally. "That's not a put-down. That's just simple fact."

"Then help me, please. Aren't we on the same side?" But in a sense, they weren't anymore, Georgia realized with a jolt. Marenko had suffered a humiliating loss of face last night. She could see it now in the slump of his shoulders, the way he rubbed the back of his neck. When his blue eyes met hers, they looked worn and defeated.

"Mac," Georgia offered gently. "I know you're in a difficult position here. Most men would walk away. Only the strongest would put their egos aside for the greater good of catching whoever did this. . . . Please—I need you. I need *all* of you. Stay and help me."

Marenko wiped a thumb across his lips and studied her now. She knew he was trying to read her—her ambitions, her intellect, her level of sincerity. He was entitled to that. She wouldn't rush him. He shook his head and cursed under his breath. "You could talk anybody into anything, couldn't you?" He sighed. "You shoulda been a lawyer."

Georgia laughed, relieved at the break in tension. "Right now, you probably wish I was."

The phone rang. Suarez picked it up, then held the receiver to his chest.

"Yo, Skeehan. That Jose you were trying to find is on line two. You wanna take it?"

"Yeah." She picked up. She could hear traffic in the background and a buzz of static. The guy was calling from a cell phone on some street corner.

"Hey, are you *really* a lady fire marshal?" He had a slight Spanish accent, and the breathless distractedness of a low-level street dealer.

"Sure am."

"So you won't pull my rap sheet if I give you a statement?"

"I'll pull it, Jose. I just may decide not to read it too closely if you help me out here. Alison tells me you worked for Fred Fischer."

"I used to fix locks and shit like that for Fred."

"And deal drugs for him, too, right?" Silence. "C'mon, Jose, don't get cute with me."

"Okay, okay. We had some business dealings—know what I'm sayin'? Fred stored my stash in his room. Monday's fire cleaned me out."

"I'm not falling over with sympathy here." Georgia frowned at her notes. "When you say 'Fred's room'—do you mean he *lived* in the building?" Spring Street was a commercial structure. There was no certificate of occupancy, or CO, for residential usage.

"Yeah. He lived in the basement. His brother owned the building, I think."

Obviously, Jose had no idea who Fred's brother was. Fred probably never told him.

"Alison said you think Fred burned the building down."

"He was always talkin' 'bout it, 'cause his brother wanted to put him in rehab. . . . And the night before the fire—Sunday night? Fred's brother made him go down to Atlantic City on some errand. Gave him a wad of cash and told him to keep his ass down there until at least Tuesday. I had some business I wanted to do with Fred, know what I'm sayin'? So it was a problem—"

"Wait a minute," said Georgia, startled. "Are you telling me Fred said his brother *told* him to stay out of the building?"

"Yeah. Made it real clear he wasn't s'posed to come back until Tuesday. But Fred, man, he takes the money and gets fucked up on blow. By Monday, he's broke, so he comes back and crashes. Maybe he got to thinkin' . . ."

"Why would Fred's brother want him to stay away?"

"I don't know, man. But that was Fred. He never fucking listened."

CHAPTER Twenty-four

Sloane Michaels's secretary told Georgia that her boss often went to New York Hospital on Friday afternoons to visit his wife. But when Georgia got to Amelia's room at the hospital, the door was wide open, and neither of them were there.

"She's getting bathed," a nurse explained. "They should be back any moment."

Georgia idly scanned a wall of photographs opposite Amelia's bed while she waited. The pictures showed a tiny, dark-haired sprig of a woman in running shorts and tank tops with numbers pinned to her back. In some, she was in full stride, her jaw set firmly against the pain, sweat pouring off her sinewy body. In others, she was collapsing over the finish lines, a look of relief mingling with something sad around her eyes.

There were medals, too—big, garish gold discs strung with ribbons that had faded from their once-brilliant hues. And newspaper articles that had yellowed with age. On a bedside table, a hardcover book lay open along a cracked spine: a biography of the runner Prefontaine. Michaels had been reading to her.

Georgia turned at the sound of rubber wheels on polished linoleum. Two nurses were wheeling Amelia into the room. Sloane Michaels walked behind them. His suit jacket was off and his shirt sleeves rolled up. His brown eyes registered shock and a certain wariness at Georgia's presence.

"I'm sorry to intrude," Georgia stammered. "I just needed to speak to you for a few minutes. This was the only place I could track you down."

She glanced over at Amelia lying on the steel gurney, her body twisted and emaciated, her freshly shampooed hair matted to her head, threads of gray sprouting like weeds among the black strands. "Would you rather I call you later?"

Michaels folded his arms across his chest. The smile that had beamed back at her from countless television interviews and newspaper articles was gone. He was reserved, protective. He leaned over and told Amelia who Georgia was. The woman's dark eyes focused clearly. She parted her lips to say something, but the words were garbled.

"I suppose you might as well stay." Michaels sighed, tenderly stroking his wife's hand. "Amelia loves company."

The nurses settled the woman back into her bed, then left.

"Amelia can't talk much anymore," Michaels explained. "But she understands everything."

Georgia, accustomed to death but not to the process of dying, had no idea how to respond. Embarrassed, she nodded and smiled, then leaned on the edge of the bed, nearly toppling a monitor. Michaels pulled up a chair and Georgia sat stiffly on it, fidgety and nervous in the sour, stuffy room. She'd thought herself so tough, so superior in life experience to Sloane Michaels the other night. But watching the kindness and patience he showed with his wife, she wondered which of them was really the more cocooned.

"Amelia wanted to be a firefighter, too," said Michaels. "Right after she got out of grad school. But that was before they let women on the job." He took his wife's limp hand between his. "Amelia's quite an athlete."

The present tense took Georgia aback. For a man so shrewd in business, he seemed willfully boyish and naive in his wife's presence. Georgia sensed it wasn't an act. Sloane Michaels was used to controlling every aspect of his life. Yet his wife was dying before his very eyes. Georgia suspected that, on some level, he couldn't accept what he couldn't control.

Michaels's cell phone rang. He cleared his throat and took the call—sounding, to the world, like a man in charge. He dispatched the caller quickly, then explained that he was due back for a meeting at three P.M. "If we walk out together, will that give you the time you need?" he asked Georgia.

"That's fine," she said.

Michaels leaned over and murmured something to his wife, then gently pressed his lips against hers. In the hallway, his pace quickened until he was nearly at a gallop. He seemed to need the physical release. His way of decompressing, perhaps. Georgia wouldn't speak until he was ready.

"She loves people," Michaels murmured when they reached the lobby. "God, she was a talker. Talked to everybody. . . . I worry that if something were to happen to me . . ." His voice trailed off and he seemed suddenly embarrassed. Georgia rescued him.

"I shouldn't have intruded upon your time with her today. It was bad judgment."

"No harm done." He unrolled his sleeves, slipped back into his gold cuff links, then wiped a hand down his face. He reminded Georgia of an actor getting ready to go onstage. "What did you want to see me about?"

"Your brother, Fred. I understand you sent him to Atlantic City last Sunday?"

"I have property down there. I asked him to pick up some rental receipts."

"When was he supposed to return?"

Michaels shrugged. "I don't think I gave him a timetable. I may have told him to take a couple of days down there and enjoy himself."

"Didn't you specifically tell him not to come back until Tuesday?"

"Ms. Skeehan, you couldn't *tell* my brother anything. He always did what he wanted."

"Were you aware he'd returned Monday?"

"Not until they pulled his body from the wreckage."

"You never told me he lived in the building."

"Because you're a fire marshal and it was an illegal occupancy. Look, I let my brother have a small room in the basement. Otherwise, he'd have been homeless. He was too messed up most of the time to pay rent. If I'd put him in any of my residential buildings, the other tenants would've complained. Spring Street was funky, the building commercial. He didn't cause any harm down there—"

"Except probably deal drugs."

Michaels sighed. "He may have. I'm sorry if he did."

He barreled through the revolving doors. His limo was waiting at the curb. "I know that to you, Ms. Skeehan, my brother was a lowlife. But sober, he was a good guy, and I loved him. Just because he came back early from some errand doesn't mean he set any fires."

The chauffeur got out and opened the rear passenger door. Michaels offered to drop Georgia someplace. She declined.

"He talked a lot about burning the building, you know," she told him as he got into his car. "He wanted to hurt you."

"He hurt me, all right—he died. I buried him yesterday." Michaels looked up at the hospital and shook his head. "People get sick. People die. All the money in the world, and you can't do a damn thing about it. That's the biggest hurt of all."

CHAPTER Twenty-five

Walter Frankel's lab was pitch-black when Georgia arrived. The shades were drawn, the overhead fluorescent fixtures off. The only light in the room emanated from a long table with a steel hood. Frankel, dressed in safety goggles, was hunched over it, a shifting array of colored light reflecting in his lenses— from deep red to amber to blue-green. Overhead, a ceiling fan whirred noisily.

"What are you doing?" asked Georgia.

"Can you get the light switch?" he yelled over his shoulder.

She did, tripping over Frankel's calico cat in the process. Two bright bands of overhead fluorescents buzzed to life. Frankel turned off the table light and lifted his goggles. "I'm trying to find the best wavelength of spectroscopic light to highlight this thumbprint from the plastic bucket you found at Howard Beach. We still haven't got a matchup."

"I don't know why you're still fooling with that when we've got so much else to do." She flopped into his duct-taped orange chair. "You wanted to show me something. This better be good, Walter. I've got Gene and Randy out interviewing witnesses at the Howard Beach blaze and overseeing the collection of evidence. And I've got Mac and Eddie chasing down former firefighters, some of whom would just as soon deck them as speak to them."

Frankel laughed. "I see you've whipped these guys into shape already. What's your secret?"

"I ripped the cord out of the task-force television and threw it out the window."

"Whatever works." He wheeled himself over to a sink and handed her a disposable paper cup.

"I'm not thirsty."

"I didn't say you were." He put a finger to his lips, striking a thoughtful pose. "Question: How fast would this cup burn if I suspended it over an open flame?"

"Walter." She rolled her eyes. "I flunked chemistry in my sophomore year in college. That's why I dropped out."

"Indulge me."

"Okay." She sighed. "I'll say five seconds."

Frankel clamped the empty paper cup to a Bunsen burner stand and turned on a flame beneath it. Fire spread evenly over the bottom of the cup, then up the sides. Ten seconds later, the blackened cup shriveled into ash that dissolved in the fire.

"So?" said Georgia.

"Wait," Frankel urged. He took another cup, this time filling it to the brim with water. "Now, how long do you think it will take to burn up?"

Georgia shrugged. "I don't know. Maybe twenty seconds?"

"And how will it burn?"

"The same way. The bottom will catch fire, then travel up the sides and blacken it until the whole thing's reduced to ash."

"So you say." He smiled. He clamped the filled cup to the Bunsen burner and turned on the flame. Ten seconds went by. Then twenty. The water inside the cup boiled and turned to steam, but still the base didn't catch light. By thirty seconds, the rim was burning where the water had evaporated. And it continued to burn that way— from the top down—for another twenty-five seconds, until all the water had turned to vapor and the sides of the cup had burned away. Frankel shut off the flame and grinned at Georgia's surprised expression.

"A simple paper cup, with a hot flame underneath. And yet the bottom doesn't burn. Why?"

"Because the water in the cup's keeping it from burning," said Georgia, amazed.

"The energy is being transferred from the flame to the water, turning it into vapor," Frankel explained. "Only when there's no more transference does the heat consume the cup. The base is the last thing to burn."

Georgia snapped her fingers. "Those plastic bucket bottoms found at the fires—"

"Exactly. I'm willing to bet they were filled with accelerant, Georgia. Had the buckets just been lying around, they would've been consumed. But we know fire travels upward in a V-pattern. So those buckets heated up, but the heat was transferred to the fuel inside. By the time the fire was going good, it was in the vapors above the bucket, burning so hot, so fast, the base never had a chance to melt—something our torch probably never realized. My opinion? I think our guy may be building his HTA devices in five-gallon hardware-store buckets, then dropping them, ready-made, at the scene."

"Can we do a trace on the buckets?"

"That's what I'm trying to do now. All the buckets were made of high-density polyethylene—HDPE. Unfortunately, ninety-four percent of all recyclable plastic is HDPE, so that doesn't give us much to go on. I've done a GC on the bucket samples to see if I can pick up any manufacturing variations. So far, they're all coming back identical."

GC, or gas chromatography, is a test in which a sample of material is heated until it turns into vapor. The vapor is then broken down and graphically analyzed, component by component, to determine its exact chemical composition.

"The problem is," Frankel continued, "many different stores buy the same kinds of buckets. I don't know if we'll be able to say our guy bought these at a Sears in Long Island or Joe's Hardware in the Bronx."

"Sounds like a dead end to me." Georgia sighed.

"Maybe, maybe not. In the meantime, I've uncovered something else interesting." He thumbed through some notes. "I went back through the evidence on those first three HTA fires. Marshals found type-A blood on a piece of window glass at the Washington Heights blaze—sharp glass from a break-in, rather than combustion. I've ordered a DNA test."

"But we don't have a perp to match it against . . ."

"No. But if we get one, we can link him to the Washington Heights blaze, if nothing else. And we can narrow the field just by checking his blood type."

Georgia massaged her temples and sank back down on the orange chair.

"What's wrong?" asked Frankel. "You look like you need something to eat."

"No." She shook her head. "It's not that. Walter, I'm starting to have cold feet. How do we really *know* all these fires are connected? No bucket bottoms were found at Spring Street. Except for the possible presence of HTA, nothing ties these fires together. Maybe Brennan was right. Maybe I *am* putting a bunch of unrelated fires together to play hero."

"Then how do you explain the letters—from the Fourth Angel?"

"Mac and Brennan still insist they've never seen them before." Georgia read his frown. "All right, I know—they're *lying*. But forget about the letters for a moment. You told me yourself—HTA's not that hard to manufacture. Couldn't more than one person have mixed up a batch of this stuff?"

"Sure they could. But five unrelated fires in the space of five months? C'mon, darling, I'm a scientist—I don't believe in coincidences." He slapped his desk. "Okay—let's say you're right. We still have to solve *all* these fires—"

"But at least we're only concerned with one fire at a time. Maybe just a fire started by some nerdy Joe-average, looking for revenge . . ."

"And this nerdy Joe-average, I presume, isn't as dangerous." He laughed. "You know, back in the early nineties, after a bunch of these HTAs occurred, a group of guys from the ATF, the Seattle Fire

Department, and some heavy-hitting government science labs got together and started brainstorming all the ways Mr. Joe-average-American could build a bomb in his garage. They came up with hundreds."

Frankel ticked off a few now on his fingers: "Swimming pool cleaner and brake fluid . . . potassium chlorate and table sugar . . . plaster of paris and linseed oil . . . sawdust and chicken fat—no, you didn't hear wrong: *chicken fat.* These guys wrote up a report, warning how easily a bunch of nerdy Joe-averages, as you call them, could blow up just about anything they set their sights on. And you know what happened?"

"What?"

"Nothing . . . until April, 1995, when Timothy McVeigh, Terry Nichols, and his companions got their hands on forty-eight hundred pounds of ammonium nitrate fertilizer and took down a nine-story concrete-and-steel building in Oklahoma City, killing a hundred and sixty-eight people. Which means, Georgia, that even if your so-called nerdy Joe-averages *are* behind these bombs, that doesn't make them any less deadly."

"So where does that leave us?"

Frankel slumped in his wheelchair. "Hard evidence is going to be sketchy, so you'll have to look for motive. In Seattle, for instance, investigators were pretty sure the fires were the work of organized crime. But here, I don't know. There's no obvious profit motive. No mob vendetta, either. That's why I keep going back to the letters."

Georgia sighed. "If you're right, then Sloane Michaels has to be one of the arsonist's targets."

"Why is that?"

"Well, he *did* get a copy of that first letter from the Fourth Angel several weeks before the Spring Street fire. . . ."

Frankel frowned. "He told you that?"

"Of course." Georgia shrugged. "You know that. I put the letter in an evidence packet and asked you to check it for prints."

"You didn't tell me he gave it to you."

"How else would I have gotten it?" Georgia rose to leave, then paused in the doorway. "Walter, if what you say is true and these fires are all related, yet easy enough to put together, how come we've never seen any in New York before?"

Frankel's calico jumped on his lap. He stroked her back as a knowing gaze came into his dark eyes.

"Who's to say we haven't?"

CHAPTER Twenty-six

What do I have to link these five fires together? Georgia asked herself as she drove her motorcycle back to Queens. Three cryptic letters that could've been written by a nut? Some plastic bucket bottoms? A bit of type-A blood on a broken pane of glass?

And what about Ron Glassman? she thought as she nosed her Harley into the driveway, with fifteen minutes to spare before Richie returned from school. Marenko had developed some pretty incriminating stuff on this guy. Glassman had motive: a pregnant mistress. He had opportunity: a surveillance camera had recorded him leaving the building right before the fire. And when confronted about it, Glassman had lied and threatened to lawyer up. Plus, he had a history of fire-setting. Georgia had seen people get twenty-five-to-life on less than that.

Still, that left Howard Beach and those other three unexplained fires. They couldn't be Glassman's. Or even Fred Fischer's. Brennan said they weren't related; Frankel said they were. Who was right?

Georgia sat on the cement stoop in front of her house, waiting for Richie's schoolbus. In one folder, she'd collected the dispatch printouts from each of the suspected HTA fires. The dispatch printouts were second-by-second records of activity at each fire scene. The fires were labeled—as they always were—by a four-digit number corresponding to the nearest alarm box to the blaze, even if the blaze was called in to 911.

In another folder, Georgia had collected copies of each of the fire's face sheets—summaries of the cause-and-origin investigations. She propped a yellow legal pad on her lap and tried to draw up a very basic fact sheet about each fire.

HTA Fire Number One
Date: December 16th (four months ago)
Alarm box number: 1608
Building: Vacant, single-story furniture warehouse in Washington Heights, Manhattan.
Ownership: Private
Insurance: Adequate
Fatalities: None
Point of origin: Unknown, but plastic bottom of bucket was found in basement.

HTA Fire Number Two
Date: January 29th (less than three months ago)
Alarm box number: 1008
Building: Vacant, five-story apartment house in Red Hook, Brooklyn.
Ownership: Land is city-owned. Records missing regarding building.
Insurance: Probably none specific to building. Records missing.
Fatalities: One
Point of origin: Unknown, but plastic bottom of bucket was found on first floor.

HTA Fire Number Three
Date: February 3rd (less than a week after HTA number two)
Alarm box number: 1114
Building: Vacant, four-story apartment house in East Tremont, the Bronx.

Ownership: Land is city-owned. Records missing regarding
  building.

Insurance: Probably none specific to building. Records
  missing.

Fatalities: One

Point of origin: Unknown, but bucket bottoms found on first
  floor.

Georgia looked up the street and stretched. She could see a pattern, more or less. Three vacant, or nearly vacant, rundown buildings in fringe areas of the city, torched within a two-month period. With the building records missing and two of the properties city-owned, she couldn't see insurance profits as a motive. The torch looked instead like a classic pyro—someone who got his kicks setting fires, then hanging around to see the show.

So far, so good. She tried the same technique with the Spring Street fire.

HTA Fire Number Four

Alarm box number: 2310

Building: Fully rented, six-story commercial loft in SoHo,
  Manhattan, occupied on the sixth floor.

Date of Burning: Last Monday night, April 5th

Ownership: Private

Insurance: Adequate

Fatalities: Fifty-three civilians; one firefighter

Point of origin: Unknown.

Everything about this fire was different from the first three. It was an occupied building in a high-rent district. Public access to most of the building would have been limited. No plastic bucket bottoms were found in the wreckage.

Questions flooded Georgia's brain. If the fires were unrelated, who took the building records, and why? If Glassman set this blaze, how did he get the materials into the building? If Fred Fischer did it, how did he remain sober long enough to engineer a relatively sophisticated accelerant? And why didn't he get out?

Where did the fire in Howard Beach fit into all of this? She tried to sort out what she knew about that fire now.

HTA Fire Number Five

Alarm box number: 1912

Building: Fully occupied six-family row frame in Howard Beach, Queens

Date of burning: Thursday night, April 8th

Ownership: Private

Insurance: Adequate

Fatalities: Six dead; fourteen wounded

Point of origin: Unknown, but at least one bucket bottom found in basement.

The hiss of air brakes startled Georgia. She folded the list of fires into her pocketbook and stood, plastering an extra-cheerful smile across her face for her son as he stepped off the bus.

Richie's school uniform tie and jacket were off, his white shirt already untucked from his pants. He looked hot and tired as he trudged up the front steps. She longed to hug him and offer him a Coke while they sat on the stoop and talked about his day. But something in his face—a wariness around those hazel eyes—made her pause.

She reached out a hand to tousle his hair, but the gesture froze in midair. Somehow, over these past few months, they'd lost the ready intimacy that had been so much a part of their lives together. And, like an estranged lover, she had no idea how to get it back.

"I saw the basketball award, sweetheart," Georgia said in a voice so bright it made her throat hurt. "That was terrific. I'm really sorry I couldn't be there to watch you get it."

"Yeah." He opened the front door and threw his school jacket and knapsack across a chair—a challenge of sorts. She was always nagging him to hang things up.

"Did you celebrate afterward?" She pretended not to notice the jacket and knapsack.

"The team went to Mario's for ice cream." He kicked his sneakers into the closet. They thudded like two bullets against the back wall, where a dozen other shoeprints had long ago made their marks.

In the kitchen, he grabbed a chocolate doughnut from an open box and bit off a huge chunk. The sight of those perfectly bowed lips rimmed with dark brown icing made her heart ache for the days when he loved her without reservation.

"Look, Richie, I know you're mad at me for missing your game last night. But I had no choice. It was a big fire, lots of people died, and I'm now in charge. I can't walk away from something like that for a basketball game. If you think about it, except for my job, I'm always here. Day in, day out . . ."

Richie put down his doughnut and wiped his face with the back of his hand. "You want a medal or something?"

The words stung. He'd meant them to. She grabbed the first thoughts that popped into her head. "You're sitting in judgment of *me*? You write letters to a man you don't even know, a man who walked away—"

She stopped cold as a look of shock and betrayal flashed across her son's face. She could've slapped him and done less damage. "I'm sorry . . ." Georgia sputtered. "I didn't know what I was reading until I read it. . . . Richie, why didn't you talk to me first?"

"Because you don't want me to know him . . ." He wiped at his eyes, still child enough to cry, but just man enough now to feel embarrassed by it. A year ago, she'd have taken him in her arms. Now, she sensed he'd prefer her not to notice.

"I'd love for you to know him," she protested. "But it's not my decision."

She'd always known this conversation would come. Yet she was still unprepared for it. Richie had been fascinated by fathers since he could talk. When he was three, he saw a friend's father at the supermarket and asked Georgia if she could buy him a daddy there. At four, he told the kids in his preschool that his father was a firefighter killed in the line of duty. Georgia never had the heart to tell the teacher otherwise. She promised herself that she'd sit him down one day and explain it. She just never figured that that day would coincide with the biggest arson investigation in department history.

"Richie, I'm beat. I'm under tremendous pressure here—"

"His name's Rick, isn't it? I'm named after him, right?"

The conversation from hell. Talking to him about sex would be a cakewalk after this. She sighed. "Honey, this isn't exactly a great time to discuss—"

"Do you know where he lives?"

"Contacting him's not a good idea . . ."

"Why? Is he in jail?" The boy brightened. An outlaw dad would not only be cool, it would give Richie a clear reason for his father's absence.

"No. He lives in Jersey." She could see her son doing the math. New Jersey wasn't far. Two hours' drive—tops. A death-row dad would be preferable to a disinterested one. Hell, she'd be happy to execute him herself.

"Richie, honey, he didn't leave because he didn't love you. He left because we were changing into different people, I suppose. He never really got to know you."

"Can I send him my letter?"

"It won't . . . he won't . . ." Georgia wanted to list a dozen reasons why Richie shouldn't mail the letter. But they were *her* reasons. Because, as much as she hated to admit it, the letter embarrassed *her*, confirmed *her* darkest fears—that she'd failed as a mother.

"Please, Mom," the boy pressed.

"What if he doesn't write back? Can you handle that?"

"Yeah," he said woodenly. It was a foolish question, Georgia knew. The unfairness of life is a learned adult response. In Richie's mind, his father simply couldn't—wouldn't—do that to him. She just hoped she wasn't erasing some part of his innocence on a whim.

"All right," she said finally. "I'll get his address and mail the letter. Deal?" She held up a hand, and he high-fived her with a brave smile.

"Deal."

The phone rang. She debated whether or not to answer it, then decided she didn't really have a choice.

"Turn on channel five." It was Marenko. He sounded angry.

"What's wrong?"

"Turn it on, you'll see."

Georgia grabbed the remote and pushed the channel button until she hit five. A grainy home movie played across the screen. It showed a windowless hall filled with men, some in FDNY uniforms.

"What is this? A shriner's convention?" The men were gathered in a circle, raising what looked like paper tumblers of beer. Just beyond the circle, several more men, some in uniform, were wearing afro wigs and black pancake makeup. Parts of the tape were blacked out because the men seemed to be dancing with naked women.

"Where . . . ?" was all Georgia could stammer.

"The party at the VFW hall last night," fumed Marenko. "While that building was burning and people were dying—kids, a *brother*, for Chrissake—those jerkoffs were getting plastered in blackface."

"Who was stupid enough to film this, let alone give it to the press?"

Marenko paused. "Not stupid, Scout. Just the opposite. I checked with some of the guys in attendance—no one was videotaping. This was done by a hidden camera. A copy of this same tape arrived through the mail at the task force an hour ago, along with a letter and a quote from Revelation . . . uh . . ." He stumbled. ". . . addressed to you."

"To *me*?" Georgia could feel a prickly breeze travel down her spine. "Are you saying," she whispered, "this tape's from the Fourth Angel?"

"And that isn't even the worst of it," he said grimly. "His letter seems to be implying that he's gonna set an even bigger fire on Monday. If that's true, it means we've got, what? Three days to stop him?" He let out a string of expletives. "I coulda sworn this scumbag was a harmless wacko. I never believed this would happen. No one did—"

"Because the department would've had to admit they screwed up. Three times in a row. And they would've had to produce the building records for those two vacants."

Marenko didn't answer. Georgia suddenly got a hunch. "Where are the records, Mac?"

"I told you, I don't—"

"Oh, for crying out loud," she yelled at him. "We've got a serial arsonist promising a major fire on Monday, and you're *still* playing games? Brennan knows where those records are—and so do you."

"I'm not . . . it's just that . . ." Marenko sighed. "Why do you want to look at them, anyway?"

"Because the fires don't fit together. Something's missing and I'm hoping those records will provide a clue.

"They won't."

"Well, maybe I'll just bring the matter to the commissioner and let *him* decide."

There was a pause on the line. Marenko sucked in his breath. "Don't do that," he said wearily. Georgia heard the crumple of a cellophane wrapper, then the click of a butane lighter.

"Are you smoking? I thought you'd quit."

He took a long drag, then exhaled. "I thought I did, too. You just gave me a reason to start again. Take down this address. Three-seventeen West Fifty-second Street. Meet me in an hour. You'll have your records."

"Is that a firehouse or something?"

"No," he said stiffly. "That's my apartment."

CHAPTER Twenty-seven

Mac Marenko lived in a six-story brown-brick tenement in the middle of Hell's Kitchen, a drab, semi-industrial neighborhood on the far west side of midtown Manhattan. The hallway was overheated and dim. The air smelled of spaghetti sauce and roach defogger. She could hear the soundtrack to a movie filtering through a door as she passed.

Marenko was waiting for her at the top of the last set of stairs. He was leaning in his doorway, clad in a gray sweatshirt and jeans, a toothpick wedged in his mouth.

"I got a penthouse apartment," he joked. "The climb makes up for the Marlboros."

"I'm not here for the views, Mac."

"Yeah, yeah, I know." He put his hands over his head to feign warding off a blow. "You're gonna bawl me out." He opened the front door wider and gestured for her to enter.

The apartment was pure bachelor. There were no framed pictures on the walls, no plants along the windowsills. The shelves were crammed with books and papers in disarray. In the living room, to make up for a dearth of furniture, Marenko had set up his weight bench and exercise bike. A pile of *Sports Illustrated*s took up most of the plastic coffee table. The well-thumbed swimsuit issue was open beside a plaid couch with fraying armrests and a sagging middle.

Marenko caught her assessment of the place. "I only got home ten minutes ago," he apologized, tossing his toothpick into the garbage. "I didn't know this morning I was gonna have company."

"I'm not company."

He went into the galley kitchen, grabbed two bottles of Heineken from the refrigerator, and popped their caps. Then he pressed the cold green bottle into her hand. "In that case, I can't offer you this."

"Mac, this isn't a date."

"I didn't ask you for one. I want a beer and I hate to drink alone, okay? You some weird-ass teetotaler or something?"

"Oh, all right," she said, taking a sip. "Did you happen to bring home a copy of that letter from the Fourth Angel?"

"Yeah. I thought you might want to see it. I sent the original on to Frankel to get it tested for prints." He rummaged through an accordion folder on his kitchen table, where a dozen empty beer bottles competed for space.

"You've got enough five-cent refunds there to fund your retirement," she teased. "Don't you want to keep the place nice for when your kids sleep over?"

"My kids don't sleep over. Patsy doesn't want 'em to." He avoided her gaze, burying his eyes in the folder.

"Here it is." He handed her a copy of the letter. It had been written on cheaply printed stationery from a hotel called the La Guardia Arms:

TO FIRE MARSHAL GEORGIA SKEEHAN:

His eyes were as a flame of fire, and on his head were many crowns, and he had a name written, that no man knew, but he himself.

Ready thyself for the final Armageddon, for it will come, eleven a.m. Monday. You cannot stop me.

—THE FOURTH ANGEL

Georgia's knees gave out, and she sank into a chair. "He addressed it to me," she said softly. "Why? It hasn't even been officially announced that I'm heading the task force."

Marenko straddled another chair, facing her, and rested his forearms on the back. "Maybe it's 'cause you're the only woman on the team. Look, we can get NYPD protection on your house, you know, twenty-four hours a day."

"Yeah. I should. For my family," Georgia mumbled. Just thinking about the letter was paralyzing. She tried to shake off the fear. "Have you checked out the La Guardia Arms Hotel yet?" she asked. "The address looks near here."

"I thought maybe we'd go together."

She shook her head. "Not tonight. I have a headache . . . you gave it to me." She stared at the letter again. " 'The final Armageddon'? He's planning something bigger than Spring Street for Monday."

"You don't know that for sure."

"Like hell I don't. The guy goes to elaborate lengths to secretly *film* an embarrassing fire department party? The only reason he'd do that is because he knew that while the brothers were making asses of themselves, an occupied row frame was going up in smoke. . . . Mac, listen to me—he's not just a letter writer. At the very least, he's the Howard Beach torch. And if he's planning a fire for Monday, I have to believe that at this point, it's no hoax."

Marenko put his forehead in his hands. "Then we're screwed."

"That's why I want those records."

He got up from his chair and opened the refrigerator like he hadn't heard her. "Want something to eat? I'm starved."

"I already grabbed a quick dinner at Burger King with my son."

"I could order dessert. There's a place around the corner that delivers—"

"Look, Mac," she cut him off. "I just want the records. Then I'll be going."

He closed the refrigerator and leaned against it, then took another gulp of beer, wiping his mouth with the back of his hand. "What will you do with them?"

"I'm going to see if they offer any clues that might link these blazes together. Then I'm going to return them to the Buildings Department and explain everything to the commissioner—"

"Who'll have Brennan's head, and Brennan'll have yours and mine both." He drained his beer and put the empty bottle down on the table next to all the others. "And what are you going to do to me?" he asked softly. "That is, after Brennan's eighty-sixed my career and just before he eighty-sixes yours."

"Mac, this isn't about looking bad anymore. I can't help feeling there's something about these first three fires that keys into what happened at Spring Street and Howard Beach. The missing building records, the missing letters, they're all part of a chain that could help us find this guy before he strikes on Monday."

Marenko fished around in a drawer for a pack of cigarettes and tipped one out.

"Why are you smoking?" she asked.

"Why are you nagging?" He jabbed the cigarette into his mouth and lit it. "Geez, Scout," he said, taking a drag. "I wish I'd never told you anything. I broke my own rules." He shook his head sadly. "I've got two kids to support. I need this job."

"I know," Georgia said softly. "I do too." It wasn't like she could go out and earn $50,000-plus a year anywhere else. Her educational credentials consisted of a half-finished bachelor's degree. Her entire work experience prior to the FDNY amounted to a summer as a burger flipper, a short-lived bartending gig, and a secretarial job at a plumbing supply firm.

"Then why are you doing this?" he pressed. "For glory? Shit, there's no glory on an unemployment line."

"I . . ." Georgia thought about Randy now, about the little girl in cornrows sitting on his lap in a dog-eared photo that he could never again look at without breaking down. His grief spoke to her on so many levels. She could see the love of her own father in Randy. She could see the guilt he was wrestling with in her own dealings with her son. "I can't say, Mac. Please, you just have to understand. It's important. If you knew why, you'd do the same."

He stubbed out his cigarette. "The records are in my bedroom closet. I'll get them for you."

A few moments later, there was a loud crash, followed by a string of colorful Marenko expletives.

"Are you all right?" she called out.

"Yeah, sure. I like hitting myself in the head with a couple of two-by-fours. It'll make gettin' it up the other end from Brennan and the commish seem like a picnic."

She found Mac standing in front of his open bedroom closet, surrounded by fallen junk, his arms outstretched to prop up a shelf.

"What happened?"

"I went to get the box of records and the damn shelf collapsed on me. Can you give me a hand?"

"Sure." She grabbed a chair to stand on and positioned herself in front of him. Then she snaked between his arms and grabbed the shelf. "I've got it," she said, propping the shelf temporarily back into position. "It looks like one of the brackets gave out. It wasn't drilled into a wall stud like it should've been—"

"Thank you, Bob Vila."

Georgia turned to him. He was still behind her, their bodies almost touching. "You're bleeding, Mac."

"Huh?" He touched his forehead. "Yeah, I guess so. I'll just tell the guys you came to my apartment, had a couple of beers, and took advantage of me. Hey, since you're the boss now, maybe I can plead sexual harassment."

"Very funny," she said, stepping down from the chair. "Let me get you some ice."

"I'm all right."

"You don't know that. Lie down on the bed and I'll get some ice from the kitchen."

She opened his freezer. The ice trays were bone-dry and the freezer bare, except for a mostly empty gallon of crystallized vanilla ice cream and a frozen pizza that had been in there so long that the tomato sauce on it had turned pink. Along the freezer's perimeter, however, ice crystals were gathered a half inch thick.

"You don't have any ice cubes," she called out to him. "For that matter, it looks like your freezer hasn't been defrosted since the building was built."

"Geez, you're supposed to defrost it? I thought that's how you got ice," he yelled back. "Just take a knife to the edges. I'll take whatever you can scrape into a plastic bag."

She came back in the bedroom with a sandwich bag of ice crystals. Marenko winced as she gently placed it on his forehead. The gash wasn't bad, but the skin around it was already turning purplish.

"I'm sorry about your head, Mac."

"Forget about it. I deserve it. Shit, maybe all this time we could've been focusing this investigation on catching a serial arsonist. I feel like it's all my fault."

"Brennan told you to get rid of the records, didn't he?"

"He just made some comment about if *The New York Times* gets ahold of these, we can all kiss our pensions goodbye. I knew what he was telling me to do. We go back a lot of years."

"You think Brennan had any other reasons?"

"Nah. He's interested in bureaucratic self-preservation, nothing more. I didn't see any harm in keeping this part of the investigation quiet. I figured if we got the torch on fifty-four counts of murder, we could worry about a bunch of vacants at grand jury time."

Georgia followed Marenko's line of vision to a chest of drawers. On top was a foldout frame with two color portraits of children.

"Your kids?" she asked, examining the frame. Marenko nodded. The boy looked a lot like Marenko. He was about ten, with a face that promised to grow more handsome and chiseled with age, and those same sparkling blue eyes underneath a mop of wavy, blue-black hair.

The girl, maybe six or seven, was brown-haired with hazel eyes and a string of freckles across the nose. Georgia could almost see what Patsy looked like.

"How long have you been divorced?"

"Long enough," he said, wincing as he repositioned the ice pack. "I deserved that, too."

"I don't know." Georgia smiled. "The longer I'm around you, the harder it is to hate you."

"That's 'cause I'm not making you work with Lightning anymore," he teased. "So, like, maybe in fifty years we can be friends?"

She laughed. "I'd have to trust you first."

He raised himself on an elbow and grinned. "Oh, forget about it, then. I'm completely untrustworthy."

"You cheated on your wife, huh?"

"Never."

Georgia raised an eyebrow.

"I swear. That one, I swear, Scout. I bullshit about a lot of things, but I don't go around pinching all the peaches in the supermarket to get a ripe one. That ain't me. I find the one I want, I stick with her."

She laughed again and they locked eyes for a long moment, neither of them moving. Then he smiled that boyish, innocent smile and she returned it. Slowly, he lifted himself off the bed and moved toward her. She didn't resist, even after he brushed his hand against the sleeve of her shirt and drew her closer. Gently, he folded her into his embrace and brought his lips down on hers. Their tongues found each other while he combed a hand through her hair and slowly snaked it down her spine and across the firm outline of her buttocks.

Georgia's breasts began to tingle. She felt sweat cool against her neck and a fiery warmth build up between her legs, gradually radiating through her whole body until even the shafts of her hair felt erogenous.

He undressed her slowly, his warm, moist lips christening each new patch of bare skin. A light stubble on his unshaven cheeks heightened the sensuousness of his caresses. When he held her breasts in his hands, he massaged them gently, then kissed them, running his lips tenderly along her skin. He didn't race into her pants. And when they were both naked, staring at each other's yearning bodies, he paused and held her close. She could feel his erection hard against her abdomen.

"Are you sure you want to?" he whispered, stroking the side of her face. "I don't want you to hate me tomorrow."

She gulped, letting her eyes wander the length of his body. He was well-built, with broad shoulders, strong, sinewy arms, and a fine, dark dusting of hair across his chest. His eyes were a deep, rich blue, set off by fine black eyebrows. The effect would have been almost too pretty if not for the fact that his nose was slightly flattened across the bridge, probably from a fistfight or two, knowing Mac. It gave him the right combination of toughness and tenderness that was hard to resist. But what made him really sexy was the nonchalant way he carried himself, as if it never occurred to him she might want him at this moment as much as he wanted her.

"Do you have a condom?"

He grinned and nodded. "I'll take that as a yes."

Afterward, lying naked and sweat-soaked in the bed, still warm from his gentle, constant touch, she couldn't even remember how it had all begun. An evening drizzle played at the edges of sleep. Car horns and alarms echoed from the street, and tires hissed on the wet pavement.

She propped herself on one elbow and watched him doze. His face, despite the gash, was soft and angelic, bathed in the reflection of streetlamps through a rain-speckled window. She stroked his damp hair, wanting desperately to feel him inside her again. She longed to experience once more the weight of his chest on hers, to delight in the rough sandpaper of his stubbled face across her abdomen, her cheeks, her thighs, as he probed her with his tongue. He rolled over and wrapped a muscular arm around her. She sighed and snuggled close. She wished she could stay, but it was impossible. One of them had to talk to somebody at the La Guardia Arms. And she was awake. *What time is it?* she wondered.

She searched for a clock on the upended crate beside Mac's bedside that doubled as a nightstand. There was none. So she slithered out of his embrace and rummaged through the only other piece of furniture in the room—the chest of drawers. She didn't find a clock, but in the top drawer, she found his wristwatch, draped across his wallet, next to his nine-millimeter. She turned to see whether he was awake enough to help her, but he was breathing deeply now. The wallet was stuffed with cash and bits of paper that made it bulge open to the picture on his driver's license. *Stanley Marenko, Jr.,* it read. She grinned. So "Mac" was just a nickname. She'd tease him about that tomorrow.

She lifted the watch to the thin band of streetlight coming in between the venetian blinds. Nine-fifteen. She would let him sleep. She rummaged in the drawer for some paper to leave him a note. Her fingers brushed along a notebook, like the kind used on investigations. She opened it now and scanned his messy scrawl to make sure she wouldn't be ruining something important. The notes, she quickly realized, were from their interview with Ron Glassman on Thursday evening. She flipped to the next page, where he had scrawled:

> *Call Brennan. GS unstable? Check out incident with dead firefighter in Queens. Way to get her off case???*

Georgia stumbled to the edge of the bed. Her insides burned with a mixture of shame and fury. She longed for a shower to erase his scent from her skin. How could she have been so stupid as to confide in him about Petie Ferraro? The only reason Brennan was able to humiliate her in front of the commissioner the other night was because Mac had fed him the lines. And to think she actually thought Mac was trying to *rescue* her. What a joke.

She tried to stuff the notebook back in his drawer, but it jammed on some papers. She moved them aside. Three sheets of painstakingly scrawled biblical passages she knew only too well.

Her breath was quick and shallow as she grabbed her clothes, hastily throwing them on. There was only one reason Georgia could think of why Mac Marenko would deny seeing the Fourth Angel's first three letters—copies of which he'd had in his apartment all along. That's because he knew—had known from the start, perhaps—that the person who had penned those letters was no outsider.

More than likely, Georgia began to realize, the Fourth Angel was one of them.

CHAPTER Twenty-eight

The La Guardia Arms was a gray twelve-story hotel on Thirty-eighth Street and Tenth Avenue, on the far west side of Manhattan. It had small, boxy windows, a neon marquee running down the side of the building with the letter "M" burned out, and a front awning that had once been red but was now faded to something between orange and pink.

The lobby was small and sparsely furnished. Behind a high black counter, a chunky Asian woman regarded Georgia warily. *Hardly a Big Apple welcome.* She stepped up to the counter and flashed her shield.

"I promised no trouble. No trouble," the woman said excitedly.

"Excuse me?"

"No police raids. No fire summonses. That was deal."

"Deal? I don't follow."

The woman froze. "What you want?" she asked tersely.

So this is why the Fourth Angel sent me this note on hotel letterhead, Georgia thought. *This is the game. Chalk up another embarrassment for the FDNY.*

"You know," Georgia told the woman, "if I didn't know better, I'd figure you've got a little sideline business going on upstairs. And this being a hotel and all, well, the only kind of sideline business I can think of in this neighborhood might have to do with working girls, am I right?"

The woman pursed her lips and didn't answer.

"So maybe some cops and firemen figure, why should out-of-towners grab all the fun? And you figure, hey, they don't raid me.

They don't write summonses for code violations. So what if they enjoy a little hospitality on the house now and then? Tit for tat. Or maybe in this case, tat for tit, yes?"

The woman stared at her stonily, arms folded across her chest. Georgia slammed a fist on the counter and she jumped.

"Personally, I think it stinks. But that's not why I'm here. So you tell me what I want to know, and maybe I'll just go away and let these guys get the clap and explain it to their wives."

"What you want?" the woman asked again.

"Something nice and simple. A guy. I'm guessing he's white, maybe a firefighter or ex-firefighter. Ticked off at the department. Maybe he was fired or disciplined in some way. Talks about getting revenge. He had a piece of your letterhead stationery. Maybe he had a piece of one of your girls? He work for you? Is he a client?"

"I don't know anyone like that . . ."

"Think harder. This could be your last day as a police/fire liaison. The guy I'm looking for likes to throw around quotes from the Bible."

Something in the woman's eyes changed. Nervously, she played with the nylon band of her watch, pressing it into the subcutaneous fat of her wrist. "There was man," she said hesitantly. "A few weeks ago. White. Late thirties, maybe early forties. Blond. Nice-looking. Well built. He . . . he wanted . . ."

"He wanted to get laid." *Marenko was rubbing off on her.* The woman looked uncomfortable.

"He said he was firefighter. I ask for badge. He didn't have. He had some other ID. 'No good,' I say. He knew about our . . . service. I say, 'No freebies without badge.' I . . . offer discount. He got angry. When he leave, he say, 'A whore is a deep ditch.' This is from Bible, yes?"

Georgia froze. To pass the time in catechism as a kid, she used to look up the R-rated passages in the Bible. This phrase was one she recalled.

"What did the ID look like that he showed you?"

"I don't remember. Something with flame on it. But not a badge. I've seen badges. Many, many badges."

"I'll bet you have," she noted dryly. *Was this guy a buff?* Georgia wondered. Every firehouse had buffs—groupies who hung around, basking in the firefighters' reflected glory. Some of these usually single, lonely guys knew more trivia about firefighting than the thirty-year veterans. Or maybe this guy was a volley—volunteer firefighter—from some town upstate or out on Long Island.

"I told you what I know," said the woman. "Now, do we have deal? You keep quiet, yes?"

"I promise not to open my mouth any wider than your girls do. The rest, you'll just have to sweat."

Georgia walked out the front door just as Marenko was about to walk in. He took her by the arm.

"Why didn't you wake me?" he asked, his blue eyes bleary with sleep, his hair looking as if he'd barely had time to run a comb through it. "I'd have come with you. You get anything from the clerk?"

She shook her arm from his grip. Two streetwalkers in fishnet leggings and miniskirts stood on the opposite corner, eyeing their encounter.

"Leave me alone," Georgia hissed through clenched teeth.

Marenko stepped back. "Whoa, talk about postcoital regret. I didn't force—"

"This isn't about sex, Mac," she yelled, then blushed. The women on the opposite side of the street guffawed.

"It's *always* about sex, girlfriend," one of them shot back.

Mac stared at her. Then a flash of recognition crossed his face. "You went through my drawers. You saw the letters from the Fourth Angel."

"I was *looking* for a sheet of paper to leave you a note. And by the way, I also found your little missive to Brennan. 'GS unstable'? So that's what you think of me?"

He dropped his head against the wall of the hotel and cursed. She noticed that the purplish gash on his forehead from earlier in the evening had feathered into a lovely mixture of greens.

"Listen to me, Scout." He turned and tried to put both hands on her shoulders. She shoved him away. "I was just letting off steam. It was dumb, okay? I know that. When the chief tried to use that stuff against you, didn't I step in?"

"And I suppose you just *forgot* you had copies of letters from the Fourth Angel, huh?"

"When this whole thing started, Brennan didn't think those letters were for real. I didn't either. Then Howard Beach happened. . . . What was I gonna do—tell you *now* I had them?"

"I *am* a Girl Scout, Mac," Georgia said, shaking her head in disgust. "Only a Girl Scout would've ever believed you. Then or now. And by the way, if the clerk's description is accurate, the Fourth Angel is definitely connected in some way to the FDNY. Now you tell me: Who's protecting this guy?"

"No one. Scout, there's no conspiracy here."

"Liar." She began walking away.

He started after her. "Where'd you park?"

"Eleventh and Thirty-seventh."

"Then at least let me walk you to your car."

"No."

"But it's dark, and this isn't the greatest—"

"I've got something more reliable than you," she said, patting the nine-millimeter holstered to her hip, underneath her bulky beige cable-knit sweater and windbreaker. "I don't need your help." She walked down the street, leaving him standing on the corner with his hands in his pockets.

"Hey, I thought we had something good going tonight," he called over the whoosh of traffic along the wet pavement. But she didn't turn around to answer. She wouldn't give him the satisfaction.

CHAPTER *Twenty-nine*

The walk to her car seemed endless. On the avenue, street-lamps filled the darkness with a coarse, shallow light. But along this far western stretch of Thirty-seventh Street, the murky blackness enveloped Georgia. Cellar doors and entranceways lost all form, and metal trash cans bulged with strange, menacing shadows.

She kept to the middle of the deserted sidewalk, pulling her jacket around her and clutching her keys tightly in her fist. Too late, she remembered the green laundry bag on her car's backseat, bound for the dry cleaner. She hoped some kid wouldn't bust a car window for the privilege of discovering that laundry bags do, indeed, carry dirty laundry.

Her Ford Escort was wedged in between two vans, which half buried the car in shadows. She fumbled with the lock for only a second before inserting the key. A pallid interior light instantly welcomed her, like the glow of a diner sign from a highway. She threw her pocketbook on the front passenger's seat and jumped in. The door closed with a resounding thud, and she punched down the lock.

There was a soft rustle from behind.

"Turn, and you're dead."

A weight settled on Georgia's chest. Every muscle tensed. Her pulse quickened, and she breathed rapidly.

"My bag's on the seat. I have about eighty dollars in it—"

"I don't want your money."

If this wasn't a robbery, then it had to be a . . .

No. Please. Not that. A thousand showers could never make her feel clean again.

Slowly, Georgia tried to maneuver her right hand to the holster under her windbreaker. The intruder caught the movement, highlighted by the pale green glow spilling out from the car's digital alarm clock. He grabbed her arm and yanked it behind the seat. Pain seared through Georgia's shoulder socket.

"I could burn you and this whole friggin' car in the time it'd take to shoot me."

With his other hand, the man reached under her jacket and dug through a layer of sweater before he was able to slip the nine-millimeter out of its holster. "You buried the goddamn piece, anyway. What's the matter? Afraid you might kill someone? It wouldn't be the first time, now, would it?"

A shudder traveled up Georgia's spine, electrifying the hairs on the back of her neck. She didn't recognize the voice, but the tone, the references—the *familiarity* of it chilled her.

"Do . . . I . . . *know* . . . you?"

The intruder chuckled to himself. "You do now." Then he let go of her arm. It still ached at the shoulder. Her feet had grown numb. She could no longer move them. "So . . ." he exhaled. "You meet any of the brothers at the hotel while they were engaged in their . . . um, civic activities?"

His words tore through her like a hot poker. A bitter, metallic taste settled on her tongue. A pins-and-needles tingling washed over her whole body.

"You're . . . the Fourth Angel," Georgia whispered, as if the name itself had the power to ignite. All at once, her conscious mind seemed to bail out of her body, then hover in the air above, like a spectator at a movie. The earthly vessel it left behind—in the driver's seat—barely had the power to talk.

"What do you want?" she managed to choke out.

"Something you took from me and can't give back." He paused, watching her fidget and tremble as she tried to make sense of his words. Then, abruptly, he leaned forward. Georgia could feel his hot, soggy breath on her neck and the polyester fibers of his ski mask.

"But hey, this little chat's been grand. We'll have to do it again some-time . . . real, real soon, *Georgia*. I promise."

The blow came sharply and swiftly from behind. A crack, then darkness, then a cool burst of air. Shattering glass. Voices . . .

. . . The sound of her back window being broken.

CHAPTER Thirty

"Scout? Jesus Christ, you're bleeding. Hold on."

Strong arms opened Georgia's door and began pulling her from the car.

"Can you hear me, girl? An ambulance is coming."

The words ebbed and flowed, like shoreline chatter to a swimmer. Those hands, that voice—she knew them well. They belonged to Mac Marenko. Her dilated pupils tried to take in her surroundings. Monitors beeped and blinked red. A bag of saline bulged at the end of an IV running to her vein. A plastic valve mask lay pressed against her face. She went to sit up, but a callused hand gently pushed her back down. Her head felt like it was going to explode.

When she came to in the emergency wing at Saint Vincent's Hospital, Randy Carter was hovering over her, his basset-hound eyes looking sad and shaken. She tried to lift her head to speak to him, but it felt like a firecracker was ricocheting around in her skull.

"Lie still, okay?" Carter pleaded, easing her back down. He went to the examining-room door and called for a doctor. Georgia had never seen him so jittery. Or gaunt.

"You want something?" he asked. "Hungry? Thirsty? Name it and I'll get it."

"A date with Mel Gibson." She tried to smile, and it hurt.

Carter made a face. "This is no laughing matter, girl. Have you blanked or something? You got hit upside the head."

She put her hands over her face to blot out the glaring fluorescents. Her skin felt too tight across one cheek. Probably swollen. She was afraid to look in the mirror.

"Not for nothing, Randy, but you don't look so hot these days, either."

"Forget about me. I want to know what happened back there. It wasn't a robbery. Your gun was on the backseat, a full sixteen rounds in the clip, and your purse was retrieved with eighty-six dollars still in it—and a screwdriver, girl, though it's beyond me why y'all carry that thing . . ."

"Tell me about Broph."

He stopped and squinted at her. "Huh?"

"Your ex-partner, Paul Brophy."

Carter ran a hand down the sides of his mustache and frowned at her. "You want to talk about that *now*? Why?"

Silence.

"You're a doozy, Skeehan—you know that? There's nothing to tell." He shrugged. "Broph was a gambler, he turned dirty, and he went down."

"You mean, you took him down."

"Yeah, okay. So? *You* want to crucify me along with the rest of the department?"

"I want you to tell me the truth."

"I just did," he said. "End of story."

"End of story? How do you know?" Georgia asked angrily. "You're always so fucking sure of yourself, aren't you? How do you know Paul Brophy isn't so pissed at you—at this whole department—that he'd torch anything just to get revenge?"

"You ain't making any sense, girl."

Georgia tried to sit up, but nearly keeled over. Carter caught her just in time. His embrace was firm and paternal, and it melted the thin layer of anger she'd been clinging to to keep from dealing with the wild, dark tumor of fear beneath. She sobbed into his shoulder and he held her close. "It's all right," he murmured. "It's gonna be okay . . ."

"Oh, Randy . . ." The scene in the car began to come back to Georgia in fractured snippets like a jigsaw puzzle. "The man who attacked me? He was the Fourth Angel. He knew stuff . . . about this department . . . about *me*." She shivered as it sank in.

Carter pulled a blanket over her shoulders and frowned. "You don't seriously think Broph—?"

"Maybe. I don't know." She wiped her eyes. "But I do think the Fourth Angel is, or was, FDNY. That makes everyone we know a suspect. I'm so scared."

"What you need is rest," he told her, trying to ease her back down on the examining table.

She bobbed up on him again like a cork. "Where's my car?"

"Frankel's having it dusted for prints."

"Can I get anything out of it?" She was thinking of the building records—and her laundry. Most of the pants she used for work were in there.

"You'll get it back Monday—"

"But I need those records. And my laundry."

Carter looked at her, puzzled. "What records? What laundry?"

"A pile of reports on the front seat. And the big green duffel bag in back."

"Skeehan, there were no reports. There was no big green duffel bag. I saw the car when they were dusting it. There was nothing in it but your gun and pocketbook."

"Who saw the car before you?"

Carter sighed, then ticked off the possibilities. "Half a dozen cops, Frankel, the technicians on loan from the NYPD. And Mac, of course. He was first on the scene."

Mac took the records. She was sure of it. *But the laundry?*

"I need my laundry," she whined like a little kid. *Amazing what a normally rational mind can choose to focus on under stress.*

A nurse walked by the examining room and checked her vital signs.

"I want to go home," Georgia insisted.

"The doctor wants you to stay overnight for observation," the nurse explained.

Georgia turned to Carter. "Randy, get me out of here, will you?"

"I can't. I'm on duty. Stay here, girl," he pleaded. "You're not thinking straight. You can't work. Y'all can't even sit *up*." Carter always got more southern when he got mad.

"I still want to go home."

"Marenko's getting his arm stitched up down the hall from busting your back window. He'll take you."

"I'd sooner have root canal."

Carter clicked a retractable ballpoint pen in his jacket pocket. Up and down. Up and down. "You're not a . . . ?" He gestured, embarrassed, running two fingers down the sides of his graying mustache. "You two aren't . . . ?"

"What, Randy? Spit it out."

"I thought you and Marenko were, you know. . . . Actually, first I thought maybe you and the commissioner were, you know. But then, I figured you couldn't be, you know . . . doing it with both, you know . . . I guess I was mistaken."

"I guess you were," she said flatly. "But hey—*you know.*" *What have I done to my career?* "What's today?"

"Saturday. Why?"

"Jimmy Gallagher's working the six-by-nine over at Fifty-seven Truck. Call him, will you? Ask him to get early relief. He'll take me home."

Carter shook his head. "I don't know who's gonna collapse first on this case, you or me."

"We'll get her killer, Randy. I swear," said Georgia.

CHAPTER *Thirty-one*

Dawn was peeking over the Whitestone Bridge by the time Jimmy Gallagher began the drive to Queens. Georgia hadn't seen him since Quinn's funeral on Tuesday. In the car, she realized how much she'd missed him.

She could smell the faint charred odor of smoke on his clothes, mingled with sweat and Old Spice aftershave. His bearish hands were embedded with dirt that couldn't easily be scrubbed off. And along the knuckles and cuticles, he sported a colorful assortment of fresh scrapes and bruises that told the tale of a hard night's work. It reminded her of when her dad used to come home after a tour of duty.

"Thanks for getting early relief and driving me home," she said.

He shrugged his burly shoulders. "I wouldn't have it any other way, love."

Georgia reclined the passenger seat slightly, moving a carton of unfiltered Camels to one side. "These things'll kill you," she chided, shaking the box.

"Terry Quinn didn't smoke or drink and he's six feet under," Gallagher reminded her. "When the good Lord tells you it's time, it's time."

Georgia laughed. "What was the good Lord trying to tell me when he gave me this?" She pointed to her cheek. An eggplant-colored lump swelled across it. On her nose and lips were scabs the color and texture of sun-dried tomatoes. It was a face only an Italian cook could love.

Gallagher sneaked a sideways glance at her and shook his head. "The good Lord didn't do that, love. You put yourself in that situation, you did."

"By doing my job?"

He frowned. "I know you think I'm old-fashioned, but the department's no place for a woman—"

"Oh boy, here it comes. The lecture . . ."

"Look what just happened to you. And that's not the only kind of concern your mother and I have. You know what we were both worrying ourselves sick about Thursday night while you were at that fire in Howard Beach?"

"What?"

"That you'd step in a soggy basement, touch the hot leg of an electric wire somewhere, and pow! No more Georgia."

She rolled her eyes. "I was a firefighter, Jimmy—just like you. I'd know better than to touch electrical current with my feet in water. Now, tell the truth, Ma put you up to this talk, didn't she?"

"She didn't put me up to anything. She just loves you and she's worried about you."

"Feels more like control to me."

Gallagher raised a bushy, silver-streaked eyebrow. "Then you don't know her like I do, love. I still remember . . ." His voice trailed off and he shook his head.

"What?"

"The day of your father's funeral. It rained. Oh, how it rained . . ."

"I remember."

"And you and your brother were each carrying key chains that your father had given you, with his badge number on them—your badge number now. And you dropped yours as you were coming out of the funeral mass . . ."

Georgia smiled at the bittersweet memory. She could still feel the solid weight of the Maltese cross—the emblem of firefighters everywhere—between her fingers, its smooth, cool, beveled edges touching her skin as if for the very first time.

"I think I cried more about losing that key chain that day than about Dad."

"Do you remember your mother? On her hands and knees in the rain over that thing?"

Georgia closed her eyes, humbled and embarrassed at the memory of her mother's black crepe dress matted and soggy, her nylons snagged, and her hair plastered to her forehead—all for a key chain. On the same day she was burying her husband. Children can be cruel sometimes. She was learning that as a mother herself now.

"Ma couldn't find it. And you guys were crawling all over the pavement, in your dress uniforms, soaking wet . . ."

"Ah, that we were . . ."

"And then a few days later, that new one came in the mail." Georgia smiled at him. "I still cherish it, you know. Even if it *is* just a replica."

Gallagher started. "But it's not a replica. The company that made the originals went out of business."

"Then how did you . . . ? Ma said it went down the storm drain—"

"It did." He laughed and shook his head. "Me and this other firefighter, Ray Farnsworth—we went back with a couple of good souls from the sanitation department and took the whole drain apart. Took us four hours in the dead of night in the pouring rain. Lord, what a mess."

Georgia turned to him now as the full weight of what he was saying sank in. "You didn't, Jimmy. For a key chain?"

"For a kid who'd just lost her father. But I never forgot the image of your mother in the rain, on her hands and knees over that thing." He palmed his forehead, as if even the memory were too potent to let linger. "So if you want to know how much she loves you, just think of that."

Georgia stared out the window and thought with a pang of that key chain. The brass had long since tarnished to black. It lay buried in a kitchen drawer, beneath a stack of yellowing mass cards from old memorial services at Saint Patrick's Cathedral. Georgia never ventured in that drawer. The past was in there—a past she'd never entirely reckoned with.

"I'm touched, Jimmy," she said finally, unable to find the right words after so many years. But he didn't want thanks. She could see that now. He just wanted her to love her mother—as he did—faults and all. "When I lost Dad, I kind of focused on myself . . ."

"You were a child." He shrugged. "You would."

She thought of Terry Quinn's widow up in Yonkers, and the two little girls he'd left behind. "I imagine Quinn's family's going through the same thing now. . . . Maybe they'll turn that halfway-house property he fought so hard for into a park in his memory."

"Maybe. The county doesn't own it anymore, though. After the house burned down, Terry convinced some muck-a-muck to cough up the dough and buy the county out."

"Really? Who'd buy a piece of scorched earth in a marginal neighborhood?"

"Don't know. But it worked out well for the community." Gallagher laughed. "I tell you, Quinn could sell ice to an Eskimo, he could. Gift of the blarney."

"I trust that was his *only* influence in the matter."

A taxi slammed its brakes in front of them, and Gallagher muttered under his breath. When he turned to her, his eyes were narrowed, cautious. "I don't make it a habit to speak ill of the dead."

"Jimmy, you're not saying he had a *hand* in burning that halfway house, are you?"

Gallagher frowned at her. "You should know better than to ask that. But think about it, love. Here was a neighborhood of working stiffs who spent their life savings to buy a little bungalow with a yard for the kids and a street to play ball on. Then one morning they wake up and pow! . . . The county's put perverts next door. They're scared—who wouldn't be? Their kids can't play outside. They can't sell their homes when they retire. They're trapped. And who trapped 'em? A bunch of high-and-mighty judges who don't even live in Yonkers."

Georgia gave him a sour look. "That doesn't justify arson."

"I never said it did."

"But if Quinn was involved—"

"Jesus, Joseph, and Mary." Gallagher hit the dashboard in frustration. "Do I have to spell it out for you, lass? Terry Quinn didn't burn down that halfway house. The fire was ruled accidental; the case is closed. Leave the family alone, love. *I'm* begging you. They've suffered enough."

Georgia and Gallagher rode in silence the rest of the journey. As they turned the corner onto her street, by some unspoken agreement, they both dropped the matter. Maybe it was the sight of the police cruiser parked outside Georgia's house for protection. Suddenly, there were more important things to worry about.

Margaret was waiting at the front door. She ran out when she saw them, crossing herself at the sight of her daughter. "Oh, dear Lord. That's it—you're off the case."

"Ma," Georgia whined. "You can't tell me . . ." She caught Gallagher's frown. "We'll discuss it later, okay?" she said to her mother.

Richie hovered by the front door, clearly taken aback by her appearance, but slightly awed, too, she noticed. The bruises had clearly elevated her coolness. He hugged her tightly, something he hadn't done in ages.

Just walking from the car made her head spin, so she flopped on the living room sofa. Something small and hard rubbed up against her back. She reached around and fished out a nub of pool-cue chalk.

"Ma," she said, holding up the chalk, "I hope you're not playing in any seedy dives again. I swear, some of those places—the clientele have more tattoos than teeth."

Her mother turned to Gallagher. Georgia caught the girlish blush. "What?" she asked.

"Grandma won a pool table," Richie blurted.

"You won a *what*?" Georgia looked at Gallagher, who shrugged.

"Kelly's Bar was going out of business," he explained. "They had a tournament. Your mother won."

"A good pool table costs at least two grand."

Gallagher laughed. "You haven't seen the table. A real mess. It's in the basement. I'm bringing my tools over to start work on it tonight—" Gallagher caught Richie's look of disappointment and checked himself. "That is, right after Richie and I finish building that slot car. Right, kiddo?" He gave the boy a chuck on the shoulder and Richie beamed.

The cordless phone rang. Gallagher found it on top of the glass case of Hummel figures. He answered, made a face, then handed it to Georgia.

"It's Randy Carter," he whispered. "You're recuperating, remember?"

Georgia nodded, puzzled. Carter wouldn't call unless it was important.

"I'm sorry to bother you at home, girl, but you're the only one who can approve this." Carter sounded shaken. "Marenko ordered a scan of Ron Glassman's Visa receipts. And it shows he bought a bucket of spackling compound and lawn fertilizer last month."

"Randy, he *does* own a house—"

"But that's not all. This morning, Cassie's momma faxed me a humdinger of a letter Cassie wrote her a couple of weeks ago. She told her momma she was afraid of this Glassman guy, that she'd contacted a lawyer to get an order of protection against him."

"That goes to motive, all right," Georgia said.

"Marenko wants to put some pressure on Glassman, get him to talk. I agree."

"Sounds good to me."

"And I want to do the questioning."

"No. That's where I draw the line."

"But Mac won't get diddly-squat from the guy. You said yourself— Glassman hates him. Suarez hasn't been involved in this end of the investigation. And Lightning . . ."

"I'll do it," said Georgia. "Look, if he's willing to spill his guts to anyone, it's probably going to be me."

"But y'all not in any condition to—"

"Randy, the only way I'm gonna get well is when this thing's over and the perp's behind bars. Set it up." She sighed. "I'll come in."

CHAPTER Thirty-two

Ron Glassman agreed to talk to Georgia without an attorney present under two conditions. First, she had to meet him on his turf—not at the task force. And second, she couldn't bring, in his words, "that jerk Marenko."

Her assessment precisely.

Georgia was in no condition to drive to Chappaqua. So Jimmy offered to go home, take a shower, and come back to chauffeur her up there and keep an eye on her. "You rest a while, love." he said, shaking a finger at her. "No working."

"I won't," she promised. But sleep eluded her. Something dark kept moving across her emotions. *How did that halfway house in Yonkers burn? And who would buy a scorched piece of earth?* A few phone inquiries wouldn't hurt Quinn's family. They—and Jimmy—wouldn't even know.

Georgia dialed the Yonkers Fire Department. Five phone calls later (the department being two phone calls more efficient than the FDNY), she was put in touch with the marshal who had investigated the burning a year before. Williams, his name was. Georgia identified herself and asked him what he remembered about the investigation.

"You want to know why it was classified as accidental, is that it?"

"In a word, yes."

"Off the record? Or on?"

That startled her. She wasn't prepared for multipart questions. Not with a brain that felt like it had been used as a basketball.

"Everything you know or have a gut instinct about. And I didn't get it from you."

"You're not taping?"

She shut the tape recorder off. "I'm not now."

He took a deep, raspy breath. He sounded like a smoker. "The place burned to the ground. Every inch of it, in something like fifteen minutes. Even the five-hundred-gallon cast-iron oil tank in the basement. Our guys couldn't get near it. They put water on it and—I know this sounds crazy—the fire got hotter."

A chill ran down Georgia's spine. "And I'll bet you couldn't find a point of origin, an ignition device or any accelerant residue."

"Yeah, that's right." The fire marshal paused, suddenly feeling uncomfortable with the line of questioning. Probably wondering if this conversation would cost him his pension.

"Hey, you guys had no choice, right?" Georgia quickly chimed in. "You had no arson evidence, so you had no arson."

"You got it." He seemed to exhale. "We're a small department, and there was a lot of pressure from the mayor's office and the community to leave the matter alone, it being an election year and all. No one wanted these mutts in the neighborhood, anyway. You know how it is."

"Sure. Tough situation all around." She was on a roll. She decided to keep going. "So, who owns the land now? I heard some civic-minded big shot bought it."

"You got me. The tax receiver's office might know, though. Somebody has to pay the tax bills. Their payment window is open until noon on Saturdays."

He transferred her over, but the clerk who handled the records was on the phone. Georgia left a message, along with her name and the number at the task force. Then she slipped into the last clean white blouse she had to her name and a pair of dark blue pants with a fire marshal ring around the cuffs. As she dabbed some water on her face, she caught the blur of a blue Buick pulling into the driveway. Gallagher was here. Quickly, she patted on some base makeup and blush to try to hide her bruises. It didn't work. When she got into the car, Gallagher frowned.

"What's wrong?"

"I don't think you should be doing this, love. Why can't Marenko talk to him?"

"He did. That's why we're in this mess."

"What about Carter?"

Georgia shook her head. "Don't ask . . . and Suarez is out on interviews with ex-firefighters. And Lightning, well . . . let's just say Gene couldn't catch a cold in flu season."

Gallagher laughed. "Okay, you know best. I'm at your service."

CHAPTER Thirty-three

"My lawyer said I'm making a mistake talking to you."

Ron Glassman was dressed in a Cornell sweatshirt, Levi's, and a baseball cap. He stood next to Georgia, in a park overlooking a serene pond rimmed by stately ashes and maples just beginning to turn green. The air smelled of moist earth and new-mown grass. A yellow latticework of forsythia graced a railroad-tie fence near the road.

"Then why *are* you talking to me?" she asked him.

"I don't know. I'd like to think I've got a conscience." Ducks sunned themselves along the banks of the pond. Glassman pulled out a plastic bag with two slices of white bread and handed them to his older daughter. The seven-year-old, dressed in overalls, her long dark hair pulled back in a ponytail, skipped down to where her four-year-old sister was standing. Gallagher was squatting next to the younger child, showing her how to skim rocks across the pond. He took the bread and balled it up for the little girls to feed to the ducks. Georgia smiled. Gallagher was always so good with kids. She was sorry he and his late wife, Rose, had never been able to have any of their own.

"If I tell you what I know," said Glassman, "does it have to get back to my family?"

"That depends on what you know and how you know it."

Glassman's hand trembled as he took a sip from his cup of Starbucks coffee. He made a face as it went down. "I know what I'm facing here. . . . It looks bad, doesn't it?"

"You've got a record for fire setting. You were at that party. You've got motive aplenty. And the raw materials to have pulled it off. So, yes, Mr. Glassman, it looks bad."

Glassman wiped a hand across his eyes. "I can't believe this is happening." He watched his daughters giggling as Gallagher quacked at the ducks. "I blame myself. I was drinking and I just get irrational when that happens."

Georgia froze. *Was this a confession?* This was usually how they started. The perp can't bear the truth, so he backs into it. First it's an accident. Then a mistake. Then it becomes something the victim deserved. Any reasonable person would've done the same thing. And finally the raw details. If Ron Glassman confessed, she'd have to arrest him and read him his rights. In front of his daughters. In front of Gallagher, quacking at the ducks. God, his was going to be a tough one. She gritted her teeth and pushed ahead, keeping the image of Carter collapsed on that morgue floor in her head.

"Being under the influence can be a mitigating factor in situations like this, you know," she offered. "If you didn't realize your actions . . ."

Glassman blinked back tears and stared at her. "No, you don't understand. I was drinking, so maybe I got a little belligerent. But I didn't set that fire." He brought his coffee to his lips.

"You wrote Cassie Mott threatening letters. She was seeking an order of protection against you."

He stopped in midsip. He probably didn't think she'd know that. "I . . . I was angry, yeah. Cassie wanted to have the baby and I didn't. She was planning to sue *me* for child support. But I never touched her. Never. I went to that party because I knew she'd be there. A guy she used to date worked at *Nuance* magazine. Cassie refused to talk to me except through her attorney. What was I supposed to do?"

"Why did you leave the party?"

"I . . ." He lowered the brim of his baseball cap and looked around. A man walking his dog nodded and waved, calling Glassman by name.

He waited until the man had passed before answering. "I got thrown out."

"Why?"

Glassman squinted out at the pond. "I got into an argument with Cassie . . ."

"You hit her?"

"No," he said indignantly. "I'm not proud of my behavior, Ms. Skeehan. But it never went further than words." He grimaced at the memory. "Two security guards escorted me to the elevator. I was so frustrated and blitzed, I didn't even pay attention to what buttons I was pushing. I pushed 'LL' instead of 'L,' and it took me to the basement."

His lips started to tremble. "When I got to the basement, I realized my mistake and hit 'L' for lobby. Then, just as the doors were closing, I heard this telephone start ringing from somewhere in the basement. And right afterward, I heard this little—explosion's too strong a word. It was kind of like the sound a stove makes when the gas jets light up. A kind of whoosh."

"*Right* after the phone rang?"

Glassman furrowed his brow. "I think so."

Had a ringing telephone triggered some kind of ignition device? Georgia had read about arson jobs where a telephone was used as the ignition trigger. The phone's relay could be hooked up to an electric match and activated simply by dialing the number. However, it was an old and unreliable type of ignition device—rarely used because a wrong number could set off a fire at the wrong time. But if for some reason the torch needed flexibility or was concerned about being in possession of a detonation device, starting a fire by placing a phone call could prove a clever way to conceal involvement.

"What did you do after you heard the whoosh?" she asked.

"The elevator doors were already closing. I was in the lobby maybe ten seconds later." He shot her a quick, nervous glance, then looked away. "You probably think I got scared and ran. But I didn't know it was a fire. It was cold in that basement. I figured maybe the oil burner was just kicking in or something." He swallowed hard, averting his gaze. "I should've known that it was a fire, right? That's what you're thinking—that I ran away and left all those people to die."

Like she was any expert in the bravery department.

"Look, I had too much to drink. I'll admit it," he explained, misreading her silence. "I wasn't thinking clearly. But I didn't just run away."

Georgia could see the drama of that night unfolding in his pale gray eyes, that sick hindsight sensation of loathing and remorse that is the agony of those who *can* act and don't. She wanted to tell him about the days ahead, when he'd vacillate between self-righteousness and self-doubt, always seeing that last moment he could've altered the equation, always asking the unanswerable: *Why didn't I?*

"I'll check out your account," Georgia assured him. "If the call came in as you say it did, it'll show up on phone records. But I still want a videotaped statement from you."

"I have to talk to my attorney first."

"Twenty-four hours." She pointed to her watch. "After that, I'm getting a subpoena."

"But tomorrow's Sunday," he protested.

"Hey," she said. "If I can work weekends, so can your attorney."

On the drive back, Georgia dialed the task force and briefed Carter.

"He's lying."

"Maybe, but we'll know soon enough. Call Bell Atlantic and get them to forward the phone records on One-thirty-one Spring Street, ASAP. I want to know what calls were made and to whom. And if any came in at eleven P.M. the night of the fire, have Gene trace them back to the callers."

Ideas were coming fast and furious to her now. "Randy? Can you phone UPS as well? The accelerant had to come into that building somehow. I'm beginning to wonder if it wasn't delivered. Also, can you touch base with Walter Frankel? Ask him what he thinks about a phone triggering an HTA device."

"Uh-huh," said Carter. He seemed distracted.

"Have you got all that?"

"Yeah. Sure . . ."

"Look, do you need off the case? We can invent a reason, you know."

"I'm fine, Skeehan. Quit asking, all right?" He caught himself. "I'm sorry. I'm okay, really. . . . By the way, did you call the tax receiver's office in Yonkers this morning?"

Georgia had almost forgotten. She flicked a look at Gallagher in the driver's seat. She didn't want him to know she'd made that call. "Yeah, I called. What did they say?"

"You wanted to know who bought a Yonkers property once owned by the county, right? It was bought by a group called Concerned Citizens of Yonkers. But the taxes are paid by a friend of yours . . ."

"I don't have any friends with money."

"Does the name Sloane Michaels ring a bell?"

CHAPTER Thirty-four

Georgia had expected to find Sloane Michaels on a yacht in the Hamptons on a Saturday afternoon. Or playing squash in TriBeCa. Or perhaps opening a new art exhibit at the Guggenheim. Instead, when she called his beeper, an assistant told her she could meet up with Michaels in the basement of the Knickerbocker Plaza Hotel. Gallagher dropped her off in front of the hotel. He looked beat.

"Go home," she told him. "You've done enough." Georgia planned to take the subway back to Queens from here. "Are you coming over for dinner tonight?"

"That I am, love."

Georgia kissed him on the cheek. He blushed.

"Tell Ma I won't be late."

"Ach, sure you will." He frowned, then drove off.

In the hotel, Georgia was directed to a private bank of elevators that led down to a small garage-level room with brass lamps, a beige linen couch, and a television. A middle-aged black man in a chauffeur's uniform got up from the couch as Georgia approached. A college basketball game was on behind him.

"I'm sorry to bother you. I'm looking for Mr. Michaels."

From the corner of her eye, she spotted a figure emerging from behind a steel door. It was a man dressed in grease-stained blue pinstripe coveralls opened halfway to a faded black T-shirt. The T-shirt sported a Harley-Davidson insignia across the front. Georgia took in the face now and stared, dumbfounded, as the man wiped his hands on an oil-smeared cloth. His brown eyes stared back, equally surprised. She'd forgotten how bad her bruises looked.

"Marshal, what happened? Are you all right?"

"Occupational hazard." Georgia shrugged. "It comes with the turf." She nodded to Sloane Michaels's grimy hands. "So, you're a closet mechanic, huh?"

He grinned. "You caught me." He motioned for his chauffeur to sit down. "I'm not leaving yet, Charlie. Maybe ten minutes, okay? Relax, enjoy the game."

"Yessir, Mr. Michaels. Thank you, sir."

Michaels turned to Georgia. "When I'm not riding, I tinker. I've done a lot of the custom work myself. Would you like to see my bikes?" he asked eagerly.

She hesitated. "I'm not here for a social visit . . ."

"Good. On my own time, I'm not very social. C'mon."

Michaels ushered her through a steel door with a small window in it. On the other side was a large, L-shaped room, separated from the rest of the underground parking garage by tinted windows. Georgia could see out—at the parking attendants, the rows of Mercedeses, Jags, and BMWs. But no one, she guessed, could see in.

"I'm shocked you're not out playing cricket or flying a Lear jet or something," she said.

Michaels made a face, retrieving a wrench he'd casually tossed on a grease-stained tool bench. "You know, I'm not the rich prick you seem to think I am. I grew up very modestly. Most of the stuff I do, I do because I have to. This is how I relax." He led her around a corner to a room as well equipped as any mechanic's garage. There were shelves full of spark plugs, motor oil, nuts and bolts. There were tanks of compressed air. And in the middle of all this sat the bikes. In the presence of their gleaming chrome, their lace wheels, their customized engines and jazzy paint jobs, Sloane Michaels seemed more relaxed than Georgia had ever seen him.

"This"— he gestured—"is my freedom. My escape." Georgia couldn't have said it any better. She stepped closer, oohing and aahing over a big red Harley Ultra Classic with custom bodywork, a light, nifty pearl-blue Ducati, a delicate Bimoto—another Italian racing bike— in violet. And, set up on custom-made supports, a retro-stylish Vincent Blackshadow shimmering under track lights. She'd heard that the Blackshadow, an English motorcycle from the 1950s, was so rare and coveted that it could fetch as much as $100,000 on the open market.

"They're beautiful," said Georgia.

"I can tell by your face you mean it." Michaels toyed with his wrench. "But you're not here to discuss bikes, are you?"

"No . . ." She sighed. "What's your connection to Concerned Citizens of Yonkers?"

He pocketed the wrench, then leaned against the tool bench, folding his arms. "I grew up in Yonkers. Met my wife, Amelia, there," he explained. "A local citizen's group was having a problem with the county and I forked over a very small sum to buy some land and help them out."

"You bought the land anonymously?"

"Yes, Marshal. I help out a lot of causes anonymously. I'm not looking to have three hundred charities lined up at my office door every morning, begging for money."

"You knew the building burned down."

"So I'd heard." Michaels ran a hand against the grain of his close-cropped beard. "I didn't get involved with the purchase until *after* the building had burned. I had nothing to do with it before. The land was county-owned."

"But you knew the dead firefighter, Terry Quinn?"

"In passing. His widow, Kathleen, is a nurse. She took care of Amelia for a time at our apartment on Sutton Place before my wife needed round-the-clock hospitalization."

"Why didn't you tell me you knew him?"

"I didn't think it mattered. And more to the point, it seemed rather tacky after Quinn died to be boasting about how I'd given money to help out his neighborhood." He stroked his beard and studied her now. "Is that what this is all about? You're upset because I didn't tell you I knew Terry Quinn?"

"I'm not *upset,* Mr. Michaels. What I am is *concerned.* That you don't tell me things until it suits you—about your brother, about your relationships with people."

"You're right." He shrugged. "My apologies. How 'bout we change that?" He opened up a cabinet above his tool bench and unfurled a set of blueprints. "Do you know what these are?" he asked her. "They're plans for turning that land up in Yonkers into Quinn Memorial Park. I was going to announce the groundbreaking tomorrow. I've already hired architectural and landscape firms. So I'm hardly hiding anything."

Georgia took in the blueprint notations for playground equipment, benches, and fountains to be installed. She nodded with satisfaction. It promised to be a beautiful park. "I'm sure Terry's family and community will appreciate the generous gesture. Sorry to bother you."

"Never a bother." He rolled up the plans and walked her to the elevator.

"Just one last question," said Georgia. "Your brother lived in the basement of Spring Street, is that right?"

"Illegally, yes. Don't shoot me for it, okay?"

"Did he have a phone?"

Michaels started. "Of course."

"Did you know his phone number?"

"Sure. 212-673-1702. Any special reason you need it?"

Georgia jotted it down. "Just being thorough."

CHAPTER Thirty-five

The smell of greasy Chinese food hit Georgia before she even opened the door to the task-force office. Inside, Gene Cambareri was at his desk, wolfing down a double order of spare-ribs.

"What's this?" Georgia held up the empty white cardboard carton. "I told you to trace those Spring Street calls, and you go out for Chinese?"

Cambareri wiped barbecue sauce off his sausagelike fingers and frowned at her. "Youse worry too much, you know that, Georgia? I traced the calls. The last one was to a Chinese restaurant on Twenty-third and Seventh called Ho Yen. So whiles I was there, I figured, why not kill two birds with one stone?"

Georgia stared at the plate of bones on his desk. "Looks like you ate them, too, Gene."

"Youse want some?" He held out a carton of fried rice and ribs to her. The smell was overpowering.

"No, thank you. What did you find out?"

He licked his fingers and rummaged through some phone records splattered with barbecue sauce. Georgia rolled her eyes. "The Bell Atlantic printout came up with only one call made to the entire building after nine-thirty Monday night—to a number listed for a Mr. . . ." He held the printout at arm's length and squinted. He'd probably forgotten his glasses. ". . . Fred

Fischer. Here it is: 212-673-1702. Came in at exactly eleven P.M." Cambareri scratched his belly. "Fischer . . . he's Sloane's brother, right?"

Georgia nodded. *So Glassman was telling the truth.* "Was the call made from a pay phone at Ho Yen?"

"Yep. I spoke to the owner . . ." Cambareri checked his notes. "A Mr. Sam Chu. He was there Monday night, but he doesn't remember anybody unusual in his restaurant. You know, Georgia"—Cambareri spread his fleshy palms—"this brother of Sloane's, he was a street mutt. Them guys lead strange lives, have strange friends. A call from a Chinese restaurant at eleven on a Monday night don't mean nothing in their world—"

"Where's Randy?" Georgia interrupted. She wanted to hear Carter's opinion on this, not Cambareri's. "Isn't he supposed to be on duty until six?"

Cambareri frowned. "Everybody's looking for the guy. You, his wife, Chief Brennan . . ."

"Chief Brennan?"

"Yeah. He wants youse to call him."

"Did he say why?"

"Georgia . . ." Cambareri shook his head.

"I know. You don't ask."

"Right."

Georgia dialed the chief's beeper and waited for him to return her call. Below, in the firehouse kitchen, she could hear the clatter of lunch dishes, a television blaring a stock-car race too loudly, and above it all, the static-filled drone of the department radio.

Fires, medical emergencies, car wrecks, and collapses—twenty-four hours a day, seven days a week, the radio hummed with the steady rhythm of dispatchers relaying 911 calls to fire companies and acting as the department's eyes and ears.

Though she heard their voices every day, Georgia had never met most of the dispatchers. She didn't even know their names. Unlike firefighters and marshals, dispatchers—civilian employees of the FDNY—didn't refer to themselves by name on the airwaves, only by number. Once in a while she'd meet one and it was always a strange feeling, for not only did they know *her*, they often knew virtually everything about the fire department. Yet they wandered faceless and nameless along its perimeters.

And he had a name written, that no man knew, but he himself.

Georgia froze as the line of scripture came back to her now. She shook her head, surprised it hadn't occurred to her before.

"Gene," she called over. "Phone Walter Frankel. Ask him to get an update on that AFIS manual search of FDNY fingerprints. Tell him I want special attention paid to the fingerprints of the fire dispatchers."

"Gotcha," said Cambareri.

Stacked neatly on a shelf beside Georgia's desk were the dispatch recordings of each of the HTA fires. She popped them in a tape recorder and listened to the disembodied voices now:

Box one-six-oh-eight. Report of a ten-seventy-five at a single-story tax-payer at one-one-eight-four Amsterdam Avenue, corner of One-seven-five Street . . . Box one-oh-oh-eight. Report of a ten-seventy-five at a five-story multiple dwelling at eastern corner of Bay Street and Fifth . . .

Nothing about the recordings seemed unusual. Different dispatchers. Different boroughs. The phone rang. Georgia picked it up. "Special operations, Fire Marshal Georgia Skeehan," she droned.

"All right, Skeehan. What the hell is going on?" fumed Brennan.

Fatigue had made her giddy. "Which part of 'the hell' are you referring to, Chief?"

"Don't get smart with me."

"I'd never do that."

He paused, and Georgia grinned in spite of herself. She'd pay big-time for this when the investigation was over. But it was so much fun right now, she was too tired to care.

"Where's Carter?"

The question sobered her up fast. "I . . . I'm trying to locate him, sir."

"Now, listen to me, Skeehan. I'm going to ask you something. And I want a straight answer. Is there any reason why Carter shouldn't be on this investigation?"

Georgia stiffened. She'd promised Carter she'd cover for him. She'd given her word.

"I . . . that is . . . Marshal Carter . . . is a very capable investigator. He's checking an important lead for me right now, sir—"

"Bullshit, Skeehan. I just got a call from his wife. She said Carter's been distraught since this case started. Twenty minutes ago, he apparently left their house talking about how he wanted to kill a suspect in this case. Now, I want to know what's going on."

"Oh God," Georgia mumbled. She felt sick. "Please, Chief, let me find him."

"One hour. Find that son of a bitch, get his ass straitjacketed to a chair and see to it that he hasn't said so much as 'good afternoon' to any suspect without prior written authorization. Because we're not talking getting kicked out of the *bureau* here. You'll both be out of the FDNY. Your ass is mine on this one, Skeehan."

Brennan hung up. Cambareri called over to Georgia, his pudgy Italian face all smiles.

"I just spoke to Frankel. He thinks youse are on to something with that dispatcher theory. He's gonna get AFIS to do a manual scan of prints, but he said you could speed the whole thing up if youse just hike over to Manhattan dispatch now and talk to 'em yourself, see if you can't narrow the field of suspects."

"I can't." Georgia sighed. "I gotta find Randy first."

"I'll find him."

Georgia gave Cambareri a dubious look.

"Young lady, I been doing this job since youse was in diapers. I'll hunt up Marenko and Suarez and we'll play baby-sitter, okay? Keep Carter outta trouble."

"You haven't asked why I need to find him," Georgia noted.

"It's like I always say—"

"I know, I know," said Georgia. "You don't want to know."

"Youse got that right."

CHAPTER *Thirty-six*

The afternoon sun brushed golden against the white marble building as the chief double-parked his Ford Econoline van by the service entrance. He wiped his sweaty palms on his paint-splattered carpenter's pants and considered his week.

The loft in TriBeCa was finished; four rooms covered over in plum, chartreuse, and lemon yellow that would make a dog barf. But it had earned him a cool $3,500 profit off the books. Today, he was on to his next job. His biggest job yet.

Three construction workers with tool belts strapped to their waists walked out of the building's service entrance. Above them, a latticework of scaffolding draped like a cobweb across a window. It was four P.M. Saturday. Quitting time. They wouldn't be back at work again until Monday.

The chief opened the back doors of his van. Paint, plaster compound, tools, and a reel of eight-gauge stranded heavy copper wire lay spread across the interior. He slipped on canvas work gloves, then loaded his materials onto a small metal pushcart and headed for the service entrance. He could feel the heat of the late-day sun through his plaid flannel shirt. He could see the light, as thick as spun maple syrup, pour over the bronze reliefs on the main entrance doors.

He maneuvered his cart down a ramp by the service entrance and through a set of doors to the building's basement. The walls were granite block, the hallways long and winding, with storage rooms off to the sides and gothic arches leading to narrow spiral staircases carved in stone. The overhead fixtures, despite their heavy wattage, were cold and subdued, and a thick odor pervaded the air—a combination of mildew, stale incense, and tallow.

The metal wheels of his cart rumbled noisily across the concrete floor. It accentuated the pounding in the chief's chest and made his stomach turn slow somersaults in anticipation. He had only the vaguest sense of the crush of bodies and cars along the avenues above him, of the size and majesty of the building he was now traveling beneath, a monument of stone, wood, and glass that rose three hundred and thirty feet in the air and had taken more than twenty years to build. He was struck, as always, by the contradictions he found here— the placid, gleaming, symmetrical exterior, the cobwebbed, labyrinthine passageways within. Compassion and cruelty, mercy and misery springing from the same dark well of the human soul.

At a bend in the hallway, he found the service elevator, barely large enough for his cart. He pressed the second-floor button and the elevator slowly ascended, opening onto a small wood-paneled room. He maneuvered through the room and onto a balcony where drop cloths encircled a section of damaged wrought-iron railing. A portable construction lamp hung from a timber beam above the railing. The bulb inside the mesh cage was unlit. The chief nodded with satisfaction. He didn't want any live voltage to interfere with the job he had to do.

Not right now, anyway.

The job took about twenty minutes. He worked quickly, deftly. When he'd finished, he stood and admired the beauty of the marble walls around him. There was an aura of spectacle about this place that moved him, in much the way he was moved by a good fire. He loved the order men tried to bring to both environments—the rituals, the sense of bonding, that ever-present connection between life and death. Firefighters loved a good spectacle.

And on Monday, he thought as he wheeled his empty cart back to the service elevator, *I'm going to give them one.*

CHAPTER *Thirty-seven*

Manhattan's fire dispatch station was located in the middle of Central Park on Seventy-ninth Street. For New York City, it was a strangely bucolic place to work. The small, one-story fieldstone building was surrounded by sycamores and white dogwoods just beginning to bloom. Behind the adjacent parking lot, bike trails meandered through hilly, daffodil-spotted terrain, and children's voices drifted over from a nearby playground. It looked more like a park-service headquarters than command central for the busiest fire department in the world.

A female dispatcher buzzed Georgia through the solid steel front door. The woman was in her twenties, tall and thin, with long, dark, wavy hair, parted in the middle. Her angular face was pale, the skin as taut as a trampoline, the lips slightly pouty. Georgia recalled hearing a dusky, Brooklyn-edged female voice over the department's Manhattan frequency. The voice definitely fit the face—young, sort of tough, but with a lot of common sense. Georgia flashed her shield and asked to see the supervisor on duty.

"His name's Bello. He's in the operations room. At the end of the hall." The woman gestured. "You want some coffee?"

"That'd be great."

The operations room at Manhattan dispatch looked as if it had been lifted wholesale from a B-grade science-fiction flick. The overhead lights, set into water-stained acoustic tiles, were dim and diffuse. Ancient computers the size of Dumpsters lined two of the room's four beige walls. On a scattering of dented metal desks in the center, outdated video screens glowed green with information about fires in progress. Tabletop fans sputtered from dusty file cabinets in a vain attempt to circulate the humid air.

Bello was leaning over the desk of a middle-aged Latino dispatcher—one of seven on duty—when Georgia approached. The supervisor was a short, beefy man in shirtsleeves and a knit tie that followed the curve of his gut. A fringe of hair surrounded his bald pate, making him vaguely resemble a Franciscan friar. Georgia extended her hand. It hung there for a moment before Bello thought to shake it.

"I can spare five minutes," he said, checking his watch.

"My name is Georgia Skee—"

"I know who you are," he said impatiently, walking over to his own desk, slightly above and apart from the others. He plopped down in a well-worn swivel chair without offering Georgia a seat. "What I don't know is what you want."

The woman dispatcher returned with a Styrofoam cup of coffee and handed it to Georgia. "You want milk or sugar?" she asked. "Sugar" came out "sugah." Definitely the voice Georgia had been hearing on the radio.

"Black is fine. Thanks."

The woman retreated to her desk. Georgia located a spare chair beside a metal bookcase of fire department reference manuals. She sat down and pulled out a tape recorder and pen under Bello's glare. Clearly, this was going to be an adversarial encounter—not, she sensed, because Bello didn't like firefighters. On the contrary, like many dispatchers, he'd probably wanted to be one and either failed the physical fitness test or never scored high enough to get the job. He probably had a lot of friends—maybe even family—in uniform. It was Georgia he didn't seem to like.

"I'm looking for a man who might be a dispatcher," she explained. "White, blond, well built. Late thirties to early forties . . ."

Bello squinted at a map of Manhattan on the wall across the room, winking red and green like a Christmas tree. The lights were the locations of Manhattan firehouses—red, out of service or responding to an alarm; green, in service and ready. No fires were coming in at the moment.

"Is this guy you're looking for a suspect in these fire bombings?"

"Could be. He's familiar with stuff—embarrassing stuff—that only someone in the department would know."

"And he couldn't *possibly* be one of New York's Bravest . . ." Bello's voice dripped with sarcasm.

"We've come into some evidence that suggests he's probably not an FDNY firefighter at the present time." *Evidence?* What a joke. The guy couldn't get laid at the La Guardia Arms because he lacked a badge. *Some evidence.* She'd love to see a lawyer present *that* to a grand jury.

Bello rubbed a thick hand across the shiny dome of his head and leaned back in his chair. "The guy could be a buff. He could be a volley from upstate or Long Island . . ."

"His knowledge is too inside for that. We think he might be a dispatcher."

"Of course." Bello threw up his hands. "Anything goes wrong, the uniforms always blame the dispatchers. *You* should know about that, Marshal."

Georgia caught the reference and stiffened. People in the FDNY had long memories.

"So it's *me* you don't want to help, is that it?"

"When you give me something solid, I'll help. But you come in here with these accusations, honey, you ain't *my* friend, badge or no badge."

Georgia put down her pen and stared at him. The heavy stone walls resonated like ocean waves with the steady whoosh of cars cutting across Seventy-ninth Street.

"I'm doing my job here, Mr. Bello," she said softly. "I was doing it eight months ago, too. And I won't apologize for that. I missed the chance to collar an arson suspect—a suspect who went on to set a fire that killed two people a week later."

"You blame the dispatcher for that?"

The Latino man Bello had been speaking to earlier walked over to the shelf of reference manuals next to Georgia. He eyed her with curiosity. They probably all knew she was the marshal who'd filed that formal complaint against Dispatcher Number 35. Georgia shifted in her seat as the man skimmed the binder titles on the shelf. The *Cole Directory,* a kind of reverse telephone book, lay on top. Look up a listed phone number in Manhattan and the directory will give you the corresponding street address—very useful for tracking down civilians who report fires. Georgia returned her attention to Bello.

"Last August, a witness phoned in a fire," she explained. "All I wanted was her phone number and the callback address so I could get her statement. *Three times* I called Dispatcher Number thirty-five. By the time he walked over to this"—she slapped the *Cole Directory*—"my witness had skipped to the Dominican Republic. Without her, I had nothing to arrest the torch on, and two people later died because of it. How would *you* feel?"

The Latino dispatcher turned now and nodded to Georgia. "The dude's gone, you know," he said.

"Ramirez . . ." Bello muttered tightly. Ramirez ignored him.

"The dispatcher who didn't call you back? He was fired."

Georgia blanched. "I didn't mean to get the guy—"

"You didn't." Ramirez shrugged. "He was fired on an unrelated incident. But I figured you'd like to know." He closed the manual he was looking at and began to walk back to his desk. Georgia spoke up.

"He wasn't by any chance blond, in his late thirties to early forties, was he?"

Ramirez frowned. "You think he—?"

Bello jumped to his feet. "This has nothing to do with these firebombings."

Ramirez called across the room to the woman who had gotten Georgia coffee. "Hey, Annette. Are you tied up? You should hear this."

The woman finished handling a call, then sauntered over, tucking a wad of black hair behind an ear pierced with a silver cross and two tiny silver hoops.

"Tell her," Ramirez urged Georgia.

"The task force is looking into the possibility that the serial arsonist behind all these superhot fires may be—or have been—a dispatcher," said Georgia.

The woman took a moment to process the news, then sank into an empty chair and massaged her temples. Her hands were trembling.

"Ramirez." Bello leveled a stubby finger. "You wanna play detective, do it on your own time."

"C'mon, Annette," Ramirez pleaded softly, squatting on his haunches in front of the woman and pointedly ignoring his boss. He could see over to his computer. At the moment, no calls were coming in—for him *or* Annette. "You *know* he's been doing this stuff to you. Maybe he's a lot more dangerous than you thought."

Bello paced like a caged tiger. "Back to work, Ramirez. You too, Nolan," he snarled at the woman.

Georgia turned on him. "Supervisor Bello, you are interfering with a criminal investigation. And let's not forget how good I am at filing complaints."

Bello stopped pacing. He folded his arms across his gut. "I still don't see how any of this—"

"It's not related," Annette Nolan interrupted. "This guy . . . he's just got a problem with me, that's all. But it's not related."

"Bullshit, it's not." Ramirez straightened, then looked at Georgia. "In November, Annette's tires were slashed. In December, she found sugar in her gas tank. In January and February, a bunch of false alarms were called in on her apartment building."

"That's not even the worst of it," Annette said, a dark look in her eyes.

Bello shrugged, as if all this was news to him. But the surprise seemed too feigned. Georgia suspected Annette's situation was anything but news to the dispatchers and supervisors here.

"Who's doing this to you?" Georgia asked.

Annette sighed, shooting quick, sideways glances at Bello. "I've only been on the job two years. I don't want to get a reputation as a troublemaker."

Georgia regarded Bello with disgust. The words, she knew, were his, most likely delivered during a fatherly speech about the need to keep such matters quiet. *You cowardly bastard,* she thought, watching him squirm under her scrutiny. *You let this woman deal with this harassment for six months—six months—because you didn't want to make waves with superiors.*

"I think maybe you and I need to get some fresh air," Georgia said, taking the woman's hand. Annette looked at Bello, who made a face then caught Georgia's glare and relented.

"All right, go ahead," he said. "Ramirez and the others will cover for you. Take all the time you need."

"Believe me," said Georgia. "We will."

CHAPTER Thirty-eight

What Georgia hadn't realized was that taking a walk *anywhere* from Manhattan dispatch was like crossing out of a medieval fortress. Although the place sat in the middle of Central Park, it was entirely cut off from it. A high, spiked wrought-iron fence surrounded both the building and the adjacent parking lot. Only a padlocked gate on Seventy-ninth Street—which was more highway than street where it bisected the park—provided access to the compound. The wooded trails of Central Park, a stone's throw from the building, could be reached only by walking a quarter mile east along Seventy-ninth Street—essentially, *under* the park—then backtracking west from Fifth Avenue.

Annette Nolan and Georgia did that now, walking single file below a park overpass and along a narrow sidewalk flanked by ten-foot-high stone walls. At Fifth Avenue, they turned back into the park and hiked across a wide grassy field dotted with sunbathers. There, Georgia decided to break the uneasy silence.

"Bello told you not to make waves about this guy, didn't he?" she asked softly.

Annette pulled a pack of cigarettes out of her handbag and offered one to Georgia, who declined. The woman's hands were still shaky.

"His name's Ralph Finney, by the way. Bello said if I ignored him, the harassment would stop." She took a deep drag and exhaled. "You must know how it is, being in the department and all. The men expect you to take whatever gets dished out, without complaint. If you don't, they figure you're weak and freeze you out. I couldn't decide which would be worse."

"I know the feeling." Georgia sighed. "The macho code—put up *and* shut up."

On the other side of the field, they spotted a playground. Fair-haired tots climbed monkey bars, their laughter as warm and sweet as the dappled late-afternoon light through the trees. Nannies shot Georgia and Annette suspicious glances as they sat down on one of the playground's benches. They made an odd pair: Georgia, with her bruised face; Annette, towering above her, smoking—neither of them with kids or strollers.

"I probably shouldn't be smoking in a playground," Annette ventured.

"Forget about it," Georgia said, staring down a frowning nanny. "The kids' rich parents will air them out in the Hamptons later this weekend. They'll live." She leaned back on the bench and closed her eyes, catching a shaft of sunlight across her bruises. The warmth felt healing.

"Annette?" she asked, keeping her face pointed up at the sun. "Do you mind my asking *why* Finney had it in for you?"

Annette laughed, a breathy sound. She'd have made a good disc jockey, Georgia decided.

"Do you know, when I first came to work here, Ralph was the only dispatcher who'd even *talk* to me? Teddy Ramirez is a sweetheart. You see him. But he barely said hello."

Georgia glanced over at Annette's hands. She didn't see a wedding ring. "Maybe Finney wanted to date you."

Annette shrugged noncommittally, stubbing out her cigarette.

"Maybe I should rephrase that," said Georgia. "*Did* Ralph Finney date you?"

"Ralph's good-looking and all. And he can be charming. But . . ." her voice trailed off. "The thing about Ralph is . . . he likes people to look up to him. And I did, big-time—for a while. Nobody knows more about fires and fire operations than he does."

"So what happened?"

"He was supposed to move up to supervisor. And he—" Annette stopped, suddenly embarrassed.

"What?" Georgia opened one eye.

"That incident happened. He didn't give you the callback number and you filed that grievance. So his promotion got delayed."

"Oh boy . . ." Georgia massaged a thumb and index finger across her eyelids. She'd known Ralph Finney simply as Dispatcher Number 35. Maybe Annette wasn't the only woman he was nursing a grudge against.

"He must hate me," Georgia suggested.

Annette grew red-faced without answering. Georgia could only guess at the venom Finney had unleashed about her.

"Look, you didn't do anything that bad to him," she reassured Georgia. "He was still going to become a supervisor—it was just a six-month delay. In any case, they made him a supervisor-in-training, which, in the end, was probably what did him in."

"What do you mean?"

"One night tour last November, I got this ten-twenty-eight transmission from the captain of Engine Company Sixty-two. They were investigating a smoke condition in a subway tunnel, and the captain requested backup. I wanted to dispatch the nearest engine, but Ralph told me not to."

Georgia bolted upright now. "He *what*?"

"There was a three-alarmer going on in the neighborhood. Ralph wanted those companies available in case the fire got worse. He told me to wait ten minutes, check with the captain, and if things still weren't good, to dispatch an engine outside the immediate vicinity."

"Did you?"

Annette toyed nervously with the tiny silver cross in her right ear. "I had to. Ralph *was* the acting supervisor. By the time I dispatched another engine company, the captain had taken some pretty serious smoke. When the shit hit the fan, it looked like I might lose my job because of the delay. I told my supervisors the truth: that Ralph had ordered it. The audio tapes and my computer notes backed me up—"

"And they fired him," said Georgia.

"Yeah," mumbled Annette. "I didn't want to see that happen. But really, by that point, what could I do? He must've thought otherwise, because bad stuff's been happening ever since."

"What kind of bad stuff?"

Annette kicked at a patch of grass. Her hands were still shaking. "You know, before all this happened, Ralph was actually very sweet. He used to bring me flowers on my birthday. And he helps out this family . . . bought one of the kids a bike . . . takes them out to McDonald's when their mother's welfare money runs out."

"Was he religious?"

Annette furrowed her brow. "I don't think so."

"He didn't read the Bible or like to quote from it?"

"Ralph could look at a piece of paper for ten seconds and quote from it a week later. He had a photographic memory. He could tell you alarm box locations and street addresses in his sleep. But he wasn't religious, as far as I know."

The two women sat in silence for a few minutes, watching the children scamper between the monkey bars and their nannies, trailing cookies, juice, and an assortment of toys.

"So, um . . . ," said Annette nervously. "Do you really think Ralph could've set those terrible fires?"

Georgia turned to her, her gaze sober and direct. "Yes, Annette. I do. What's more, I think getting fired may have been what set him off. In his mind, you put him there. That means your life's in danger, too. Do you live alone?"

"Yeah," she said glumly. Georgia sensed she always answered the question this way.

"Move in with somebody right now, okay? Keep a low profile until we find him and question him." She checked her watch. "Are you ready to go back?"

"I suppose we should." Annette sighed.

They took the same circuitous route back to dispatch. On the way, Georgia called Cambareri on her cell phone. "Any luck finding Randy?"

"None," replied Cambareri. "Ditto for Marenko and Suarez."

"How about Ron Glassman—the witness? Is he safe?"

"Don't know. He's gone."

"Gone?" Georgia started. "Gone where?"

"Youse won't believe it. His wife said somebody called him, said they was from the task force, and asked to meet with him right away."

"Did she say where they were supposed to meet?"

"No, but Georgia—Carter wouldn't do anything stupid."

"Let's hope you're right." She asked Cambareri to pull an address on Finney and have Marenko and Suarez bring him in for questioning. "And get Frankel to run a check on Finney's prints and blood type off personnel files."

By the time the two women reached dispatch, the sun was beginning to set. Already, the trees were darkly silhouetted against the brilliant blue sky, and Seventy-ninth Street was bathed in shadow. The padlock on the parking lot gate was unlocked. A shift would soon be ending, no doubt. Annette punched in the alarm code on the front door, and Georgia followed her back to the operations room to thank Bello and Ramirez for their time.

At Annette's desk, Georgia paused, staring at a black-and-white video monitor perched atop a file cabinet. It was trained on the parking lot. A pair of legs in dark sweatpants stuck out from underneath a late-model Toyota Corolla.

"Looks like one of your colleagues is having car trouble." Georgia nodded at the monitor.

Annette looked up at the screen, then frowned. "That's *my* car."

The figure slid out from beneath the vehicle. His face was covered with a black ski mask. Georgia sprang into action.

"Radio the NYPD," she told Annette. "And Gene Cambareri at Engine Two. Don't let anyone in the parking lot. And don't let anyone touch your car."

"Will do," said Annette, getting on the headset.

Georgia raced outside. The parking lot gate, not thirty feet from the entrance to Manhattan dispatch, was still ajar. There were no pedestrians on Seventy-ninth Street. He had to be trapped inside this wrought-iron cage. This was the only way out. Instinctively, Georgia reached for her hip holster and unfastened the safety latch on her gun. She'd hold him here until help arrived.

She took several cautious steps forward until she spotted him. He had scrambled to the roof of a pickup truck on the far side of the lot. If he managed to jump from the roof over the fence and into Central Park, she would never find him. She swung the gate wide open and trained her gun on him.

"FDNY. Hands in the air," Georgia shouted, moving cautiously into the lot. The man hesitated for only a second. Then he grabbed the fence with both hands and lobbed his body over it, landing awkwardly on an asphalt bike path on the other side. He seemed to be betting she wouldn't shoot, betting that the woman who wore a sweater over her holster wouldn't fire unless her life depended on it. It had to be him.

Shit. I'm going to have to go over that fence or lose him, Georgia realized. She holstered her weapon, then clambered up the roof of the truck. Grabbing two spikes in the fence, she wedged her right foot onto a lateral crossbar and hefted herself over. Her exhilaration at clearing the spikes was short-lived. She landed heavily on the asphalt. Blood spurted from cuts and scrapes along her arms and legs. Her palms stung.

He was still in sight, about fifty feet straight ahead. But Georgia would lose him if she didn't hurry. He was limping into the hilly, winding section of Central Park known as the Ramble—full of blind curves, rocky crevices, and densely wooded thickets. Georgia fought back the pain and pushed forward, reaching for her gun.

Once inside the Ramble, she lost him almost immediately. The narrow, deserted trails were like a maze; the paths splintered again and again. Lamps flickered to life, but instead of bringing clarity, they merely defined the shadows. Every twitching branch or rippling leaf brought forth a new, warm spurt of adrenaline in her veins. The winding paths, flanked by huge granite boulders, closed in on Georgia, making her feel lost and claustrophobic, like a child in a sea of legs. Her pulse raced furiously at each bend in the trail.

Desperate and exhausted, she scrambled over an outcropping of rocks, perhaps ten feet above the trail, hoping to get a better view. That's when she heard it. A scrape of sneakers on loose dirt, an audible gurgle somewhere on the other side of the vegetation below. She couldn't be sure it was him, yet she had to take that chance. She crossed over the rocks, crouched behind some bushes and waited. When the figure passed beneath her, she pounced.

He was large and powerfully built. Georgia had hoped to land on top of him and let gravity do the rest. Instead, she managed to catch only the back of his sneakers. But it was enough to make him tumble onto the muddy, unpaved earth, where he lay on his stomach, moaning.

She sat on his back and pulled off his ski mask. A burst of static crackled from his fine wisps of blond hair. Georgia could see only the side of his face, smeared with grime and contorted with pain—the strong, square jaw, the slight upturn of his nose. Still, a small quake rippled through her body. A prickly sense of déjà vu. She took out her gun and trained it on him.

"You've got a lot of explaining to do, Finney."

He answered with a groan. Georgia fumbled for her radio, then called in her approximate location to dispatch. *I'm beside the huge granite boulder—which huge granite boulder? I'm a city girl, for Chrissake—not a park ranger.* She frisked Finney and began to rattle off his rights. But as she went to cuff his wrists, Finney surprised her. In a sudden burst of strength, he thrust his shoulders upward, jerked his arm from her grasp, and tossed her off his back.

Georgia landed elbow-first on the packed earth. The gun tumbled from her hand, landing in a pile of last winter's leaves not six feet from her grasp. Finney, neither as hurt nor as weakened as he had pretended to be, pinned Georgia on her back and sat on top of her. Dirt streaked his face and hair, giving him a wild, otherworldly appearance. Yet he still looked familiar.

"You'll never shoot me, *Georgia,*" Finney mocked. He spit a wad of saliva onto the ground for emphasis. "You know me, and it's bothering you."

"You were a dispatcher," she stammered. "I filed a complaint against you."

He yanked up her white blouse, now smeared with grime, and fingered her lace bra underneath.

"I like the other bra better—the one with the little pink bow in the middle?"

My green bag of laundry. That bra was in there. He has my clothes.

"You sick son of a bitch!" she screamed, squirming out from under him and jerking her right knee up quickly into his groin. He grunted. She twisted her right hand from his grasp and poked her fingers deep into his eye socket. He shrieked, pushing her away from his face. It bought just a second or two, but that was all she needed. She rolled over to the pile of leaves and grabbed her gun.

"Freeze, asshole," she yelled, aiming her semiautomatic at him with both hands. "Face the rocks, hands above your head."

He did as he was told, but kept talking. "You beat me, Georgia," he said hoarsely as she cuffed his hands behind his back. "That's what you like, isn't it? To beat men?"

"Shut up."

"That guy you were dating? Back when you took the test to become a firefighter? You beat him too, didn't you?"

"Shut up, goddamnit!"

"You got the job and he didn't . . . and he dumped you big-time after that . . . left you to raise his kid . . ."

"What the hell?" She could hear sirens somewhere in the park now. She sucked in a couple of deep breaths and tried to fight off the excruciating cramp in her side. Then she turned him around. The face was older, but even in the dim lamplight she recognized him now—after ten years, she still recognized him.

"The fire department physical," she mumbled, staring into his pale blue eyes. "You were in my recruit group. You dropped out after you hurt your ankle on the mile run—"

"You tripped me, bitch."

"No, I . . ." Georgia frowned. "If I did, it was an accident . . . I don't remember . . ." She massaged her forehead. "My God, Finney, you wanted to be a *firefighter*. You *were* a dispatcher. How could you set these fires? How could you kill sixty innocent people?"

He leaned against the damp rocks, his face bathed in shadows, his hair backlit by a streetlamp twenty feet down the path. A small mocking exhale escaped his nostrils. She couldn't see his eyes—only his icy smile when he spoke. "What makes you so sure I did?"

CHAPTER Thirty-nine

By the time Georgia, filthy and dazed, arrived at the Midtown North Precinct to book Ralph Finney, the television news vans were parked two deep, and dozens of reporters and cameramen were already on the scene. It seemed they'd put the case together before she'd even had a chance to make it.

Although the NYPD's bomb squad had indeed found an incendiary device under Annette Nolan's car, Georgia was alarmed at the level of extrapolation in the news reports as she hustled Finney through the front doors. Somebody was leaking stuff she couldn't even prove yet.

"Preliminary word tonight is that the fire department has apprehended a suspect in a string of deadly arsons. . . ."

"Fire department sources say the suspect, Ralph Finney, a former fire dispatcher, let go from his job for unspecified reasons last November, is likely to face charges for last Monday's fire in SoHo that killed fifty-four people, including Nuance *editor Rubi Wang and a firefighter. . . ."*

"No official word yet, but it appears New Yorkers can breathe easier tonight with the arrest of a serial arsonist. . . ."

Inside the station house, the scene was just as chaotic. Burly cameramen and newspaper photographers jostled one another and Georgia to get a good head shot of Finney. Men with freeze-dried hair and women with too much makeup—television reporters, Georgia guessed—paced the worn linoleum tiles and shouted into their cell phones. Lawyers tried to muscle their way to Finney and press their business cards into his manacled hands.

Everyone else seemed to be sporting some kind of badge—FDNY, NYPD, FBI, ATF.

Commissioner Lynch and Chief Greco were there. So was Brennan. The mayor was on his way. Georgia saw Gene Cambareri standing next to a vending machine, a Milky Way in hand, and began to walk over, as much for the candy bar as for word on whether Carter or Glassman had surfaced. She hadn't eaten since early morning. The commissioner got to her first.

"Congratulations, Marshal," Lynch said, pumping her hand. "A superb collar. Superb. There's just one thing troubling me."

"Me too, sir. Those reporters outside. They've got the story—"

"My concern, Marshal, is why you've booked Finney only for the attempted murder of that female dispatcher. Are you waiting to get a search warrant for Finney's apartment?"

"Well, sir, I'd like to get a search warrant, yes. But—" Georgia looked over at Cambareri. He was licking the last of the Milky Way from his fingers. She could taste the caramel from here.

"You'll get your warrant before the weekend's over, I promise," said Lynch. "In the meantime, why not pile on the charges and let the district attorney sort it out later? Spring Street, especially. That's the biggest charge of all."

"I would, Commissioner. Except I'm not sure he did it."

Lynch's beady blue eyes scrunched up, leaving his jowls as loose and unresponsive to gravity as a water balloon. He smiled condescendingly, a small set of lips in a big, fat face.

"And may I ask why, after days of convincing everyone that a serial arsonist was on the loose, you've had this sudden change of heart?"

"Sir, I know this sounds crazy, but I think Finney may not be responsible for all—"

"Skeehan," he barked, then took note of the scores of cameras and reporters milling around the station house and softened his tone. "Ask him again," he said tightly. "Until he gets it right."

Georgia found a sympathetic female police sergeant who loaned her some soap, shampoo, and a clean red sweatsuit. She showered quickly, then found Cambareri, Suarez, and Marenko in a small file room beyond the chaos of the precinct lobby. She closed the frosted glass door, shutting out the noise that seemed to resonate like a tuning fork through the old building.

"Did you find Carter?"

Marenko rose from a chair and spoke first. "No. What's going on? Tell us the truth."

"Oh, there's a good one," said Georgia. "Coming from you—"

"Skeehan," Suarez interrupted, laying a firm but gentle hand on her shoulder. "We've been all over. We've got all-points bulletins out on Carter's and Glassman's vehicles. And we can't find either of them."

"My bunions have bunions," complained Cambareri.

Suarez looked at Georgia levelly now. He was a compact man with warm brown eyes and the kind of soft-spoken demeanor that always calmed people down. "You've got to tell us what you know."

Georgia sighed. "Cassandra Mott, the pregnant victim from the Spring Street arson? She was Randy's daughter . . . by a prior relationship."

Marenko fell back against a desk and cursed. "And you knew this?"

"Not right away. And then Randy asked me not to—"

"That was a dumb-ass rookie mistake, girl." He slammed the desk for emphasis. "Rule number one: *never* work a case you've got a personal stake in. Carter knows better. And so should you. We've finally got our perp, and instead of celebrating, we're baby-sitting—"

"We don't know for sure Finney's our perp," Georgia interrupted.

"It's looking mighty likely," said Marenko. "Walter Frankel was able to match the guy's right thumbprint with the print from that bucket bottom at Howard Beach. And Finney's fire department medical records list his blood type as A positive—same as the blood found on that broken glass at the fire in Washington Heights. Suarez and I have already started the paperwork for a search warrant on his apartment.

When that comes in, we'll probably have all we need to make the case stick."

"Gee, Mac," said Georgia dryly. "Thanks so much for letting me be a part of *your* investigation."

"Hey, you screwed up with Carter. You think I'm gonna let you screw—"

Suarez threw himself between them. "Cool it, you two. You're both playing mind games. Meanwhile, Finney could be sitting in his holding cell, laughing his ass off because we've got that letter promising a big fire for Monday, and we don't even know if he wrote it, let alone where that fire could be."

"You're right, Eddie," said Georgia. "We've got to get a formal statement from the guy before he lawyers up."

"And I think Gene and I should take it," said Suarez. "Mac's got his hands full with the evidence chain. And you had a problem with Finney when he was a dispatcher. Mac's right, you know. You can't get personally involved in a case."

Georgia glared at Marenko. "Yeah. Good piece of advice, Mac. Never get personally involved. I'll remember that."

THE INTERROGATION ROOM had gray cinder-block walls, bright overhead lights, and a scattering of molded, light blue plastic chairs. In the center stood an oatmeal-colored metal table, covered with graffiti. There were no windows, only a large one-way mirror. Behind it, in a darkened, soundproofed room, Georgia, Brennan, and Lynch observed the interchange.

Suarez sat at the table, smoking a cigarette and drinking a can of Coke. Cambareri waddled about the small room, his belly hanging over his pants and straining at the buttons of his shirt, while he loudly slurped coffee and munched a stale doughnut that had been lying around the station house since this morning. Cambareri being Cambareri, he didn't seem to mind.

A police sergeant led Finney in, still dressed in his navy blue sweat-shirt and black sweatpants, stained from their tussle in the tunnel. But he'd had a chance to wash his face and, for all the scuffling, looked sur-prisingly cool and handsome. Even with the cuffs on his wrists, he managed to lean forward and shake Suarez's and Cambareri's hands. If Georgia hadn't interviewed Annette Nolan, hadn't arrested Finney in the tunnel, hadn't felt what she was certain was his hot breath on her neck last night in the car, she'd have sworn they'd gotten the wrong man.

Finney sat down in a plastic chair opposite Suarez and smiled shyly at the trim, compact marshal with the coppery skin. Then he gestured to Cambareri, leaning against a wall. "You were a union delegate when you worked in One-thirty-eight Engine, weren't you?"

Cambareri reared back, astonished. "Yeah. How youse know that?"

"My old man, Bob Finney, was head of the UFA for fourteen years." The Uniformed Firefighters Association was the all-powerful New York City firefighters' union.

"*Your* dad was Bobby Finney?" asked Cambareri, nearly spilling his coffee down the front of his shirt. Suarez was staring wide-eyed, the ash from his cigarette burning a new pockmark in the table. Behind the one-way mirror, Lynch got up from his chair and stormed about furi-ously.

"What the hell is this?" he boomed. "A high school reunion? The guy's a friggin' mass-murder suspect and he's talking to Cambareri like they're having a few beers in a bar after work."

Georgia said nothing, which was just as well. Brennan was ignoring her anyway.

"It's not gonna make a difference who we put in there, Bill," said Brennan. "Hell, if this joker's Bobby Finney's son and he's got that kind of memory, he probably knows every son of a bitch in the department, down to what size underwear they buy. Jesus, *I* knew Bobby Finney. This asshole probably knows *me.*"

They turned their attention back to the interrogation room. Cambareri and Finney were laughing. Georgia flinched. She just hoped Suarez had the presence of mind to work this to their advantage.

"Ralph," said Suarez, his voice soft with just a trace of Spanish accent. "My man, you're in a lot of trouble here . . ."

Finney nodded and pursed his lips. "Yessir. I lost my head. A lover's quarrel, it was. And . . . well." He made a face. "I feel really bad about how it got out of hand."

Georgia leaned forward, confused.

"A lover's quarrel?" Suarez repeated.

"Yessir. I wanted to break things off with Annette, and well . . . she started hollerin' that if I did that, she'd make up stuff about me, make me lose my job. And"—Finney shrugged—"you know how much power these women carry in the department. I mean, look at you. You're a class act. A guy with what? Ten years in rank? Fluent in Spanish, I'll bet. Hardworking with a good conviction rate, right? And you're taking orders from a political appointee with less than two years as a marshal, because she's a woman."

Georgia seethed. She could see Suarez tapping a pen vigorously on his notebook. She couldn't quite read his dark, deep-set eyes, the smooth planes of his face, the set of his muscular shoulders on his solid frame. *Was there a shade of agreement there? Had Finney managed to touch a nerve? Gain some sympathy?*

Suarez took a puff of his cigarette, blinking away whatever emotions Finney had managed to call up from the recesses of his brain.

"Where are we going with this, Ralph?" he asked evenly.

"I'm telling you, sir, why I did such a stupid, impetuous thing. I stopped dating Annette, so she blackmailed me. And the department being the department, they took her word over mine. I lost my job, sir. I'd been a good dispatcher for eight years and I lost everything. I just wanted to scare her, that's all. Not hurt her—just scare her . . ."

Georgia blanched, replaying her conversation with Annette in her head. The woman had been somewhat evasive about the extent of her relationship with Finney. Georgia hadn't pressed too hard. Now she wished she had. *Was it possible Ralph Finney was telling the truth?*

In the interrogation room, Suarez seemed to wonder the same thing. He frowned. "Okay, Ralph. I see what you're saying. But I'm talking more serious stuff even than that car bomb. I'm talking about those fires—the one in Howard Beach . . . the one on Spring Street . . . that warehouse in Washington Heights and those two vacants . . ."

Finney leaned back in the molded plastic chair. "I didn't set any fires."

Suarez held out his pack of Newport Lights and Finney declined. The marshal stubbed out his own, then licked his lips, stringing out the moment to make Finney as nervous as possible.

"Your thumbprint was found on a bucket in the basement of that row frame in Howard Beach—"

"My old man used to be a firefighter in the firehouse next door. I'm a housepainter. I gave him stuff all the time. Maybe he gave the super some of my leftover materials."

"Your blood type matches a smear on a broken window at that burned-out warehouse in Washington Heights. We can do the DNA, if it comes to that."

Finney cocked his head. He looked first at Suarez, then pleadingly at Cambareri. "Mr. Cambareri, sir, tell the marshal here. I didn't set any fires."

"How about the letters?" Cambareri mumbled. "You write those letters, kid? Hide a camera and make that videotape at the VFW hall?"

"The tape that was on the news?" Finney shook his head. "Why would I do that? I *love* the guys in Howard Beach. My old man worked there. I went to Sean Duffy's wake. . . . Went to school with his older brother."

Suarez pushed his notebook and pen across the table at Finney now. "Write something for us, Ralph, will you?"

Finney stared at the blank page of notebook paper and licked his lips. His eyes were wide when he looked at the men. He tried to cross his legs, but a jingle of manacles made that impossible. "Why are you guys trying to frame me?" he asked softly.

Cambareri put a fatherly hand on Finney's shoulder. "Maybe youse didn't mean to kill anybody, Ralph . . ."

"No. That's not it. Don't you believe me, Mr. Cambareri?" When Cambareri didn't answer, Finney looked down and kicked at an imaginary speck of dust on the floor. "I want to speak to an attorney."

Suarez's eyes flicked to Cambareri's. This was the moment every marshal—every cop—dreads. Once the suspect asks to speak to a lawyer, the game's over.

"You can do that anytime, my man," Suarez said slowly, reasonably. "But then we gotta handle this whole thing differently, see? We gotta charge you with all these fires. Tell the press—the people in the FDNY who knew your dad—that you did this stuff. That'd be mighty embarrassing for your family, not to mention the stain it'd leave on your late father's name and reputation."

Finney put his head in his hands. Georgia assumed he might be breaking down. It wasn't uncommon at this stage of an interrogation, when a suspect was confronted with cold, hard evidence, for the person to break down and cry. But when Finney took his hands away, his expression was icy, almost serene. The eyes that just a minute ago had been so warm and seemingly sincere were now two little chips of hardened granite. The half smile on his lips was creepy enough to make Suarez push back from the table.

"Go ahead, Marshal, *sir*," Finney said softly, almost mockingly. "Tell them. Tell them anything you want. You're the ones who are gonna look like fools—not me."

"How's that?" asked Suarez.

Finney leaned back casually in his chair now and studied his nails. "Well, here are the two scenarios as I see them." His voice took on the same timbre it had last night in the car, Georgia noticed. A sort of flat, nasal tone, full of surface calm with only a fleeting hint of the menace beneath. He flicked dirt from his nails on the floor.

"One is, you got the wrong guy. Oh, you got a few little damaging pieces of evidence, but you don't have shit on the fire you really want—Spring Street—do you? And without that, all you've got is a guy with no criminal record who went a little overboard in scaring his ex-girlfriend. That ain't gonna make your lady boss happy, is it? And since she's got you and the whole friggin' department by the *cojones,* you gotta do what she says, don't you?"

Georgia shifted uncomfortably in her seat behind the one-way mirror. She sensed Finney knew she was watching. She shot a sideways glance at Brennan, who was drumming his fingers tunelessly on the armrests of his chair. Even Lynch sneaked a look at her. Finney knew the right buttons to push. Suarez was fighting hard to stay in control. His jaw was clenched. His fingers were pressing so hard on his pen, they were white.

Finney had gotten to him. Georgia could see that. He knew how to rub against that splinter of resentment that must have been festering inside Suarez—inside all of them—since this case started.

"What's your second scenario?" Suarez grunted. He didn't sound as cool anymore.

"Two is, you got the right guy." Finney shrugged. "But that doesn't help you much either. 'Cause you know if you've got the right guy, the fires aren't over."

"What do you mean?" Suarez straightened. In the control booth, Georgia leaned forward. *Was Finney talking about the fire that had been promised in the letter? The fire that was supposed to take place at eleven* A.M. *Monday?*

"I'm not saying more unless I get the deal I want."

"What do you want?"

"For starters? Keep that Skeehan bitch away from me."

"We can accommodate you there, Ralph." Suarez said the words without hesitation. It was the right answer, of course. But Georgia felt a twinge of betrayal. None of them wanted her on the case, it seemed. Not even the suspect.

Seconds ticked by. Finney stared at the ceiling. Cambareri's wheezing was the only audible sound in the room. Finally, Finney spoke.

"Check out Our Lady of Mercy Catholic Church. Four-ten Dupont Street, Brooklyn."

"What'll we find there?" asked Suarez, trying to sound casual.

"A surprise."

"There it is!" whooped Brennan. "We got a bead on the location of Monday's fire." He reached for an intercom and buzzed the precinct captain with the details. "We'll need that forwarded to the NYPD bomb squad, ASAP."

"You see, Skeehan." Lynch beamed. "We find that device and disable it, the investigation's a wrap."

There were high-fives all around when Suarez and Cambareri met up again with Georgia, Brennan, and Lynch. Suarez seemed quietly pleased, Cambareri had a big sloppy grin on his face, and Brennan, for once, managed to mumble a couple of words of praise—for Suarez and Cambareri, of course. Not for her. In the precinct lobby, there was a feeding frenzy of reporters. Bright spotlights blinded Georgia. The commissioner took her hand.

"Why don't you stand beside me while I say a few words?"

Georgia pointed to her oversize red sweatsuit. "I'm not really up to it, sir. I think I'd just prefer to go home." Her mother, Richie, and Gallagher would be waiting for her. That's what she needed right now.

The commissioner shrugged. "If you wish, Marshal. Go out tonight and celebrate."

"Celebrate. Right," Georgia said woodenly. Celebrating was the last thing she wanted to do. She was tired—and confused. Finney had manipulated everyone in that interrogation tonight. He'd suggested that Annette Nolan was nothing more than an ex-lover hell-bent on revenge. He'd offered no motive that would tie him to the Spring Street blaze. And he'd tossed out the supposed location of an HTA device—

which everybody else seemed to believe not only existed, but was the "Armageddon" he'd been promising for Monday. More than likely, Georgia decided, Finney had sent them all on a wild goose chase. They'd find that out soon enough.

She stopped by the station-house front desk to get the address of the sergeant who'd loaned her the clothing so she could mail it back in a day or two.

"You're Georgia Skeehan, right?" asked the desk officer on duty.

"Yeah . . . ," she said uncertainly.

"There's a call for you on line one." Georgia picked it up.

"Scout? I found Carter." Georgia never thought she'd be so happy to hear Mac Marenko's voice.

"Is he okay?"

"He's alive, which is more than I can say for Ron Glassman. The transit cops are scraping his body off the subway tracks now."

"Oh God, no. Was it a suicide?"

Marenko paused. "Let's hope so."

CHAPTER Forty

"Honest, girl. I swear. Ron Glassman was already dead on the tracks when I got to the platform. I never touched him." Randy Carter rolled a nearly empty cup of cold Starbucks coffee between the knuckles of his fingers. "I came straight upstairs, called my wife. She got in touch with Marenko, and here I am, in this doozy of a mess."

Carter slumped on the bottom step of a sweeping marble staircase in the cavernous concourse of Grand Central Station. He was wearing a blue suit and paisley tie beneath a brown leather bomber jacket. The tie had been loosened—unusual for Carter. And his right leg jiggled nervously under a golden light that oozed over him from the graceful chandeliers above. Underneath the landmark station's hundred-foot-high ceiling of star constellations, he looked especially small and beaten down.

"This is a real humdinger, all right," he mumbled as he watched a janitor push a broom across the sparkling granite floor.

"Did Glassman throw himself on the tracks? Did somebody push him?" Georgia asked softly.

"I wish I knew." He nodded down a long corridor of closed kiosks to the entrance of the Lexington Avenue subway. "Mac's down at the crime scene with the transit police now. He told me to stay away and not say a word to anybody."

"All right." She sighed. "Sit tight till we check things out."

"Yeah, sure," he said dully, staring at the floor. "Y'all think I'm going somewhere?"

It was seven on a Saturday night—a quiet time at Grand Central. The station's weekday commuters from upstate New York and Connecticut were replaced by a more subdued scattering of suburbanites off to concerts, dinner, and Broadway shows in the city. Only the red flashing lights of police cruisers parked on Forty-second Street, and the clusters of blue uniforms leading down to the subway, gave any hint of what lay below.

A set of concrete steps, darkened to an indefinable shade of gray-black and smelling faintly of urine and stale sweat, led down to the dank, windowless subway platform. Yellow crime-scene tape sectioned off the low-ceilinged platform, and a grimy silver subway car was stopped halfway along the tracks. Georgia peered over the edge. Two police technicians in coveralls were taking samples and measurements six feet below. Glassman's body was gone, but she could still see dark red splatters along the rails and little bits of what looked like gray gelatin—brain tissue, in all likelihood—stuck to the dirty white tile wall behind. There was a heavy, earthy smell to this concrete tomb, she realized now. The smell of death.

She found Marenko by the base of the stairs, talking intently to a cluster of transit cops and a couple of men in suits—NYPD detectives, she guessed. When he saw her, he broke away from the men with a round of hearty handshakes and pats on the shoulder. Georgia vaguely recalled that Marenko had a brother in the transit police. They'd give Mac more leeway than they would her. For once, she was glad he was here.

"What did you find out?" she asked him as soon as they got out of earshot.

He pulled a cigarette out of his pocket and jabbed it into his mouth.

"You can't smoke down here," she scolded him.

"I can pretend, can't I?" He pulled a notebook from his pocket. "It happened around six-forty this evening. There were about thirty people on the platform at the time. A witness said she saw a black man in a suit walk up to the dead man a few minutes before the train came and whisper something in his ear."

Georgia started. "But Randy said he never spoke to Glassman. He said Glassman was dead when he got down here."

"I know." Marenko's unlit cigarette bobbed up and down on his lips. "Could be a different black man in a suit, or the witness could be mistaken. In any case, the cops don't know about Carter. They think I'm here 'cause Glassman was our witness—and that's the way we're keeping it. I already told Randy he's faking a back injury and putting himself on medical leave first thing tomorrow. He shoulda never been working this case to begin with." Marenko's bright blue eyes held hers a moment, a silent reproach. Georgia let it pass.

"Why was Randy tailing Glassman anyway?"

"Carter told me he was trying to work up the courage to confront this guy and find out the truth about his daughter's death."

"How'd they end up here?"

"Glassman drove in, parked at a garage on Forty-eighth and Sixth. Nobody knows why he chose to park there." Marenko pointed to the sign above them. "Or why he was catching an uptown train."

Georgia nodded. "The whole thing's strange. Who phoned him? Gene said Glassman told his wife the call was from someone at the task force."

Marenko jotted a note to himself. "I'll get the telephone company to run a trace on that call to Glassman's house. You know, Scout. It still could be a suicide. The conductor swears he never saw anyone but Glassman throwing himself onto the tracks."

"It doesn't sound like a suicide."

Marenko pulled the cigarette from his mouth and frowned. "You don't think Carter really pushed him, do you?"

Georgia gazed over at the police technicians carefully bagging a smashed gold wristwatch and sighed.

"Somebody did."

———

MARENKO TOOK CARTER home while Georgia rode the E train back to Queens. It was a familiar ride, but on this Saturday evening, there was something disquieting about the lurching subway car, the glassy-eyed riders all staring straight ahead, and the lights that periodically flicked on and off as the wheels screeched along the tracks.

Nothing in Ron Glassman's demeanor this morning had suggested he was planning to kill himself. And if he was, why drive all the way into Manhattan?

Then there was the matter of the phone call to Glassman's house. Only someone who knew about his eyewitness testimony to the Spring Street blaze could've placed that call. But there were only eight people besides Georgia for whom that was true: the commissioner, Chief Brennan, Walter Frankel, Jimmy Gallagher—who knew next to nothing about the case but had driven her up to Chappaqua—and the guys on the task force—Carter, Marenko, Cambareri, and Suarez. Yet within eight hours of that news, Glassman was dead, his face pulverized beneath the wheels of a subway car. The facts were alarmingly indisputable, at least to Georgia. Glassman had not only told her the truth about Spring Street, but someone close to her didn't want anyone to know it.

When Georgia arrived home, Richie rushed into her arms. His concern touched her, and she held him close.

"You caught the bad guy."

"Yes. Everything's okay now," Georgia lied. Margaret came out of the kitchen and hugged her daughter tightly.

"We've been watching it all on the news." She looked down at her daughter's oversize sweatsuit. "Where are your clothes?"

"Damaged beyond repair. I borrowed these."

Richie thrust a red race car into her hands. "Look what me and Uncle Jimmy finished."

"The slot car. That's terrific." Georgia noticed Gallagher now, standing by the entrance to the living room. He was wearing a button-down shirt and dark blue slacks, his gray hair slicked back like a little boy's in church. Behind him, the television was blaring news reports of Finney's capture.

"Cheers to the hero," Gallagher said, raising a glass of beer.

"Nah. I had a lot of help." She shrugged. "You, Eddie, Walter, Randy—even Gene." She couldn't bring herself to mention Marenko.

"Yes, but if you hadn't collared him, that church might've been bombed and all those parishioners killed."

Georgia furrowed her brow. Gallagher gestured to the television.

"It's all over the news, love. The bomb squad found a firebomb at Our Lady of Mercy in Brooklyn—right where that creep Finney said it would be."

Georgia walked into the living room and stared at the screen. The camera panned a large stone church with yellow crime-scene tape around it.

"You don't look happy," Gallagher noticed.

"I am." She forced a smile. "I'm just in shock and kind of tired, that's all."

"What you need is a drink," he said. It looked to Georgia like he'd had a few of his own already, though he wasn't drunk, just happy and relaxed.

"I think I'll wash up first."

"Good," he said. "Then I'll show you your mother's new pool table in the basement. I've already started taking off the brass hardware." He looked as excited as a kid with a new toy. *Just like my dad,* thought Georgia as she trudged upstairs to the bathroom. She could still remember tagging along behind her father, handing him tools as he fixed hinges, soldered pipes, and rebuilt cabinets. She wished he were here now to talk to. Maybe he could help her fix this case.

At the sink, Georgia splashed cold water on her face and thought about Ralph Finney. Everything he'd done up to this point had been a game. So how come he gave up his last fire to Suarez and Cambareri with no struggle at all?

Or did he?

In her bedroom, Georgia stepped into jeans and shrugged on a crew-neck sweatshirt. And suddenly, it came to her. All this time, she'd been trying to make sense of the fires—when it was the letters she should've been trying to make sense of. The game was in the letters. She walked over to her desk and pulled out an envelope. Copies of the letters were neatly stacked. She read them again, in order.

Letter number one:

> *And the Fourth Angel poured out his vial upon the sun; and power was given unto him to scorch men with fire.*
>
> Revelation. Chapter sixteen, verse eight

Letter number two:

> *And the voice which I heard from heaven spake unto me again, and said, Go and take the little book which is open in the hand of the angel which standeth upon the sea and upon the earth.*
>
> Revelation. Chapter ten, verse eight

Letter number three:

> *The second woe is past; and behold, the third woe cometh quickly.*
>
> Revelation. Chapter eleven, verse fourteen

Letter number four:

> *His eyes were as a flame of fire, and on his head were many crowns, and he had a name written that no man knew, but he himself.*
>
> Revelation. Chapter nineteen, verse twelve

All the passages were from Revelation. All spoke of fiery destruction, angels, and death. But there had to be more—something else about them she couldn't see. The answer wasn't at Our Lady of Mercy. It was still here—locked inside these lines of scripture she couldn't make sense of.

Gallagher knocked on her door. "You all right, love? Your mother waited until you came home to get dinner ready."

"Be right there." She shoved the letters back into the envelope and followed Gallagher downstairs. The dining room table, rarely used, was set with her mother's fine china and linens. Two long red tapered candles rose from crystal candlesticks at either end. She didn't even know her mother had *candles,* never mind candlesticks.

"Looks great, Ma," said Georgia as Margaret put the salad on the table. She could smell roast chicken and mashed potatoes in the oven. "You didn't have to go to all this trouble for me."

"I didn't. I'm bribing Jimmy to refinish my pool table before the summer."

"So she can beat the pants off me." He laughed. "I'm glad I never played your mother for money. I'd be broke." He winked at Georgia. "So, what do you say we all have a quick round on that hunk of junk before dinner?"

"I thought you'd already taken it apart."

"I'm taking the legs off Monday. It's still in one piece for now."

"I'll watch," said Georgia. "I've been beaten enough these last few days."

The pool table sat in the middle of the basement, smelling of smoke and mold. The legs had white, wavy lines from water damage, the wood was pockmarked with cigarette burns, and the green felt was knobbly and worn down to a sheen in sections.

"Ma, you outdid yourself," said Georgia, popping open a beer. "I *never* thought you'd win something more useless than those Engelbert Humperdinck recordings."

"Now hold on, lass," said Gallagher, coming to her mother's rescue. "This wood?" He rapped a knuckle on a faded, splintered corner. "That's solid mahogany. They don't make things out of solid mahogany anymore. When I'm done with it, it'll be a thing of beauty, it will. Good-looking as your mother—"

"And a fair bit younger." Margaret grinned, racking up the balls.

Gallagher looked at her tenderly. "Wine, women, and wood, love," he said softly. "All get better with age." Margaret blushed, but concealed it by chalking up her cue.

"Eight ball? Or straight pool?" she asked.

"Eight ball," said Gallagher, rubbing some chalk on his own cue. "I'll break."

Gallagher popped the tab on a can of Budweiser and clinked it against Georgia's and Margaret's beers and Richie's Coke. "Cheers." He took a sip, then gave the white ball a solid smack. A striped one went into the hole. He took aim at another stripe and missed. He straightened and rubbed his back.

"I'm going easy tonight, I am."

"Excuses, excuses . . . ," Georgia ribbed. Richie giggled as his grandmother brought a step stool over and helped the boy line up a shot. He rarely got anything in—he had Georgia's lack of talent at pool—but he enjoyed being part of the action.

"No, honest," Gallagher explained as Richie missed the shot. "I'm going fishing early tomorrow, I am."

"Not for nothing, Jimmy," said Georgia. "But the last time you went fishing, all you caught was a cold."

"I brought back three pounds of perch," he said defensively.

Margaret leaned in low and aimed a backspin shot at the number-six ball. "Yes, you did." She grinned. The ball thudded cleanly into the far right corner pocket with the white ball still in place. She dispatched two more balls in quick succession. "Cleaned, filleted, and wrapped—from Sal's Seafood."

"You're not staying over?" asked Richie with disappointment.

"No, lad. But I'll see the three of you Monday."

"You'll see Richie and Ma," Georgia corrected.

"Working?" asked Gallagher, but he caught Margaret's frown and already knew the answer. Her mother had a solid number ten in position to sink, but she missed. Georgia sensed she was the reason.

Margaret put down her cue. "I'll check on dinner," she said stiffly. Gallagher touched her sleeve as she brushed by—a gesture of understanding that made her visibly exhale. He always knew the right thing to do. Margaret turned to Richie. "Want to help me with the rolls?" she asked him.

"Sure," said the boy. Margaret padded up the stairs. Richie ran after her. Georgia waited until they were out of earshot to speak.

"I'm sorry, Jimmy," she said. "I'm not trying to cause trouble, but it's the same thing every year. Ma thinks I'm dishonoring Dad when I don't go to that memorial mass. But I take one look at all those pompous chiefs and clergy and all that Catholic rigamarole. I can do the funerals, but this?" She took a sip of beer and rolled the can, gorgeously beaded with sweat, across her forehead. "Religion died for me the day that bodega ceiling fell on my father's head. An inch to the left or the right and he'd have lived. I can't listen to some priest stand there smugly telling me there's a God in that. I just can't."

"I understand, love." Gallagher squeezed her shoulder, then began putting the cues away. "Things happen and they change people—maybe in ways we don't even want to be changed." She sensed he was talking about himself. He laughed. "Me? I believe the good Lord must have a plan. But, that said, I'll be damned if I can figure it out. Sometimes I just think He has a wicked sense of humor."

Margaret called out that dinner was ready, and they went upstairs. Gallagher grabbed a knife to carve the chicken. Margaret began rummaging through drawers while Georgia dished out salad.

"What's wrong, Ma?"

"I thought I had matches. To light the candles."

Gallagher patted his pants pockets and tossed a book to Georgia. "Here, love, take these."

Georgia caught the shiny red book and walked into the dining area. She flipped open the cover, removed a paper shaft, and struck it. Instantly, the flame sprang to life, and she coaxed it to the wicks of the brand-new red candles. A flicker of honey-colored light spilled across the white linen table. She refolded the matchbook and read the gold stenciled writing on the cover. HO YEN CHINESE RESTAURANT. It listed a Manhattan phone number and an address on West Twenty-third Street.

It took her a minute to place the name. By now, Gallagher was opening the kitchen door, and Margaret was placing the chicken on the table. Georgia handed the matchbook back to him with a mumbled thanks. Firefighters probably ordered food at Ho Yen all the time. Ladder 57, Gallagher's company, was just a few blocks away. Hell, Cambareri liked the place enough to order a double portion of spareribs there. So what if Jimmy Gallagher had been to that restaurant? *So what?*

"WHERE ARE YOU going?" Margaret asked later that evening as Georgia was grabbing her coat and keys. Richie was already in bed.

"I just want to get a couple of videos. I'll be back in a little while."

At the video store pay phone, Georgia called directory assistance and got a number for Ho Yen. A man picked up with that annoyed, hurried attitude of Chinese waiters and short-order cooks in New York.

"This is Fire Marshal Georgia Skeehan, is Sam Chu there?"

"He go home already."

She asked if anyone at the restaurant had been working the front counter Monday night.

"I work counter. You got order?" She could hear voices and commotion in the background. The restaurant always seemed busy.

"No," she said. "I just need to know one thing. Do you recall any firefighters in your restaurant around eleven on Monday night? Maybe they made a call from your pay phone?"

"You no got order, I can't help . . ."

"Look, please. I'll give you my Visa number. Anything. Just don't hang up."

There was dead air on the line. Then she heard the rattle of paper and throaty conversations in Chinese and realized he was talking to another worker.

"Yes. Two firemen in here. They pick up big order. They have uniforms and radios."

"They made a phone call?"

"Yes. They ask where pay phone is."

"Do you remember what they looked like?"

"One young with funny accent. Not American . . ."

Irish, thought Georgia. Maybe Terry Quinn. Then again, to this guy, maybe they all sounded funny.

"Other man older. Heavy. Gray hair. He smoke. I say, 'We no allow smoke at counter. Only in smoke section.' This what you want?"

No, thought Georgia, bitter bile gathering at the back of her throat. *This definitely not what I want.*

CHAPTER Forty-one

An early-morning light glanced off the red bricks of Manhattan's Ladder 57 and Engine 11 as Georgia nosed her Harley into a parking space out front. An American flag flapped crisply over the firehouse doors, breaking the street's Sunday stillness. It wasn't until Georgia unstrapped her helmet and dismounted that she noticed the black-and-purple funeral bunting draped across the entrance. It had been just six days since Terry Quinn had died in the line of duty. For firefighters here, it was still a raw wound.

Georgia took a deep breath and tried to still the quake in her stomach. *You're about to commit the worst crime a firefighter can commit,* she reminded herself. But even this knowledge couldn't stop her.

A firefighter buzzed her through the metal side-entrance door. He was in his mid-twenties, with the dark eyes and olive skin of an Italian. His black hair was shaved to a crew cut that accentuated his broad shoulders. *Rick, had he scored high enough to get the job,* thought Georgia. She remembered Richie's letter to him in her purse. She still hadn't mailed it.

"My name is—"

"Georgia Skeehan—Marshal Skeehan," the firefighter corrected himself, leaning forward to shake her hand. "I saw you on TV. Jimmy talks a lot about you."

"Nice to meet you," Georgia stammered, feeling the tremble of anxiety again. "I need to look at some files in juvenile. Can you ask the captain if he has a key to the room?"

Georgia knew from Gallagher that the hundred-year-old building's labyrinthine back rooms had been reconfigured a dozen or more times to house everything from a battalion headquarters to a short-lived juvenile fire-prevention unit. For once, Georgia was thankful for the inefficiency of city bureaucracy. If Gallagher had worked in a single-engine house, she would have had no plausible excuse to get inside.

"Captain Hessler's doing drill, but I'll get him," said the firefighter.

Hessler emerged from the kitchen now, a thin man with prematurely gray hair and the deeply lined face of a longtime smoker. She had met him through Gallagher once before. He took in her jeans, T-shirt, and fire department sweatshirt underneath her cropped black leather motorcycle jacket—hardly fire marshal attire. All her good clothes had either been stolen by Finney or chewed up on the job. She had nothing left.

"Glad to see you collared that creep," Hessler said as he walked her up a flight of stairs to his office on the second floor. "I've dealt with Finney over the radio. A very smart, capable dispatcher. Who'd have figured?"

"People will surprise you," said Georgia. *Take me today, for instance,* she thought.

Along one wall of the captain's office, a gray metal cabinet and a chest-high set of file drawers competed for space with two ripped brown vinyl chairs. A simple cot, crisply made, hugged the wall in the back corner, across from the officer's bathroom and shower. Except for the computer humming on the battered metal desk, it looked like a prison cell. But then again, so did every fire officer's bunkroom.

"Are you and Gallagher going to that ceremony this afternoon?" asked Hessler.

"What ceremony?"

"Here." He tossed a folded-up Sunday *Daily News* to her. "See for yourself."

Splashed across the front page were pictures of Ralph Finney's arrest. Georgia was reduced to a blur in the shot, which was just as well, since between her bruised face and muddy clothes, she didn't think of it as a Kodak moment. On an inside page was a picture of a patch of green in Yonkers with an inset photo of Sloane Michaels, detailing his plans to turn that land into a park in Quinn's memory. The groundbreaking was at five-thirty P.M.

"Jimmy's somewhere off the Long Island Sound, fishing," said Georgia. "I don't think he knew about the ceremony."

"No one did, it seems. Very last-minute," Hessler agreed. "But I know a lot of my men are going." The captain jiggled open the center drawer of his desk and sorted through an enormous ring of keys. "What do you know? I have it," he said, holding up a key that looked identical to all the others.

He walked her to the third floor and unlocked a small room with only one window overlooking an air shaft. "The bureau wanted you to read files—on a Sunday—and didn't give you a key?"

Georgia shrugged. "You know how the department is—right hand doesn't know what the left is doing."

"You got that right."

The room had three file cabinets and one desk, all covered with a layer of dust. "I'll get a couple of my guys to clean the place out for you," Hessler offered.

"Thanks," said Georgia. Anything to buy time. She couldn't do a thing until both the engine and ladder were out on runs. Worse, she had only until one P.M. Richie had softball practice at two. If she missed that, she might as well turn in her mommy credentials.

It was a slow morning. The truck went out twice for false alarms, the engine three times, for two medical emergencies and a water leak. It was eleven-thirty before both the truck and engine went out together—but not for a fire. Just to get groceries to fix lunch. Georgia had been on enough meal runs to know that they usually took about half an hour. It would have to be enough.

She crept downstairs into Hessler's office as soon as the automatic garage doors closed. Already her heart was pounding. The plank floors creaked. The heating ducts rumbled. The computer, still on, hummed. In the kitchen below, the telephone rang, and she jumped as the answering machine spewed out a recorded message and a beep for the caller. The sounds resonated through the cavernous interior.

The enormity of what she was about to do made her as skittish as a wild animal. Inside Hessler's office, a dozen black and blue loose-leaf binders gazed back at her from shelves. She read the spines and was disappointed to realize that they all dealt with fire department procedures, not the company itself. The computer might have helped her, but Georgia surmised that poring over disks could take too long. She would have more luck finding what she needed in some binder. By process of elimination, she settled on the metal file cabinet behind Hessler's desk. She pulled the handle. It was locked. The metal doors puckered, sending a thunderous rattle through the building. It was eleven-thirty-five. Five minutes had passed. In about twenty-five more, the men would be back. The key to the lock was probably on that ring of keys in the desk drawer. But which one? Her hands shook with the possibilities.

The phone rang again downstairs, and the answering machine clicked on. A layer of cold sweat formed on her fingers, making the keys slippery beneath her touch. The first, second, and third keys failed to open the lock. She eliminated the fourth and fifth as too big and too small. The sixth looked right, but wouldn't turn and nearly got lodged in the cylinder. The seventh one slipped in. She turned it to the right and heard a click—

And a voice.

"Hey Cap, you up there? I just want to get my paycheck."

Her blood froze. An off-duty firefighter. She could hear his heavy footsteps lumbering up the stairs. The light in the office was on; the key, wedged in the cabinet lock. Georgia was trapped with no escape.

The officers' bathroom. It was her only hope. The door was open. She backed up and stepped behind the shower curtain. She was breathing hard now. If the men came back, she would have no reasonable explanation for being in the officers' shower, fully clothed. Nor would she be able to explain why Hessler's keys were stuck in his cabinet.

The office door squeaked open wider. "Cap? Anyone around?"

The firefighter opened the captain's desk drawer and cursed as he thumbed through the contents. Georgia's limbs were locked so tight, her thigh muscles ached. She heard the crunch of paper and the rattle of pens in a drawer. He was leaving Hessler a note.

She closed her eyes and breathed in slightly at the sound of his heavy footsteps trudging down the stairs. Firefighters were never quiet. They walked as if they had cement in their shoes. That was her one salvation. She heard the door by housewatch slam. He had left the building.

Slowly, she crept back into the office and opened Hessler's cabinet. A row of looseleaf binders greeted her eye—all meticulously labeled. *Thank God for the anal retentives who run this department,* thought Georgia. *Every friggin' thing in a firehouse is coded.* She found a binder with the company roster and thumbed through it. *Gallagher, James J.,* one entry read. *Locker number 27. Combination 07-63-82.*

Georgia copied the numbers onto her palm, then read them twice for accuracy before putting the book away and returning Hessler's ring of keys to his drawer.

She slipped out of the office and into the locker room adjoining the communal bathroom. Eleven-fifty-three A.M. She had under ten minutes left. She spit into her palm and rubbed off Gallagher's combination number while mentally chanting it to herself. "Oh-seven. Six-three. Eight-two." Her hands were so sweaty, she feared losing her grip on the dial and having to start over. Yet somehow she managed to open the locker on the first try.

The dark, narrow space looked orderly and unremarkable. A couple of clean uniform shirts. Fire-retardant bunker pants. A black turnout coat with bold yellow stripes. A helmet. Two $20 bills. Nothing that seemed even remotely worth the risk she was taking. Then her muscles clenched as she looked down at the bottom of the locker, at an oval black frame surrounding a clear plastic shield.

In five years of firefighting, Georgia had worn facepieces to breathing masks dozens of times, simply grabbing one off the apparatus floor at the beginning of a tour and returning it at the end. She'd never stashed one in her locker. For who would need an extra?

You know who I belonged to.

Her legs wobbled unsteadily. She could smell the smoke on Gallagher's turnout coat. She could see him now in her mind's eye, last Monday night at the fire. Him and Quinn and Lieutenant Russo, climbing the fire stairs in that adjoining building, through a veil of smoke that grew darker with each step. Three men from Ladder 59 went into that building—but only two came out. She stared again at the oval frame, at the round hole in the plastic shield where an airtank regulator could be hooked up to supply air. It looked like a face with a shrieking mouth. It mocked her.

You know who I belonged to.

On the locker shelf, Georgia noticed a plain brown padded envelope. It was open and unaddressed—empty but for an unlabeled floppy disk. She frowned. Gallagher couldn't even type, never mind use a computer. Her mother did all his paperwork.

It was eleven-fifty-six A.M. No sign of the firefighters yet. Maybe they had hit traffic. She prayed for an accident, a fire, anything to keep them away as she scrambled back to Hessler's office and slipped the disk into his computer.

The disk contained more than two dozen files—all with names that appeared to be abbreviations for building addresses: *Htsmn Twrs* had to be an abbreviation for Heightsman Towers, a luxury apartment building off Central Park West. *Bll-Chbrs Thtre* looked to Georgia like an abbreviation for the Bell-Chambers, a prominent Broadway theater. *Knck Plz* . . . Knickerbocker Plaza? Knickerbocker Plaza was owned by Sloane Michaels. Georgia recalled with a sudden jolt that he'd also been involved in the purchase and renovation of the Bell-Chambers Theater a few years back.

Georgia opened the Knickerbocker Plaza file now. It was a spreadsheet. Down the vertical entry lines were names she'd never heard of. Some sounded Latin—*Locasa, Bardellin, Sopras.* Some sounded Russian—*Mirakov, Grushenko, Paglinsky.* Next to the names were dollar amounts that ranged from $2,000 to more than $500,000. Her head spun. *What was Jimmy doing with a computer disk of this stuff in his locker?*

A high-pitched series of beeps on the apparatus floor startled her. The rigs were backing into quarters. And across the hall, Gallagher's locker door was still wide open.

Georgia pulled the disk out of Hessler's computer and shoved it down her T-shirt. She would send it to Walter Frankel later, via departmental courier. Right now, she dashed across to the locker room. Already, the men were bounding up the stairs—all seven of them, minus the engine and truck officers. They would find her next to Gallagher's open locker. They would know she had broken in—broken trust, the most unforgivable crime a firefighter can commit. Georgia shoved the empty padded envelope back on the shelf and closed Gallagher's locker by slamming her body against the door.

"Hey, you morons deaf or something?" she shouted as soon as they came upon her. No defense like a good offense. She was a Queens girl. She had a mouth that could stand up to anybody when she had to. *Fugedabowdit.*

"Didn't you jerkoffs hear me pounding the lockers?" She pretended to zip up her jeans. "Not for nothing, I had to take a leak. Do you mind giving me two friggin' seconds of privacy?"

"Relax, Skeehan," said one of the firefighters, patting the air. He was a beefy older man whom Georgia vaguely recognized from firehouse parties Gallagher had invited her to. The firefighter flicked a look at the other men, who shrugged. "What are you getting so upset about, Skeehan?" he asked, nodding at her hands. "You're shaking like a leaf."

Georgia saw the men look quizzically at her now. She had to deflect their curiosity. She never thought she would say something this stupid. But Marenko would buy it, and so would they.

"Hey." She shrugged. "It's like you guys always say: must be PMS."

CHAPTER Forty-two

She was late for softball practice. She expected Richie to chew her out. What she didn't expect was to pull up to the curb on her motorcycle and see her son in his green jersey, baseball mitt in hand, playing catch with a stranger in the front yard.

The stranger was dressed in loose jeans and a burgundy sweatshirt, a baseball cap on his head. Though his back was to her, he exuded athletic confidence. His throws were casually well placed, his catches graceful. He heard the sound of her bike, tossed Richie a high pop, then sauntered to the curb. She frowned as soon as she realized who it was.

Marenko. What was he doing here?

Georgia unstrapped her helmet and unzipped her jacket, feeling his radiant blue gaze upon her. He was a good-looking man who didn't seem to put much stock in it, and that alone always made her pause and take notice.

He jingled a set of keys in his front pocket. "So, you ready? We're late for Richie's practice."

"*We're* late?"

Marenko shrugged. "If you didn't show up in five minutes, I was gonna take Richie and leave you a note. By the way, the kid's got a good arm. I'd work on it, if I were you."

"And who gave you permission to do that?"

"Work on his arm?"

"No. Drive my son to practice. I don't know what you think you're doing here, but now's not the time." Georgia turned to Richie. "C'mon, honey, let's find Grandma's car."

"But Mom," the boy protested.

"Richie, no whining. We're late as it is."

"But Mom . . ."

Georgia looked in the driveway, then down the street. "Where's Grandma's car?"

"With Grandma. Mr. Marenko's driving us."

Marenko rubbed the back of his neck and looked at her sheepishly. "Your mother asked if I could drive you both to practice, seeing as your car's tied up till Monday and I wanted to talk to you anyway."

"*My* mother asked a complete stranger to drive her daughter and grandson somewhere?"

He made a face. "C'mon, Scout. Your mom knows I'm a marshal. I'm doing you a favor here. You *could* be a little nicer about it."

Georgia was trapped. She didn't let Richie ride farther than around the block on her motorcycle. Her car was still impounded. And now her mother had driven off and left her no choice but to catch a ride with Mac—on purpose, she suspected. Her mother probably liked his eyes, and the absence of a wedding ring on his finger.

"The practice takes an hour."

"No problem." He shrugged. "That'll give us time to talk."

"There's nothing to talk about."

"You might change your mind when you hear what I have to say." He stuck his thumb and middle finger in his mouth and whistled for Richie. "Come on, sport." Then he turned to Georgia. "My car's pretty beat up, but at least it runs."

Marenko drove a seven-year-old silver Honda Accord—probably his portion of the divorce settlement. There were still marks on the back upholstery from where his kids' car seats used to be, and ancient, sticky stains—most likely juice—on the carpet. She used to think it would've been easier if she and Rick had married, then divorced. But looking at Mac's car gave her pause. The hole left by his wife's departure was bigger—and probably more painful—than anything she'd experienced with Rick.

In the car, Mac managed to carry on a pretty knowledgeable conversation with Richie about his beloved Mets. When Richie switched to Pokémon characters, however, Mac was left in the dust.

"You may have a Charizard, but I have a thesaurus," he offered with a grin.

Richie rolled his eyes. "That's an old joke."

"Well, I'm an old guy."

By the time they pulled up to the field, the teams were taking warm-up shots, and the bleachers were already crammed with parents. Georgia's gait slowed and her gaze turned downward.

"What's wrong?" asked Marenko, cupping his palms around a Marlboro and lighting it.

"I know a lot of people here."

"So?" Then he caught her drift. "You're uptight about them seeing you and Richie with some guy, is that it?"

She didn't answer.

"You want me to leave? Pick you up in an hour?"

"No." She sighed. "I just don't want anyone getting the wrong idea . . ."

"You mean like you might actually have a sex life?"

"Ssshhh," she said sharply. "Keep your voice down."

They took a seat at the far end of the bleachers, away from the other parents, some of whom smiled and waved and let their eyes linger a beat too long on the handsome man in the baseball cap next to her.

"How's Randy doing?" asked Georgia.

"Holding up, I guess. He's officially on medical leave. At least he didn't get our butts in a sling over that stunt."

"So, Carter's not the reason for your visit, then?"

"No." Marenko stubbed out his cigarette, then rubbed his palms along the thighs of his jeans. "First, I want to say . . . I mean . . . what happened on the investigation . . ." He looked out at the worn baseball diamond and wiped the back of his hand across his lips. Richie's team was up at bat. The boys were seated behind the chain-link fence surrounding the dugout. Marenko kicked a pebble across the sparse grass. "I can't get the words out," he finally admitted.

"I think the word is 'sorry,' " said Georgia.

"Yeah . . . Not sorry about us, I mean. I wish . . ." He let the thought trail off and rubbed the back of his neck. She was tempted to fill in the spaces. She was still attracted to him, much as she hated to admit it. It was as if the very molecules in the air resonated with his being. Still, she felt foolish for the other night. He had played her too easily. She wouldn't be such a pushover again.

"Okay," said Georgia slowly. "I'm ready for a truce, though I don't know what difference it makes. For all practical purposes, the investigation's over—"

"Not for me, it ain't. This morning? The commish told Brennan he's gonna roast his *cojones* for breakfast. And when Lynch is finished with him, he's gonna start on me."

"Why? We made an arrest pretty quickly. Carter didn't get us in any trouble."

"Ralph Finney, the little shit, still won't cop to Spring Street or Howard Beach. But he *did* give a nice lengthy piece of testimony last night in jail about how easy it would be to torch vacants in this city because the bureau never follows through on demolition. And he gave Red Hook and East Tremont as examples."

"So? The proof's gone, *remember*?" Georgia said icily. "You took the records from my car."

Marenko gave her a blank look. "No, I didn't."

"Mac, don't pull this wide-eyed crap with me. Those records were in my car the night Finney attacked me. Carter told me they were gone by the time the car was dusted for prints. You were the first one on the scene—"

"Yeah. And I was a little too busy saving your ass to worry about a bunch of papers." He saw the dulled edge to her eyes. She didn't believe him anymore. "I *swear*, Scout." He ran a hand through his hair. "Honest to God. I *don't* have the records. Hey, that's the reason I'm *here*—to beg you not to hand that stuff over to Lynch. Now why would I do that if I had them?"

"That's the reason you're here, huh?" She couldn't hide her disappointment.

"Not the only reason . . ."

Her heart leaped.

"I got a trace on that call made to Ron Glassman."

"Oh." She should've known better. She brushed the moment aside, pretended it didn't exist. Marenko, oblivious, plowed ahead.

"The call was made from a pay phone in the lobby of the Knickerbocker Plaza. Your friend Sloane Michaels's place."

"He's not my friend."

"You went to some jazzed-up party at his hotel—"

"And I went to bed with you. And I wouldn't qualify either of you as bosom buddies."

He stared at her, a hurt look on his face. Now it was his turn to feel slighted. "For the record, I had a good time Friday night," he said softly.

Georgia shielded her eyes and looked at the dugout. Richie was next at bat. "For the record," she mumbled without looking at him, "I had a good time, too."

Richie stepped up to the plate now. Marenko put his thumb and middle finger between his lips and whistled loudly.

"C'mon, sport, a homer. Follow through on the swing, like we talked about."

The boy turned and smiled radiantly at Marenko. Georgia shrank into a corner. "What do you think you're doing?"

Marenko rested his elbows on his thighs. Richie swung at the first pitch and missed. The umpire called a strike.

"I'm not doing anything." Marenko shrugged, then shouted, "Eye on the ball, Richie."

"Yes, you are. Playing ball with him and cheering him on, talking about the Mets with him in the car. You're trying to win him over. You think you can buy me by buying him."

A second pitch sailed over Richie's shoulder. He didn't swing, and the umpire called a ball.

"Good eye, sport," Marenko shouted, then turned to Georgia. "You're paranoid. He's a sweet kid. Would you rather I treat him like dirt?"

"I'd rather you not play head games with him—or me. You get him to like you and then you're gone. And who gets hurt by that? Not you. Him. He's been hurt enough."

Richie swung at the third pitch and made contact. Both Marenko and Georgia stood and cheered him on. The boy ran to first, then beamed proudly up at Marenko when he was declared safe.

"You see? He's happy I'm here. I'm not hurting him. I wouldn't hurt anybody."

"That's what every man says."

He stiffened. "And you know every man, I suppose?"

"Enough of them. I've worked, eaten, and slept beside them," she reminded him.

"And you figure if you've seen a guy with his pants down, you know what's going on in his head? Scout, that doesn't work with a man any more than it does a woman."

Georgia rummaged through her hip bag and handed him a wrinkled, legal-size white envelope. "Here. Read this."

"What is it?"

"A letter Richie wrote to his father. He wants me to mail it. I know Rick won't answer, and it's breaking my heart."

Marenko read the child's scrawl and swallowed hard. Georgia could see that he was thinking about his own kids. "You're gonna mail it, aren't you?" he asked, handing back the letter.

"Yeah." Georgia sighed. "But I already know nothing's going to happen." She put the letter back in her bag. "I'm showing it to you because when you tell me you're not trying to hurt Richie, I'll tell you that neither was his father. Intentions don't matter. He's hurt all the same."

"I'm sorry," said Marenko, shaking his head.

"Me, too."

They sat in silence for several minutes, watching the game. Richie got as far as second base before his team made three outs and they were in the field, the boy playing shortstop, his green jersey so large it practically skimmed his knees. Finally, Marenko spoke.

"I know this case is sort of over, but I don't buy Glassman offing himself over Carter's daughter, do you?"

"No," Georgia agreed.

"And I don't buy Carter making that call to Glassman or pushing him under a train . . ."

"Where does that leave us?"

"Remember you asked for a record of deliveries to Spring Street?" Marenko reminded her.

"Yeah."

"On the Friday before the fire, four fifty-pound UPS packages were delivered to Fred Fischer, all from companies that now have disconnected telephones, post-office-box addresses that were opened with what now appear to be fake IDs, and no listing in any phone book or business directory."

"Fred *was* a cokehead. These could be drug transactions."

"Maybe. But he's dead, and his brother Sloane ain't. And there's something more," said Marenko. "At the start of this investigation, I did what I always do whenever anybody in a case has any bread—I run a check of their financial affairs: Do they have insurance claims against them? Are they in debt? Are they in trouble with the IRS?"

"And?"

"Sloane Michaels came up clean as far as insurance and debt. The IRS, though, was a little slow getting back to me. So last night I called a couple of ATF agents I go drinking with. I had them put a little pressure on their Treasury Department brothers. This morning, the agency finally faxed me the highlights of a two-foot-thick file on Sloane Michaels."

"The IRS was investigating him?" asked Georgia.

"Better than that, Scout. For the past eighteen months, the Feds have been reconstructing what they believe was an elaborate money-laundering operation. They think Michaels sets up dummy trusts for cocaine dealers to buy into real estate he owns and manages. They give him the bread, and he hands them back clean rental income and an equity stake in some of the properties."

"The IRS has proof?"

"An accountant who used to work for Michaels tipped them off that the guy keeps two sets of computerized records: the ones he pays taxes on, and the real ones detailing all the laundered cash and the names of recipients. The Feds think Michaels stored the real records in a computer in the basement of Spring Street where his brother lived. The agency was fixing to subpoena the computer and files when the fire broke out."

The computer disk in Gallagher's locker. Georgia froze. *No. It couldn't be.*

"Of course, all of this is sort of moot now," Marenko admitted. "As far as the FDNY's concerned, Finney's their boy. And the Feds can't prove otherwise without the records—"

"I saw them." It was an impulsive response. Georgia wasn't ready to tell anyone about the disk. Not without knowing more.

Marenko frowned at her. "What do you mean, you *saw* them?"

"I saw a computer-generated spreadsheet listing buildings, people's names, and dollar amounts."

"In Michaels's office?"

"No."

"Where, then?" She didn't answer. Marenko misread her silence and drew back. "You didn't sleep with him, did you?"

"What is it with you guys? You think I sleep with every man I meet in the course of my work?"

"You slept with me."

"And that was the only—underlined, *only*—time I mixed work with pleasure."

"Really?" He brightened. "I mean about the pleasure part."

"Press me on it and I might change my mind."

He grinned. "So, what do you want to do with all this? It's your case, Scout. You gotta decide."

She sighed. "I know we're missing something here. Finney gave up that last device too easily. He's got something else planned for tomorrow morning. Something really big. I can feel it. Maybe Michaels is connected in some way to all of this. If we find out how, we can stop this bomb before it's too late." Georgia squinted past the bleachers. The practice was nearly over.

"There's a groundbreaking ceremony for a park in honor of Terry Quinn. It's at five-thirty today, up in Yonkers," she said. "Michaels is supposed to be there. Want to come up with me and talk to him?"

Marenko cocked his head. "You mean you actually *want* me along? Hey, I'm flattered. But I can't. I've gotta be at this party."

Georgia felt a stab of pain in the pit of her stomach. She shouldn't have cared. But she did. "A wild bash, huh?"

"Yeah. Real wild." Marenko winked at her. "Lots of young, cute, giggly girls . . . Barbie dolls everywhere . . ." He caught her look of disappointment and laughed.

"Scout, I'm talking about my daughter Beth's birthday party. She's turning seven."

"Oh."

CHAPTER *Forty-three*

People are just like dogs, Ralph Finney reminded himself as he sat down on his stiff metal bunk in the suicide-watch section at the Manhattan House of Detention. *Always hungry for praise and affection. So trusting. So willing to cede control.* Get a dog to like you and you could bash in his skull while he licked your face. Same with people.

He scratched at the stiff polyester fabric of his bright orange jumpsuit and leaned his back against the cold beige cinder-block walls of his one-man cell. His eyes smarted from the harsh fluorescent lights of the walkway. His skin burned from the shower disinfectant. But otherwise, he wasn't particularly troubled about being here.

He found himself surprisingly able to deal with the physical insults—the fingerprinting, the booking, being poked and prodded in every orifice. And he'd even enjoyed that little session yesterday with Suarez and Cambareri. Cambareri was a moron, but Suarez—that was a treat. Finney loved working his way below the marshal's skin like a tapeworm, telling him things he couldn't admit even to himself. He liked, too, the throngs of reporters who seemed to follow his every move. They turned his name—his moniker—into a household word overnight. Already, half a dozen TV tabloids were lining up for interviews. Even correctional officers were asking for his autograph.

The guard on duty—a stocky, nervous white guy named Harlen—walked to the door of his cell.

"Those fire marshals are back to talk to you some more before your bail hearing. Stand against the wall." Harlen attached a leather belt around Finney's waist and handcuffed his wrists to it. Then he led him down a bleak corridor to a room similar to the one they'd talked to Finney in at the precinct yesterday, except the table was gray and the walls dark brown. Hell, it made that chartreuse and plum he had painted in the TriBeCa loft look positively pleasant.

Suarez was sitting at the table again, tapping a pen nervously and smoking. Cambareri was munching a bag of chips. At the sight of Finney, Suarez rose partway and forced a wary smile. It looked like a real effort. Cambareri, his dark brown eyes weighed down by bags, wiped salt and grease off his fingers and patted Finney on the back.

"How youse holding up, Ralph?" Cambareri asked.

Finney hung his head and made his lips quiver. "Not good, Mr. Cambareri. I can't eat. I can't sleep. Remember when Tony Savone at Engine One-thirty-eight got that DWI? And you called my old man to help straighten things out so he wouldn't get axed? That's how I feel now. Only a thousand times worse."

Cambareri's fat lips flapped open. "Geez, youse got a good memory, kid. Tony Savone? I remember that. Your dad got him into rehab and he stayed outta trouble after that . . ."

"Went on to make lieutenant," Finney mumbled, then paused. "Thanks to you, sir." He flashed an open, ingratiating smile at Cambareri. Just like he would a dog. A big, fat, slobbering Saint Bernard.

"Savone just had a bad turn, that's all." Cambareri shrugged, returning the smile. "It happens."

"Yeah," said Finney. "Tell me about it." Suarez cleared his throat. *The nervous little Pekingese,* thought Finney.

"Ralph, my man, this isn't a DWI," said Suarez. "We've got your thumbprint at one fire, your blood at another. Your handwriting's been matched to those Fourth Angel letters and a search warrant's coming through on your apartment. You gotta stop playing games with us and come clean. 'Cause after today, it's Rikers Island for you until you make bond or get a trial date. And then your lawyer takes over and we're not in a position to help you anymore."

"You want a confession. Is that it?"

"You're a religious man, aren't you?" Suarez asked him softly. "From your letters, I'd guess you must read the Bible a lot. A confession airs out the soul."

Finney stared at his wrists, cuffed in front of him. "It's hard to make a confession in chains. Do you think we can get rid of these?"

Suarez nodded to Cambareri, who waddled to the interview room door and asked Harlen to uncuff Finney's wrists. Finney made a show of massaging his muscular arms. "Thank you both," he said. "You've both been very decent to me." He turned his blue-eyed wattage back to Cambareri again. *Always cut at the weakest link. The drooling Saint Bernard over the jumpy Pekingese.* Finney cocked his head at Cambareri.

"You're about due to retire, Mr. Cambareri, aren't you?"

"Three months to go." Gene smiled proudly. "Then me and the missus are headed to Pensacola, Florida."

"You got a place there already?"

"A place. A boat. The works."

"Paul Ahearn and Doug DeStephanis retired there, too. You know them?" asked Finney.

"Know 'em?" Cambareri patted his chest. "Dougie's the guy convinced me and Barbara to move down there. . . . Hey, youse want some coffee or a doughnut or something, Ralph?"

"No, thank you." Finney nodded to Suarez's pack of Newport Lights. "Actually, if Marshal Suarez doesn't mind, I'd like to bum a cigarette."

A small crease appeared between Suarez's brows. "I thought you didn't smoke."

"Calms me down."

Suarez pushed his pack of Newport Lights and a red butane lighter toward Finney, along with a small tin ashtray. Finney pulled a cigarette from the pack, cupped the red butane lighter around it, and lit it. He took a long drag, then exhaled slowly across the table.

"Maybe you can clear up something for us, Ralph," Suarez said evenly. "All of these fires seem to have been set as revenge fires—to punish and embarrass the FDNY. Am I correct?"

Silence. Finney smoked casually, confidently. The marshals shifted in their chairs.

"Are you choosing not to answer, Ralph?" Suarez finally asked.

"You're divorced, Marshal, aren't you?" Finney asked Suarez.

Suarez frowned. "I don't see where that's any of your business."

Finney gestured with his cigarette to Suarez's right hand, to the ruby-colored stone on his ten-karat gold fire department ring. "You don't wear a wedding ring, but you *do* wear a department ring, so you're not opposed to jewelry."

Suarez pulled his hand away self-consciously.

"You're not gay, and I don't get the feeling you've never been married," Finney continued. "So that leaves us with divorce. Maybe more than once. . . ."

"Where's this going, Ralph?"

"You never wanted revenge on someone who jilted you?" Finney asked with a slick smile. "Maybe some woman who slept with another guy first before she said *Adios, Eduardo*?"

Suarez's eyes narrowed to tiny, dark slits. The smooth planes of his face grew taut as a trampoline. Finney licked his lips. "She did, didn't she, Eddie? Cheat on you, I mean."

Suarez clenched his jaw, but the tremor in his hands was unmistakable. "Listen, Ralph, you can play all the games you want. The bottom line is, the evidence is stacking up against you—"

"But not Spring Street," Finney interrupted, gesturing with his cigarette. "That's what's bothering you. That's why you're here. You think you've got everything, but you can't quite put it together."

"All right, Ralph. *You* put it together for us."

"Help you send me to death row?" Finney stubbed out his cigarette with an overly brusque motion, as if to accentuate his point. The tin ashtray slid across the table, knocking the cigarettes and butane lighter to the floor. A flurry of black ash flew like week-old Manhattan snow across the cement.

"I'm sorry," Finney apologized. "I didn't mean that." He stooped to pick up the cigarettes and ashtray, then palmed the lighter and stuck it in his shoe. The motion was so fluid, the marshals so intent upon his words, that they only saw him wipe his hands on his orange jumpsuit before settling his gaze back on them.

"Give it up, my man," Suarez reasoned with Finney. "We might be able to work something out if you give it up. Otherwise, all bets are off."

"Okay." Finney sighed and hung his head. "You win."

Suarez tapped a pen nervously. In the bleak, windowless room, every noise was magnified. Cambareri took a seat and massaged his swollen ankles. He wheezed the same way Finney had as an asthmatic kid. It brought back the sensations again. The tight breathing that turned raspy as it traveled down the windpipe. The racing pulse. The short, panicked gulps of air that can easily induce hyperventilation. Finney placed both palms on the table and began gasping.

"I . . . think . . . I'm . . . having . . . an . . . asthma . . . attack," he choked out. "I . . . need . . . to go . . . to . . . the . . . infirmary."

"Do you get these often?" asked Suarez, rising from the table, alarmed. Finney shook his head. "Only when I smoke."

Suarez let out a string of Spanish expletives. Cambareri alerted Harlen at the door. The guard fumbled with the handcuffs on his belt.

"Will youse forget those?" Cambareri yelled. "Finney dies, we gotta answer a lotta questions. And I hate questions."

Finney kept up the gasping, his body jerky from the effort to get air. The three men half carried, half dragged him down the hallway and two flights of stairs to the infirmary. A middle-aged doctor in a white coat regarded the sudden intrusion sourly. She was a heavyset black woman with short, frizzy hair flecked with gray.

"What do you think you're doing?" she asked in a Caribbean-flavored accent, folding her arms across her ample chest.

"Finney's having an asthma attack," said Harlen. The guard was sweating heavily now as he grabbed Finney underneath his armpits and hoisted him onto the paper-covered examining table.

"All of you, clear out," barked the doctor.

"One of us has to stay," Suarez explained to the doctor.

"I'll do it," Cambareri volunteered. "Seeing as I kinda know him and all."

Harlen closed the examining room door, but kept watch through a small glass window with wire mesh across it. Suarez stood behind him. In the examining room, Cambareri hugged the wall, trying to stay out of the doctor's way. Even so, she kept backing into his fat belly.

The doctor poked roughly at Finney's neck until she found his carotid artery, then stuck a finger on it to check his pulse.

"Sit up and lean forward," she barked. She made harrumphing noises as she pulled down the top part of Finney's jumpsuit, lifted his T-shirt, and ordered him to breathe while she listened to his back with her stethoscope.

"Your pulse is normal, there's no blueness around your lips, so we'll hold off on a corticosteroid. But since you seem in distress, I'm going to give you a nebulizer."

The doctor turned to a contraption on the counter the size of a lunch box. Inside was a face mask, which she intended to put over Finney's nose and mouth to help him breathe. Finney watched her reach for a vial of bronchodilator preparation.

What happened next was part luck, part knowing what to do with it. For as Ralph Finney sat on the table, wheezing and seemingly list-less, he spotted a plastic half-gallon jug of isopropyl rubbing alcohol on the countertop. He didn't have to read the red lettering on the label: FLAMMABLE, KEEP AWAY FROM FIRE OR FLAME. He already knew. And he knew, too, that he would have just seconds to succeed. The doctor was out of his grasp, but Cambareri was right next to the metal table, his cheap polyester knit tie practically dangling in Finney's face. Nobody had a gun—prison rules. And besides, Finney was in terrific shape. Cambareri had a body the consistency of pizza dough. *Go for the Saint Bernard.*

"Mr. Cambareri," Finney gasped out. "I . . . got to . . . tell you . . ."

Cambareri leaned in close. "What, Ralph?"

Finney grabbed the marshal by his knit tie and spun him around in a choke hold before Cambareri had a chance to react. In a flash, Finney sprang from the table, reached for the bottle of rubbing alcohol, and twisted off the plastic cap. The doctor let out a little gasp and flattened herself against the far wall. She was a civilian. Finney'd have no trouble with her.

"Ralph—what're youse . . . ?" Cambareri cried out as a pungent odor of disinfectant filled the room. With Finney's knee to the small of the marshal's back, he managed to push Cambareri's head forward and douse the wispy strands of his thinning black hair.

Alcohol flowed down Cambareri's face and into his eyes, stinging them and temporarily blinding him. It soaked his white shirt until it was translucent, revealing a sleeveless white T-shirt beneath. His blue knit tie was saturated with rubbing alcohol. A small cry escaped Cambareri's lips. Part pain, part disbelief.

Harlen kicked open the door, his truncheon ready to strike. But Finney was faster. From his shoe, he pulled out Suarez's disposable red butane lighter and held it just inches away from Cambareri's soaked tie.

"You want him to burn?" he hissed at the guard, at an ashen Eddie Suarez behind him. "That's rubbing alcohol on him. I so much as touch this lighter to it, he's gonna fry, I promise."

Gene Cambareri, his eyes screwed shut from the pain, began to whimper. Harlen let his rubber baton fall to his side. Suarez came up behind the guard, also frozen by the enormity of the situation and how quickly it had spun out of control. They exchanged glances and by some unspoken agreement decided that Suarez should be the one to talk. Cambareri was, after all, his partner.

"C'mon, man," Suarez urged softly, patting the air. "Put the lighter down . . ."

"Get me out of this place, I will."

"You know I can't do that."

"Then the fat man burns."

The only sound any of them could hear was the static from Harlen's radio, buzzing with alarmed voices about what was transpiring on the third floor, and the choked whimpers from Cambareri.

"What's this gonna get you, Ralph?"

"A front-row seat at tomorrow's blaze. The one you morons'll never figure out."

So there *was* going to be another HTA fire. Suarez tried not to betray his astonishment. They had maybe fifteen hours to stop *that* disaster. This one could be all over within seconds.

"C'mon, my man," Suarez reasoned. "Think about what you're doing here. You *know* Gene. He's not just a badge to you. He was on a first-name basis with your dad. And Tony Savone. And Dougie DeStephanis. You *can't* wanna do this to him."

Finney laughed and shook his head. His pale blue eyes were wild now—deep and sparkly, as if lit by a demon fire within. Suarez could feel the pulsating thrill behind that glare. It made him shudder.

"I can't wanna do this to him? Well, I have news for *you, my man*," Finney said mockingly to Suarez. "Those are the only kinds of burnings *worth* doing."

CHAPTER Forty-four

FUTURE SITE OF QUINN MEMORIAL PARK, proclaimed a colorful banner strung between two large oaks. Georgia checked her watch and frowned. Six-thirty P.M. She was late. Already families and television crews were dispersing. Street lights were ushering in the evening. She'd have been here earlier if not for the fact that she was down to a heel of bread and a can of Yoohoo in the refrigerator. The guilt was so overwhelming that not only did she do a quick food shop, she also mailed Richie's letter to his father. Hell, if there'd been so much as an orange in the house, Rick wouldn't have seen that letter until July.

The event was bigger than Georgia would've expected. Sesame Street characters handed out the last of the balloons and ice cream sandwiches, while a parade of bagpipers in kilts blanketed the two-acre stretch of sycamores and willows with their shrill wail.

Michaels was standing to the side of a newly planted hedge of English boxwoods, looking regal in his navy blue silk suit. He was talking on a cell phone. A black stretch limo was parked nearby, the motor running. She wouldn't have much time.

"Mr. Michaels," she called, waving to him.

Two assistants in expensive suits hustled over, neither smiling. One was black and built like a linebacker. The other was a Latino with a shaved head and an earring in one ear.

"Can we help you?" the black linebacker asked. Georgia noticed one of his incisors was capped in gold. So much for the company dental plan.

"I need to speak to your boss."

"No can do. He's already late for a meeting."

"This is important."

"So's the meeting."

Georgia caught Michaels's eye just as the bald Latino was about to put a less-than-friendly grip on her arm.

"Marshal Skeehan, I'm so glad you came," Michaels said, walking over. "Congratulations on arresting that arsonist." He shook her hand warmly. She stumbled over a reply.

"There are some things I really need to discuss with you, sir."

He checked his watch. "I have to be at an event at the Four Seasons in an hour, but if you walk me to my car, we can talk."

The limo was only about fifty feet away, but Michaels had to stop three times before he got there, to smile for photos, sign autographs, or simply engage in small talk with adoring residents. Georgia sucked in a deep breath. This wasn't going to be easy.

"What were in the four fifty-pound UPS packages delivered to your brother the Friday before the fire?"

"I have no idea." He ran a hand against the grain of his silvery beard. "Why?"

"Because the packages all came from dummy companies."

A cluster of neighborhood residents passed by, giggling and waving. Michaels kept a smile plastered across his face and shot it in their direction as he spoke.

"If I had to hazard a guess, knowing my brother, I'd say they contained drugs."

"Maybe. But *you* were the one who sent him on an errand designed to keep him out of the building Monday. *You* knew the department finally had a witness to the Spring Street fire. And now that witness is dead—under suspicious circumstances—after receiving a call traced to the lobby of *your* hotel."

Michaels touched his chest. "You don't think *I* made that call, do you? I don't even know who you're talking about."

"Where did you get that Fourth Angel letter that you showed me, Mr. Michaels? Did Finney *really* send it to you? Or were you just looking for a convenient way to take the heat off yourself—in case the department started tracing those UPS packages and discovered they were filled with HTA?"

"You're talking nonsense." They were at the door to his limo now. The motor was running.

"I'm talking motive," said Georgia. Behind her, children scampered on the sidewalk and car engines revved up along the curb. Burly men with television cameras strapped to their shoulders walked by, readying themselves for their next assignment.

"You see," Georgia continued, kicking at an ice cream wrapper at her feet, "the only one with a motive to burn down Spring Street"—she looked up, fixing her gaze on him—"was you. I know about the IRS investigation, Mr. Michaels."

Michaels's root-beer-colored eyes registered shock and profound sadness. He shook his head. "Why do you have it in for me, Marshal? Is it rich men you don't like? Or men in general?"

"This isn't personal."

"The hell it isn't."

"Why are the Feds investigating you for money laundering?"

He opened the back door of his limo. "Get in," he said tersely. She hesitated. "You want to level allegations at me, the least you can do is not broadcast them all over the goddamn park."

She followed him into the car. There was a bar, a television set, and a bank of phones. She could see out, but no one could see in. Her heart thumped in her chest. Michaels told his driver to close the soundproof windows and kill the engine. Then he turned to her.

"Just because I'm investigated from time to time by the IRS doesn't make me a crook. A man of my stature gets investigated." He frowned at her. "You see that, don't you? To judge me by that would be like"— he snapped his fingers—"like judging a doctor's competence by the size of his malpractice premiums."

"Okay," Georgia said slowly. "I'll buy that. If you can tell me one thing . . ."

"Anything." He gestured expansively, sinking into the black leather upholstery.

"Who's Locasa?"

Michaels sat up straight and stared at her now. She reeled off two more names: "Who's Grushenko? Who's Sopras?" His eyes narrowed into dark little orbs. His fingernails dug into the upholstery. Even his voice became flinty.

"Where did you get those names?"

"They're your clients, right? Drug lords who invest dirty money in your buildings, then get paid back with clean rental income." Georgia could read it in his face. "Knickerbocker Plaza, the Bell-Chambers Theater, Heightsman Towers—they were all built on the backs of junkies, weren't they?"

Michaels didn't move. It was as if he couldn't quite believe what was happening.

"That son of a bitch made a copy," he muttered to himself. "A firefighter . . . a goddamned firefighter."

Tears welled up in Georgia's eyes. *Not Jimmy Gallagher. Dear God, no.*

"You had Ron Glassman killed, didn't you?" Georgia prodded. She'd expected Michaels to protest, but instead, he laced his trembling fingers in his lap and stared at them without speaking.

"It's true, then," she whispered, horrified at the realization. "You had him killed because he could testify that the Spring Street fire started in the basement—an area only you and your brother would've had easy access to. But who gave you Glassman's name?"

The question seemed to snap Michaels out of his daze. He punched the seat behind her. "Where are the files?" he demanded.

Georgia flinched. "I don't have them anymore," she stammered. "They're out of my hands." She put a palm on the limo door, but Michaels grabbed it.

"Do you understand what you've done?" he hissed. He was breathing hard.

"Let go of me."

"Do you know what will happen to you if those files become public?" Michaels's voice began to crack. He ran a hand down his face, fighting for control. "Look, Marshal—*Georgia*—listen to me. We can work out a deal—"

"A *deal*? Fifty-four people died that night—my partner's *daughter,* his unborn *grandchild*—and you want to work out a *deal*?" She regarded him with disgust. "I was right the first time about you. We *are* different."

He flopped back on the seat, looking defeated. And in that instant, Georgia saw her chance. She fumbled with the lock on the door for only a moment, then bolted.

The sky was dark now. The streets were emptying. Lights were glowing behind pulled-down shades. She thought one of Michaels's assistants might run after her. But when she finally looked back, out of breath, the car had sped away. Michaels was too smart, too powerful, to risk a public confrontation. But until Georgia got that computer disk copied and recorded into the official case file, she knew she was far from safe. She'd sent it via departmental courier to Walter Frankel's lab. He probably wouldn't get it until tomorrow, but she couldn't be sure. She had to warn him.

Frankel picked up his home phone midway through the answering-machine message. Breathlessly, Georgia began to pour out what had happened with Michaels in the limo. A Camaro roared down the dark street. Georgia stuck a finger in her ear.

"Where are you?" Frankel interrupted.

"Still in Yonkers. I need you to meet me at the lab in case the disk's in the evidence drop box. We can't have it floating around."

"Forget about the disk and listen to me. You've got to get home, right now . . . Georgia," he said in a quavering voice. "Finney's on the loose."

Georgia cradled the phone, transfixed, as a cold finger of sweat trickled down her spine. Even with her black leather motorcycle jacket pulled tightly around her, she was shivering. Finney had nothing to lose now—no job, no stature, no false sense of pride or belonging. The absence of those things would narrow his will to a single sharp focus: revenge. And of all the targets he could aim at, none would be more satisfying than taking down Georgia Skeehan, the woman who—in his mind—had cost him the only thing he really coveted: a place in the uniformed ranks of the FDNY.

"Georgia? Did you hear what I said?"

"I heard you," she choked out. "Tell me what happened."

Frankel explained how Finney had threatened to burn Cambareri, how Suarez felt he had no choice but to let Finney go. Cambareri was in the hospital now, unharmed, but getting checked out. Suarez was with him.

"At least Gene's okay," Georgia offered in her most sober, rational voice.

"Darling, I haven't told you the worst," Frankel explained. "That fire Finney promised? For eleven A.M. tomorrow? He told Suarez it's still out there—"

"Armageddon," Georgia mumbled to herself.

"What?"

"He called it *Armageddon* in his letter. Walter, we could be talking hundreds of deaths in what—?" She looked at her watch. It was almost seven-thirty P.M. "Under sixteen hours?"

"I'm so sorry," Frankel said softly. "I let you down. I let everyone down . . . I hope one day . . . you'll forgive me." There was a long pause, followed by an audible intake of air. It sounded like Walter Frankel was crying.

"Shit, Walter—we *all* blew this one," Georgia said with a trace of annoyance. "How could you know? You can't let it get to you like this."

"I'll take care of the disk," he promised hoarsely. "Michaels won't get it."

"It's you I'm worried about."

"Look, darling, whatever happens . . ." His voice trailed off. Georgia sensed he wanted to say more but couldn't bring himself to. "Watch out for yourself." He hung up.

CHAPTER Forty-five

Ralph Finney crouched in an alleyway and pressed the striker on Eddie Suarez's red butane lighter, listening for a familiar metal click as the flame punctuated the darkness. He stared at the plume of orange. Shimmering. Contained. Then he removed his thumb, feeling the blackness surround him as if it had weight and mass. He did it again. On and off. On and off—intermittent as a flash from a lighthouse beacon. He liked the rhythm. The contradictions. In darkness, there is danger. But, he thought as he watched the flame flicker and grow again, there is danger in light, too. Maybe more.

He waited until nearly eight P.M.—a busy time—before he breezed through the front doors of an Upper West Side fitness center and flashed his membership card at the spandex-clad brunette at the front desk. She barely noticed him. At first glance, there was no reason she should. "Ray Flynn"—the assumed name Finney had taken out the membership under, three months ago—was wearing a Syracuse University T-shirt and gray sweatpants. Nothing out of the ordinary.

The little peculiarities about him would have taken a more alert mind to pick up. The fact that he carried no gym bag. That his sweat-soaked blond hair was plastered beneath a knit hat, though the temperatures outside were balmy. That his hands and fingernails were filthy—the result of keeping a low profile in the tunnels of Central Park until dark. Or that he was wearing sneakers without any laces—suicide prevention at the Manhattan

House of Detention. No matter, thought Finney. All those peculiarities would soon be erased.

Standing in the men's changing room, turning the combination lock on his locker, Finney allowed himself his first deep breath since his escape. The initial run was the hardest. He had waited out the first hour at a bad Spanish movie. A busy laundromat was his next stop. From an untended dryer, he swiped the T-shirt, socks, sweatpants, and hat.

By early evening, he had made his way to a Barnes & Noble bookstore. His health-club membership card was stashed there in an obscure reference book. He wasn't too worried about finding the book, however. He had told the club twice that he had lost his card and paid for replacements. Two other books in two other bookstores held those.

He opened his locker. Fresh clothes, a bottle of men's black shampoo-in hair color, money, fake IDs, and some interesting items he had retained as souvenirs greeted him. A good long shower, a dramatic change of hair color, some horn-rimmed glasses, and he could finish business in this town. He had plenty of business to finish.

He stripped down and stepped into the shower, feeling its soothing warmth across his skin. With a small gel bottle, he squeezed coloring along the fine blond shafts of his hair, feeling a tingle of excitement as he imagined himself walking up to Georgia Skeehan without her realizing who he was.

Finney caught an odd reflection of himself in the chrome faucets. *Who was this man?* Celia Maldonado and her kids thought they knew— and they were wrong. And so was that fat old marshal, Cambareri. The Duffy family, whom he'd known all his life, didn't have a clue that the man who'd held their hands at their son's funeral had also sealed his fate. A one-way mirror, he was. He could see them all so clearly—their petty lies and hypocrisies, their jealousies and sorrows. But they never saw him until it was too late.

He turned off the shower and rubbed a towel through his hair. Men wandered in and out of the locker room. Finney kept his distance. He wasn't worried about the FDNY or NYPD finding him here. If they had managed to pinpoint his whereabouts, they would have made a big production out of it. He would have seen it coming.

No, his real problem—his real fear—was the sudden bullet from behind or the tight band of twine around his neck.

And that would only come from a man he'd never met.

CHAPTER Forty-six

Georgia nosed her Harley alongside Walter Frankel's lab on West Thirteenth Street, in the shadows of an abandoned elevated-freight bridge. Beneath it, two transvestite prostitutes stumbled about in high heels, their garish silhouettes framed by streetlights misty with the damp haze off the Hudson River.

She cut the bike's engine and listened. On a Sunday night at nine P.M., the only sound that punctuated the darkness was the clinking of rusty meat hooks under corrugated-tin awnings.

A single lightbulb hung above the entrance to Frankel's one-story building. Georgia leaned on the buzzer that was marked FDNY, FORENSIC INVESTIGATION DIVISION. She didn't have a backup plan. *Please be here, Walter,* she prayed. She banged on the door, then noticed it was ajar.

Inside, a fluorescent cylinder flickered from an overhead fixture, throwing odd shadows across the checkered asphalt tile and disappearing into darkness at the end of each hallway. Only the thin white glimmer of light coming from a frosted glass door at the end of the west hallway told her that Walter Frankel was in his office. She called to him, but he didn't answer.

The office door was open, the lights on. Frankel's calico cat was mewing anxiously around his desk. Georgia called for him again but got no answer. A mug of coffee next to the telephone was still warm.

He went to the men's room. She'd take a seat and wait. Then she'd scold him for leaving the door open again.

There was a faint sense of the macabre about the place, about the various pieces of equipment humming for unknown purposes and the cold, dull pewter gleam of the lab tables. Even the Arnold Schwarzenegger poster had a menacing edge to it in the harsh overhead glare.

The calico leaped onto Georgia's lap, and she jumped. The movement toppled a folder from a pile of papers on a side table, spilling its contents. Georgia picked up the papers. Building records of some sort. She glanced at them more closely and froze. These were the records Mac had given her, the ones that had disappeared from her car the night of the attack. *What was Walter doing with them?*

A brief gasp, then a gurgling sound, emanated from Frankel's inner office. The door was closed. Georgia tried to open it now. It wouldn't budge. "Walter?"

Frankel answered with a hoarse moan. Georgia threw her weight against the door and managed to push it open.

He was lying on the floor, half wedged against the door. A dark red mass radiated from the middle of his chest where an assailant's bullet had penetrated. His pulse was weak, his skin ashen. She elevated his feet in a feeble attempt to keep him from going into shock.

"It's okay. You're gonna be all right," she said. She pulled out her radio. "Ten-eighty-five. Marshals in need of assistance. Corner of West Thirteenth and Washington streets. Request an ambulance." She spoke calmly, as she'd been trained to do, but inside she was shaking.

Frankel fluttered his eyes up at her now. His skin was cold and clammy. "Let me die," he choked out. "It's better that way . . ."

"Stop talking like that," Georgia snapped at him. She took off her jacket and propped it under his head. "You leave the doors open, what do you expect? The Avon Lady?"

"Michaels," he gasped. "His guys . . ."

Georgia's stomach went into free fall. "Michaels came for the disk? But I never told him—"

"You . . . didn't . . . have to." Frankel looked up at her darkly. Georgia reared back.

"He *knew* you'd have it? Walter, you weren't *helping* him, were you?"

Frankel didn't answer. A weight settled on her chest. She felt like crying.

"But why? Why would you do a thing like that?"

"I . . . never meant . . . to hurt you . . ." He coughed violently several times, then took a breath and continued. "I went to Michaels . . . to try to . . . stop the cover-up."

"You mean of Finney's first three HTA fires?" Georgia frowned. "The ones the department didn't want to make public?"

Frankel closed his eyes and nodded. A logical chain of events began to percolate in Georgia's brain.

"Because you figured if you went directly to the commish about them, Brennan would retaliate and force you out of the job. So you went to Michaels—gave him copies of the Fourth Angel's letters—because he was friends with Lynch. You assumed he'd prod the commish to investigate and you'd be off the hook, is that it?"

Frankel winced and turned away. Georgia thought it was from the pain, but as she bent over him now, she could see it had more to do with the embarrassment and shame of her scrutiny. "Oh, Walter." She sighed, stroking his forehead.

"That's why . . . I took the . . . records . . . from your car," he croaked without looking at her. "I still want the truth . . . to come out."

"But how do you know Michaels?"

"Amelia . . . at the hospital . . ."

"Ah."

"I didn't know he would . . . use it this way." Frankel blinked back tears. "I didn't know until—"

"Until I showed you the letter," Georgia gasped. "The one Michaels claimed to have gotten from the Fourth Angel . . . but he really got it from *you,* didn't he? He used Finney's fires as a smokescreen to destroy records under subpoena by the IRS."

"He . . . didn't get . . . the disk." Frankel turned and gave her a wan smile. "The poster . . ." He looked up at her like a child wanting to please.

Georgia thought she understood. In Frankel's outer lab, she tore back a glossy corner of the Schwarzenegger poster. A white legal-size envelope was neatly taped to the wall behind it. The envelope rattled about with the weight of a floppy disk inside. *Please deliver to Fire Marshal Georgia Skeehan, FDNY,* the lettering on the outside read.

She ran back to Frankel waving the envelope, but he no longer seemed to see her. His skin was cold and a bluish tinge had settled in his fingers and across his lips. She held him close and stroked his face and hair. He couldn't die. Not this way, not with all this unfinished business between them.

"Hang on," she whispered. He grimaced, and his breathing became raspy and inconsistent.

"Don't . . . search Finney's place . . . Michaels . . . has it rigged."

"I'll let the bureau know." Georgia heard the squeal of an ambulance siren. "Our guys are here, Walter," she told him, squeezing his hand. "You're going to be okay."

His lips barely parted. She leaned in close.

"Hasta . . . la . . . vista . . . baby," he said. Then his jaw dropped open and his pupils became fixed and dilated. Frantically, she felt for a pulse. There was none.

Fire department EMTs were running down the hallway now. They burst into the room. Georgia stepped back and numbly watched them check Frankel over and shake their heads. Police came and ushered her into the street while they secured the crime scene.

She'd been calm until now. But as she watched the EMTs wheel out Frankel's body with a sheet over it, she began to shake violently—so violently, she thought she was having a seizure. She stood by the curb, feeling a cool night breeze, listening to the spaced-out chatter of street people. There was no place to sit down, so she sank onto the sidewalk and rocked back and forth, sobbing.

The if-onlys came fast and furious. *If only the fire department had heeded Walter's warnings about Finney's early fires . . . If only the mar-*

shals hadn't screwed up the demolition paperwork in the first place . . . If only Walter had been honest with her about what he'd done . . .

And the worst wasn't over—not by a long shot. It was nine-thirty P.M. She had under fourteen hours to stop Finney's last fire. And arrest Michaels. And confront Jimmy Gallagher. She slipped the disk into her purse.

Her peripheral vision caught the shadow of a tall, lean, gray-haired black man talking to a couple of police detectives while he rubbed a crick out of his shoulders. Randy Carter was here. She looked up with gratitude as he walked over, dressed impeccably as always in a gray pin-striped suit and tie. He squatted down beside her and grunted with the realization that such a maneuver was becoming difficult for a man pushing sixty.

"How you holding out, girl?"

"Oh, Randy." She blinked back tears. "You don't know the half of it." Then she remembered. "You're supposed to be on medical leave."

He patted her on the shoulder. "I heard about Finney escaping. Y'all think I'm gonna sit on my butt after that?" He let a moment of silence pass between them. "I saw Frankel . . . damn. What happened?"

"Am I giving you a formal statement, or are we just talking here?"

"The statement can come when you want it to. You decide."

Georgia took a deep breath. "Are you up for Dunkin' Donuts?"

"Long story?"

She nodded.

"Long *humdinger* of a story?"

She nodded again and smiled. He was teasing her. She needed that right now. They both did, actually.

"All right," he said. "But one thing. Don't you be ordering no king-size coffees, then telling me you've got to pee, okay? I been there with you, remember?"

CHAPTER *Forty-seven*

Carter knew of an all-night Dunkin' Donuts in Chelsea, just north of Frankel's lab. There, he treated Georgia to a large coffee and a cream doughnut, which she barely touched. She called her mother and Richie to tell them she'd be working overtime tonight, but didn't elaborate. She didn't want to alarm them—not yet, anyway.

The Dunkin' Donuts was surprisingly busy for ten-thirty on a Sunday night. Four of the six booths were full and there was a pretty steady stream of take-out customers as well. Most were young and garishly dressed—rings in their noses, uncombed green and purple hair, clothes that were either so baggy the wearers looked like kids playing dress-up, or so tight they looked like hookers.

Georgia had always thought of herself as pretty young and hip. Yet sitting in one of the booths, hunched over an orange-laminated table under the overly bright lights, she felt suddenly very old. Maybe it was just that she hadn't slept much since the case began. Or that she'd suffered enough physical punishments to feel rain in her bones.

But there was something else that set her apart from the young women with green hair, she decided. It wasn't chronological or even sartorial. This past week, she had risked more of herself—emotionally and physically—than she had in all the thirty years preceding. And it had changed her in a subtle way—opened her up. She would never see people in such black-and-white terms again. That was bad in the case of men she loved, like Frankel and Gallagher. But it also, strangely, made her able to see *herself* in a more forgiving light. She wasn't the only human being who was haunted on dark nights by the what-ifs and maybes of life.

Carter needed some kind of formal statement from Georgia, but he went easy on her, to his credit. So she turned over the computer disk and gave him a thumbnail sketch of what she believed had happened at the lab: that Michaels had demanded the incriminating disk, Frankel had refused and been shot—by Michaels or his men—then left to die in what was supposed to look like a botched robbery.

Georgia left out any mention of Frankel's complicity. Or Gallagher's. Walter had screwed up, unintentionally, it seemed. In the end, he had given his life to protect the only real piece of evidence they had against Michaels. As for Gallagher, she'd have to handle that one herself. She wanted to look into his eyes when she told him what she had found in his locker. She wanted to be sure.

Carter wrote everything down, then rubbed a hand across his face, which was as tired and sad as her own. "Michaels will try to bump off Finney, you know. If Finney's dead, then all the fires will probably die with him."

"I know," said Georgia. "Before Walter died, he told me Michaels had booby-trapped Finney's apartment—probably with that same idea in mind."

Carter jotted a note to himself. "The search warrant's supposed to come through soon. I'll make sure the NYPD's bomb people comb Finney's place before our guys."

"Finney's smart," said Georgia. "He won't go back there."

"We'll find him," Carter assured her.

Georgia gave him a dubious look. "I don't know. We're what, maybe twelve hours away from probably the biggest of his firebombs? And nobody has the faintest idea where he's put it . . ." She tried to choke down some coffee. "Have you been able to reach Eddie and Gene?"

Carter nodded. "Cambareri's asking for seconds on hospital food. Can you believe it?"

Georgia grinned. "Not too much wrong with him. He'll be sneaking doughnuts by tomorrow."

"Suarez and a couple of marshals at Manhattan Borough Command have already been dispatched to arrest Michaels at his duplex on Sutton Place," said Carter. "As for Mac, I can't reach him. No answer at his apartment."

"His daughter's seventh birthday party was this afternoon. Maybe he's still out on Long Island."

Carter grinned. "You know his schedule, huh?"

"Yeah, so?"

"You know *my* schedule?"

"Listen, I'm not . . . that doesn't make me . . ." Georgia blushed.

"Okey-dokey. Ten-four. Anything you say, Skeehan."

"Screw you."

"I'd return the compliment, but I think you're already spoken for."

She blushed some more and they both laughed, feeling good at being able to release some of the night's tension. Then her beeper went off, and the color drained from her skin.

"You want me to call that in for you?" Carter offered kindly. He could see she still needed to decompress. He dialed the number on his cell phone, then frowned and grunted into the receiver.

"What's wrong?" Georgia asked when he hung up.

"That was Suarez. Michaels wasn't home. His housekeeper said he got some kind of urgent call, then told her he was going to visit his wife at New York Hospital. That was about an hour ago, but he never showed up." Carter shook his head. "Wherever he is, though, I can tell you one thing: he's been a busy boy."

"How's that?"

Carter turned up the volume on his department radio. A static of voices filled the airwaves. Something about a 10-24—a car fire—under the FDR Drive at Sixtieth Street. Georgia heard the fire lieutenant at the scene mention a 10-45, code one.

"A car fire with a dead body inside—so?"

"Skeehan, that's not just any car. It belonged to Ralph Finney."

CHAPTER Forty-eight

Georgia and Carter could see the dense cloud of luminous, gray-white smoke a block away, drifting over a scattering of Seagrave pumpers and police cruisers. The flames had already been extinguished, but the smoke was biting. Georgia's eyes stung and her nose and mouth felt dipped in pepper as she stepped closer.

"You smell the gas?" she shouted to Carter over the whoosh of traffic above on the FDR Drive and the surge of water from the firehoses. "The fuel tank must've ruptured."

Great plumes of noxious smoke hovered in the air, opening and closing around the vehicle like a fog. Through the drifts, Georgia made out an older-model beige Ford van. It was surprisingly intact in the back compartment, yet hideously disfigured in the cab. The passenger doors were burned black, the windows shattered, and the seats razed in places to the coiled springs. Yet for all the charring, the vehicle's framework appeared structurally intact, a fact Carter pointed out now. The car had not been in a collision.

"Look," he said, shining his flashlight on the slick runoff from the hoses. A slimy, swirling sheen of oil ran through the cascades of water. "The gas tanks on these vans are toward the back. Yet the burning occurred in the cab. So it's not a gas-tank rupture."

"Then where'd the gas come from?"

"From somebody putting it there—in the passenger compartment. That's my guess," he said.

They flashed their badges at the battalion chief in charge, then found Suarez. He looked tired, rubbing the back of his neck and muttering to himself in Spanish, an unlit cigarette between his lips. He was probably dying for a smoke, but couldn't so close to the fire. He shook his head over the news about Walter Frankel. Though none of the men were close to him the way Georgia was, he was a fixture in the fire department. Not having Frankel around was as unsettling as if you told them that all the FDNY's trucks and pumpers were going to be painted phosphorescent yellow. The FDNY's rigs were *always* red. And Walter Frankel would *always* run the department lab.

Suarez told them Brennan and several Manhattan marshals were directing the manhunt for Michaels. Then he gestured to the burning vehicle's back license plate, which drifted in and out of the smoke.

"The plates went through the computer and came up as Finney's. The van matches the make and model of Finney's registered vehicle as well."

The smoke parted for an instant across the passenger compartment. On the upper rim of the steering wheel, a hand—gray-white and skeletal—flashed before them in all its grisly splendor. Suarez took the cigarette out of his mouth and gestured with it now. "We just don't know if that's Ralph Finney."

"What's a guy who lives in Manhattan doing with a van?" asked Georgia. "That had to be a bitch to park."

"Finney worked on the side as a painting contractor," explained Suarez.

Georgia snapped her fingers. "Those plastic spackling buckets—the ones we found at Howard Beach and Red Hook—that's probably how Finney gained entrance into all these buildings without being noticed. He pretended to be a painting contractor, then carried the fuel in the buckets."

"Marenko's running a check on area paint and hardware stores to see if Finney had an account with any of them," said Suarez. "Hell, as a contractor, he could walk into any hardware store, buy all the aluminum powder and ammonium nitrate fertilizer he wanted, and no one would bat an eyelash. All contractors buy in bulk."

Georgia looked again at the smoky wreckage. "So we know *what* Finney did and *how* he probably did it. Yet we're still no closer to finding out *where* he set tomorrow's fire."

The smoke began to dissipate. Four firefighters opened the driver's side of the vehicle and extricated the body. The blaze had badly charred both car and victim—but only in front. The victim's backside, which had been pressed against the seat, remained mostly intact, as did the fabric of the seat where he was sitting. Georgia gave a passing glance to the skeletal face, to the frozen, bluish eyes, like overcooked egg yolks, that seemed to follow her, to the teeth nearly glowing in their whiteness, untouched by the ferociousness of the flames. Even for Finney, it was a hellish way to die.

The firefighters rolled the body on its right side. The burning had already tightened muscle tissue so that it lay, legs bent, in a semifetal position. Georgia squatted down to look at the unburned backside now. She paled when she noticed the sweatpants—light blue with a pattern of orange and yellow palm trees. An unusual design—hard to find, and about a size too small for the wearer. She stood up, feeling woozy and lightheaded.

"What's wrong?" asked Carter.

"The pants."

"Tacky, ain't they?" joked Suarez. "My ex-mothers-in-law could dress better."

Georgia didn't laugh. Instead, her lower lip began to quiver.

"Those were *my* pants," she said softly. "They were in the laundry bag in the backseat of my car the night Finney assaulted me."

Carter and Suarez traded nervous glances. "Well, now we know it's Finney, all right," said Suarez.

Then Carter donned a pair of latex gloves and rolled the body a little farther onto its stomach. "And we know something else, too," he said, stepping back to let Georgia and Suarez take in the large, reddish-black hole in the chest cavity.

"He shot himself?" Georgia asked with amazement.

"Humdinger of a trick, I'd say," said Carter. "Shooting yourself in the back."

"Especially," said Suarez, "when he's got someone who'll be glad to do it for him."

CHAPTER *Forty-nine*

Sloane Michaels owned a beachfront house in Southampton, New York, a ski chalet in Aspen, Colorado, and a winter retreat in West Palm Beach, Florida. Georgia took the precautions of alerting authorities in all three locations. But in her bones, she sensed Michaels was still in New York. He'd never leave Amelia.

"Still, he hasn't shown up at the hospital or his office at Knickerbocker Plaza," Carter reminded her. "He's probably got some rich friend who's hiding him until he can find a good lawyer."

"I don't think so," Georgia argued. "I know Michaels a little. I don't sense that any of those rich people he hangs out with are his friends. And I think he'd be afraid that his drug-dealing clients would rather shoot him than save him."

"So, where do you think a man worth eight hundred million might escape to?"

My freedom . . . my escape . . .

"A place no one who doesn't know him would think to look."

THE KNICKERBOCKER PLAZA'S night manager was all of twenty-six, yet he possessed the haughtiness of a dowager. He regarded Georgia's bruised face and black leather jacket sourly as she and Carter flashed him their shields and asked to be let into Sloane Michaels's office.

I've already accommodated the NYPD." He sniffed. "I can't have people traipsing willy-nilly through his office without a search warrant."

"It's not the office I'm interested in," Georgia shot back.

The manager went to open his mouth, but Carter put a hand on his jacket sleeve. "Son, I think it's best if you just let us in." The "son" was deliberate, Georgia knew. The manager might take an attitude with a disheveled white woman from Queens, but he would be reluctant to give offense to a black man in a suit who was old enough to be his father.

"Don't touch anything," the manager warned, wagging a finger at them as he led them up the mezzanine stairs. With an electronic key card, he unlocked the suite's door. The reception area's carpet had the thick, brushy look of a recent vacuuming, and the Queen Anne chairs smelled of lemon oil from a fresh waxing. Georgia and Carter each put on a pair of latex gloves and followed the wainscoted walls to the elevator. Georgia pushed the down button.

"Where's this lead?" asked Carter.

"To Michaels's private garage."

Carter grinned. "He show you his etchings down there or something?"

Georgia made a face. "Every firefighter's got a one-track mind."

A smoldering smell, like rubber tires, greeted them as the elevator doors opened. Georgia sniffed at her clothes and noticed Carter doing the same. They had been in a lot of smoke at the car fire. It wouldn't be the first time they came away smelling like pork chops. But then Georgia noticed the night manager wrinkling his nose as well.

In the middle of the lounge, a beige linen couch sat across from a television. Something brown had dripped along the couch's armrest. Carter scratched at the stain through the sheer covering of his latex gloves.

"Blood," he said, a puzzled look on his face. He turned the seat cushion over. On the other side, all that was left of the fabric was a jagged edge of brittle black cloth along the perimeter. The cushion had been burned.

Georgia walked into the garage and fumbled around for a light switch.

"Do me a favor, Randy? Find the light for this room, will you?"

"Affirmative," he said. "I think it's back here, in the lounge."

Georgia pulled her flashlight off her duty holster now and shone it across Michaels's tool bench and equipment, trying to locate his bikes. He had four of them, she recalled. A Ducati racer, a vintage Vincent Blackshadow, an Italian Bimoto, and the monster Harley-Davidson Ultra Classic. If one was missing, Georgia would be able to call in the description to police and track Michaels down.

Her heart sank as she counted all four sets of chrome. She went to lower her flashlight when a metallic red motorcycle helmet caught her eye. It was resting on the cement of the garage floor, just behind the rear wheel of the Ultra Classic.

Georgia took a step forward, noticing for the first time that there was something inside the helmet, something dark but glistening. She shined her beam on it and stepped closer. The burning smell intensified. She recognized it now. Not just a burning smell—a *human* burning smell. Like rotten meat. Her stomach roiled. A buzz reverberated overhead as the fluorescent lights kicked on. Georgia looked up while they flickered to life, then, with the full force of their wattage on the room, she looked back at the helmet.

The face inside was hideous. The skin was blackened and swollen, the nose and lips burned away. The eyes were just slits of brown-red blood. But what really scared her was what she found as she stepped closer to get a full glimpse of the rest of the body. It wasn't burned—at least not like the face. The horror was more personal than that.

The victim was wearing Georgia's sweatshirt.

It was the navy blue one, with an FDNY insignia on the left shoulder and the number of her old engine company stitched on the right front pocket. *Her* sweatshirt—from the laundry bag in *her* car. People were dying hideous deaths in her clothes.

Carter came up behind her now and got a good look at the body. "Holy mackerel," he said slowly, drawing out each syllable. "You think this guy is Michaels?"

Georgia nodded as if in a trance. "Finney did this to him."

"Finney's dead, girl."

"No, he's not. The sweatshirt? It's mine. Finney stole my laundry that night he attacked me in my car. He's the only one who could've put it here. It's a terrible, terrible joke, Randy—don't you see? A joke on me."

Carter put a hand on her shoulder to steady her. "Why don't you get some air?" he said gently, helping her to the door of the lounge. "I'll call Suarez, tell him we've got another body, and see what he's coming up with."

Georgia sat on the steps by the front entrance of the Knickerbocker Plaza, across from Central Park, breathing in the midnight air as if it had the power to wash thoughts from her head. Above the dense, dark thickets of trees in the park, the sky seemed nearly colorless, the streetlights having sucked up the darkness the way a child sucks the flavoring from a snow cone. Georgia rubbed her neck, feeling tired and distracted. A headache throbbed at the base of her skull. She thought suddenly of Richie. It seemed like years since she'd seen him, rather than just hours. She felt heartsore with longing.

A couple of police cruisers screeched to a halt at the curb, along with a van from the medical examiner's office. Georgia turned to see Carter racing toward them, out of breath. He briefed the cops and the ME's assistant, then shot Georgia a panicked look.

"What's wrong?" she asked.

"I just spoke to Suarez," he sputtered, trying to catch his breath. "Marenko's gone."

"Gone where?"

"The search warrant for Finney's apartment? It came through."

"Now?" Georgia asked, alarmed.

"Brennan convinced the judge it was an emergency, what with Finney on the loose. When Mac called Brennan for an update on the case, the chief asked him to start the search himself."

"But Michaels has that place rigged to blow—"

"I know," said Carter. "I just told Suarez and Chief Brennan. They called Mac's brother's place, but he'd already gone. Our frequency doesn't work on Long Island. Dispatch is gonna keep trying to reach him, but nobody can say for sure if he'll pick up."

"But surely the police have Finney's place under surveillance in case he shows up—"

"The patrol car had another emergency. They're dispatching a backup, but it may come too late to stop Mac from going inside."

Georgia rubbed the ache between her shoulders. A series of blunders and bad luck. That's how stuff happens. It's never just one thing. One thing, you can work around.

"How fast can we get to Finney's place?"

Carter jingled his car keys. "We'll find out."

CHAPTER Fifty

Marenko wasn't answering his handie-talkie. Dispatch tried him. Suarez tried him and Georgia tried him. He had probably turned it off in Long Island where he wouldn't have been able to get reception anyway. It was possible he had never turned it back on.

Carter floored the accelerator north on Riverside Drive. "Did you radio for an engine to meet us?" he asked.

"Engine Eighty-four's closest to Finney's place, but they're out on another emergency," she said. "Engine Sixty-seven's coming. Forty-five truck has also been dispatched." Georgia noted the street sign as it flashed by. They were already up to 137th Street themselves and Mac still wasn't answering. It would be a toss-up who got to 158th Street first.

"Hope they drive better than you," she said as Carter snaked through car lanes and squeezed past traffic at a red light. "I don't even like the guy, and here I am about to get killed for him."

"So you *didn't* sleep with him?"

"I plead the Fifth."

Carter smiled. "I won. I won."

"What are you talking about?"

"Suarez said Mac'd never be able to talk you out of your pants. I bet him he was wrong."

"Glad my private life is so enriching. How much you stand to win?"

"Twenty."

"That's all?"

"Hey, it wasn't like we were betting on Mother Teresa . . ."

"I wouldn't go for double or nothing. It's not going to happen again."

"Not if we don't get up to Finney's place fast, it ain't."

Carter took a sharp right and tore down 158th Street. Marenko's seven-year-old silver Honda Accord, a portable red flashing light stuck to the roof, was double-parked in front of a graffiti-covered tenement. Smoke was seeping out a sixth-floor window.

"Jesus, Randy. We're too late. Mac's inside." Georgia jumped out of the car. "I'm going in. Give me a radio."

"I'll come with you," said Carter.

Georgia ran ahead into the building's vestibule. She slapped indiscriminately at doorbells until someone finally buzzed her through the entrance.

Carter followed her down the shabby, dimly lit hallway. They pounded on doors yelling "Fire" in English and Spanish. Then they bounded up the stairs, repeating the procedure on each story. Locks disengaged and bleary-eyed faces popped out. It was, after all, one o'clock on a Monday morning. Few of the residents made any attempt to leave.

"Fire. Get out," Georgia pleaded with them. Most moved slowly or not at all.

"Y'all get your *butts* on the street—now," Carter, the former drill sergeant, roared. "C'mon." He clapped his hands together. "Move, move, move." His manner had the desired effect. People started heading for the stairs. Georgia grinned.

"I'll bet you were a *load* of fun in the marines."

"A real doozy."

By the fifth floor, a light veil of smoke filtered through the hall. Carter was winded. His face was ashen as he leaned on his thighs, head down, straining for air. At the apartment below the fire, a large cardboard Easter bunny had been taped to the front door. Georgia roused a young heavyset Dominican woman and her three boys from the apartment and led them over to Carter. The littlest one, with two front teeth missing, was holding so tight to his mother's fleshy waist that Georgia thought he was probably hurting her. He seemed deathly afraid, not of the fire, but of being separated. Perhaps, Georgia thought idly, a fire wasn't the worst of the traumas he'd known.

"Randy, take them to the street."

"What about you?" he wheezed.

"I'm gonna get Mac."

He frowned. "Skeehan, you can't. You haven't got any gear. The place could explode."

"I have to do this."

"For Mac?"

"For me. Now go." Brusquely, she pushed Carter and the family toward the stairs, then went back into the woman's apartment. The kitchen window by the fire escape was painted shut. The sash cracked and gave way when Georgia threw herself against it. Finney's window—directly above appeared closed and locked. She'd have to break it open.

She searched the kitchen for something heavy. Under the sink she found a cast-iron skillet and swung it to test its weight. It would have to do.

The fire escape swayed as Georgia stepped onto it. Flecks of peeling paint floated to the pavement forty feet below like snow flurries. Engine 67 was just maneuvering into position below. The company would bring in a hose line, but rescues were generally handled by ladder companies. And Ladder 45 was probably another minute or two away—a lifetime, in terms of a fire. She had to get in. She swung the cast iron skillet at the window—

And it bounded off. *Thermopane glass. Double-insulated.* She could swing forever and never break it. The interior would be tight, well insulated—and deadly hot.

She put down the skillet and pushed at the window sash. It opened easily. *Great going,* Georgia said to herself. *Next you'll be chopping down doors instead of just trying the knobs.*

A burst of heat hit her as the window opened. Smoke poured out, stinging her eyes and making her cough. She called to Marenko but got no answer. Gulping a lungful of air, she dropped into the room and sank onto her belly.

At floor level, the air was hot but manageable—about 100 degrees. But as Georgia lifted her hand, she felt a stinging sensation. It was probably 300 degrees Fahrenheit just inches above her head. If she stood, she would probably encounter temperatures of about 1,200 degrees. No one could survive that.

She had been able to see a little when she first dropped into the room. But a fine shroud of black smoke now choked off all light. *If I leave this wall, I'll never find my way back to the window.* So she kept one foot on the wall and felt the floor in front of her.

"Mac," she cried out, her voice raspy from smoke and fits of coughing. Adrenaline pumped through her veins like a broken water main. Her eyes stung as if shot with pepper spray, and a thick coating of oil clung to her skin like nicotine. Light-headed and dizzy, she was on the verge of collapse herself.

Suddenly, her fingers brushed against the stubble of a man's face, the sinewy muscles of a shoulder. He was lying stomach-down on the floor—probably crawling to the window before he lost consciousness. She couldn't see him, but she knew. She had felt his body before.

"Hold on, Mac."

To drag him to safety, she had to crawl another three feet forward and grab his chest. But that meant taking her foot off the wall. It was her only trail out of this maze. If she couldn't move him, if she couldn't find the window again, they'd both die. For all she knew, he was dead already.

"Hang on, you bastard," she choked out, clawing her way forward. Her head throbbed from the smoke. Her lips began to blister. She grabbed his unconscious body under the armpits and dragged him in the direction of what she thought was the window. Because she had to stay low to the floor herself, it was an arduously slow, painful task. Her foot touched a wall and she let go of Marenko with one hand to check above the rough, pockmarked plaster for the window.

But there was none. She had lost her bearings.

Her hands began to shake, her lungs to hyperventilate. She could feel herself about to black out. She had to choose a direction—more to the right or more to the left? She didn't know, but something told her to move to her right. Her hand reached up weakly and encountered a burst of cooler air. *The window!* She got behind Marenko and began to shove him over the sill and onto the fire escape.

She didn't have to push far.

"We got you," a voice called out beyond the smoke, yanking Marenko from her arms. Then two strong arms in a turnout coat reached in and grabbed Georgia.

The fresh air on the fire escape was the sweetest sensation she had ever experienced. She gave in to it now, gasping in great lungfuls, letting herself be carried down the escape to an ambulance below.

"Anybody else in there?" a firefighter asked her. She couldn't talk. Her throat felt rubbed with sandpaper. Fire department EMTs placed her on a stretcher and put a valve mask over her face. She kept trying to get up to find Marenko.

"He's gonna be okay," one of the EMTs said, easing her down. "You saved his life."

The man's words were punctuated by a thunderous roar. Georgia lifted her head in time to see the sixth floor's Thermopane windows finally giving way as a fireball burst through them. Georgia watched in a daze as the battalion chief pulled his men back and ordered more trucks and ladders into position.

That could've been Mac. That could've been me.

She took the mask off her face and forced herself to her feet when the EMTs were busy filling out forms. Marenko was a few feet away, in another ambulance. She didn't know if he'd still be unconscious. He had a valve mask on his face, but his eyes were open.

"Mac?"

He offered a small, crooked, parched-lip smile as he tried to sit up, then fell back against the stretcher.

She brushed a gentle hand through his soot-choked hair. "You're gonna be okay," she said, only half sure of her words. She knelt beside him and put her head on his chest.

He pulled the mask off his face.

"I was wrong," he said hoarsely. "You're a hell of a firefighter."

She smiled. "Yeah, right. But if I were a man—"

"Then I wouldn't do this," he said, reaching up a soot-blackened hand and bringing her face toward his. Oblivious to the chaos and commotion around them, they touched lips.

An EMT intervened, clearing her throat. "You both need to go to the hospital," she said.

"I'm fine," Georgia insisted, waving the woman away.

"You're not, Scout," Marenko croaked out.

"Sure I am." She climbed down from the ambulance and took two steps before the pavement began to spin. It rose up to greet her with all the softness of a baseball being lobbed at her head.

CHAPTER *Fifty-one*

Georgia awoke to the cold steel of a hospital bed rail pressed against her skin and sheets as crisp and starchy as canvas. Voices echoed down a waxed-floor hallway. She sat up, wondering what time it was. The room spun, so she sank back down and forced herself to look at her hands and arms. The knuckles were bruised and reddened with first-degree burns. Her blue and white hospital gown was wrinkled and smelled of sour sweat and smoke. She ached everywhere—her arms, neck, shoulders. But the biggest ache by far was inside. She remembered with a piercing stab that Walter Frankel was really and truly dead.

The flashing lights and sirens in the night had given everything a cinematic, fantastical air. Adrenaline had muted the pain, dulled the fear and disorientation. But inside this hospital room, with its soothing light blue walls, monitors, and badly painted florals, the night came back to her in still-life snapshots of memory and sensation. Walter was gone. She'd had no chance to grieve before, but she felt heavy with the burden now.

A sudden, overwhelming urge to retch seized her. She raced to the bathroom, barely making it in time to empty her insides into the bowl. Then she crouched in a corner, without even the strength to stand, and started to sob.

That's where the nurse found her. She was a short, chunky woman with a Filipino accent and a motherly air, and she helped Georgia back into bed, checking her blood pressure and temperature. She reinserted an IV into a vein.

"Where am I?" Georgia croaked.

"New York Hospital–Cornell Medical Center."

"What day is it?"

"Monday. You were admitted around two this morning. It's nine-thirty now. We tried to notify your family, but there was no answer at your home."

Home! Georgia had nearly forgotten. Her mother and Richie often visited her aunt's house when she worked a night tour. By now, they'd be on their way to the memorial service—with Gallagher. She should have said something to her mother last night. But what could she have said that would have made any sense?

"When you're up to it," said the nurse, "some fire marshals are here to see you." Georgia noticed a shuffling in the hall now. Carter and Suarez peeked around the corner, looking as awkward and nervous as school-boys killing time in the principal's office. Carter was carrying a small bouquet of drooping red carnations. Suarez held two chocolate Easter bunnies wrapped in gold foil. One of them, Georgia noticed, had no head.

"Hey guys," she said, feeling suddenly self-conscious in her hospital gown.

"We brought you some presents," Carter said, placing the wilting flowers on a side table by the phone.

"Yeah," said Suarez. "Mine's the rabbit *with* the head. Cambareri's still recuperating, but he wanted to send you something, too. Only he couldn't contain himself."

"Let me guess." Georgia grinned. "Gene ate the head."

"Says he didn't have enough dinner last night." Suarez laughed.

"Can't be much wrong with *him* . . . how's Mac?"

"He's here at the hospital," said Suarez. "Doing fine. Cussing up a storm. He's got some second-degrees on his arms and back and they're treating him for smoke inhalation, but he'll be out in a day or two. The jerk even arm-twisted me into bringing him some clothes—like he's going somewhere."

That sounds like Mac, all right, thought Georgia with satisfaction. He must be doing okay. She asked for an update on the investigation.

"The bodies have been ID'd," Carter told her. "That *was* Sloane Michaels in the Knick's garage, but you were right about the body in the van. It wasn't Finney. The vic was a street mutt, just released from Bellevue."

"So Finney's alive."

Carter and Suarez exchanged nervous looks.

"What?" asked Georgia.

"The NYPD combed Michaels's murder scene last night," Carter explained. "They found this under the body." He handed her a letter.

DEAR GEORGIA:

And a mighty Angel took up a great millstone, and cast it into the sea, saying thus, with violence shall that great city of Babylon be thrown down, and shall be found no more at all.

—THE FOURTH ANGEL

"How about we get some police protection on your room?" Suarez offered.

"Yeah, okay." Georgia sighed. "Not that it'll make any difference. If Finney could give you the slip at Manhattan Detention, he can surely outwit some rookie assigned to protect *me*." She stared out the window at the sliver of bright blue morning sky and cursed. "Why the letter? He's free. We've got no leads on his bomb. He's already *won*."

Carter pulled out a black, vinyl-bound Bible from the inside pocket of his jacket and flexed it like a deck of cards, fluttering the gilt-edged pages in quick succession. "I swiped this from the chapel downstairs, to look up the scripture in his letter. It's from Revelation again. Chapter eighteen, verse twenty-one. Other than that, it's sort of a dead end."

"Dead end . . . great," said Georgia. "What are we gonna say to the people who burn today? To their families? 'We're sorry, but we were too *dumb* to know what else to do'?"

"Now hold on, girl." Carter frowned. "We're still working this thing."

"That's right, Skeehan," Suarez added. "Maybe we can't stop the fire, but Finney won't get far. We'll catch him."

"What am I supposed to do in the meantime?"

Carter tossed the Bible on her bed. "Pray."

THE MINUTES TICKED by on the big black arms of the clock just outside Georgia's door. It was nine-fifty-six. Idly, she thumbed the Bible Carter had swiped. She could see why Finney would love Revelation, with all its talk of fiery demons and damnation. She came across the first set of lines he'd sent the department back in December:

> *And the fourth angel poured out his vial upon the sun; and power was given unto him to scorch men with fire.*

Georgia squinted at the Roman numerals beside the passage, wishing for once she'd paid more attention in school to such things. XVI— *sixteen.* The selection was from chapter sixteen, verse eight. *16:8.*

She turned over a corner of the page to mark her place, then leafed through more verses until she found his second quote:

> *And the voice which I heard from heaven spake unto me again, and said, go and take the little book which is open in the hand of the angel which standeth upon the sea and upon the earth.*
> Chapter ten, verse eight

Her eyes blurred from the tiny print and repetitive lines. It took a while to locate the passage from his third letter:

> *The second woe is past; and behold, the third woe cometh quickly.*
> Chapter eleven, verse fourteen

He'd sent her that line about eyes being a flame of fire, too. Chapter nineteen, verse twelve:

> *His eyes were as a flame of fire, and on his head were many crowns, and he had a name written, that no man knew, but he himself.*

Georgia sat up straight. She thumbed the dog-eared pages again. Her hands grew sweaty with excitement. Her pulse began to race. She fumbled for her bag in a drawer of the side table. Inside a zippered pouch, crumpled but undamaged, was that list on yellow legal paper she had pulled together several days ago, summarizing the fires.

With a pen from one of her medical charts, she scribbled the chapter and verse numbers, in order, on a margin of the list: *16:8, 10:8, 11:14, 19:12.*

She stared at the numerals, then at the alarm box numbers of each HTA fire. A slow smile spread across her cracked lips.

Alarm box 1608 was Finney's first HTA, at the furniture warehouse in Manhattan. Box 1008 was that vacant in Brooklyn. Box 1114, the vacant in the Bronx. And Box 1912 was the row-frame apartment house in Queens.

All this time, she had thought it was the verses that held significance. But it was the *numbers* that mattered—numbers a dispatcher like Finney would know in his sleep.

But what about Spring Street—Box 2310? Georgia flipped to the end of Revelation. It stopped after twenty-two chapters. This couldn't have been his fire.

So that means . . . Georgia's fingers trembled as she tried to locate Finney's latest passage. Chapter eighteen, verse twenty-one . . . *Alarm box 1821?*

Could it be that simple? Was there an HTA device at a building near alarm box 1821? It was ten-oh-seven. The letter promised a fire at eleven A.M. She had fifty-three minutes. She reached for her phone to dial 911, but it rang before she could pick it up. The familiar nasal voice wiped the smile from her lips.

"Did you get my letter?"

Georgia gripped the cold steel rails of her bed, willing herself to be calm.

"Yes, I got it. And I know about this morning's fire . . . at Box eighteen-twenty-one."

Silence. She heard him breathing hard. *I'm right,* she realized with a jolt.

"And where *is* Box eighteen-twenty-one?"

"I'll know when I call your old pals in Manhattan dispatch and ask them to order an emergency evacuation."

"Go ahead." He laughed. "Call in the alarm. By the time you convince those jerk-offs to believe you, I'll be in a position to blow up half *this* fucking building."

The receiver fell from Georgia's hand. It clanged against the steel bed rails. She barely noticed. *He's in the hospital.*

CHAPTER Fifty-two

Save yourself, save the hospital, save the people at *Box 1821.* Her priorities had to run in that order, or no one would survive.

Georgia couldn't call security. Finney's firebombs had been capable of leveling whole buildings. She couldn't chance his being strapped with HTA in a wing full of infirm patients and highly flammable oxygen. Luring him away from the hospital was the safest course. But in her flimsy gown and bare feet, she wouldn't get far. And her own clothes were ruined. She gritted her teeth and yanked the IV out of her arm. Blood oozed from the needle-mark. *Where can I find a bandage?* Then she remembered Richie's Pokémon stickers in her handbag. He had gotten them the other night at Burger King. She plastered a smiling Pikachu to the wound. If Finney didn't get her, the germs probably would.

She slipped out of her room and scanned the ninth-floor corridor, searching for a room with a heavily sedated patient. She found one three doors down.

A closet beside the sedated man's bed revealed a pair of brown trousers, a white short-sleeve undershirt, a blue-and-brown-plaid flannel shirt, and a Mets baseball cap. *Sorry, mister,* she thought as she changed into the man's clothes, laced up his oversize Keds sneakers, and headed for the fire stairs.

A clock in the hall said ten-twenty-three. The ninth-floor fire-exit door squeaked as Georgia opened it. She stepped onto the landing and peered down the vertical shaft of concrete, steel, and cinder block. Sounds echoed through the stairwell, washing over her in a distorted, dreamlike manner. A dropped coin somewhere below had the clarity of a Buddhist chime. Fragments of voices ebbed and flowed, as if borne on the wind. The thud of Georgia's sneakers down the steps mimicked a heartbeat. She became dizzy, fighting the urge to pitch forward. Her stomach sloshed about with queasy uncertainty.

By the sixth floor, she felt too weak to continue. *Best take the elevator from here,* she told herself. *Less physical exertion. More safety in numbers.* She tried the sixth-floor fire door. It was stuck. A small wire-mesh window was cut into the metal. She peeked through it. A face shot back at her—a man with horn-rimmed glasses and jet-black hair. Their eyes locked for one surprised moment, the man's glasses magnifying the chill in those pale blue irises. Then his lips pressed together with mocking certainty. Georgia recoiled. She'd know that face anywhere.

He pushed hard on the door, sending Georgia reeling to the opposite wall. She stumbled down a half flight of stairs, so weak that only the rough porousness of the cinder block kept her from collapsing.

"You think you can outrun *me*?" Ralph Finney laughed. "You couldn't do it ten years ago. You sure as hell can't do it *now.*"

Trembling and wheezing, Georgia scrambled into the fifth-floor hallway and flattened herself against a wall. Her lungs burned as she felt her way forward, keeping an eye on the door. A cool metal cylinder twanged against her outstretched hand: a familiar sound.

Now, her reflexes shouted as Finney opened the hallway door. Sweat poured off her body. Her heart pounded wildly in her chest. She peeled away from the wall as Finney lunged for her. Then she grabbed the CO_2 fire extinguisher, pulled the metal pin, and aimed the hose. A white cloud of CO_2 blasted Finney's face. He retreated into the stairwell, clawing at his stinging eyes.

"You're dead, bitch," he screamed.

Georgia put the canister down and raced toward a bank of elevators down the hall. It wasn't until she was nearly upon them that she noticed something different about this wing. A mobile of black and white ponies hung above a nurses' station. The wall behind a lounge sported a colorfully painted clown and blocks. Tiny cries floated from a patient's door, which was taped all over with pink balloons.

She was in the maternity ward. Worse, Georgia realized, as she neared a large glass viewing window filled with palm-size infants, oxygen tanks, and monitors, she was in the *premature* nursery.

Finney was half a corridor behind her now. His eyes were red-rimmed from CO_2. His shoe-polish hair was damp. His bulked-out jacket was pulled loosely around him.

Goose bumps puckered along Georgia's bruised arms. Finney was in the perfect place to launch an HTA device. She had to do something fast.

Then she noticed it, just to the side of the nursery viewing window. A red metal box, chest high. *A fire alarm!*

Georgia pulled the handle. A sharp clanging echoed through the wing. Finney started as hospital staff, patients, and visitors poured into the hall. Maintenance men appeared. Nervous parents pressed anxiously against the nursery windows. Finney was jostled by the crowd, his moment gone. There was too much commotion to set a bomb or slip away.

The babies are safe, Georgia decided. The false alarm would bring fire trucks. The trucks would be a ready connection to Manhattan dispatch—and the location of Box 1821.

A beefy security guard grabbed Georgia's wrist.

"That's her," yelled a nurse, gesturing over the crowd. "That's the crazy woman who pulled the alarm! I saw her."

The guard spun Georgia around and began to frisk her.

"I'm a fire marshal," she shouted over the alarm. "If you'll just give me a minute—"

"Yeah, yeah," said the guard, patting her down. "You can tell it all to my boss the easy way"—he reached for a set of handcuffs on his belt—"or the hard."

"But *I'm* not the one you want . . ." Georgia lifted herself up on tiptoe and peered over the guard's shoulder at the throngs of patients and staff milling about the hallway. Finney had disappeared. It suddenly dawned on her how off balance she looked in her baggy brown trousers and flannel shirt with her bruised face and tangled hair, and how useless any explanation would be. As the guard fumbled to unhitch his cuffs, she bolted. Painful spasms ripped into Georgia's gut. Her windpipe constricted to a pinhole, making every breath feel like a punch to her solar plexus. She couldn't keep this up. She had to find a way out.

Beyond a supply room, an unmarked door led to a flight of stairs. Georgia stumbled down them now. The guard, it seemed, was in pursuit. She could hear the metal clang of the door above her and footsteps thudding overhead.

The stairs ended in a windowless room of gray-painted cement. The sub-basement. High-pressure steam boilers rose twenty feet in the air, and generators hummed like giant washing machines. At the far end of the room, beyond dozens of color-coded pipes, catwalks, gauges, and dials, a glowing red exit sign loomed. Georgia held her side and raced toward it.

A metallic click from behind stopped her in midstride. It resonated over the white noise of the generators. Georgia froze, gasping for breath. Hospital security guards don't carry guns.

"Turn around, bitch."

She turned. Ralph Finney stood before her with a nine-millimeter semiautomatic aimed at her head. The dyed-black hair and glasses accentuated something odd in his face that had been easier to cover up before.

He stepped closer. "You've always been afraid of guns, haven't you?" he asked with that deadly nonchalance he could slip into on a moment's notice. "Maybe you knew you'd die this way." He shook his head. "Funny, I'd planned to burn you. But with all the flammable stuff down here, *I* can't take that chance."

Georgia didn't answer. All she could feel now were sensations—the rumble of the boiler behind her, the whir of the generators, the stark glare of the overhead fluorescents, the ceaseless noise and heat.

Finney grinned. "Too bad, really. You'd have burned pretty as a matchstick. Sort of like, oh . . . I don't know . . . Petie Ferraro? How'd it feel, Georgia, to watch him fall into that fiery hole? To know you crapped out on a brother?"

She gritted her teeth. "Leave his memory out of this."

"Why? Can't face the truth? That you fucked up someone's life? Like you did mine?"

"I never did anything to you."

"You're the reason I'm not a firefighter. . . . You're the *reason!*" he screamed, his voice reverberating through the cavernous interior. "You took something from me . . . ten long years ago . . . and you can't give it back." He aimed the gun close-range at her forehead. "So now I'm gonna repay the favor."

She heard the safety click. The sound stripped her of everything but reflex and impulse. Instinctively, she ducked and rolled away as he fired. Above her head, a high-pitched whistle resonated, followed by a hissing. And then Finney hit the floor, screaming as a white cloud of vapor enveloped him. When it cleared, his skin was as pink as a slice of boiled ham. Blisters as big as jellyfish filled with fluid on his neck and face. Alarms rang. Buzzers sounded. Overhead, an invisible stream of deadly high-pressure steam continued to whistle from a small bullet hole that had pierced a pipe.

Georgia ducked under the invisible jet of steam and dragged Finney away, but already, his body was going into convulsions and shock. He jerked violently and gasped for breath. She tilted his chin up to do CPR. His eyes remained steady, his pupils dilated to the size of dimes. He was already starting to swell. He wasn't screaming anymore. He was whimpering. A sound like a cat in heat. It made her skin crawl.

An engine company lumbered into the boiler room now—drawn, no doubt, by Georgia's false alarm. One firefighter went to find the engineer to turn off the steam pipe and stop the deadly spray. The others began first aid on Finney. Georgia stepped back to let the men take over.

"What happened?" the captain asked, eyeing her suspiciously. Georgia looked at the clock on the wall. Ten-thirty-three. She had twenty-seven minutes.

"I'm a fire marshal, Captain. My name's Georgia Skeehan. Please, I need to use your radio. There's going to be a big fire at eleven A.M. A lot of lives could be at stake."

He regarded her warily. "You have ID?"

"No . . ."

"Look, lady," he explained. "The police are going to have to sort this out. Why don't you just stand over there."

Finney was convulsing. Georgia backed up to the exit door. When the captain turned away to direct the rescue effort, she ran for the lobby.

CHAPTER Fifty-three

The uniforms were everywhere by the time Georgia made it into the lobby of New York Hospital. She searched for a familiar face among the firefighters, but with their helmets on, they all looked the same.

And then she saw him. He was perched awkwardly on a chair, dressed in gray sweatpants and a fire department sweatshirt, talking to a couple of the arriving firefighters. His face was red and slightly swollen, with a shadow of black stubble across it. He winced as he shifted in his seat. She never thought she'd be so happy to see Mac Marenko.

He stood tentatively as she approached him, towering above her as he took in her baggy clothes and tangled hair beneath a baseball cap. It took him a moment to realize who she was.

"Scout?"

"I pulled the alarm . . ."

"You *what*?" He led her by the elbow away from the other firefighters.

"I know where Finney's fire's gonna be. At alarm box eighteen-twenty-one. At eleven A.M. I just don't know where that is. Please, Mac, help me."

He frowned at her. "How can you be sure?"

"There's no time to explain. You've just got to trust me."

Marenko licked his blistered lips, then wiped them with the back of his hand, still bandaged from where an IV had been inserted. He squinted at an engine double-parked outside the revolving doors.

"C'mon," he said.

"Where?"

"Just follow my lead."

A jowly firefighter with thinning gray hair stood beside the rig, smoking a cigarette.

"Johnny?" Marenko called out.

"Mac?" said the man, stamping out his cigarette and breaking into a smile. "Jesus Christ, I heard what happened. How ya doin'?"

"Okay. Listen, this is Marshal Skeehan. She needs to use your rig's radio."

The big man took in Georgia's clothes and furrowed his brow. Then he looked at Marenko and shrugged. "Yeah, okay, Mac. Whatever you say."

"Thank you," Georgia said to Mac and the chauffeur. Then she climbed into the rig and depressed the button on the radio.

"This is Fire Marshal Georgia Skeehan. Request mixer off." "Mixer off" was a fire department term that meant the message would not be broadcast over the airwaves.

"Mixer off. Go ahead," said the dispatcher.

"I have information about a possible firebomb threat at box alarm one-eight-two-one. Can you give me a location on one-eight-two-one, K." The "K" meant the transmission was over. Her voice sounded smooth and in control—totally in contrast to what she was feeling. The radio had a way of doing that.

"Affirmative. Will run that check. K." She heard the dispatcher tap in the numbers on his computer, then return to the line. "Box number one-eight-two-one is in Manhattan. Eighteen blocks due south of your current location. Five blocks due west. Corner of Fifty-first Street and Fifth Avenue."

A lead weight settled on Georgia's chest. She couldn't speak. She couldn't breathe. The blood drained from her extremities, replaced by a pins-and-needles sensation. Her hands refused to work, though strangely, all pain from her injuries ceased to exist. Every neuron was focused on that address. On the people inside. On her mother and son.

Mac, sensing something awful, hoisted himself into the rig.

"What's wrong?"

The dispatcher's voice crackled over the radio: "Box alarm one-eight-two-one is located at the northwest corner of Saint Patrick's Cathedral."

Saint Patrick's Cathedral. Georgia couldn't believe it, even after the dispatcher said the words, then gave the time: 10:43 A.M. She closed her eyes and pictured the cathedral. The annual Fire Department Memorial Mass was always a standing-room-only affair. Twenty-four hundred people would already be jammed into the pews of the white marble landmark—firefighters, widows, children, all the department brass, and, at some point, though probably not yet, even the mayor. It was the perfect event for a man hell-bent on revenge against the FDNY.

Georgia's voice cracked from the strain. "Call it in to Battalion Eight. Advise Battalion Eight to evacuate Saint Patrick's immediately."

"On whose orders?"

"On my orders. I'll take charges if I'm wrong."

"I need higher clearance."

Marenko grabbed the speaker from Georgia's hands. "Jesus Christ! You goddamned prick! Pretend she's the bomber, okay? She's telling you an HTA firebomb's gonna take the fuckin' roof off Saint Pat's at eleven. Do you wanna take that chance or not?"

The dispatcher hesitated. "This is on record."

"Fine," said Marenko. "Bronze it on my ass if you'd like. Just get those people out of there." He clicked off the radio.

Georgia rubbed her palms together, trying to fight the panic thrumming through every organ in her body. She was drowning in it—the what-ifs, the why-didn't-I's. Finney's plan seemed so clear to her now. Why hadn't she seen it before?

"I've got to get down there," she mumbled, listening to the calm, expressionless voices over the airwaves. In seventeen minutes, the service would begin. A wall of sound, rich and resonant, would spring forth from the organ and vibrate through the clerestory. No one would hear the first pop and crackle of flames until it was too late.

"Okay. Just relax," Marenko told her, rubbing a hand tenderly across her cheek. "I know you're worried about your mom and Richie. Maybe we can get the rig to take us down."

"It'll take ten minutes to get clearance. And another ten to go two feet in midtown traffic. By then, everybody could be dead."

He looked up at the ceiling of the cab as if he were trying to sort through the possibilities. Then he exhaled and cursed. "Scoot over," he commanded.

"Why?"

"Could you just not question me for once?"

Georgia obeyed as Marenko released the emergency brake and turned over the engine. The rumble of the diesel and the hiss and pop of the air brakes startled her. Johnny, the chauffeur, took a moment to process what was happening. He did a double take as Marenko slammed the cab door shut.

"Hey, what the—?"

"I owe you one, brother," Marenko called to him. "I'll take the heat." Johnny banged on the side and cursed as the truck inched past him onto First Avenue. Traffic was at a crawl, but they had the advantage of being in an emergency vehicle. Marenko pulled into the fire lane, then asked Georgia to flip the lights and sirens. He had to point out where they were. The burns on his back made him grit his teeth when he lifted his arm.

"I was in the department's chauffeur school when I got made a marshal," Marenko explained. "Even with my injuries, I figure I can still drive this baby."

"Mac, this is crazy. You could get fired for this."

"Hey, I owe you my life. Least I can do is let you screw it up. Besides, even if that dispatcher doesn't call in the rigs, every cop and fire truck in Manhattan's gonna be at Saint Pat's to bust my ass."

Marenko turned up the department radio and nodded with satisfaction as a stream of information flew across the airwaves. "You see?" he said. "They're sending our guys to evacuate Saint Pat's. Your mother and Richie will get out of there. Don't worry."

Marenko leaned on the horn as they tore through red lights and down sidestreets double-parked with rush-hour cabs, limos, and buses. The dispatcher called out the time: 10:46 A.M. They got as close as the corner of East Fifty-first Street, across from Rockefeller Center and the great golden statue of Atlas with the world on his shoulders.

Already the scene was a mess. Police barricades were being set up to block off Fifth Avenue. An NYPD cruiser, in its zeal to beat out the fire department, had collided with a taxi, blocking traffic on East Fiftieth Street. Swarms of civilians streamed like ants from the church vestibule doors, spilling onto the steps and the street. Even if the NYPD had dispatched the bomb squad immediately, Georgia suddenly realized, there would be no way for them to get through this gridlock in time.

She looked up at the great white marble cathedral, spread out over an area larger than a football field. There wasn't a wisp of smoke or flame in sight. God, she hoped this wasn't another one of Finney's "games." Then again, maybe she hoped it was.

"I can't park any closer," Marenko apologized, wincing as he repositioned himself across the wheel. His skin looked clammy and gray. Fresh blood had begun to ooze through his sweatshirt. "I'll come with you."

"No." She brushed her fingers across his face. "You need to get back to the hospital." She stepped down from the rig. "Mac, I—"

He waved her away. "Go find your kid."

The sidewalks were already clogged with people, the curbs with dozens of double-parked emergency vehicles and clusters of firefighters and cops trying to keep order. Some of the brass were probably still inside, a fact that would further complicate the chain of command.

Georgia looked at the faces coming out of the church now. Hundreds of people were already out of the building, pressing at her from all sides. A drop in the bucket, she realized. Even if the twenty-four hundred attendees streamed out of every door three abreast, it could take at least twenty minutes to completely evacuate. They didn't have twenty minutes. It was ten-forty-seven.

She pushed through the crowd to the command post on Fifth Avenue, opposite the front doors of the cathedral. Chief Greco, in a starched white shirt and blue dress uniform, was pacing, the medals across his breast pocket gleaming in the late-morning sun. He had obviously planned to attend the mass and was saved only by the fact that he was running late. His aide, conferring with officers on his handie-talkie, stared at Georgia with reproach. She'd forgotten how much she looked like a street person.

"I know I don't look like it, but I'm Fire Marshal Georgia Skeehan," she told the aide. "I called in the alarm."

Greco walked over, then narrowed his gaze as the full weight of who she was and what she'd done began to sink in. "Skeehan"—he looked about nervously—"as if this department hasn't had a bad enough week already."

"Have you found anything?"

"Negative. And I've got uniformed personnel inside, searching. The bomb squad can't get within ten blocks of this gridlock. Con Ed's deploying an emergency foot crew to shut down the power forthwith." *In other words, immediately,* thought Georgia, stifling the urge to roll her eyes. Even in a crisis, Greco was still a bureaucrat.

She suddenly remembered her conversation with Suarez by Finney's burning car. "Chief? Finney's a painting contractor. My guys think he delivered the fuel for his other firebombs inside five-gallon plastic spackling buckets. Can you ask the men to see if they can locate any?"

"Affirmative," said Greco. Behind him, at the bronze vestibule doors, two firefighters lifted a woman in a wheelchair down the front steps. A crowd surged behind them, some with disheveled hair, some screaming in panic and trying to shove their way past the bottleneck.

Georgia turned to Greco now. "My son and mother were in there, too. Is there some way to confirm if they've made it out?"

The chief started. He hadn't realized this was personal. His handlebar mustache twitched, and his normally bewildered expression dissolved into a kind of awkward embarrassment. He suddenly lost the nerve to look her in the eye.

"We've initiated a CRC," he said, then caught her blank look and checked himself. "A civilian rendezvous checkpoint. But a lot of people have simply gone home."

"Can you radio over there?" Georgia prodded. "See if my mother and son are there?"

Chief Greco nodded to his aide, who tried to make radio contact. As Georgia stood waiting, she spotted a little girl in a white bonnet standing to one side of the church steps, enduring the crush of adults, crying for her mother in a sea of legs. Georgia leaped over the barricade and picked up the crying child.

"It's all right. We'll find your mom," she cooed, then motioned for Greco's aide to radio the child's description to the post as well.

The aide frowned. Georgia thought it was because he resented taking "orders" from a rookie marshal. But his eyes looked more frightened than annoyed. "You, ah . . . better get over to the CRC yourself," the aide stammered. "The captain there has a firefighter's widow with the same last name who can't find her grandson."

Georgia dashed out of the command post and pushed through the crowds until she found her mother behind a cordon of firefighters, looking pale and disoriented.

"I had his hand . . . I had it," Margaret sobbed. "People kept running and pushing and I couldn't hold on . . ."

"Richie's still in there?" Georgia staggered back against the barricade. Her head buzzed. Her insides felt as cold and hard as marble.

"I'm not sure," said Margaret, wiping her tears. "He's not with the paramedics. Jimmy insisted on going back inside."

"*Jimmy's* looking for him?"

"Of course," her mother said, a puzzled look on her face. "If anyone can help—"

"Don't talk to me about help!" Georgia screamed. "I'm going in."

"You can't. They won't let you—"

"I'm not asking." She ducked under a barricade and walked past a line of fire trucks. In the back of one, some overheated firefighter had carelessly tossed his turnout coat, along with his handie-talkie. Georgia grabbed the coat and slipped it on, shoving the handie-talkie in a pocket. Voices crackled across the rig's radio in the cab compartment up front.

"Field communications to Manhattan, Chief Greco requests mixer off."

There was only one message that would cause the chief to request the mixer off in such a tense situation. *Someone had found the device.*

Georgia crawled under a second set of barricades near the north-side doors of the cathedral and pushed against the crowds tumbling onto the sidewalk. The press of bodies was frightening. Firefighters had been asked to stay inside until everyone else was evacuated, and for the most part, they had. But in their zeal to get their families out, people had formed a bottleneck at the doors, trampling one another under a sea of legs.

Inside, sunlight turned shadowy and otherworldly. Panicked voices echoed off the marble arches like the tortured laments of the damned. Blank-eyed saints stood sentry, their hands raised as if passing final judgment, their silhouettes ghoulishly outlined in the ever-shifting flicker of votive candles.

Hymn books, coats, and prayer cards were strewn across the aisles. Lumpy bagpipes lay in heaps on the ground, like roadkill. Georgia could almost hear their plaintive wail.

She searched behind statues, in confessionals, and under pews for Richie. Every cry, every terrified face made her heart burst with expectation. But she couldn't find him. She was not a praying woman, but she prayed now—prayed that Finney had gotten it wrong, prayed that her son had gotten out, prayed that Con Ed could work some kind of miracle by shutting off the power.

Georgia heard a soft sobbing behind one of the statues and looked down with a brief stab of anticipation. But it wasn't Richie. Instead, a young Latino mother was cradling an infant, mumbling prayers through her tears. Georgia squatted before her.

"You're not going to die," she said, lifting the baby from her arms. Then she yelled across to a firefighter helping civilians out one of the doors.

"Start a chain!"

The firefighter was young, freckle-faced, and wide-eyed with fear. Probably not unlike Sean Duffy the night of the Howard Beach fire, Georgia surmised. He was a few feet from the exit. It would've been so easy for him to bolt. But he stood firm, his lips pressed together—steeling himself for the worst—and reached out his arms to retrieve the infant over the heads of the crowd.

"We'll get the baby," he promised.

The infant was screaming now as Georgia passed it through a sea of hands until at last it was in the firefighter's arms.

"My baby! My baby!" the woman cried.

"You're next," said Georgia. "Help me lift you onto my shoulders."

"Bless you! Bless you!" she said as she climbed on top of Georgia's turnout coat and scrambled over people's heads to the exit, where she was safely reunited with her baby.

I can't save them all. I can't even save my own son, thought Georgia now as she looked up to the choir loft forty feet above the front entrance of the church. Three middle-aged men in dress uniforms were peering intently at something near the main organ. Georgia made out the rosacea-scarred face of the man in the center. Chief Brennan. She recognized the other two—a bald man and another with a shock of white hair—as high-ranking staff chiefs from headquarters. *They've found the device.*

She raced to a stone spiral staircase in the north vestibule, then stopped short at the top. A cold, bare bulb from a construction lamp shone brightly from its wire-mesh cage, backlighting the three men, raking their monstrous shadows across the wall. The real monster at their feet looked timid by comparison: six five-gallon buckets once filled, according to their labels, with spackling compound. All white plastic. All labeled with a logo that read ACE HARDWARE. They were lined up inconspicuously on the wood plank floor near an arc welder's grip and face mask. Only the thick, sinewy strands of copper wire protruding from the buckets and snaking along the door frame gave any hint of the danger lurking within.

The gleaming copper wire, braided like rope, was stripped of all insulation and tacked along the doorframe, then poked through a hole in the wall, presumably attached to a power source—traceable, if you had an hour. But not traceable in nine minutes. It was now ten-fifty-one. Georgia could already see the events as they were about to unfold.

Somewhere inside these buckets, there had to be a timer. At eleven A.M., the timer would complete its circuit. Electricity already humming through the copper wires would spark fuses in the buckets.

But that jolt of power, however intense, couldn't burn a solid metal fuel like HTA, she reasoned. It was the same principle that explained why a match touched to a log wouldn't incinerate the log. Georgia guessed that Finney had poured a layer of diesel fuel or kerosene over the granular mixture. Once sparked, the fuel vapors inside the buckets would burn rapidly, and the heat would ignite the HTA.

She studied the six buckets now. Each could carry five gallons—about fifty pounds—of what was essentially solid rocket fuel. Three hundred pounds in all. The combination of chemicals and sealed containers made the device not only extremely flammable, but highly explosive as well. It could take under a minute for such a mixture to topple the cathedral's three-hundred-and-thirty-foot twin spires across Fifth Avenue—and little more than that to send flames skyrocketing forty feet in the air. Not a lot of difference between this and the fertilizer bomb at Oklahoma City, except that this would burn as well as explode.

The three high-ranking chiefs before her recognized the danger, too. Beads of sweat glistened across their brows. The chief with the shock of white hair hoisted a fire extinguisher and attempted to spray the uninsulated copper wire with water. Georgia knew what he was trying to do—submerse the wire in enough water to short it out. But the spray merely sizzled as it dripped down the vertical strands and pooled on the plank floor. Everyone stepped back. Touching the bare wires, especially in water, would be suicide. Even if the wires *could* be ripped from the buckets, anyone who even attempted would be fatally electrocuted before he could succeed.

Brennan noticed Georgia now. His blotchy, pitted face was grave and stony. "What are you, Skeehan? My purgatory? I've not only got to die, I've got to suffer you before I go?" He turned his back to her and spoke into his handie-talkie.

"Brennan to Greco: Is Con Ed here yet? K." From the looks of it, Finney's device appeared to run solely on electrical power—probably because Finney wanted a big jolt to maximize the bomb's speed and efficiency.

"Con Ed has rendezvoused," Greco radioed back. Brennan made a face. He was no fan of Greco-speak, either, it seemed. "They're terminating power at street level forthwith. Stand by. K."

The bodies of the chiefs slumped with visible relief. If Con Ed could shut the juice to the building, there'd be no spark to start a flame. Plus, the stripped copper wiring—the device's ignition-delivery system— could be handled and removed. And not a moment too soon. It was now ten-fifty-four. They had six minutes.

CHAPTER Fifty-four

The two staff chiefs began to radio fire officers in the nave. News spread across the crowd. People crossed themselves and prayed as the air system shut down and the amber chandeliers winked out. Quiet cries of relief reverberated through the cathedral, now lit only by filtered light through stained glass windows and votive candles at the altars.

Georgia scanned the nervous faces below her, hoping to see Richie's. But he wasn't there. *He must have gotten out,* she told herself. *He must have.*

Suddenly, Brennan let out a string of expletives. She turned, noticing for the first time that the light in the choir loft was too bright to be pouring in from the twenty-six-foot stained-glass rose window behind her. And then she saw it—the bulb in the construction lamp dangling from a rafter above the men. It was still burning.

"What the—?" the bald staff chief exclaimed. He grabbed the thick black insulated electrical cord running from the base of the bulb and began snaking it through the loft. But it, too, disappeared into a space in the wall. Firefighters and civilians in the nave saw the bulb now. A murmur of panic rose through the crowd. The light attracted attention outside as well. Greco came back on the radio.

"Greco to Brennan: Where's that light coming from? K."

Georgia's eyes scanned Finney's uninsulated copper wiring and the arc welding equipment near it. Her dad once borrowed some arc welding equipment to fix the wrought-iron railing along their front stoop. A friend in his firehouse loaned him a portable generator to supply the 250 amps needed to melt the iron. In arc welding, standard current is never enough.

"Chief?" Georgia ventured. "Finney may have hooked up his device to a backup generator the welders were using. It's probably in the basement somewhere, running off a diesel engine."

Brennan nodded at the logic. He got on the radio and immediately dispatched two fire companies to the basement of the cathedral to find the generator and shut it off. Then Brennan and the staff chiefs hustled down the stairs to supervise.

Georgia went to follow, but her attention was diverted by the sound of shattering glass. A group of panicked parishioners, sensing the bad news, had snagged a maintenance ladder and broken one of the stained-glass panels. A new surge of people raced toward it, clinging to the ladder and throwing themselves through the sharp glass, slicing up their arms and legs. Georgia scanned the mob of people with hungry eyes. Still no sign of her little boy.

Brennan's voice crackled over the department radio. He was speaking to Chief Greco. A midtown ladder company had found the backup generator, but it was locked against theft in a tamperproof steel cage. Like an airline pilot, Brennan spoke in a tone that betrayed none of the panic he had to be feeling. Firefighters were trying to break the lock, Brennan reported to the chief. Georgia shook her head at the irony. The contractor was probably on the street somewhere with the key. But even if he explained who he was, the young, overzealous cops on duty already had strict orders not to let anybody inside. It would take too long to get clearance.

It was now ten-fifty-six, and many firefighters—memorial service attendees and guys on duty—were still inside, knowing full well what price they might pay for staying to help the hundreds of civilians remaining.

And how will we die? Georgia wondered as she stared up at the muted prisms of blue light filtering through the stained-glass windows of the clerestory. *Will there be a burst of white-hot flame and an end of consciousness? Will the fire rise up slowly, choking off our air as we struggle over one another for the door?* She hadn't been in a church since she was a kid. And now she was going to die in one.

Her brooding thoughts were broken by a set of heavy footsteps lumbering up the choir loft stairs. Georgia turned and took in the bushy silver eyebrows and grizzled, solemn expression. Jimmy Gallagher moved toward her, a meaty hand extended, then stopped, sensing some boundary between them. The hand hung in the air an instant, then flopped back at his side.

"I've looked for Richie everywhere, love. Lord knows, he's probably out. Let's at least take cover."

Georgia recoiled. "Get away from me! I know what you did." She rubbed a grimy hand across her face and fought back tears. All the misery of the last twenty-four hours came back to her in waves and she inhaled deeply, trying to suck it all back into some corner inside herself to keep from breaking down.

Gallagher froze and stared at her, pain bunching up the deeply etched wrinkles around his watery blue eyes. He went to say something, then simply shook his head.

"Not now, love," he said softly, reaching again for her hand. "C'mon. Now's not the time."

He tried to lead her to the stairs, but Georgia pushed him away. "I found Quinn's mask in your locker. And that computer disk—"

"We've got to get out of here," he mumbled as if he hadn't heard her.

"Jimmy, are you listening?" she shouted angrily. "I know you killed Terry Quinn. I trusted you. Every man I trust just . . ." Her voice trailed off.

He winced as if struck by a blow, then shoved his hands in his pockets, swallowing hard to regain his composure. He didn't look at her. Instead, he leaned over the choir rail.

"Father in heaven," he said softly. "I wanted to tell you everything . . . so many times . . . but then what? How would that help you?

Or Quinn? Or his family?" He turned to face her. "I had to make a choice, love. Do you understand?"

"Yeah," she said coldly. "I understand your choice: freedom or prison."

"No." He frowned. "Not that kind of choice. I could tell the world that a brother had screwed up and killed all those people—or I could let him die a hero."

The words tore through her like a bullet.

"Are you saying that *Terry Quinn* set the Spring Street fire?" *Not Quinn. Not a dead hero with a wife and two little girls.*

"I never looked at what was on that disk Terry gave me. I wouldn't know a floppy from a hard drive. But I *did* know Terry was in trouble. I just never put it together until the fire . . ."

"Put what together?"

Gallagher paced the choir loft now, the stark light of the construction bulb refracting off his silver hair. "Terry tried every legal means to stop that halfway house for sex offenders from being opened in his neighborhood. Nothing worked." Gallagher ran a callused hand, hardened from a lifetime of firefighting, through his hair. He took a deep breath and continued.

"Kathleen Quinn used to work for Michaels. Terry figured a rich man like that could put pressure on the right people. Instead, Michaels had the house burned, then fixed it so that if Terry ever said anything, it would look like *he* did it."

"Why?"

"Because, love . . . when Sloane Michaels does a favor, he expects one in return. A year later, he ordered Terry to burn down Spring Street in repayment."

Georgia felt her head spin. She stepped to the railing and looked out over the vastness of the cathedral, at the high altar with its gleaming bronze canopy and the overturned vases of lilies lining the red-carpeted aisles.

"Jimmy, you *knew* this?" she asked.

"I knew Michaels was pressuring Terry to burn a building. I didn't know which one until the fire." Gallagher closed his eyes and shook his head. "You gotta understand, love. Terry didn't know about that party. He figured the building was empty and the fire would burn so fast, it'd be over before anyone got hurt. He was a good man in a bad situation, he was."

Georgia wiped a hand across her forehead. She tried to shake off the incessant thrumming, like a swarm of bees, that vibrated through her—a mix of fear, exhaustion, and confusion. At every exit, there were still civilians pushing to get out and people lying beneath them, crushed and in need of medical attention.

"But *you* killed Terry," Georgia said, her voice cracking with the realization of it all. "*You* took his mask . . . *you* stuck that cheater in his pocket."

"I was angry at what he'd done—the stupidity, the waste. I knocked him out, I did . . . I could've pulled him out of there, unconscious . . . and I . . . chose not to." Gallagher paused, smearing the back of his hand across his red-rimmed eyes. "I let him go. For his sake—and the department's. He couldn't have lived with those deaths on his head."

Gallagher braced his trembling hands against the railing beside her. "What would you have done, love?" he asked softly. "Would you have wanted to see the department dragged through that? Or his widow and kids?"

He pinched his eyelids together. Tears spilled down his leathery cheeks and he looked away, embarrassed. He'd spent twenty-eight years crawling through the ashes. Twenty-eight years walking through walls of fire and bringing brothers back from the dead. And it had all come down to this. She sensed his deep lament and it touched her.

"Please, Georgia," he said to her. "Please let me try to get you out of here. I don't want another life on my conscience."

She looked at her watch. It was ten-fifty-eight. She turned away from the railing. Suddenly, an anguished voice called up to her.

"Mama!"

He hadn't called her "Mama" since he was two. He stood, arms out-stretched, his navy blue jacket torn on the sleeve, his shirttails untucked, his black wavy hair matted on one side. Tears streamed down his swollen, bruised face. "Mama," he sobbed again. He must have been knocked unconscious and trampled in the stampede.

"I'm coming down, baby."

Georgia raced to the top of the staircase. When she turned around, Gallagher was still on the balcony, staring at the gleaming copper wire, sinewy and alive with its poisonous energy. The light from the construction lamp reflected in the pool of water beneath the strands.

"This thing works on electricity, right?" he called over to her.

"Yes, but those wires carry two hundred and fifty amps of current. And you can't disconnect the power."

"I wasn't planning to." There were tears in his eyes.

"Take care of yourself, love. Tell your mother I love her, always have . . ."

"Jimmy, you can't." Georgia took a step toward him, but he crossed himself and ordered her to stay back.

"Tell 'em, love, if they ask, that this is still the greatest job in the world."

Then he stuck his left shoe in the puddle of water and clamped his right fist hard around the stripped copper wire. His body jerked vio-lently, and he shrieked. Waves of convulsions racked him, and a halo of sparks buzzed overhead. Georgia stood back, waiting for the flash of the HTA firebomb. But it didn't ignite.

Her knees gave out and she sank to the floor, shaking. Richie raced up the stairs now, and Georgia ordered him to stay back from the elec-trically charged site. Two firefighters came rushing over. One took the sobbing child; the other smelled the sickly-sweet odor of burned flesh, saw Gallagher, and made the sign of the cross.

Georgia reached for her handie-talkie and attempted to depress the button three times before she could get her fingers to work.

"Mayday! Mayday!" she croaked out across the airwaves. "Fire-fighter down in the balcony." Greco came on the line.

"Can you evacuate him? It's eleven-oh-two. The device was set to blow two minutes ago."

"But Chief, it's Gallagher who's down," she stammered. "He shorted out the device. He spared the cathedral."

"How bad is he hurt?"

She looked across the balcony at his lifeless body. "Chief," she said, trying to stave off the rising emotion in her voice. "Firefighter Gallagher made the supreme sacrifice."

CHAPTER *Fifty-five*

The department buried Jimmy Gallagher with full honors. His flag-draped casket was paraded before a throng of firefighters from all over the country. Georgia and her mother attended the funeral, which was held, fittingly, at Saint Patrick's Cathedral. Margaret put on her best face. At home, she cried a lot. She'd buried two men in her life. She seemed to age overnight.

Georgia tried to think of words of comfort, but there were none. Gallagher couldn't have lived long with the shame of knowing he was a de facto accomplice to the Spring Street fire. Or that he'd given a lifetime to saving people, yet made a choice to let Quinn die rather than risk the good name of his friend or the honor of his beloved department.

Walter Frankel wouldn't have fared any better under the scrutiny. For his funeral, Georgia bought a wide-screen version of *The Terminator* and stuck it in his casket. Maybe the next world had DVD and Dolby stereo.

For both Gallagher and Frankel, giving up their lives in the line of duty was the only way they could've ever—in their hearts—set things right. They knew it. And so did Georgia, though it was something she couldn't share with her mother. So she became the mother for a while, cooking and consoling and arranging activities to bring some order to her mother's loss. One afternoon, she started taking apart the pool table to refurbish.

At first, Margaret was appalled, insisting she could never play again. But gradually, as the white, mildewed wood turned to a rich, chestnut-colored hue in Georgia's hands, her mother began to understand what Georgia had all along: Jimmy Gallagher wouldn't have wanted them to grow old and musty in his absence, any more than he would have the pool table.

Wine, women, and wood get better with age. Wasn't that what he'd said? Georgia's efforts brought her closer to her mother than she'd been in years. Gallagher would have liked that. These days, she carried her father's key chain with her everywhere—in honor not only of her dad, but of Gallagher as well.

Ralph Finney survived, if one could call it that. He spent two months in the hospital before being released to stand trial on multiple first-degree murder and arson charges. The prosecutor wanted mandatory life in prison. The defense pleaded insanity. Nobody spoke about the death penalty, probably because a jury might be disinclined to convict a man so horribly disfigured by his own actions. He had no facial hair, no lips, and only a small, strange lump of what looked like candle wax for a nose.

He had to be in a lot of pain. But when Georgia gave her deposition and looked into that hideous face, she thought of the brave young firefighter, Sean Duffy, who gave his life to save a little girl's. She focused on his pain, fear, and suffering, and that of Finney's other victims who could no longer speak for themselves.

Newspapers hailed Georgia as a hero. The publicity embarrassed her. *Hero.* What did that mean? Heroes greeted every encounter with undaunting courage and undiluted faith in themselves and the world around them. She could never be like that.

One morning a month or so after the ordeal, on a routine investigation, she bumped into the firefighter who'd helped her lift that infant and mother out of Saint Patrick's. She didn't even know his name. They nodded to each other and waved across the space of several fire trucks. And then he went back to helping a chain of fellow firefighters pack up hose in the back of a rig.

Watching him, no one would've guessed the risks he'd taken for a woman and child he'd never meet again. There was no camera to record it, no medal to note it. He didn't get his name in the paper. He showed up. He did his job and he asked for nothing in return.

Georgia wondered if her definition of heroism had been too simplistic. Maybe heroism wasn't a bright torchlight in the heat of battle. Maybe it was just a steady, smoldering ember of conscience that refused to surrender. Heroes were men and women who had suffered every bit as much despair, failure, and doubt as the rest of the world. They just toughed it out one minute longer.

Michaels's computer disk was turned over to the IRS. The agency was quickly able to match up the names on the disk with figures in organized crime and international drug trafficking, and begin the lengthy process of tracing funds and auditing records. Some of Michaels's "clients" fled the country. Others were arrested to stand trial. With Michaels gone and his name tarnished, his empire quickly crumbled. So did Amelia. Three weeks after the ordeal, she slipped into a coma and died. Georgia read later that the Knickerbocker Plaza was being sold to a French conglomerate.

Gene Cambareri, fully recovered, was given the biggest retirement party Georgia had ever seen. Half the department—or so it seemed— showed up at an Italian social club in Gravesend Bay, Brooklyn, to wish him well, which wasn't surprising, since he'd split a box of doughnuts or played a hand of gin rummy at nearly every firehouse in the city. The entire task force went—all except for Carter, who couldn't make it. He'd gone down to North Carolina—by himself—to visit Cassie's grave. He didn't mention it when he returned except to tell Georgia that his little girl had been buried in a lovely spot overlooking an open field of buttercups, rimmed with tall pines. When Carter told her about the place, he seemed at peace.

A month and a half after the fire, the mayor hosted a luncheon to celebrate the work of the Bureau of Fire Investigation. There, Lynch and Brennan circled each other like two piranhas. Nothing had changed between the commissioner and the chief fire marshal. Yet Lynch, the consummate politician, clearly saw no advantage to bringing up departmental misdeeds when his power was on the rise. Now Georgia knew those misplaced building records would never be brought to light. Nor the shenanigans at the La Guardia Arms. Nor the gambling den in Washington Heights. Crime gets punished, but corruption and inefficiency just ramble along. There was nothing more anyone could do but move on.

Georgia tried to do the same. In the weeks that followed, she spent a lot of time with Richie—taking walks, going out for pizza, and shooting hoops in the backyard. Mac Marenko stopped by often as well. His kind and steady presence buoyed their spirits and seemed to soften the disappointment Richie felt when week after week passed with no word from his father. Georgia knew there wouldn't be any word—knew the hurt would always be there. But she kept those thoughts to herself. Sometimes you just have to allow people a chance to be forgiven, even if they never take it. Georgia wondered if the same applied to her. There was only one way to find out.

On a cloudless Sunday afternoon in early June, Marenko drove Georgia to a two-story, vinyl-sided cape in Valley Stream, Long Island. It was a street of modest houses, tidy lawns, and the clutter of small children. In the cape's backyard, Georgia spotted bicycles, baseball bats, and a doll's carriage. The front door, with its oval-shaped frosted glass pane, sported a wreath of fake roses in the center. The mailbox, with an American flag etched on the side, read MR. AND MRS. P. FERRARO. It had been more than two years since Petie's death, but Melinda had never changed the lettering.

"I can't do it," Georgia stammered upon seeing the mailbox.

"Sure you can," Marenko prodded. "She's expecting you. You can't back out now."

Georgia wrapped a finger around the red-and-white string securing the box of Italian pastries in her lap. "What do I say to the woman?"

"Tell her how much you liked Petie. The good stuff you remember about him. Tell her about your own childhood, growing up after your dad died. What helped you. What got your mother through it all."

"How do I"—she swallowed—"tell her how sorry I am?"

Marenko took his hands off the steering wheel and planted them on her shoulders, giving her a little, reassuring squeeze. "Just say the words, Scout. Say them and the rest will come."

She stared again at the door and licked her dry lips. "Will you be here when I come out?"

"You bet."

"You won't leave?"

"Not if you don't want me to."

She looked at him for a long moment and thought she saw a trace of panic in those sparkling blue eyes. Like he wasn't sure what she'd say. After all they'd been through, he still wasn't sure. She opened the car door and got out. Then she shut the door and leaned in the open window.

"Mac?"

"Yeah?"

"I don't want you to."